FOR BABY ZOE?

BY
FIONA LOWE

A LOVE
AGAINST ALL ODDS

BY
EMILY FORBES

MILLS
BOON

Fiona Lowe is a RITA® and R*BY award-winning author who started writing romances when she was on holiday and ran out of books. Now writing single title contemporary romance for Carina Press and Medical Romances for Mills & Boon, she lives in a seaside town in southern Australia, where she juggles writing, reading, working and raising two gorgeous sons with the support of her own real-life hero! Readers can visit Fiona at her website: fionalowe.com.

Emily Forbes is an award-winning author of Medical Romances for Mills & Boon. She has written over 25 books, and has twice been a finalist in the Australian Romantic Book of the Year Award, which she won in 2013 for her novel *Sydney Harbour Hospital: Bella's Wishlist*. You can get in touch with Emily at emilyforbes@internode.on.net or visit her website at emily-forbesauthor.com.

A DADDY
FOR BABY ZOE?

BY
FIONA LOWE

Published in Great Britain 2016
By Mills & Boon, an imprint of HarperCollins*Publishers*
1 London Bridge Street, London, SE1 9GF

© 2016 Fiona Lowe

ISBN: 978-0-263-25422-8

Our pc   able
produc
The lo
enviro

Printe
by CP

Dear Reader,

The idea for *A Daddy for Baby Zoe?* came from some TV footage of a pregnant woman at her husband's funeral. You're not supposed to lose your beloved husband weeks before the birth of your first child; that is meant to be a time for daydreaming and planning for the happy years ahead spent in each other's company. The idea of being with someone else is anathema. Throw into this mix society's unspoken rule that committing to someone new in under a year or two is wrong, and you have a bubbling pot of grief and guilt. This is the mantle I laid over my heroine, Meredith.

Raf Camilleri has always thought he'll be a father, but the only thing he's created so far is a very successful business. Home to take care of his grumpy and elderly Italian father, who is recovering from a stroke, Raf finds himself torn between intrigue and self-preservation when he meets his heavily pregnant neighbour. Throw in a large Italian family, Meredith's in-laws, a dog and the island locals, and you have a messy, complicated and heartfelt story—just like real life!

My inspiration for Shearwater Island is Phillip Island, and you can find photos of it over at fionalowe.com by clicking on the Pinterest icon. Worried you'll miss new books of mine? Subscribe to my newsletter at fionalowe.com.

I hope you enjoy this story of love and family. No matter the turmoil they face, I promise you a happy ending.

Happy reading!

Fiona x

For Mónica. We hosted each other's sons
on a French-Australian exchange
and became friends in the process. *Bisous* x

Books by Fiona Lowe

Mills & Boon Medical Romance

Miracle: Twin Babies
Her Brooding Italian Surgeon
The Most Magical Gift of All
Single Dad's Triple Trouble
Career Girl in the Country
Sydney Harbour Hospital: Tom's Redemption
Letting Go with Dr Rodriguez
Newborn Baby For Christmas
Gold Coast Angels: Bundle of Trouble
Unlocking Her Surgeon's Heart

Visit the Author Profile page at
millsandboon.co.uk for more titles.

CHAPTER ONE

Dr Meredith Dennison's hands were tied behind her back, and her head was deep down in a large bucket, leaving her face millimetres from water as she tried to get her mouth around one of the many bobbing silicone babies' teats. The laughter of her colleagues filled her ears—she was going to kill them. They'd cheerfully ambushed her with a surprise baby shower, which had been a generous and appreciated idea, although she could have done without the party games.

'Come on, Merry, just grab one with your teeth,' Olivia, the receptionist, encouraged, her voice full of glee.

'I've got dinner at Le Goût with Richard's parents at seven,' she said rising slightly. 'I can't go with wet hair. The snooty maître d' won't let me in.'

'You've got plenty of time to restyle your hair,' Emma, her good friend and fellow GP, said firmly. 'Besides, you want your presents, don't you?'

'This is extortion,' she replied indignantly, her breath making the water ripple.

'Sure, but it's fun.' Emma's tinkling laugh rained down on her. 'Consider it payback for the humiliations you made me suffer at my hens' night.'

Meredith turned her head sideways to see her friend.

'Having a hunk of a male stripper making a fuss of you is a lot different from half drowning me.'

Emma rolled her eyes. 'It *may* have been different if I hadn't treated him the week before for a sexually transmitted infection. Instead of admiring his ripped muscles, I kept seeing his path report and going *ewww*.'

'Granted, that was unfortunate but, as I've said at least one thousand times since, I didn't know he was a clinic patient.'

Emma crossed her arms, her eyes twinkling. 'Stop stalling.'

Meredith felt a firm kick under her ribs and sighed. Even her unborn child was telling her to get on with it. Sucking in a deep breath of air, she lined up a bobbing teat, bared her teeth and dived. Two seconds later and with dripping wet hair, she raised her head triumphantly, the teat firmly clenched between her lips.

Her colleagues cheered. The baby kicked again as if to say, Go, Mum. Laughing, Meredith spat out the teat. 'Wait until I tell Richard I was all tied up and he missed it.'

'When he gets home from his week of snowboarding in the back country he won't care,' Emma said. 'He'll just want a hot shower, clean sheets and lovely, waddly you.'

'Hey, I don't waddle.'

Emma laughed again. 'If you say so.'

Meredith accepted the proffered towel from Olivia. 'I asked Richard if I waddled and he said I'm the sexiest pregnant woman he's ever seen.'

Lee Ng, the clinic's physiotherapist, sighed, the sound loaded with experience. 'If he wants an easy life, he'd be a fool to say anything else.'

'Damn straight.' Meredith smiled and hugged Richard's loving words to herself.

She'd been waiting a long time for this baby—waiting while she and Richard completed their fellowships, waiting while Richard established himself as one of the top trauma surgeons in Melbourne and now, finally, her long-held dream to be a mother was almost here. In a few weeks they'd welcome their baby into the world and as far as she was concerned it couldn't come fast enough. They were going to be parents—a team at last—and she couldn't wait to see Richard as a father.

There had been a few worrying months a year and a half ago when she'd despaired that Richard was never going to be ready for fatherhood. He worked long hours as a surgeon and he'd told her he didn't want to have any more demands put on his time. Any precious spare time he had he spent in the great outdoors, unwinding and re-energising. As much as she loved joining him in his outdoor adventures, she'd craved motherhood more. Just when she had really started to worry he would never change his mind, he'd surprised her. Last year, on his return from trekking in Nepal, he'd swept her into his arms and told her he was ready. The ease with which she'd got pregnant had delighted them both.

With the physical demands of pregnancy on her body, her life had instantly changed with the nausea and cloying fatigue in the early weeks, thankfully followed by the energy and wonder of feeling the baby move. Richard's life had stayed much the same and he'd continued to work hard and play hard. She'd buried any niggling concerns she had that he wouldn't be the hands-on father she hoped for because right now there was no need for him to change a thing. After all, the baby wasn't here yet so why shouldn't he go hiking and kayaking and do all the things he loved just because she was too big now to join him?

There was no rational reason at all but that didn't stop irrational reasons booming in her head. All she wanted was one free weekend so they could paint the nursery together. Perhaps he'd sensed her disquiet or finally the reason behind her burgeoning belly had registered in his brain as *baby coming*. Either way, last week as he'd packed his gear for his alpine snowboarding trip, he'd tucked her hair behind her ears, kissed her on the forehead and told her this was his last recreational trip away until the baby was a few months old. Next weekend—medical emergencies excepted—they were painting the nursery together. She felt dizzy with excitement.

Having towelled her hair dry, she grinned and tossed the damp towel into the hamper. 'So, Emma, did I hear you say presents?'

Raf Camilleri stood in the kitchen, immune to the lulling sound of foaming waves rolling rhythmically onto the beach. With his chest heaving, he was trying to gulp down water and quench his ragged thirst while he waited for his blood to pump out of his legs and back to his brain. Running along the white, sandy beaches of Shearwater Island was completely different from pounding the concrete pavements of Melbourne and his calves reminded him of that every day. After draining the water bottle, he pressed the palms of his hands against the island bench and lowered his heels to the floor, welcoming the burning stretch of his Achilles tendons. It was a case of the pleasure of the pain—without it he'd end up a lot sorer.

'You're back.'

'I am.' Raf swung his head sideways, glancing under his arm towards the familiar male voice. He caught sight of his father's orthotic shoes—shoes Mario Camilleri hated, shoes Raf laced up for him each morning—and he was reminded, not just by his burning calves, that both his and his father's lives had changed.

'So,' Mario said, his voice tinged with a hint of an Italian accent, 'now you can drive me to the club.'

It wasn't a question—more of a demand, really. Mario didn't do questions when it came to him wanting or needing something. He just issued instructions as if he was still the captain of his fishing boat. Still the captain of his life.

Raf tensed, the rush of relaxation from his run taking a solid hit, but he stayed stretching. 'I thought we'd have dinner first. I bought some calamari straight off the boat at the co-op.' He stopped short of saying, *because it's your favourite.*

'I'll eat at the club.' The terse words chopped through the air.

I'll eat at the club, not *we'll eat at the club.* Okay, then. No ambiguity there. It wasn't an out-and-out surprise to Raf that he wasn't invited and part of him recognised that his father wished to spend time with his buddies like he'd always done, but just one night, an invitation to join him at the fishermen's club, might be nice.

Really? You've got as much in common with your father's mates as a steak at a vegetarian's picnic.

Raf straightened up and glanced at his father but Mario ducked his gaze. Once father and son had been the same height, but since Mario's stroke, Raf was now the taller. 'It would have been helpful if you'd mentioned your plans to me this morning,' he said, pitching for a light tone.

Mario shrugged. 'Freeze the calamari.'

His temper sparked. 'Jeez, Dad, you've never eaten frozen seafood in your life.'

Mario's brown eyes flashed in his jowly face. 'Maybe I want to start. You're not my keeper, Rafael.'

'No.' He deliberately closed his mouth hard to prevent himself from saying anything more. He wasn't his father's keeper but right now he was his carer. A job fraught with more unexploded mines than the fields of Cambodia. It made the taking of his medical IT company public and its subsequent sale look like a walk in the park. 'Do I get to take a shower first?' he asked, hating that he sounded like the petulant teenager he'd been twenty-three years ago.

'Suit yourself. I told them I'd be there at six.' Mario's four-pronged cane thumped against the faded linoleum as he turned towards the door that led to the living room.

As Raf made his way to the bathroom, he heard the blare of the television and the sounds of a soccer game. Situation normal. It was just another happy day at Casa Camilleri.

Meredith checked her watch. Damn it, she was going to be late. Again. It had taken longer than anticipated to open all the lovely presents her colleagues had showered her with, including the cutest selection of baby clothes and the generous gift of a baby car seat. Lee and Emma had helped her load everything into the car and she'd raced home in an attempt to rescue her hair. It had been a bad move because now there was no way she was going to be able to fight her way down Brunswick Street with its heavy traffic and trams, and arrive at Le Goût on time.

Although Richard had carte blanche with his parents to arrive late, that courtesy wasn't as easily afforded to Meredith. As her mother-in-law, Linda, often said, surely, as a GP in an inner-city practice with six large hospitals in a five-kilometre radius, most emergency patients bypassed the clinic.

They did and, truth be told, most days Meredith ran late at the clinic because she didn't want to rush her patients. At home she ran late because even though she and Richard had a cleaner come in once a week, the bulk of the domestic tasks fell to her. Raised on a dairy farm, where either the cows or the farm machinery had the uncanny knack of causing chaos at inopportune moments, she'd come to believe that being ten minutes late was considered on time. Linda wasn't of the same opinion. Meredith knew the look that would dart across the restaurant at her as she walked in late—the one that said Richard could have done better.

She sighed. *Stop it.* It didn't matter that she hadn't gone to one of Melbourne's elite private schools or that she hadn't studied medicine at Melbourne University. It was Linda's issue, not hers, and to keep the peace she hadn't objected when Linda had mentioned she already had the enrolment forms for Melbourne Grammar on her desk and that Derek, Meredith's father-in-law, had the application form for the Melbourne Cricket Club on his. Both were ready to be lodged the moment the sex and the name of the baby were announced.

As far as Meredith was concerned, she and Richard had years ahead of them before they had to worry about schools. The baby kicked again and she put her hand on the foot that kept digging her in the ribs. 'You telling me you're starting to feel squished in there, Sprocket? Sorry, but I need you to stay put for another six weeks.'

Feeling the cloying tendrils of fatigue starting to pull at her, she didn't dare sit down to put on her shoes in case she gave in and didn't stand up again. As much as she appreciated Linda and Derek insisting that Richard's absence was no reason for them to cancel dinner plans, the idea of slumping on the couch and eating a green curry from the Thai takeaway down the road was very appealing. 'Come on, Merry, you can do this,' she told herself as she took one final glance in the mirror—lipstick on, hair mostly under control, clean black dress. 'You'll do.'

She picked her keys up from the key dish and then remembered her phone was resting on the charger. She doubled back to the kitchen to retrieve it and as she picked it up, the doorbell rang. Her heart skipped in delight. Despite Richard being adamant he couldn't cut a day off the snow trip and that he'd be home tomorrow night, he'd known that she and his parents had been disappointed he was missing this long-anticipated dinner at the popular restaurant. Turning up unannounced and making it to dinner after all was just the sort of surprise Richard would pull.

She slipped her phone into her handbag and rushed back to the front door, letting her excitement take control. Oh, how she wanted to find Richard on the other side and not a power company or a cable television salesperson. Turning the deadlock and the door handle in tandem, she opened the door. Neither Richard nor a sales person stood on the tiny veranda of her inner-city terrace house. Disappointment sank through her like a stone.

'Dr Dennison?' a young police officer asked quietly, her expression serious.

'Yes.' She was used to the police ringing her doorbell, given that out of all her colleagues she lived the closest to the clinic and the police station. If there were any out-of-hours problems with the clinic security system or if there was a break-in, the police knocked on her door. She instantly thought that Olivia had probably drunk one glass of champagne too many at the baby shower. 'Did Olivia set off the alarm system when she was locking up?'

The policewoman shot a confused glance at her male partner. His shoulders rose almost imperceptibly. The policewoman looked back at her. 'May we come in?'

Come in? She checked her watch again. 'I'm already running really late for dinner so how about we go straight to the clinic and I'll override the security, okay?'

The policewoman shook her head slowly. 'We're not here about a security system, Dr Dennison.'

'Oh?' She stared at the officers in their distinctive blue uniforms with all the necessary accoutrements from holstered guns to radios. Her brain snagged on the motto, *Tenez le droit.* Why French? With a shake of her head she marshalled her thoughts. 'Why are you here?'

'Please, may we come in?'

Had she forgotten to pay her speeding fine last month? Did they send the police to your door for that sort of thing? She automatically stood back from the doorway to allow the officers access and they crossed the threshold before standing uneasily in her living room. She was struck by how their black heavy-duty work boots seemed glued to her polished Baltic pine floorboards.

'Is this going to take long because if it is I really should call my in-laws and let them know I'll be even later for dinner than I already am.'

The officers sat down. 'Can you please sit down?'

For the first time, confusion gave way to something akin to fear and like an obedient child she sat. 'What's going on?'

The policewoman set her cap on the coffee table. 'Dr Dennison, is Richard Nichols your husband?'

'He is.' Merry's breath hitched in her throat as her hand gripped the arm of the couch. 'Why?'

The policewoman swallowed and her tongue moistened her lips. 'I'm afraid there's been an accident and your husband—'

'What sort of an accident?' She heard her voice loud and strident bouncing off the floor-to-ceiling bookshelves, only it didn't sound like hers. 'What hospital is he in?' Her head spun with the logistics of getting Richard transferred out of a small country hospital and into Melbourne City where they were assured of the best medical care in the country.

The male officer moved his head back and forth very slowly. 'This year there was a lot more snow than there's been for many years.'

The policewoman leaned forward, her official expression now full of compassion and empathy. 'According to your husband's friends, they'd hiked to Mount Feathertop and enjoyed two days of back-country activities. It snowed heavily last night and Mr Nichols went out early this morning for a last snowboard before he returned home this evening.'

Meredith nodded. 'He lives for fresh powder.'

The officer didn't respond to her comment but continued talking. 'Your husband was caught by an avalanche.'

'No.' Merry shook her head so hard her brain hurt. 'No, that's not possible. Avalanches don't happen in

Australia, they happen in places with real mountains, like Switzerland.'

Sympathy glowed in the policewoman's eyes. 'By the time his friends found him it was too late and there was nothing they could do to revive him.'

Noooooooooo! Merry stared at the two of them as a slow and insidious shake started at her feet, vibrating up her legs until it consumed her entire body. 'No! He can't be dead. I won't let him be dead.' Her pitch rose sharply as hysteria took hold of her with a tenacious grip. Her throat narrowed and her eyes burned. 'We're having a baby in six weeks. We've got a nursery to paint.'

'We're so very sorry, Dr Dennison.' The male police officer proffered a box of tissues. 'Is there someone we can call for you? You shouldn't be alone.'

The baby chose that moment to kick and a ragged sound left her mouth. Her dream of a family—of her and Richard as parents—shattered into tiny, jagged pieces. She was going to have a baby but now she'd be facing parenthood alone.

CHAPTER TWO

Three weeks later

AFTERNOON SPRING SUNSHINE poured through the window, setting up a glare on Raf's laptop screen and making it hard to see. He was working on his current project—designing an app for cardiologists to use to explain conditions and procedures to patients. So much had changed in health care since his mother's sudden and unexpected death from a heart attack it made that time look like the Dark Ages.

After an overcast and drizzly morning, he took the warm rays as a sign and closed the computer. His father was dozing in his recliner—weary after his hydrotherapy session earlier—and his ageing schnauzer and extremely elderly cat were both curled up on his lap, snoring louder than their master.

The brightness of the light cast Raf's childhood home in an unforgiving glow. What had once been one of Shearwater Island's state-of-the-art homes was now looking very tired and dated with its 1970's arches, the faded and worn Berber carpet, and the wood-panelled feature wall with its geometric clock. The only things that had stood the test of time were the beautiful, clean lines of the Scandinavian furniture. His mother had decorated the house as a bride and twenty years later, when she probably would have redecorated, she'd died. That had been nineteen years ago and apart from the addition of a big-screen TV, his father hadn't changed a thing.

The pounding surf combined with the warbling and happy song of the magpies and the sounds slipped under the open window, calling to Raf. He stood, stretched and walked over to the glass, leaning his hands against the sill and fingering the bubbled paint. He didn't know why he often stared out this window—it wasn't like he could see the sea. All he got was a view of the modern house next door. Perhaps that was the reason. Something about it reminded him of his new home in Melbourne—a house he'd designed and spent all of two nights in before his sister had telephoned with what he'd assumed was the daily Mario poststroke update.

'The rehabilitation centre wants to discharge Dad,' Bianca had said briskly.

'I guess he'll be happier at home,' he'd replied, wondering if he'd really notice a change in his father's mood. Happiness and Mario were two mutually exclusive things.

'They won't send him home alone.'

'Can't he live with you for a while?' he'd suggested, as he'd ripped open another moving box.

Bianca's sharp intake of breath hissed down the line. 'I've got a business, Raf, a husband and two teenagers, all of whom are driving me crazy. I can't add Dad into the mix or I'll go under.'

He ran his hand through his hair, running options through his mind. 'What about live-in help?'

She snorted. 'He can't afford that.'

He unwrapped a beautiful piece of glass art he'd bought from the Wathaurong in Geelong. 'I can.'

'It wouldn't work. You know how difficult he can be and, besides, down here on the island in winter we're not exactly overflowing with candidates for the job.' He heard her click her tongue. 'You've been a volunteer with St John Ambulance since Mum died.'

'That's first aid and emergency work. It doesn't qualify me as a carer.'

'Well, I've never done first aid but I've been looking out for Dad for years and now, little brother, it's time for you to step up. Besides, it will give you something to do now you've sold your company.'

'I'm designing an app and I've got plenty of things to do.' Things that didn't involve living on Shearwater Island with Mario.

'I'm sure you do but for now you're going to be the good Italian son you haven't been in years and come home.'

Anger meshed with guilt and then, reluctantly, resignation followed. When Bianca got an idea in her head she didn't let it go until it was a done deal, and he grudgingly conceded that she did have a point. He'd stayed away a very long time. 'Exactly how long do I need to be there?'

'For as long as it takes.' Her snappish tone immediately softened. 'His rehab coordinator said they'd review his independence in three months. Look at it this way, winter's on the run and spring on the island is always pretty. Bring your computer and think of it as a working holiday.'

The thought of him and his father sharing a house was so far removed from his idea of a holiday that it made his gut churn. 'Exactly when did you add being a stand-up comedian to your many skills?'

She gave a hoarse laugh. 'You never know, Raf, Dad might surprise you.'

Over the last six weeks, Mario hadn't surprised Raf in the least.

As he gazed at the house next door, he admired the soaring timber beams and the floor-to-ceiling windows. Every inch of it had been built to maximise the view of the Southern Ocean. It was a view his father had seen from his fishing boat all his life right up until four months ago. Now the only time Mario saw the sea was when he left the property—an event he was dependent on Raf and others to provide. He probably missed the glorious vista that on a sunny day promised the world. No wonder the old bastard was grumpy a lot of the time.

His father cleared his throat—his sign that he was now awake. 'What are you doing?'

Raf turned from the window, an idea suddenly taking hold of him with a zip of excitement. 'I'm thinking you should extend this house upwards and get the same view as your neighbours.'

His father jerked the lever on his easy chair, snapping the leg rest back with a bang. The animals scattered. 'And I can climb stairs so easily now, Rafael.'

His father's sarcasm swirled around him. 'There's a thing called a lift, Dad.'

'And there's that thing called money.' Mario thumped his cane to emphasise his point that he could no longer work.

Raf closed his eyes and counted to five before opening them again. 'I'd be happy to finance it.'

'Why would you want to do that? You hate living on the island.'

He sighed. 'I don't hate it.'

His father's mouth flattened into a hard line. 'Could have fooled me. You stayed away long enough.'

And just like that, they were back to the circular argument that had dogged them for eighteen years. He could have said, *I'm here now*, but that would only remind his father of the reason why, which was like throwing a lit match onto a petrol spill. He changed the subject to something neutral. 'Who lives next door?'

Mario grunted, the sound derogatory. 'Weekenders.'

The locals had a love/hate relationship with the holidaymakers who flooded the island each year from December until Easter. There was no doubt the money the tourists poured into the economy helped keep the island's businesses alive but that money came with city attitudes, which frequently scraped up against country sensibilities. A community needed more than money to thrive and apart from the surf lifesaving club, the holiday home owners didn't usually get involved.

'They're not doing a very good job at being weekenders, then,' Raf said wryly. 'I've been here a few weeks and I haven't seen them once.'

'Probably too busy working to pay for that house. You know your cousin Rocco made a pile of cash building and selling it.'

His father rose laboriously and Raf held himself back from rushing forward to help. The staff at the rehabilitation centre had been firm that he should wait for Mario to ask if he needed assistance. It was logical on paper but in reality it meant by the time Mario asked for help he was furious at himself for failing and, by default, furious at Raf for being the one there to help.

The role of a carer was a catch-22 situation, no matter which angle he viewed it from.

His father walked slowly to the kitchen. Although Mario no longer skippered his boat, the habits of a lifetime were hard to shake. At three o'clock each afternoon he made coffee and listened to the detailed coastal weather report as if he still had to make the decision about whether or not to navigate across the treacherous bar and enter Bass Strait.

With Mario occupied, Raf usually took this time to go for a run and as he turned away from the window the soft drone of an engine snagged his attention. He looked back. A silver BMW four-wheel drive was pulling into the neighbours' driveway. The tinted windows made it impossible to see how many occupants were in the vehicle but given the style and make of the car he thought it a pretty safe bet there'd be two adults and at least two children. The perfect nuclear family to match the beautiful house.

A ripple of sadness and disappointment rolled through him and he immediately threw it off. He had more than enough money to live his life as he pleased. He had *nothing* to be sad about.

He glimpsed a flash of blond hair as the driver's door opened. 'Yes!' His prediction was on the money—make that a blond-haired, blue-eyed family.

'What?' Mario yelled from the kitchen.

'Your neighbours have arrived.'

Mario didn't bother to reply—the weather report took precedence over weekenders—but Raf stayed at the window to see if the rest of his conjectures would be accurate.

The driver stepped out from around the door and surprise shot through him. It wasn't a blond man but a woman. A very pregnant woman wearing large, dark sunglasses that hid half her face. She arched her back as if she'd been driving for a long time without a break and the clingy top she wore stretched over her full, round breasts and fecund belly.

Lush. So lush, so beautiful. The words pinged unbidden into Raf's mind and he gave himself a shake. Hell, what was wrong with him? It was one thing for a bloke to think a woman pregnant with his own child was sexy. He was certain that thinking that about a pregnant stranger was totally wrong.

No one else had alighted from the car. Had she just come with the kids? He waited for her to open the rear passenger doors but instead she turned so her back faced him. With her left arm akimbo, he assumed she was stroking her pregnant belly. Her head tilted back and her hair swung against her shoulders as she stared up at the house, looking at it as if it was a tall mountain she had to climb.

Why would you think that? More to the point, why are you even watching her? You're not that creepy guy who stares out of windows at people.

He rubbed his face with his hands. Exactly how small had his world become over the last few weeks if he was looking out a window and imagining things about a pregnant woman he'd never met. He really needed to get out of the house and talk to someone other than his father.

He dropped his hands from his face and saw she was still standing and staring at the door. Suddenly her shoulders rolled back, forming a rigid, determined line, and she marched up to the door and inserted the key. The door swung open and a moment later it closed behind her.

Raf had the ridiculous urge to follow her inside.

* * *

'Hello.'

The deep, male voice pulled Meredith's attention away from the horizon. She had no clue how long she'd been standing in the dunes, staring out to sea, but it had probably been a while.

In the three weeks since Richard's death she'd lurched from focused, rapid decision-making to being lost in a miasma of grief. Four days ago she'd escaped Melbourne, coming to the island for a much-needed change of scenery. Each day she walked along the beach early in the morning and again in the afternoon, welcoming the whip and sting of the salt-laden wind. The exercise was supposed to help her sleep but the baby and her grief had other ideas.

She turned her head towards the source of the voice. A tall, dark-haired man with tight, curly hair peppered with grey stood jogging on the spot on the beach just below her. She'd seen him from a distance every afternoon. Like her, he seemed to come to the beach at this time every day, no matter the weather. She felt her cheeks stretch minutely as she tried to muster a smile. 'Hello.'

In contrast, his wide, full mouth curved upwards into a friendly grin, sending dimples swirling into his dark stubble-covered cheeks. 'Everything okay?'

Not even close. But she wasn't going there. She'd spent days contacting everyone from the internet service provider to the bank, requesting that Richard's name be removed from the account. There were still organisations that needed to be told but she wanted a whole day off from saying, *My husband died.* She was worn out with having to deal with the sympathy of the person on the other end of the line or, in one situation, counselling the call-centre woman who was also recently bereaved.

'There's something hypnotic about the waves,' she said. 'I lose hours, watching them.'

He nodded as if he understood and ran his hand across his forehead, preventing a trickle of sweat from running into his chestnut-brown eyes. 'You could do it from the wind-free comfort of your home.'

A spike of unease washed through her. How did he know where she lived?

'We're neighbours,' he said quickly, as if realising he needed to reassure her that he hadn't been stalking her. 'I'm Raf Camilleri.'

'Oh,' she said, her sluggish brain trying to make connections. 'Is the street named after you?'

'No. It's named after my *nonno*, who paid for the road to be sealed. He was very proud that it was the first sealed road on the island.' His smile became wry. 'I think he took it as a tangible sign that he'd made good in his adopted country after the war.'

She extended her arm out behind her to encompass the row of houses further along the beach. 'So the Camilleris own a lot of this land?'

'Once, but not any more. Over the years it's been sold or gifted to family. Today it's prime real estate and my cousins are busy selling lots to holidaymakers so they can build their dream holiday homes.'

She remembered exactly when she and Richard had driven past number six Camilleri Drive and had recognised it as their dream home. Sadly, Richard had barely used it.

Raf's kind eyes continued to gaze at her and she realised she hadn't introduced herself. 'I'm Meredith Dennison.'

'Good to meet you, Meredith.'

His eyes crinkled at the edges as he smiled at her

again. She braced herself for the obvious and inevitable questions the Shearwater Island locals always asked her—when was the baby due and when was her husband joining her or how long did she plan to visit.

'If you ever need anything, Meredith, don't hesitate to call out over the fence.'

Before she could reply he'd pushed the ear buds into his ears, waved, turned and run off along the beach.

Meredith stood watching him run—his athleticism obvious as his long, strong legs strode out, quickly eating up the distance. Her phone vibrated in her pocket and she fished it out, checking the caller ID. She sighed before pressing accept call. 'Hi, Linda.'

'Meredith, thank goodness.' Her mother-in-law's voice combined worry with reproof. 'I've left three messages.'

She'd received each message but she'd been waiting until she could cope with talking to her utterly bereft mother-in-law. It often took more strength than she had. 'Sometimes the reception's a little dodgy down at the beach.'

'When are you coming back, dear?'

I don't know. 'I'm just taking it one day at a time.'

Linda's sigh sounded ominous, like the squalling wind that was chopping at the waves. 'Derek and I don't think you should be down there alone, especially not in the off season. Remember last year when they arrested that horrible man who'd been stealing underwear from clotheslines? And what if you went into labour and there's no one around to help. We thought we'd drive down on the weekend.'

Oh, God, please, no. After the emotional maelstrom of the funeral and the following days when a parade of well-meaning friends and Richard's grieving family had refused to let her be on her own, she'd almost gone crazy. She'd appreciated their concern but at the same time it had been suffocating her. Coming to the island was all about gaining some much-needed time so she could hear her own thoughts.

She saw a little dog suddenly shoot out of the dunes and race towards Raf, dancing around his running feet. Raf dodged and weaved and eventually bent down, scooping the dog up with one hand and tucking it under one very solid arm. She smiled. A man who tolerated little yappy dogs was probably not a stalker. Or a horrible man.

If you ever need anything, Meredith, don't hesitate to call out over the fence.

'That's very kind, Linda, but I'm not alone,' she said, her voice more firm and resolved than it had sounded in days. 'I have a neighbour and I can call over the fence if I need anything so I'll be fine. I'll ring you in a couple of days, promise.'

She cut the call, turned off her phone and returned it to the pocket of her coat, suddenly reminded of the many times she'd been the one to telephone Linda.

Can you call Mum for me?

Richard, she wants to hear from you, not me.

Please, Merry. I've got back-to-back surgeries.

'Richard,' she screamed into the wind. 'You bloody went and left me with your mother.'

The baby kicked and she pressed her hand against the busy foot. 'I know. She cares for us in her own way but right now, if I'm going to survive this, I have to do it my way.'

She wished she had a map to guide her.

CHAPTER THREE

RAF SURVEYED THE GARDEN, which was strewn with debris courtesy of last night's storm. The wind had raged, rattling the windows, snapping limbs off trees and redistributing the garden furniture all around the yard.

Mario stood at the front door, his expression glum as he gazed at a tree that had been sheared in half. 'Your mother planted that bottlebrush. The lorikeets love it.'

Raf had always hated how sad his father got whenever he talked about his mother. Hated that after all these years his memory of his wife was still clouded in throat-choking grief as if he was the only person to have suffered when she'd died.

'It's survived this long in the salt and the wind, I'm sure it's still got a lot of life left.'

Mario grunted. 'Get the chainsaw and cut it down,' he said authoritatively, as if Raf was still fifteen and under his instructions. Orders issued, he turned and shuffled back inside.

'Yeah, so not doing that,' Raf muttered, as he made his way down the drive and into the workshop.

Lifting the bush saw from its hook, he placed it in the wheelbarrow along with the shovel and returned to the front garden, and on the way he automatically glanced next door. He immediately cringed, remembering his conversation two days ago with Meredith on the beach. It hadn't been the first time he'd seen her in the dunes, standing and staring out to sea. Wan and drawn, and with misery and a quiet desperation rolling off her in great hulking waves, she'd made the dismal weather look positively cheery in comparison.

The sight of her had activated his first-aid training and experience—he really didn't want her walking fully clothed into the water. Before he'd even been conscious of making the decision, he'd found himself asking her if she was okay. That question had been the professional talking. There was something else about Meredith, though, that had kicked his three-year rule of not getting involved with women to the kerb, and a moment later he'd totally stuffed things up by mentioning he knew where she lived.

The look she'd given him had been a cross between horror that they'd been alone on the beach and her calculating how close she was to the road for a quick getaway. He hadn't meant to scare her and he'd overcompensated by rabbiting on about his grandfather and the Camilleri mob, before suggesting she yell out if she ever needed anything.

Oh, yeah, like she'd ever do that. Even if she'd sustained some house damage last night he doubted she'd have reached out. It was far more likely she'd call her husband ahead of him, even though chances were he was two hundred and fifty kilometres away in Melbourne.

And there was the thing. Since she'd arrived, no one had visited her. Now it was Sunday so if there had been weekend guests making the trek from Melbourne, surely they would have arrived on Friday night or Saturday lunchtime at the latest. A pregnant woman alone and staring out to sea bothered him more than it should. Although there was no rule to say a woman couldn't be on her own, being alone, pregnant and down on the island out of season seemed all wrong.

Not your problem, mate. If you want a problem to solve, you've always got Mario. He shook off the thought. Some things couldn't be solved. The tree, however, was something he could rescue. Picking up the bush saw, he started work, welcoming the push and the pull as his arm and leg muscles tensed and relaxed.

Half an hour later he was covered in the fine red filaments that gave the tree its common name and he was sneezing from pollen overload. On the flip side, he did have a growing pile of wood in the wheelbarrow. Studying his handiwork, he decided he'd take two more branches off the left side and then the job would be done. Pulling back on the saw with one hand and steadying the large branch with the other, he set to work. The weight of the wood bore down on the saw, impeding the slide of the blade, so he moved his left hand closer to apply counter-pressure.

He heard the sound of a door closing and he glanced up to see Meredith getting out of her car. Unlike at the beach where she'd been huddled in a bulky coat that hid her body from neck to knees, today she wore a long-sleeved grey-and-white jumper that fell to the tops of her thighs. Her legs, which were longer than he'd realised, were clad in black leggings that hid nothing and did everything to emphasise their toned shape. The knee-high riding boots helped as well.

She held a carton of milk in one hand while her other tried to prevent her hair from blowing around her face like a golden scarf. Despite the *Melbourne Black* clothing, which made her pale face and distinct lack of pregnancy glow more obvious, there was still something about her—something that called out to him—and it kept his gaze fixed firmly on her.

Jagged pain ripped through him.

He swore loudly, the expletive carrying on the wind as the blade of the bush saw became embedded deep in his hand. Bright red blood bubbled up like a geyser and he dropped the saw, ripped off his shirt and wound it tightly around his hand to staunch the flow. His green T-shirt turned purple.

'Are you hurt?'

He spun around to see Meredith's baby-blue eyes— eyes with unexpected variations of light and dark, like the sea on a cloudy day—fixed on him and filled with consternation. *I couldn't stop staring at you.* He felt ridiculously foolish. 'I cut myself.'

She glanced at the saw that now lay on the thick and bouncy couch grass. 'With that tetanus-waiting-to-happen blade?'

He nodded, suddenly feeling light-headed from the throbbing pain in his hand.

She pressed her hand on his shoulder, the pressure firm. 'You've gone a bit green. Sit down before you fall down. I'll just go grab my bag.'

Bag? He really was dizzy because that made no sense at all. He wanted to say he was fine but his legs felt decidedly wobbly so he sat and automatically dropped his head between his knees in the way he'd told so many of his patients to do in his role as a volunteer ambulance officer.

A minute later, Meredith's black leather boots appeared in his line of vision and a blanket slid across his shoulders. 'Pull that around you. I don't want you getting cold.'

'Thanks.' He raised his head to see her drop a back-pack from her shoulder and he instantly recognised the medical logo. 'You're a doctor?'

'GP.' She moved as if she was going to kneel down next to him on the wet grass.

'Stop.'

'Excuse me?' Her tone was both bemused and commanding at the same time, as if she wasn't used to taking instructions.

'The grass is sopping. I'll stand up and we'll go inside.'

Her light brown brows pulled down. 'Are you sure?'

'Yeah.' He wasn't sure at all but, he wasn't about to let a heavily pregnant woman kneel in wet grass.

She gave him a scrutinising look and her lips pursed into a perfect bow like those painted on dolls. 'Pull up on my hand.'

'I don't need—'

'Just do it.' Her hand hovered in front of him. 'I'm not going to break and, believe me, you don't want concussion from falling over.'

With her baby-blue eyes, dark brown lashes, pale complexion and that mouth, she looked like a fragile china doll but her firm tone said otherwise. He extended his hand. 'I think I'm too scared to say no.'

The edges of that very beautiful mouth tweaked up slightly—not quite a smile but as close as he'd ever seen her come to one. Her warm hand closed around his wrist with a surprisingly strong grip and he pushed against his injured hand to help them both. Red-hot pain ripped through him and he swayed on his feet.

'Steady.' Meredith pressed her shoulder under his and put her arm around his waist. 'Just stand still for a second and wait for everything to catch up.'

Her warmth flowed into him and he had the craziest sensation that she fitted in against him as if she was his matching piece in a puzzle.

What the hell? The pain was making him hallucinate. 'I'm good to go.' He started to walk, fighting the silver dots that danced in front of his eyes.

He thought he heard her mutter something about men taking stupid risks and then her fingers were digging into his forearm and stalling his progress. 'This isn't a race walk, okay?'

With one hand holding her bag and the other on his arm, they made their way slowly through the front doorway and into the house. 'Where's the kitchen?'

Right now it seemed a million miles away. 'Down the hall and to the left.'

A minute later Raf gratefully slid into the chrome and vinyl kitchen chair and rested his arms on the green Laminex-topped table. Meredith blinked twice as if she was clearing her vision and then she pulled up a chair and opened her medical bag.

He gave a wry smile. 'Yes, you have stepped back in time to 1975.'

She didn't say anything, just pumped hand sanitiser onto her hand before deftly rubbing it into her skin. After she'd snapped on gloves, she finally spoke. 'Let's see how much damage you've inflicted on yourself.' She gingerly unwrapped the blood-soaked shirt and more oozed from a deep and uneven cut. 'You did a good job.'

'I only ever do my best,' he joked feebly as he forced himself to look at his hand. His gut flipped as a wave of nausea washed through him. Being objective about a cut was much easier when it wasn't his hand that was bleeding.

'Wriggle your fingers for me,' she said, not taking her gaze off his hand.'

'One, two, three, four, five,' he said as he moved each one individually. 'No tendon damage.'

Surprise crossed her face as she pressed a wad of gauze against the wound and then she picked up his other hand and placed it over the top to apply pressure. 'That's right. Are you in the medical profession too?'

'Not exactly, but I've been a volunteer ambo for years. I work the big events in Melbourne like the tennis and the footy grand final.'

He heard the combined noises of shuffle and thump echoing down the hall—the new sound of his father's gait that had replaced his previously brisk and determined thwack of work boots.

A few seconds later, Mario appeared in the doorway. 'Rafael.' His voice was coolly censorious. 'You didn't mention we have a visitor.' He turned his attention to Meredith with a smile. 'Hello, I'm Mario Camilleri.'

'I'm Meredith,' she said crisply in a doctor's voice. 'I'm your neighbour but I'm not here on a social call.'

Before Raf could open his mouth she added, 'I'm a doctor and Raf's injured himself with the saw.'

Mario's gaze moved to the blood-soaked shirt and gauze and then flicked to Raf's face, his expression critical. 'I taught you better than that. Just as well you didn't use the chainsaw.'

'Meredith,' Raf said, trying to stay calm, 'meet my father.'

Meredith thought she saw Raf's jaw clench and had the almost palpable tension that ran between father and son been an object, it would have been a big, solid brick wall. Mario's hand gripped the handle of his cane and despite the fact his face hadn't blanched at the sight of the blood, she really didn't need two men down. 'I'm going to stitch Raf's hand so if that makes you feel queasy...'

'I've been a professional fisherman all my life,' Mario said. 'It takes more than some blood to upset me.' He flicked a disapproving glance at Raf. 'My wife had a rule about wearing a shirt in the house. I'll get Raf a clean one.' He turned and walked away, his left leg dragging every few steps.

As a doctor, Meredith had seen a lot of bodies in her day and she could understand how some men's torsos—especially lily-white-skinned ones with flabby abdomens—could be off-putting and a definite appetite suppressant in a kitchen. Raf's, on the other hand, was olive skinned, muscular with a hint of a six pack and not at all unappealing.

Eye candy for you, Merry. Richard's teasing voice sliced into her.

She quickly snapped open an ampoule of local anaesthetic and concentrated on drawing the clear liquid into the syringe, desperate not to think about Richard. Whenever she thought about his unnecessary death, she never knew if she was going to start screaming at him, start sobbing, or both. She'd learned in the last weeks that there was a minute distance between anger and despair.

She shot the clear anaesthetic liquid out of the needle until it measured the correct amount. 'Let's get this hand stitched up.'

Raf grimaced. 'That stuff stings.'

'Sorry.'

He shrugged. 'There are worse things.'

'Yes,' she said savagely. 'There are.'

'That was heartfelt.' His large, kind chestnut eyes—the same deep, rich colour as the eyes of the Jersey cows she'd grown up surrounded by—studied her intently, as if he was searching for something.

She dropped his gaze. 'This might hurt.' She jabbed the needle into the back of his hand and injected the local.

He flinched. 'You're not wrong.'

'We just have to give it a minute to work.' She laid out her scissors and the suture thread on the sterile paper towel from the dressing pack before swabbing the wound with antiseptic.

He sucked in a breath through his teeth. 'Okay, Meredith, you need to talk to me to take my mind off this burning pain.'

She opened her mouth to mention the weather when Raf asked, 'When's the baby due?'

'Three weeks.' She pressed the tip of a needle onto his hand, testing if the local had taken effect. 'Can you feel that?'

He shook his head. 'So really the baby could arrive any day now.'

'No,' she said emphatically, and started stitching, pushing the curved needle into the skin layers and twirling the thread around the forceps before tying the knot. 'Three weeks is the minimum and I could have up to five.'

Raf laughed. 'You've told the baby that, have you? It's my experience they come when they're ready.'

'You have kids?' she asked, wanting to turn the attention away from herself.

For a brief moment his nostrils flared and she felt sure she saw a flash of emotion. Whether it was regret or relief, it was impossible to tell.

'No. My sister has twins and they came early.'

'Multiple pregnancies always do but I've only got one baby on board.' *A baby I'm not ready to have on my own.*

A thread of panic scuttled through her and she heard herself saying, 'He or she is not allowed to come early.' He looked at her with astonishment clear on his face and she didn't blame him because she knew she sounded crazy, and, in a way, she was probably slowly going mad. Having a husband die weeks before the birth of their first child could do that to a woman. She immediately braced herself for the expected, 'Do you think you should talk to a professional?' She already had.

'You have to be the only pregnant woman I've met in the last three years who doesn't know the baby's sex. It seems to be the thing to do these days,' he said in a tone that hinted at disapproval. 'Goes along with the designer nursery and matching stroller.'

Come on, Merry, of course we need to know if it's a boy or a girl so we can plan. She kept her eyes down on the stitching as the memory of her and Richard arguing over her refusal to find out the baby's sex came back to her. 'Call me old-fashioned,' she said, 'but I didn't want to know ahead of time.'

'I guess you're going to be doing a lot of hard work during labour so you deserve a surprise at the end.'

The unexpected words made her glance up from his hand. 'Thank you.'

He frowned. 'What for?'

'You're the only person who gets that. My husband, Richard...' The words slipped out as naturally as breathing. The bolt of pain that followed almost winded her. She cleared her throat. 'My in-laws really wanted to know so they could fill out school enrolment forms.'

His brows rose. 'That's a new one. I thought grand-mothers wanted to know so they could knit pink or blue.' His tone was light but his eyes were doing that searching thing again as if he knew she was hiding something from him.

Talk about the stitches. 'This is the fifth and final stitch,' she said, snipping the excess thread and then picking up a low-adherent dressing and taping it in place. 'You need to keep this clean and dry for a week. Are you up to date with your tetanus shots?'

He nodded, his curls bouncing and brushing his in-telligent forehead. 'Yes and I know the drill. I'll see my doctor to have the stitches removed.'

She stripped off her gloves. 'I can do it for you.'

'Won't you be back in Melbourne by then? You are from Melbourne, right?'

'Yes, I'm from Melbourne,' she said briskly as she bundled up the rubbish. 'And I'll still be here.'

'But that's only two weeks before the baby's due.' Deep concentration lines carved into the skin between his eyes as he took a quick look at her wedding band before saying gently, 'You and your husband do know that the nearest hospital is on the mainland at Wongarri. That's seventy kilometres away.'

'We do.' It was both the truth and, in a way, a lie. Richard had known the distance to the hospital but he wasn't here to drive her.

'So your husband's planning on coming to the island very soon to be with you, right?'

The question froze the breath in her lungs.

Raf Camilleri's concern for her pulsed between them, reflected in the creases in his high forehead, in the depths of his rich, warm eyes and in the deep brack-ets around his mouth. She knew she should tell him that Richard wasn't coming but she also knew that the moment she did, everything would change.

People's reactions to death were never uniform but as she and Raf barely knew each other, she was pretty certain he'd feel embarrassed and that could play out in one of two ways—mortified and choking silence or prattling pity. Men usually went silent.

Thankfully, Mario chose that moment to return to the kitchen holding one of Raf's shirts in his hand. He draped it over a chair. 'Meredith, can I make you an espresso, latte, cappuccino?'

'Dad,' Raf said with resignation ringing in his tone, 'pregnant women shouldn't drink coffee.'

Mario muttered something that sounded both Italian and empathetic before saying, 'Meredith, can I offer you tea or hot chocolate?'

'Thank you, but there's really no need,' she said, zipping up her medical bag. The noise sliced through the frosty air that surrounded the two men.

'I insist.'

Two male voices—both deep, one slightly accented—collided, tumbling over each other as Mario and Raf spoke simultaneously. Mario continued, 'Indulge an old man and a foolish one.'

Raf shot his father a dark look. 'I think Dad is trying to say we're grateful for your help.'

'As you can tell, Meredith,' Mario said, 'we're sick of each other's company and we'd welcome your delightful presence a little longer.'

'You may also prevent me from committing patricide,' Raf muttered under his breath.

Mario slapped the top of a very expensive, stainless-steel Italian espresso machine. 'I can make you whatever you want and milk is good for the *bambino*.'

Meredith had a similar machine sitting on her kitchen bench next door and she'd been returning from the small corner shop with the milk to make herself a drink when she'd heard Raf's pained and loud swearing.

During the first week after Richard's death a lot of people had made her drinks, because they hadn't known what else to do for her and it had made them feel better. But right now, with Mario's coal-black eyes twinkling at her and Raf giving her a wry smile that held an element of *save me from my father*, this offer of a drink was completely different. Suddenly the idea of someone without pity or sympathy in their eyes making her a hot beverage was very tempting. 'Hot chocolate would be great, thank you.'

'And chocolate and hazelnut biscotti,' Mario said firmly, opening the fridge and lifting out the bottle of milk.

'I don't need—'

'Don't even think about fighting Italian hospitality, Meredith,' Raf said, rolling his eyes. 'You'll never win. Dad will feed you until you waddle.'

She grimaced. 'I'm eight months pregnant so I already waddle.'

'Do you?' The words were laden with query and utterly devoid of sarcasm. 'I hadn't noticed.'

CHAPTER FOUR

THE FOLLOWING AFTERNOON, Raf stood at Meredith's front door, holding a bright posy of spring thank-you flowers. Earlier in the day at Shearwater Flowers and Gifts, he'd been prevaricating between a traditional bunch of white roses and the posy. The florist had said that the riot of yellow daffodils, purple irises, pink gerberas and fragrant purple hyacinths all interspersed with blue gum leaves would make any woman smile. That offhand comment had sold the posy. He had a ridiculous urge to see Meredith truly smile.

He couldn't shake the feeling she was going through the motions of living—enduring each day rather than revelling in it. For half an hour yesterday after Mario had badgered her to stay for hot chocolate, she'd relaxed a little and although he wouldn't say she'd looked happy, she'd certainly seemed less miserable for a moment or two. But *less miserable* wasn't enough to quieten his misgivings.

It made no sense that a doctor would say so emphatically that her baby wasn't coming early. It was as if she really didn't want it to come and that, coupled with the fact she didn't know the sex, had him up at midnight and on the computer, researching antenatal depression. Apparently it existed.

He could understand a younger woman with less education and financial stability being very stressed and worried about impending motherhood. He knew he was only a stranger looking in from the outside but given the value of her house and the very expensive German car she drove, money didn't seem to be an issue. Was it the absent husband that was causing her anguish? Was the marriage in trouble because of the baby?

Bitter experience had taught him all about that. Nothing could drive the final nail into the coffin of a failing marriage faster than the emotions surrounding a child. Whether a child was wanted or not, if both parties disagreed the marriage ended in divorce.

He gripped the flowers in his uninjured hand and rang the doorbell with the other.

He heard the even tread of her walk on the stairs and then the door opened. Today she was wearing a royal-blue cable jumper that seemed to make the multifaceted blues in her eyes sparkle like the crystals in a kaleidoscope. It did nothing, however, to lessen the black shadows that stained the delicate skin under her eyes.

Beautiful and haunted.

The thought struck him hard and he almost raised his hand, wanting to stroke her cheek with his thumb and wipe away the smudges. Stunned by his reaction, he covered it by abruptly thrusting the flowers forward. 'Thank you for saving me a trip to the medical clinic yesterday.'

She stood still, staring at the posy as if it was on fire. 'You *really* didn't need to bring me flowers.'

This wasn't exactly the reaction he'd expected or hoped for. Not only wasn't she smiling, her pretty mouth had tightened into a thin line.

He brought the flowers back to his side, holding them

with the heads facing down. 'I could exchange them for chocolates if you prefer.'

The words seemed to bring her out of her trance. 'I'm sorry. Come in.' She turned and walked up the stairs, and he followed, losing the battle not to stare at her curvy behind. It wasn't big but it wasn't small either and the contours of the long jumper outlined its curves to perfection.

Married and pregnant, dude. So not available.

Under his feet the stunning jarrah floorboards gleamed red and when he hit the top stair he was standing in an enormous open living space filled with light. The view of the ocean was as spectacular as he'd imagined but it was the dozen vases of flowers—every possible shade of white, cream and green—that stopped him in his tracks. All of them had the trademark card of Shearwater Flowers and Gifts inserted into the middle of them.

'I can see why you didn't need my flowers,' he said with an ironic laugh. 'They don't match your colour scheme.'

A muscle twitched in her cheek but she didn't say anything.

'Special occasion?' he asked, hoping she'd tell him so it would break the ice and he could congratulate her.

Meredith continued to stare out to sea with her arms wrapped tightly around herself.

She was giving him nothing so he pressed on. 'Birthday? Conferment of your fellowship?'

She shook her head hard, sending her golden hair flying across her face. She quickly tugged it back behind her ears. 'Condolences.'

The word came out softly but it barrelled into him with the impact of a rampaging bull. The white roses, the white stargazer lilies, the white daisies with the green discs and the white orchids all catapulted him back in time so fast he almost got whiplash. Memories of standing next to his mother's casket, with the cloying scent of lilies clogging his throat, rushed back to him unbidden.

Suddenly it all made sense—her paleness, the black rings under her eyes and her all-encompassing sadness. She was grieving, but for whom? They were both of an age where parents might die. Hell, three months ago he and Bianca had been faced with the possibility that Mario might die. Raf wanted to offer his condolences but for whom? Was it her mother? Father? Was it crass to ask who had died?

Yes!

Meredith cleared her throat but her gaze didn't leave the horizon. 'Richard…my husband…was snowboarding with a group of back-country enthusiasts. They'd hiked to Mount Feathertop,' she said in a flat tone, as if she'd told the story many times before. 'He was caught in an avalanche and…' She sucked in a deep breath, her whole body trembling. 'He didn't survive.'

Her pain tore through him, tightening his chest and making his gut heave. He'd seen the television news reports and read the articles in the paper a few weeks ago about the talented trauma surgeon whose life had been cut short so dramatically. 'Bloody hell, Meredith. That's… It's…' He swore softly. 'So very wrong.'

She raised her gaze to his. At first he saw desolation and despair but then anger sparked bright like a flint. 'Oh, yes, it's wrong all right. I'm so furious with him for doing this to me.' She rubbed her belly. 'To us.'

Raf frowned and said quietly, 'I doubt it was his intention to die.'

'You think?' Blue jets of fury flared in her eyes and she jabbed her finger at him. 'It's just the sort of selfish thing he'd go and do.' She spun away from him and grabbed a vase of flowers, dumping them in the sink and snapping the stalks in half. 'For years I've waited to have our baby. I fitted into his life. I moved cities and countries, leaving good jobs behind to support him and his career.'

She threw the broken blooms into the bin, her actions jerky. 'Now it was supposed to be my turn. He should be here, supporting the baby and me. He owes me that. He promised.' Her voice broke and she sagged against the sink like a deflating balloon, her shoulders shaking as the emotion of her outburst caught up with her.

Her agony tugged at Raf and guilt propelled him forward. Gently and silently, he put his hands on her shoulders. The last time he'd spoken, his words had been a match to her outrage and powerlessness over her husband's death. This time he wasn't saying a word. This time he was just offering comfort in the same way he offered it when he was on first-aid duty.

Her shoulders heaved under his hands and with a choking sob she turned into his chest. Without a second thought, he wrapped his arms around her, wishing he could absorb and dilute her distress.

Shuddering, she dropped her head onto his shoulder and it seemed the most natural thing in the world to bring his hand to the back of her head and stroke her hair. The silky strands caressed his palm and he breathed in deeply, enjoying her subtle fragrance of salt, spring flowers and a touch of apple far too much.

Her gulping sobs brought tears that soaked through his shirt and the dampness was cool on his skin. He didn't care. It felt right to have her in his arms and he'd stay here for as long as she needed him.

Slowly, her ragged breathing calmed and they fell into a matching rhythm of long, slow, deep breaths.

The baby kicked him hard in the belly. Kicked a second time as if to say, *You're not my father so who the hell are you?*

He tensed and immediately dropped his arms from Meredith, feeling the chill of the spring air move between them. The baby was right. He was no one's father and he never would be.

Meredith splashed her face with water and groaned. Right now, Raf was in her living room, probably regretting that he'd rung her doorbell. After all, a virtual stranger having a monumental meltdown was the last thing any guy wanted to witness. She hoped the fact he had first-aid experience meant she wasn't the first pregnant woman to have sobbed on his shoulder and that he'd take it in his stride.

After drying her face, she peered at her reflection and sighed. It would take way more than cold water to make any impact on the red blotches on her face and she didn't have the energy or inclination to powder down. 'Sprocket, stay in there. Meeting your mother face to face will terrify you.'

Leaving the bathroom, she walked down the short hall but Raf wasn't standing by the windows where she'd left him. Neither was he sitting on one of the many couches.

'Are you feeling a bit better? If that's even really an option...'

She spun around towards the quiet sound of his voice—a sound that for some reason made her think of the slide of smooth, thick velvet against her skin. He stood in a now tidy kitchen devoid of all signs of the mess of macerated stalks and crushed flowers.

'You'll be relieved I've managed to stop crying, even if I don't look like it.'

His mouth curved up into what she was coming to recognise as his trademark smile—warm, gentle, kind and with a hint of teasing. 'I think the red splotches suit you. They add colour to your cheeks.'

She heard herself make a noise and was surprised to hear it was a laugh. 'So there are some advantages to totally falling apart.'

'Seems so.'

She pushed her hair behind her ears and said what she needed to say. 'I'm so sorry you had to see that. I've been sort of holding it together since I came down here and—'

'God, Meredith, don't apologise,' he said firmly. 'If anyone should be saying sorry, it's me. It was my damn flowers that started it. If I'd known, I would have bought something else.'

She noticed he'd put the posy in the bin. 'I left Melbourne because I needed a break from flowers and condolences and death. Stupid, right? I can't outrun this.' She sighed and tugged her hair behind her ears again. 'Richard wasn't just mine to miss. His colleagues from around the world are grieving too and their hearts are in the right place, but if I get another bouquet of flowers…'

'You'll scream? Throw them off the balcony?'

'Yes.' She couldn't believe he understood. 'And I feel so guilty. I mean they're beautiful flowers. I had those lilies and roses in my wedding bouquet.' The lump in her throat built again and she forced it down. 'I'm not sure I ever want to see or smell another lily again.'

He rubbed his jaw slowly as if he was thinking. 'What if you keep all the cards but I take the flowers to the Country Women's Association? They're fantastic. They'll divide the flowers up, rearrange them and deliver them to the sick and the elderly shut-ins. They'll get a real boost from the flowers and you'll get a break.'

A rush of gratitude filled her. 'Are you sure that's not too much trouble for you?'

He laughed. 'You'll be doing me a favour. It will get Mario out of the house and those good women will insist we stay and then they'll force me to eat the lightest scones ever made, served with island raspberry jam and island cream.'

She started plucking the cards from the flowers. One day she was going to have to find the strength to write to every single person and thank them but not today. 'None of that food sounds very Italian.'

'When it comes to scones, lamingtons, vanilla slices and pavlova, I'm a multicultural eater,' he said with a wicked twinkle in his eyes. He commenced carrying the vases to the sink and when they were all lined up, he started draining the water.

Ten minutes later, he had all of the vases washed and dried and the flowers placed carefully in a box, which he'd lined with plastic. The posy he'd brought her was balanced on the top—a slash of bright colour in stark contrast to the rest. Already the house felt less claustrophobic.

'Thank you so much for doing this.'

He shrugged as if it was no big deal. 'I'd ask you to come along because it's a pretty drive but that defeats the purpose of separating you from the flowers.'

She welcomed his pragmatic thoughtfulness. 'And you'd have to share your scones.'

He grinned. 'Good point. I share some things but never scones.'

'I'll make a note to remember that.'

He picked up the flower box and wrapped his wide forearm around it, the action making his triceps bulge. She was struck by the large surface veins that ran the length of his arm—veins that seemed to say, *safe and strong*. Looking like he was ready to leave, he unexpectedly set the box back down and met her gaze, his expression serious.

'Meredith, I totally get that you needed to leave Melbourne for a while but with the baby so close to arriving, isn't it time to go back?'

Melbourne. She reluctantly thought about the terrace house that lived and breathed Richard. The floor-to-ceiling shelves filled with his books, the many enlarged photographs that hung on the walls staring down at her, showing him doing everything from scuba diving to skiing. All of it reminding her that his love of extreme sports had stolen him from her. From their baby.

Her mind immediately flicked to the room they'd finally decided would be the nursery and to the two cans of paint sitting on the floor, waiting for Richard to open and stir them. It was a house full of memories and hope, now tainted by being the place where she'd been told Richard was dead. It had become the house Linda had taken to sleeping in to feel closer to her only child.

She shivered and rubbed her arms, far from ready to return. 'Here the days are tough but they're not as awful as in Melbourne.'

His mouth pulled down on one side as if he was weighing up her words and trying to understand. 'Okay. What about having someone come and stay here with you?'

She shook her head, remembering the parade of well-meaning people in the Fitzroy house. 'That would defeat the whole purpose of me coming down here.'

'I really don't like the idea of you being here alone.'

She'd had this conversation before and she could hear Emma's worried voice and Linda's and Derek's disapproving tones playing over and over in her head. She didn't need to add Raf's to the list. 'I'm a doctor,' she said crisply. 'I'll be fine.'

His usually relaxed face tightened. 'I may lack your medical qualifications but I do know that you don't have the objectivity to be your own doctor. And you're pregnant. When did you last have a check-up?'

'Last week, just before I came.'

'Which means you're ready for another one.'

She hated that he was holding up a metaphorical mirror to her listing all the things she knew she should be doing for herself and the baby. The idea of returning to Melbourne was enough to send her over the edge. 'I didn't realise they taught the antenatal care schedule to first-aiders,' she said waspishly.

His entire body stiffened and something close to hurt flared in his eyes. It faded quickly until all that was left was a steely glare and an implacable force. 'I'm not judging you, Meredith. Your life's been turned on its head and you're doing the best you can to survive, but it's not just about you and you can't be your own doctor. If you won't go back to Melbourne, call the Shearwater Clinic and make an appointment with one of the doctors there.'

The baby moved as if it was reinforcing Raf's words and reminding her that her obligations didn't stop just because she was grieving. She sighed. 'If I make the appointment for tomorrow, will you stop pestering me?'

His stern expression softened slightly. 'Maybe.'

'Okay, I'll look up the number and call the clinic.'

'Great.' He slapped a business card down on the counter. 'This is my number. If you're staying down here I want you to promise to call me at any time day or night if you need anything. *Anything.*' His eyes narrowed into an intransigent glare. 'I mean it.'

'I think I'll enter you in the bossiest neighbour award.' But despite her snarky comment, she knew he was worried about her and the baby. *Everyone* was worried about her and the baby—heck, she was worried about her and the baby.

She wasn't ready to have the baby. She wanted to delay the birth by a year so she had a hope in hell of being able to come to terms with Richard's death and have the energy to be a mother. 'I will ring you if I go into labour. Happy?'

Relief wove through the dark stubble on his cheeks. 'Thank you.' He picked up the box and turned towards the stairs.

As she watched him leave, she had the overwhelming feeling she was the one who should be thanking him. 'Raf, wait.' She shot out her hand to stall him and as it closed around his forearm, his warmth and strength rushed into her palm.

He stopped, his eyes fixed on her hand, which almost glowed white against his swarthy tan. 'What do you need?'

Feeling oddly comforted but rattled by his heat on her hand, she dropped it from his arm and picked up the posy. 'Thanks.'

His dark brows drew down. 'Are you sure?'

'Yes.' It was the first confident decision she'd made in over three weeks.

'You really don't have to keep them.'

'I know, but I want to. They remind me of the colour that was in my life a month ago and the excitement Richard and I had about the baby.'

He stared down at her for a long moment, his face a mixture of guarded thoughts and feelings, none of which she could decode. He finally broke the silence. 'That can only be a good thing.'

He abruptly turned and walked down the stairs and at the bottom he stopped and called out, 'Mario wants you to come to dinner on Friday, and before you say no, he also said, "Don't disappoint an old man."'

She smiled. 'Does he play that card a lot?'

'Only when it suits him,' Raf said grimly, and pulled the door shut behind him.

'Hey, baby brother, what on earth are you doing?'

Raf turned from the windowsill, paint scraper in his uninjured hand, and waved to his sister. 'The wood needs some love.'

Bianca stood with her hands on her hips, surveying their childhood home. 'The entire house needs some love but Dad resisted before the stroke and now...'

'I suggested he extend upwards.'

Bianca gave him a look that suggested she was questioning his sanity. 'Why? He only lives in four of the nine rooms he's got.'

'It's not about the space, Bianca, it's about quality of life. He could have a living room, bathroom, bedroom and kitchen upstairs *and* a view of the ocean.'

'What? And remind him of what he's lost now he can't captain his own boat?' She pulled open the screen door and walked into the kitchen.

He followed her, frustration simmering. 'Yeah, of

course that's why I'm suggesting I spend two hundred thousand dollars—just so I can taunt him.' He swallowed the sarcasm. 'You know as well as I do that the sea is part of who he is and, granted, he can't work it any more but he can still enjoy watching the weather roll in and out, and the way the clouds and light change the colours from stormy grey to turquoise green.

'Equally important, the grumpy bastard can sit, watch and grumble about the *bloody surfers* having rocks in their heads.' He shot his sister an ironic smile. 'And you know that's about as happy as he gets.'

She smiled. 'When you put it that way, I can see your point but I'm not sure we'd ever convince him.' She switched on the kettle and checked out his hand. 'How are both the invalids doing?'

'Five stitches doesn't make me an invalid. Dad's napping after the physio put him through a gruelling session this morning but the good news is I think his gait's improving.'

'That is good news,' she said, opening the fridge, scanning the contents and closing it again. 'At least you're both eating well.'

He leaned against the counter and folded his arms. 'You say that as if you're surprised.'

She cocked one eyebrow. 'I saw your empty fridge in Melbourne, Raf.'

Memories of that torrid time when his life had been turned on its head—when he'd lost a part of himself for ever—tried to resurface but he forced them back down. He made himself shrug so as not to give Bianca any reason to ask questions.

'That doesn't count. Teresa had just left me and cooking was the last thing on my mind. Since then, I've had three years to hone my skills and if you'd ever bothered to visit me again, I would have wowed you.'

Bianca poured boiling water over tea bags. 'Guilt doesn't work on me, baby brother, and the road goes both ways, remember. If you're so keen to show off your cooking skills, me, Marco and the kids will come over tonight and help you eat that large container of calamari I see you've got in the fridge.'

'You'll have to check with Dad because he's cooking tonight.'

'With hot oil?' Bianca sounded horrified. 'You're supposed to be taking care of him, not hurting him. He's got one weak hand and what if he drops the pan?'

Raf bristled. 'You were the one who insisted I come and help, and as I'm the one who takes the brunt of Dad's anger at the way his body's let him down, you don't get to say what I can and can't do.' He blew out a breath, trying to soften his outburst. 'He can still cook and as much as he hates me being in the kitchen when he does, he tolerates me because I'm a handy kitchen hand when he's making his famous salt-and-pepper calamari.'

'I'm surprised he's cooking it. He only ever made it when he was entertaining.'

'Exactly,' Raf said, thinking about Mario at the wharf this morning haggling with his mates who'd just docked after a night on the water. 'He's showing off to Meredith.'

Bianca looked confused. 'Who?'

He pointed to the white house next door and Bianca choked on her tea. 'Dad is cooking for the weekenders? Has he had a personality transplant?'

If Raf hadn't met Meredith he'd have thought exactly the same thing, but from the moment Mario had laid eyes on her in the kitchen, he'd shown more signs of paternal feeling than Raf had seen from him in almost two decades. Raf understood where Mario was coming from—there was something about Meredith that grabbed you by the throat and didn't let go.

Not that his own feelings for Meredith were paternal. They were a total mess, ranging from abject concern for her and her situation, a need to protect her, which clashed with his own need to protect himself, and an overawareness of how, despite being heavily pregnant, she had an aura of desirability he hadn't noticed in a woman in a long, long time. The memory from four days ago—her head on his shoulder, his hands on her hair, her fresh scent in his nostrils, his desire to keep his arms wrapped around her for longer than was necessary—visited him every night, heating his blood and taunting him with the irony of his attraction to her.

She was a grieving woman and pregnant with another man's child. The counsellor he'd seen after Teresa had left him would have a field day with that. He could clearly hear her saying, *You do realise you've chosen the one woman who isn't capable of reciprocating your feelings, which is exactly why you've chosen her.* His imagined conversation always stopped there. No way in hell did he want to know what she'd say about the baby.

CHAPTER FIVE

MEREDITH STOOD ADMIRING Mario's collection of model boats, which was housed in a beautiful cabinet in the living room. She was on her way back from yet another bathroom break as Sprocket seemed insistent on bouncing on her bladder tonight, along with keeping a foot firmly stuck under her ribs. It was so uncomfortable that it almost hurt.

She'd been restless ever since she'd woken up that morning and given the chance she preferred to stand, because that seemed to help the backache that had been coming and going all day.

'You okay?'

She turned to see Raf leaning loose-limbed against the doorframe, although one look at his expression and she knew the stance was deceptively casual. She was learning that he noticed things other people didn't and his incisive and penetrating dark gaze was currently fixed exclusively on her, searching and seeking.

She stopped her hand from pressing against the small of her back, which was now aching to beat the band, but as it was the end of the day and she was tired, that was situation normal. 'I'm fine. I hope Mario wasn't disappointed that I could only eat a small serving of his calamari but the baby is squishing everything at the moment, including my stomach.'

'Don't worry about it. No matter how much you eat, Mario will always think you should have eaten more. On the other hand, you've got a fan in Leo, who polished off your share along with his own, as well as three of my calamari rings that he nicked off my plate when I wasn't looking. I swear my nephew has hollow legs.'

He pushed off the doorframe, his lips pressed together in a half-smile. 'I'm sorry dinner got hijacked by my sister and her family. It was probably overwhelming and I can take you home now if you've had enough.'

She felt his understanding wrap around her like a soft blanket. 'They're a lovely family and I'm enjoying myself.'

He snorted. 'You don't have to be polite with me, Meredith. I love them but I know that the Camilleris *en masse* are a lot to handle.'

She thought about Bianca's greeting when she'd arrived this evening. *Raf told me your husband was killed in a snowboarding accident. If you weren't pregnant, I'd suggest we get drunk together but that's out so I'll just say this. I won't ask you any questions but if you ever want to talk, vent, yell or scream at someone, I'm here. If you need anything, just ask.*

'Your sister's very forthright.'

His brows hit the resident curl on his forehead. 'That's one way of describing her.'

She pressed her hand against Sprocket's foot, trying to move it off her ribs. 'I meant that in a good way. When people hear about my situation it makes them feel really uncomfortable and they immediately think two things. First it's *Thank God that didn't happen to me*, immediately followed by *That poor woman*. Bianca didn't make it about herself and for that I'm grateful.'

'Good,' he said on a sigh of relief. 'I'm glad we haven't made things harder for you.' His gaze moved to her hand, which was resting on her belly. 'Did you make contact with the Shearwater Clinic?'

'I did. I met Dr Jeglinski, and the baby and I got a clean bill of health. With two weeks to go, everything's as it should be.'

Young voices drifted from the dining room—one deep, one sweet.

'Aw, Mum, it's Friday night.'

'I've got all weekend to do my homework.'

Raf grinned. 'Sounds like the twins are negotiating to stay and watch the soccer.'

'Raf.' Bianca strode briskly into the room. 'The twins have got school sport at seven in the morning so we're leaving.' She stretched her hand out towards Meredith. 'Great to meet you, Meredith. If you do decide to have that baby down here, let me know. I can put you in touch with the new mums' group.'

The thoughtful and practical offer came on top of a lovely family evening and not for the first time that night Meredith found herself wishing yet again that her parents were still alive. Whenever she'd expressed that wish to Richard, he'd always stroked her hair and said, 'Merry, Mum and Dad love you too.' She'd always tried not to let her mouth twist wryly.

She was sure that in their own way Linda and Derek were fond of her but it was obvious it wasn't a love that came close to what she needed. Deep in her heart, she knew that just like they loved and adored Richard, they'd love and adore the baby, only the difference be-tween their level of affection for mother and child would be evident. But now they were the only family she had and family was what her baby needed.

'Thanks, Bianca, but I've been thinking it's probably wiser if I go back to Melbourne. I'm closer to the hospital there.'

'I think that's a good idea,' Raf said, his tone almost as forthright as Bianca's.

The slightly older woman with eyes similar to her brother's tilted her head. 'After the baby's born you've got plenty of time to think about giving him or her an island childhood.'

Before she could reply, she found herself being kissed on both cheeks by Bianca and then Marco, being shyly farewelled by Mietta and Leo, and then, in a whirlwind of coats and scarfs, yelled instructions and Mario pressing containers of food into their hands, the door closed behind them.

Mario leaned against his cane in the new silence. 'Hot chocolate, Meredith, and then Rafael will walk you home.'

'Sixteen again,' Raf muttered, before saying clearly, 'Dad, Meredith's looking pretty tired.'

'The hot chocolate will help her sleep,' Mario said firmly, and shuffled to the kitchen.

'Sorry.' Raf ran his hand through his hair, frustration clinging to the action. 'He was always a bossy bugger but he's worse since the stroke.'

She'd have been blind not to notice the power struggle between father and son that occurred in almost every one of their conversations. 'There's nothing to apologise for, Raf. I'm a big girl and if I didn't want to stay for hot chocolate, I would have said so.'

Turning, she walked back into the living room to look at the boats, needing to move and hoping it would encourage the baby to find a more comfortable position. 'When did he have the stroke?'

'Four months ago.' Raf moved to stand next to her, his fingers pressing against the glass of the cabinet and tracing a line of sail on the largest model. 'We weren't sure he'd live, let alone walk again.'

'Have you always lived with your father?'

'God, no.' The words spluttered out of him, horrified and indignant at the same time. 'I live in Melbourne. Have done since I left home at eighteen and went to uni. Hell, you've seen us together. We're not exactly the poster for a successful father and son relationship.'

She thought about some of her patients in Melbourne who had adult children who never visited, even when they lived in the same town and their parents were frail and in need. 'The fact you're here means you and Mario have some sort of connection.'

'Doesn't mean it's positive,' he muttered as Mario appeared at the doorway.

'The hot chocolate is ready. Rafael, bring the tray.'

She felt Raf stiffen by her side and she made a metaphorical leap between the two men, speaking before Raf could respond. 'Let's drink it in the kitchen, please, Mario. I'm more comfortable sitting in those chairs than the couch.'

'No worries.' Mario turned and started walking back to the kitchen.

She took a step forward to follow and a sharp pain ripped through her, stealing her breath and stopping her in her tracks. Raf, who was behind her, collided into her back and he instantly wrapped his arms around her to steady them both.

'You okay?' Worry and query vibrated through his baritone.

She tested a breath and the pain that had gripped her had gone. She straightened up, intending to tell him she was fine when the baby abruptly moved. God, it was like it was using her cervix as a trampoline. She tensed as a little moisture dampened her panties.

She instantly stilled, concentrating hard. Was she really wet or was it just normal pregnancy dampness? She waited a moment and when it didn't increase, relief rode through her as she reassured herself it was just normal.

Raf's strong arms turned her around as if she was feather-light instead of eight and a half months pregnant, and his huge brown eyes stared down at her full of questions. 'Meredith?'

'I'm fine. It was nothing.'

The baby moved again and this time she heard an audible pop. *No. Not yet. Please not yet.* She gasped as a massive gush of hot fluid rushed down her legs. This time there was absolutely no ambiguity about the sensation—her waters had broken.

'That's not nothing.' Raf stared at the stain darkening the carpet as if he couldn't really believe what he was seeing. That's…'

'Amniotic fluid,' she said, her cheeks burning with embarrassment. 'I am *so* sorry about the carpet.'

'Believe me, you've done us a favour,' he said with a slow, reassuring smile, which made his eyes crinkle up at the edges. 'We've been trying to get Mario to replace it for years and now he has no choice.'

His expression suddenly changed, as if the significance of the carpet stain had finally registered. 'You need a towel. I need to take you to hospital.'

She touched his forearm, wanting to allay his anxiety, and his warmth played against her fingertips. 'A towel would be great but, really, there's no hurry to get me to the hospital.'

He looked at her blankly. 'Your waters just broke, which means the baby's coming.'

The doctor in her answered. 'Not for hours. I haven't even started having contractions. If you could just get me a towel—'

'God, yes. Sorry.'

He strode out of the room as if it was on fire and she dropped her face in her hands. *This can't be happening.* If it wasn't bad enough that she was wet, sticky and utterly embarrassed, her obstetric lectures now boomed in her head.

Premature rupture of the membranes without contractions is a classic sign of a posterior labour. Common in primigravidae, these labours are long and frequently incoordinate, requiring augmentation by Syntocinon infusion. Many patients require an epidural due to exhaustion.

Richard! This is so not fair. You should be here with me. A sob rose in her throat and tears teetered on her lower eyelids. As she blinked furiously, trying to hold them at bay, her belly tightened like someone was pulling a massive band of steel around her middle. 'Ohh…' She grabbed the back of the couch as the pain hit, almost buckling her knees.

She stood rigidly still—every part of her coiled tight—fearful of adding to the pain. A thought ripped across her mind. *Early contractions aren't supposed to hurt this much.*

'Meredith?' Towels tumbled from Raf's arms and then his strong hands were on her shoulders, gently kneading. 'Breathe through the pain.'

'That's…easy…for…you…to…say,' she snapped.

Oh, God. How many times had she blithely said, *Just breathe*, to a labouring woman? Breathing meant moving and moving meant pain. She was puffing out short breaths, sounding like an asthmatic train, and trying not to give in to the overwhelming need to gasp and tense. The contraction finally faded and she dropped her head onto the couch in relief. 'It's finished.'

'*Now* we're going to Wongarri Hospital,' Raf said firmly, with a look of rugged determination on his face.

She picked up a towel. 'The hospital insists we call first and they'll want to know how long I've been in labour. If I say one contraction, the midwives will laugh me off the phone. I'll go home and have a shower and then—'

She bit down on the towel as another contraction hit her at peak ferocity, completely devoid of all the textbooks' examples of a slow and steady build-up to full force. 'Time it,' she managed to splutter as she bent over the couch again, her fingers gripping the armrest like it was a life preserver in a violent storm.

Pressure built between her legs and she had the craziest sensation of wanting to push.

No way! You're imagining it. First labours are never fast.

Finally the contraction eased and she straightened up again, relieved that full feeling between her legs had gone.

'That one lasted a full minute,' Raf said, scanning her face. 'That's not an early labour contraction.'

It definitely wasn't. First labours took hours—she knew this fact because when she'd been a medical student, the midwives had always sent her in to babysit the couples expecting their first baby. She'd worked out it had been a character test. If she'd been prepared to spend eleven hours with a couple, the midwives had let her deliver the baby.

A simmer of panic bubbled through her. If she had hours of contractions ahead of her as strong as the two she'd just experienced, she wasn't sure she was going to cope.

Raf will help.

The thought soothed her and she immediately recoiled from it. She couldn't possibly impose on Raf and ask him to stay with her during labour. Perhaps it really was time to go to hospital. Without Richard she was feeling incredibly vulnerable and the thought of a quiet, calm and caring midwife holding her hand was suddenly very appealing.

Her hand reached to rub the ache in her back—the ache that had been with her on and off since seven that morning—but as her fingers touched her spine another contraction hit. This time her legs gave way and she dropped to her knees as her body's power and strength focused on one place—surging between her legs and pushing the baby irrevocably downward towards the outside world.

Realisation hit her with the terrifying thwack of a piece of four-by-two. The intermittent back pain she'd had on and off all day, her general restlessness and discomfort—all of it had been early labour. With her mind focused on trying to get through another grief-stricken day, she'd missed every single vague sign.

The low simmer of panic that had been part of her since Richard's death—the bubbling unease that she was going to be a sole parent—hit boiling point. She could no longer ignore it. Whether she was ready or not, the baby was coming and coming soon.

* * *

Raf kneeled down next to Meredith, his anxiety rising with every rub of his hand on her back. He needed help. Hell, she needed help—she needed the security and safety net of trained hospital professionals. He was clueless about delivering a baby. Hell, he avoided just about anything to do with babies, because they brought back feelings and memories he didn't want to revisit.

Yes, two nights ago when he'd been unable to sleep he'd typed 'emergency delivery of a baby' into the search engine on his computer. Yes, he'd read three articles on the subject and all of them had told him how to deliver a baby, but they'd also stressed and reassured him that there was less than a one per cent chance of a first baby being born at home.

No, he did not want to put any of his new 'how to' knowledge to the test. 'I don't care what you say, Meredith, I'm telling you that the moment this contraction is over you're getting into the car and we're leaving for the hospital.'

Meredith slumped forward on her forearms. 'I. Can't.'

'Yes, you can, I'll help you walk to the car. I'll carry you if I have to. Everything's going to be fine.' He could hear himself jabbering. 'I know the road like the back of my hand and once we're over the bridge it's only a forty-minute drive.'

She turned and looked at him through a veil of golden hair, the beautiful blue of her eyes obliterated by wide, black pupils. 'Bathroom. Now!'

'Sure.' He wasn't going to argue with a labouring woman about a lack of manners. He hooked his uninjured hand under her arm and helped her rise to her feet. 'Ready?'

She let out a long, low moan exactly like the mournful bellow of a cow and sagged against him, her hands gripping his shoulders so hard her fingers hit bone. He braced his legs wide and, using all the strength in his arms and then some, he held her upright.

'It's okay, M., I've got you.'

Mario walked into the room. '*Mio Dio*. She's having the *bambino*.'

For some reason his father always defaulted to Italian when he was stressed. 'No need to overstate the situation, Dad,' Raf managed to say against the stinging burn of his arm muscles. 'I'm taking her to hospital.'

Mario gave him an incredulous look. 'You won't make it to hospital.'

'Don't be dramatic, Dad.'

Meredith made a long straining noise. 'Can...feel... baby's...head.'

What? Blind panic hit him.

'I'll ring for the ambulance,' Mario said, sounding flustered as he reached for his phone.

'I'm the volunteer on duty tonight, Dad,' Raf said, the irony hitting hard. 'Ring the after-hours clinic number and see if Laura Jeglinksi's still on the island.'

'*Sì*, and I'll boil water.' Mario left, his cane tapping against the floorboards faster than Raf had ever heard it move before.

'Raf! Bath. Room.' Meredith tugged at his arm, her agitation piercing his panic and centring him.

'Sorry.' He half pushed her, half carried her to the bathroom where she immediately sank to the floor on her hands and knees.

He grabbed more towels and tried to make the tiles less cold and slightly more comfortable, and all the time his blood was pounding in his ears and tapping out the tattoo, *The baby's coming, the baby's coming*.

Her fingers dug into his arm as she sucked in a breath, her entire body tensing. 'I…don't…want…this. Not…ready.'

Neither was he but he wasn't about to tell her that. 'The baby's ready.'

Her gaze found his, the blue-on-blue depths sucking him in, hauling him down deep into a place he hadn't expected to go. 'I'm scared.'

He brushed her hair from her face, tucking it behind her ear. 'Trust your body.'

'I mean, I'm not ready…to be a mother…without—'

A contraction swallowed the rest of her sentence but Raf knew the missing word was 'Richard'. Of course she wanted her husband here with her and Raf was a poor substitute.

When the contraction was over she ducked her head under her arm and looked at him, anxiety glowing in her eyes. 'Have you ever delivered a baby?'

He was tempted to lie and give her the confidence in him she obviously craved but he couldn't do that to her. He tried a smile instead. 'I know the theory.'

She made a noise—half laugh, half sob—and the strangled sound bounced off the peeling wallpapered walls. 'Me too.'

'Your body and the baby know what they're doing,' he said with conviction, as much to reassure himself as to reassure Meredith.

She didn't respond—she was too busy gripping the edge of the bath and pushing. That's when it hit him— she was still wearing her black leggings.

In first-aid situations his patients generally stayed fully clothed but today that wasn't going to be an option. 'Um, ah, M.,' he said, feeling acutely embarrassed, 'you, ah, you need to take off your pants.'

'Can't,' she puffed like a steam train. 'You do it.'

'Are you sure?'

'Just. Do. It,' she screamed as another contraction rocked her.

Step up. He just had to think about her as a patient and not Meredith of the beautiful blue eyes and the lush, curvaceous body. *Do it fast.* He blew on his fingers and carefully hooked them around the wide band of elastic. As he eased the tight leggings off her behind, her underpants came with them.

His mouth dried and he swallowed hard. He was face-to-face with a beautiful, pearly-white bottom and under any other circumstances he'd consider himself a very lucky and fortunate man. Today, the bulging perineum reminded him of exactly what was happening. A baby was coming, and fast.

'I'm putting on gloves,' he said, his hands shaking as he snapped them on, careful to cover the dressing on his hand. He desperately tried to visualise the words he'd read two nights ago.

'This *hur-r-r-ts*,' Meredith screeched. 'Get. It. Out. Of. Me.'

Her pain seared him. 'Stop pushing, Meredith,' he said loudly, surprised at the authority in his voice. He put his hand on her back, torn between his role of needing to support her and delivering the baby. 'You need to pant so we can guide the baby's head out.'

'Can't,' she sobbed.

'Can. You really can. You don't want to shoot the baby out like a human cannonball.' He used his fingers to keep the baby's head flexed. 'Pant with me. Pant, pant, pant, that's the way.'

She kept up with him and this time when the head

crowned—the skin of its scalp all wrinkly—it didn't slip back.

'Stings so bad,' she said, her voice muffled against her arm. 'Make. It. Stop.'

Watching her endure so much pain made his heart cramp. 'You're so close, M. You're doing great. Next contraction just pan—'

'Aaarrrgggghhhh!' She pushed like her body gave her no other option.

A gush of fluid hit the towels, hit his knees and the next moment the baby's head was born and he could see two closed eyes, a tiny nose and a rosebud mouth. Awe rushed through him, making him feel light-headed—it was the most amazing thing he'd ever witnessed. 'The baby's head's born. Don't move.'

'Move? Are you kidding me?' She gave an hysterical-sounding laugh.

Raf quickly wiped his fingers across the baby's mouth as the head turned just like the article had said it would. He tried not to panic at the dusky colour of the baby's face, reassuring himself it was normal. It had to be normal.

'Shoulders next,' Meredith instructed jerkily. 'Gravity should work.'

Should? God, he hoped so. 'Tell me when.'

'Contraction coming.' Pushing, she groaned long and loud and the baby moved. With a hammering heart, Raf watched the shoulders appear and a second later he was holding a small, wet and slippery baby in his large, trembling arms. He blinked away tears as he cradled it against him for a moment before putting a clean towel under the baby and passing it up through Meredith's legs.

She gazed down at her baby. 'It's a girl,' she said, her voice full of wonder.

'A gorgeous girl,' he said, his voice unexpectedly cracking. 'Congratulations.'

A moment later he heard a strangled sound and he realised Meredith was crying. *Idiot.* He wanted to smack himself. Of course she was crying. What should be one of the most amazing moments of her life was overshadowed by the fact the father of her baby was dead. Sadness for her clashed with a solid shot of protectiveness for the baby he'd just helped bring into the world—a feeling so strong he was acting before thinking. 'Meredith,' he said firmly, putting his hand on her hip to jolt her to attention, 'it's time to hold your baby.'

He didn't want her grief to wedge itself between her and the baby. He'd lost his father that way after his mother had died so he scooped up the tiny yet perfect little human being while Meredith, trance-like, rolled off all fours and propped herself up against the bathtub. She pulled her shirt off over her head so she and the baby could be skin to skin.

'Ready?'

She nodded and he placed the baby at an angle so it was head down on her chest, giving any excess fluid the chance to drain away. Grabbing a clean towel, he rubbed the baby dry to both keep her warm and to stimulate her breathing. When the baby's colour changed from dusky to pale pink, he used a fresh, dry towel to drape over mother and child.

With silent tears running down her cheeks, Meredith gazed at her daughter and then raised her eyes to Raf's. 'Thank you.'

He held her gaze as the quiet and heartfelt words socked him in the chest with the power of a punch.

They'd just shared an incredibly intimate event that in a perfect world, and under ideal circumstances, would never have taken place. Hell, he'd wouldn't have even met pregnant Meredith if her husband had been alive and yet here he was just having delivered her beautiful baby. Memories of another baby—bigger, older, darker skinned—rushed back and he cleared his throat.

'It was an honour and a privilege.' His finger brushed the baby's hand and her tiny fingers gripped his hard. He knew it was a reflex—that every baby did this—but something deep down inside him that he'd kept closed off for a very long time cracked open.

A jitter of unease made him slam that lid down hard and fast and he quickly extracted his finger. He may have delivered this baby but she was Meredith's child and nothing to do with him. Once burnt, twice shy and he'd do well to remember that.

'The doctor's…on her…way,' Mario interrupted, his breath puffing as if he'd just run a race. As he took in the scene in the bathroom, his worried expression cleared and a smile wreathed his jowly face. 'But you don't need her, you clever girl. You have *un angelo bellissimo.*'

Meredith blinked and glanced at Raf. 'A what?'

'A beautiful angel,' he said, smiling.

For the first time in a very long time Raf was in complete agreement with his father.

CHAPTER SIX

MEREDITH GAZED AT her daughter, who lay in her arms, bathed in moonlight. 'I can't believe you're here.'

Huge, dark, liquid eyes stared back at her as if to say, *Why would I not be here? It was super uncomfortable in there.*

They were lying in Raf's freshly made bed and the last two hours were still a blur to Meredith. The GP, Laura Jeglinksi, had arrived just in time to catch the placenta, check it and confirm it was intact. She'd checked Meredith and the baby, and had given both of them a big tick before suggesting Meredith might be more comfortable staying at home with the district nurse visiting twice a day, rather than being transferred to the hospital.

Before Meredith had been able to say this wasn't home, Mario had said, 'We'll look after her.'

And they had.

Bianca had arrived with the necessary toiletries a post-partum woman required, a packet of disposable nappies and some well-loved baby clothes that had been lovingly stored for fifteen years.

Raf had stripped and made his bed with clean linen, insisting she use it because it was the newest and most comfortable bed in the house.

Mario had created a temporary crib by padding the

bottom drawer of a tallboy with towels and using old soft tea towels as sheets. Bianca and Mario had argued over who was holding the baby while she'd taken a shower and once she'd been installed in bed, they'd all retreated to give her some one-on-one time with her daughter.

She kept replaying the rapid events of the birth and three things stood out—the heart-aching rush of love for her daughter, the sadness that Richard had never got to experience that type of love for his child and the amazing care Raf had shown her. The poor guy. Four days ago she'd cried all over him and today he'd seen her in her worst moments—she'd yelled and screamed at him—and if he'd been as scared as her, he hadn't shown it. He was a remarkable man.

A soft knock sounded on the door and she called out, 'Come in.'

The door opened and Raf appeared, balancing a tray on his uninjured hand, waiter-style. His lovely eyes seemed to almost caress her in a soft glance before crinkling up around the edges. 'You're looking a lot better than the last time I saw you.'

His words reminded her of the birth and mortification spun hard around her indebtedness. He'd been up close and personal with her today in a way Richard never had. Raf had seen parts of her dilated, distended and ugly, and with bodily fluids gushing, and it took every ounce of her self-control not to pull the sheets up over her head and hide. Instead, she plastered on a smile. 'It's amazing what a shower and a rest can do for a girl.'

He set down the tray and on it was a steaming bowl of pasta, a small glass of red wine, a red cloth napkin, and a fork and spoon. The pungently strident aroma of basil and garlic filled the room, making her stomach rumble.

'I read somewhere that giving birth is like running a marathon so we thought you might be hungry.'

Her already enormous feeling of gratitude over-flowed. 'That's such a kind thought.'

He shrugged as if it was no big deal. 'I'm just the errand boy. Do you really think Mario was going to let you try and sleep on an empty stomach?'

A ridiculous quiver of disappointment shot through her that the food wasn't Raf's idea. She struggled up the pillows. 'Can you take her?'

His lovely warm chestnut eyes flared with something she wouldn't call panic but it wasn't ease either, and he hesitated for a long moment. She was about to say, 'She won't break', when he reluctantly lifted the baby from her. Resting in his solid arms, she looked tiny cradled up against his broad chest. She looked safe and protected, and a lump formed in Meredith's throat.

His expression was tight as he looked at her baby and then he gave a long sigh, the exhaled breath saying, *I give up*. With the tip of his finger he traced a line down the baby's perfect cheek. 'Hey, possum, have you recovered from your speedy entry into the world?'

'She's taking it all in her stride,' Meredith said, finally finding her voice buried deep in the thickness of her throat. 'She's fed like a champ and she seems far more together about this new life than her mother.' She dug into the pasta, hoping that eating would stop all these wild emotions that had her lurching from joy to tears and disappointment then back to elation, and all in less than a minute.

Raf sat on the bed, his back up against the bed end and his long legs stretched out next to her. He immediately laid the baby between them as if he couldn't put her down soon enough. 'Does she have a name?'

No. Meredith picked up the glass of wine and took a big sip as the lovely bubble she'd been hiding in for the last hour burst, pouring real life all over her again. 'Richard and I had a boy's name all ready but we hadn't come close to choosing a girl's name.'

Raf got a wicked glint in his eyes. 'She was born to the sound of the ocean. What about Venus or Mermaid or Aqua?'

She laughed at his teasing. 'My in-laws would have a pink fit if they had to write any of those names on the private school enrolment forms.'

'What about your parents?'

She shook her head as the cool thread of sadness crawled up her spine. 'They both died a few years ago. It's just me.'

'And Richard's family,' he said gently. 'Have you called them?'

Guilt slid in under the sadness. 'No.'

Raf nodded slowly, his face filling with understanding. 'You want to name her first?'

She set the wine down, wondering how he knew. 'Is that terrible?'

He shook his head slowly. 'Not at all. Family are both a blessing and a burden and in my experience the scales are in a constant state of motion between the two. One moment they're tilting in one direction and the next they're snapping back fast and inclining sharply the other way.'

He swung his legs off the bed and gently lowered her sleeping daughter into the big drawer—now crib. 'Do your in-laws call you?'

Her fingers plucked at the doona as she thought about Linda. 'Most mornings around eight.'

He faced the bookcase and ran his olive-skinned fingers along a row of books. They came to rest on a thin volume, which he plucked out of the stack and waved at her, dust motes rising. *'A Thousand and One Baby Names,'* he said with grin. 'This has to be the only occasion Dad's hoarder tendencies have come in handy.'

He sat back down against the bed end and opened the age-yellowed pages. 'Okay. Abby, Acacia, Ada, Adelaide, Africa, Aisha, Alberta, Amanda—'

She stared at him, gobsmacked. 'You're not seriously going to read out a thousand names?'

His finger paused on the page and he looked up with a slight frown on his face. 'You've got nine hours to come up with a name that both suits possum here and that you love or else she'll be named for you.'

'Put that way, I see your point.'

He winked at her and went back to reading. 'Amelia, Angela, Aphra, Ardith…'

She settled back against the pillows, letting his melodic voice rain names down upon her, waiting for the one that said, *This one.*

'Zoe? That's…an interesting choice.'

Meredith ignored Linda's poor attempt to veil her dislike of her granddaughter's name. Last night, Raf had read out almost every girl's name in the book, complete with his own entertaining commentary on some of the stranger and more unusual ones, before she'd heard the one name that suited her daughter perfectly. She'd called Linda at seven that morning to tell her the news.

By eleven, Linda and Derek had arrived. The Camilleris, in their hospitable style, had insisted Richard's parents stay for lunch. After the meal, Raf and Mario had suggested Linda and Derek might like to see the pelicans being fed down at the wharf. Although neither

Camilleri had said the outing was to give Meredith a rest and a break from her visitors, she'd known that was their intention. Derek had accepted the invitation but Linda had declined. Now Meredith knew why.

'Zoe means life, Linda, and, given the circumstances, it fits her perfectly.'

'Does she have a middle name?'

Meredith heard the hope in Linda's voice that Zoe's middle name would be something far more Anglo-Saxon traditional, like Emma, Jane or Elizabeth. 'Riccarda.'

'That sounds Italian!' This time Linda didn't even try and disguise her displeasure as she glanced around at the Camilleris' living room with its obvious Italian influence circa 1975.

Meredith sighed. 'It is but Mario told me it's the feminine form of Richard.'

'Oh.' Linda's mouth tensed and her throat worked as if she was trying not to cry. 'I see. Thank you.'

Meredith wanted to reach out and touch her mother-in-law's hand but they didn't have that type of relationship so she said, 'Zoe's got Richard's nose, do you think?'

'She looks a lot like Richard as a baby,' Linda said, studying her sleeping granddaughter. 'I'll dig out some of Richard's baby photos for you.'

'I'd like that.' She rested her head back against the couch, her eyes fluttering closed as fatigue battered her like cyclonic winds.

'Meredith, dear.'

'Hmm?' She kept her eyes closed.

'Derek's installed the baby carrier into our car so we can take you both home this afternoon.'

Her eyes flew open as adrenaline hit her fatigue out of the park. 'I'm not ready to do that.'

Linda frowned. 'But you don't have anything here for the baby.'

She immediately thought of the empty and unpainted nursery. Of Richard's presence in the house that should be comforting but just reminded her of everything she'd lost, and she knew she wasn't ready to go back. 'All I have in Fitzroy is the car seat and a few clothes from the baby shower. I was going to shop and then Richard died and...'

'I'll take you shopping,' Linda said with an organising gleam in her eyes.

'That's very kind, Linda, but my doctor's arranged for the district nurse to visit me here twice a day. I need to rest and establish my breastfeeding.'

'You can do all that in Melbourne.'

But I don't want to.

'Surely you're not thinking of imposing on the Camilleris for a week?' Linda asked in a horrified tone.

Her gut dropped to her toes with a thud. Staying here was exactly what she'd envisaged would happen over the next few days. Resting here, with Bianca and Mario cosseting her and Zoe.

And Raf.

An ache built up behind her eyes. Oh, God, Linda was right. No matter how much the idea of staying here appealed, it was an imposition. For all of Mario's caring, he was recovering from a stroke and it was Raf who carried the bulk of the workload, carrying out Mario's instructions with barely leashed frustration. She didn't understand their relationship but her staying here was very much a burden. Raf had already done more than she could ask of anyone who wasn't family. Actually, she'd asked way more of him than she'd ever asked of Linda and Derek.

Mum will do that. Just ask, Richard had often said to her, but she rarely asked because she felt uncomfortable—as if asking for help meant she'd failed in some way. Yet now she was leaning on the kindness of strangers and the cold, hard facts declared themselves—it was time to lean on her family and to stop foisting herself on her neighbours. She laced her hands together, clenching her fingers so hard her knuckles whitened.

'Linda, would you consider staying down here with me for a few days until my milk comes in?'

'Bloody hell, Dad.' Raf waded into the flooded laundry and shut off the washing machine. It effectively cut off the water that was spraying out of a black pipe and up against the wall before falling and forming a river, which flowed out into the hall. 'What were you doing?'

Mario grunted and walked away.

Frustration lit through Raf. 'Fine,' he muttered as he grabbed towels and a mop. 'Don't tell me. I'll just clean up the mess.'

Over the past week, Mario had been difficult and more contrary than usual, and the little patience Raf had was worn so thin it was transparent. If he said black, Mario said white. If he suggested the club, Mario wanted to stay in, and if they stayed in, Mario grumbled he never saw anyone any more. Raf wasn't sure he had it in him to survive much more of this. He'd even found himself talking to whichever deity who cared to listen, asking that at the end of the three-month period that Mario would get the okay from the rehabilitation team to live alone, with some home-help assistance from the council.

Each day he counted down to three o'clock—the time when his father was occupied and he could go for his run along the beach and just be himself. He missed his life. He missed Melbourne. He missed his house.

You miss Meredith.

He vigorously twisted a sopping towel over the sink, draining the water. *I don't miss Meredith.*

He had no reason to miss her. Sure, they'd shared an incredibly intimate experience when he'd delivered Zoe and because of that he felt a special connection to her, but it was no different from the connection he'd experienced with the three people whose lives he'd saved, doing CPR. Yes, they kept in sporadic touch and traded Christmas cards and this would be no different. Perhaps he could send Zoe a birthday card each year. The idea both appealed and pained him.

On the day after Zoe's birth when he'd got back from the wharf with Meredith's father-in-law, Linda had matched Mario in the curt instruction stakes—actually, there was a slight possibility she'd outdone him. Within the hour she'd moved Meredith and Zoe next door, and he'd felt unexpectedly cheated. It had niggled and bothered him so much that he'd eventually put it down to being surprised. He'd just assumed Meredith and Zoe would stay with them for a few days but, of course, it made sense that she'd go home with her family.

What didn't make sense was that from the moment Meredith had left, he'd wanted to go next door and visit. Wanted it so badly that he found himself thinking about it constantly but he was very aware that Meredith needed time with Zoe, time to sleep and time with her family. As hard as it was, he'd struck a deal with himself—he'd wait four days.

Mario had asked him to take him to Melbourne so they could buy presents for Meredith and Zoe. Memories of shopping with Teresa for baby gear had almost made him say no to his father's unexpected request but Mario hated Melbourne so the fact he'd actually asked to go had made Raf loath to refuse.

To his surprise, his father hadn't objected when he'd studiously avoided the baby shops and had instead gone into one of Melbourne's iconic jewellery stores. As they'd wandered around, peering inside all the glass cabinets, he'd been rendered speechless by the way he and Mario had been in total sync when it had come to choosing a gift for both mother and child. It had been the only time during the week that they hadn't argued. For Zoe, they'd effortlessly settled on a beautiful pewter merry-go-round music box shaped like a carousel, complete with teddy bears riding horses. Meredith's gift had been a little harder.

He'd avoided flowers and chocolates, and the idea of a book she'd have no time or energy to read hadn't worked for him. The internet's suggestion of a flowing blouse or a designer nappy bag had seemed either too personal or too practical. He'd been starting to worry he'd have to ask Bianca for advice when he and Mario had spied the necklace at exactly the same moment. They'd exchanged a glance and a bolt of understanding had flowed between them, stunning Raf. He couldn't remember the last time something like that had happened and, if it ever had, it had been over twenty years ago. It seemed odd to him that a piece of jewellery consisting of two open hearts—one sterling silver and large, the other rose gold and small, had given them a fleeting connection.

The carefully wrapped gifts still sat in their robin-egg-blue bags because the following day as he'd driven Mario home from his exercise class, with both of them anticipating the long-awaited visit next door, Meredith's and Derek's cars had passed them, heading the opposite direction. Linda had been driving Meredith's car and Meredith had been sitting in the back seat next to the baby capsule. That had been three days ago and she hadn't been home since.

And it didn't matter, he told himself for the thousandth time, because she was getting on with her life and he was—God, he had no clue what the hell he was doing with his life. Rich, successful men with choices were not supposed to feel so adrift.

He zealously attacked the water on the floor with the mop—swipe, swipe, wring—until the floor was dry. As he reconnected the pipe that had become disconnected due to a rusted hose clamp, he realised that was probably what Mario had been trying to do when the washing machine had gone into its spin cycle. Everything in this house was old and needed replacing, and the thought of Mario living here alone made him uneasy.

Renovating would give you something to do and stop your mind from permanently wandering next door.

He walked into the kitchen where his father sat flicking through the pages of the paper. 'The hose clamp needs replacing.'

Mario's black eyes flashed. 'Tell me something I don't know.'

Raf ground his teeth. 'The whole house needs replacing.'

His father glared at him.

He sighed and opened his arms out in a conciliatory gesture. 'Dad, why not let me do some renovations while I'm here? At least replace the carpet after Zoe made a hell of a mess on it.'

Mario smiled, a dreamy look on his face. 'Such a

tiny baby for such a big mess. She will have grown.' His eyes strayed towards the gift bags that still sat on the sideboard. 'You've got Meredith's number. Call her and ask when she's coming back.'

He'd been arguing back and forth with himself about that since Thursday. 'I'm not doing that, Dad.'

Mario's mouth formed a stubborn line. 'Why not?'

Because I'm not sure I'd be doing it for the right reasons. 'Because she's got enough on her plate without me bothering her.'

Mario leaned back in his chair and crossed his arms. 'Her husband's dead, Rafael.'

'We both know that so what's your point?' he asked, matching his father's steely look.

'She needs friends.'

Raf swung open the fridge and stared sightlessly at the contents as he grappled with getting his temper under control. He wasn't strictly certain that his feelings for Meredith slotted into the friend category. 'She's got family and friends in Melbourne.'

'And they're grieving too.'

Something in Mario's tone made Raf straighten up but by the time he glimpsed his father's face over the top of the fridge door, whatever emotion Mario had just betrayed, he'd masked it again,

'We'll see her again when she visits.' He started preparing lunch. 'I'll pick up some carpet samples this afternoon.'

Mario grunted. 'And if Meredith doesn't visit again?'

Raf didn't want to think about it.

Later in the afternoon, Raf was tying the laces of his running shoes and thinking about the surprising experience of his father flipping through the carpet square samples without his usual negativity. If he'd known it only took a massive body-fluid stain to get his father to consider new floor coverings, he'd have bled all over the carpet years ago. He was pondering how he could go about convincing Mario to let him remove the very dated wallpaper and paint the living-room walls before the new carpet went down when he heard the thumping of Mario's walking frame.

'Rafael!'

His heart jumped into his mouth at the bellowing of his name. Nothing short of an emergency ever disturbed the sacrosanct three o'clock weather report. Mario had flooded the laundry that morning. Dear God, had he set fire to the kitchen this afternoon?

Raf ran from his room straight to the kitchen. Nothing was on fire, the radio was blaring and Mario wasn't there. 'Dad?' He checked the dining room—empty.

'Raf!'

He raced into the living room. Mario stood at the side window with his hands on the window sash. 'Look!'

Raf looked out across the drive and over the low paling fence until his gaze came to rest on Meredith's luxury four-wheel drive.

She's back. His heart swelled and ached all at the same time.

Meredith got out of the car and walked around to open the back door so he got a clear view of her creased cargo pants, her misbuttoned linen blouse and her crooked ponytail of silken hair. He didn't think a woman had ever looked more gorgeous.

Mario leaned out the window and waved. *'Ciao, bella.'*

'Jeez, Dad. Italian? Really?' Raf said, irritated that his father might be flirting with Meredith and embarrassed that they were both standing at the window like peeping Toms.

Meredith turned towards Mario's booming voice and

a smile broke through the shadows of fatigue on her face. She waved before leaning into the car. She tugged hard on a large cardboard box and her left leg left the ground, extending out behind her, and her blouse rode up exposing a band of golden skin. His blood instantly stirred in a way it hadn't in a very long time, sending addictive heat shooting through him and pooling in his groin.

'Leave it,' Mario yelled to Meredith. 'Rafael is coming.'

Raf choked on his intake of breath. His father's words weren't so far from the truth and he needed to get his body back under control, and fast.

Mario shut the window. 'She's had a long drive. Invite her for dinner.'

He frowned. 'She might be tired and not want to come.'

Mario rolled his eyes. 'No woman will ever refuse a meal they didn't have to cook. Didn't you learn anything from me?'

He bit back the retort that Mario had stopped teaching him anything nineteen years ago and instead walked out the front door.

Ten minutes later, after numerous trips up and down the stairs, the car was completely empty and Raf had lugged the world's heaviest and most ungainly flat pack into the living room. Panting, he managed to splutter out, 'How on earth did you get this into the car on your own?'

Meredith had the grace to look sheepish. 'An assistant took pity on me and loaded it for me.'

'What's in it?'

'Zoe's cot. I figured Mario would need his jumper drawer back.'

He instinctively took a step back from the box. For some reason—probably self-preservation—he'd assumed it was a bookcase.

Since greeting Meredith by the car with the standard Camilleri greeting of a quick kiss on each cheek—a greeting his entire family had instigated with Meredith and by default forcing him to do the same or risk looking like kissing her was a problem for him—he'd deliberately focused on the luggage instead of on Meredith or the baby. It was safer that way. It was bad enough that he had these crazy feelings around Meredith and that he breathed in far too deeply when he brushed her warm, soft cheek with his lips, without allowing himself to get attached to a baby. He'd been there and done that once before, and it had been a one-way ticket to heartbreak. Doing it again would be beyond stupid.

Zoe made a snuffling noise on Meredith's shoulder and before he'd even thought, he'd lifted his gaze and was taking in her inky hair, her enormous dark blue eyes and her pouty rosebud lips that were sucking loudly and enthusiastically on her tiny, clenched fist.

A jumble of emotions rolled through him just like they had the day she'd been born. He was filled with an overwhelming desire to stay and protect her, and an equally compelling need to run and run fast.

Not your kid to love, mate.

It was time to leave.

'The guy at the store told me the cot's part of their easy-to-assemble range,' Meredith said, patting a now squirming Zoe firmly on her back. 'It comes with step-by-step instructions and will only take ten minutes to put together, which is great because that means Zoe will be able to sleep in it tonight.'

Her naivety dug into him, putting very unwelcome

brakes on his desire to leave. 'Have you built things from
this company before?' he asked, indicating the distinctive logo on the box. *Please, say yes. Please, say all your
furniture in Melbourne comes from there and you're a
total expert.*

She shook her head as Zoe stopped sucking her fist
and started crying. 'No. That's why I bought the easy
one.'

Zoe's cry morphed into a full-throttle scream and
Meredith sat down on the couch and pulled up her
blouse. Zoe instantly attached to the breast like she
was a heat-seeking missile and right on target. Slurp-
ing replaced screaming.

Unable to look away, he gazed at the sight of mother
and child together and at peace. The image floated
through him like a soft, gentle breeze filling him with
wonder before socking him hard in the gut. Nausea
pumped through him.

*Why are you still here? Zoe can sleep another night
in that jumper drawer without any consequences. Hell,
it will be a family story Meredith can tell at her twenty-
first.*

He opened his mouth determined to say, 'Good luck
with the cot,' but instead he heard himself make a sound
that was a cross between a snort and a groan. The circles under Meredith's eyes were as dark as bruises and
if he left her alone to build the cot, the consequences
would be distress on top of her exhaustion. Even people
without a trace of fatigue failed to make head or tail of
so-called straightforward instructions.

*What about your distress? Remember, she's an intel-
ligent woman and she'll want to do it herself.*

He could only hope. 'They always tell you it's easy,

Meredith, and it's always nine circles of hell,' he said, not able to ignore the need to give her fair warning.

'That's what I was worried about. I'm not the handiest person on the planet.' She sighed and leaned back against the couch, her weariness cloaking her like a thick, woollen coat. 'I guess I'll do what I always do and call someone tomorrow and pay them to assemble it.'

You're off the hook. Take it and run.

But she looked so tired that he couldn't do it. Pushing his hands through his hair, he tugged at the roots, welcoming the pain he hoped might lessen the hurt he was about to bring down on himself. 'You stitched my hand. It seems only fair I assemble the cot.'

Her luminous eyes took on the clear blue of a hot summer's day 'I should say no…'

Please do. Saying no would be really good.

'But that would be stupid.' Her expressive mouth curved up into a smile. 'Thank you. I would love you to assemble the cot.'

The first circle of hell claimed him and he hadn't even opened the damn box.

CHAPTER SEVEN

MEREDITH SAT ON the couch, feeling like a voyeur. Poor Raf. Half of her wanted to relocate from the living room to somewhere else, because he was quietly swearing at the instructions with the look of someone sitting an exam with no preparation.

It seemed unfair to be observing his discomfort, especially as he was the one doing her the favour. The other half of her wanted to stay for that very reason— she'd feel bad abandoning him, because he was doing her a favour. A favour she hadn't wanted to ask, because today was supposed to be the first day of her coping alone. So far she'd managed the drive from Melbourne, which had been no mean feat given she'd had to stop three times for Zoe who'd needed feeding or changing or both.

'Forget the nine circles of hell,' he grumbled. 'This is Satan's theme park, complete with ride height restrictions.' He tossed the instructions at her. 'Any ideas, Dr Dennison? There are seven pieces here but the instructions start with a fully built crib.'

'What?' She caught the fluttering instruction booklet. 'That makes absolutely no sense.'

'Hah! You want sense?' He half laughed and half groaned. 'The instructions always get lost in translation on their way to English, which is why nothing is ever simple and everything takes three times as long as they tell you.'

He picked up one of the cot sides and tried it up against a cot end then snatched back the instructions from her hand and read them again. 'Bloody hell,' he muttered. 'Building one was easier than this.'

She instantly pictured his large, gentle hands—so very like her father's—working with wood, precisely measuring and cutting, sanding and smoothing, until the finished product gleamed. Wood and skill coming together in a labour of love. 'You've built a cot?'

His head snapped up and for a moment she thought she saw raw pain on his face, but then his usual warm look returned and she figured she'd just imagined it.

'Once.'

'Was it for the twins?'

'No.'

In guy terms, Raf was usually happy to chat but that *no* had had a finality to it that said, *Do not go there.* Of course she immediately wanted to go straight there, and without delay. Had he been married? Was he a father? She realised that, although she knew in her heart he was a kind and generous man, she didn't know very much about him at all.

'Oh, I get it.' Raf's brow suddenly cleared. 'This is one of those two-level cots.'

'It is. They call it a back-saver crib.'

Zoe had fallen asleep in her arms and Meredith stood and laid her in the pram that Raf had also carried upstairs. Between them, they'd made numerous trips and she conceded that she really hadn't thought about stairs and their impact on all the baby gear. Oh, well, it was one way to keep fit.

Raf grabbed the electric drill that he'd gone next door to collect after laughing derisively at the toolkit the shop had sold her. 'Can you hold these two pieces together while I use the drill to insert the screws?'

'Sure.' She did as he asked and studied his now bandage-free hand. 'That's healed up really well. Sorry I wasn't here to remove your stitches.'

He smiled his lovely smile and his eyes crinkled up in that soft, generous way. 'You're forgiven. You were a bit preoccupied with other things.' The drill whirred. 'So, how was your last week, both here and in Melbourne?'

'Okay,' she said, thinking about the steep learning curve. 'Zoe and I are finding our feet and Linda and Derek have been...' she hesitated a moment, choosing her words carefully so she didn't come across sounding ungrateful '...a great help.'

Raf laughed and the deep, full-bodied sound danced around her, making her feel warm and secure in a way she hadn't felt in a long time. 'Hey, I currently live with my father who drives me nuts so feel free to say how you feel about your in-laws. You'll get no judgement here.'

She felt herself loosen up all over and she realised with a jolt it was the first time she'd relaxed since the night he'd read out all the girl names from the name book. 'I've disappointed them by coming back here.'

He shrugged as he picked up the other side of the cot and placed her hand in position to steady the two pieces. 'It isn't real life if we're not disappointing our parents.'

'I've disappointed Linda from the start.' The words she'd always kept close blurted out unexpectedly. 'I was always too country for her and she never thought me good enough for Richard.'

The drill stopped whirring and he gave her an indulgent look as if she were clueless. 'I can tell you that no Italian mother ever thinks their daughter-in-law is good enough for their precious son. It sounds like that belief crosses all cultural divides.'

'Maybe.' She wasn't totally convinced. 'The crazy thing is that Richard wasn't that great at keeping in contact with his mum. He often got caught up at work and I ended up being the one who visited, did dinner, went to the cousins' birthdays, and filled Linda and Derek in on whatever it was he was doing.'

A slither of guilt ran through her, feeling a lot like betrayal. *God, why was she telling Raf this?*

'You sound like a godsend rather than a disappointment. They're lucky to have you.'

Was he speaking from experience? 'What about your mum? Did she disapprove of your girlfriends?' *Your wife? Ex-wife?*

'Mum died suddenly when I was almost eighteen.'

'Oh, I'm sorry.'

'It was a long time ago.' He studied the instructions again, before rummaging through the screws and bolts and selecting one. 'Believe me, Dad did enough disapproving for both of them, and he still does.'

'Does that make things difficult for you and your...?'

'Ex-wife.'

A nonsensical rush of relief swam through her as he gave her a raised-brow look—one that clearly said, *I know you're fishing for information.*

'Not really,' he continued. 'Teresa didn't care. Turns out she was immune to anyone's opinion, be it good or bad.' He gave the screwdriver a vicious twist. 'In the end, I was just pissed off that the old bastard was right. Hold this piece here,' he said, his slightly work-worn hand picking up hers again. 'When I've attached it, we can do the sides.'

His instructions doubled for, *I am not answering any more questions about me*, and, given that he was taking a series of disconnected parts and creating them into a cot for her, she reluctantly complied. It didn't stop her brain from digesting the information and sparking a hundred questions more.

'I really appreciate your help,' she said, trying to break the tension she'd created.

He grunted and switched on the drill again, the noise drowning out any conversation.

As he fitted the first side his mobile rang loudly—the ringtone the tinkling sound of a retro 1970's phone. He immediately switched off the drill. 'That's Dad. Can you answer it, please?'

'Sure.' She swiped her finger across the photo of a modern house not dissimilar to this one. 'Hello, Mario, it's Meredith.'

'Meredith,' Mario said, his accent elongating her name. 'Did Rafael tell you about dinner?'

'Ah, no.'

He made a tsking sound. 'I've made dinner for you tonight. You sound tired. I hope Rafael's looking after you?'

She watched Raf's intense gaze and unusually grim mouth as he installed the mattress baseboard. 'He's doing way more than that. He's building Zoe's cot.'

There was unexpected silence at the other end of the phone. 'Hello? Mario, are you there?'

'*Sì.*' Another silence followed. 'A cot? Can he do it?'

She knew Mario and Raf sparred a lot and even in the light of her and Raf's recent conversation about disappointed parents she thought Mario's comment harsh. 'Of course he can do it,' she said hotly, the need to defend Raf burning in her chest.

Raf's head snapped around at the tone in her voice, a frown creasing his brow. He mouthed the word, 'Problem?'

She shook her head as Mario said gravely, 'It isn't his ability I was doubting. I'm just glad he's doing it.'

The worried tone was so surprising that Meredith immediately started piecing things together—an ex-wife, a handmade cot, no mention of a baby and now a father, who more often than not found fault with his son, was suddenly sounding concerned. Something was going on but what exactly?

One thing she did know was that Raf Camilleri, the generous, helpful man with the easy-going smile, had secrets.

Right then and there, she wanted to know every single one of them.

Raf was painting a section of the lounge-room wall with paint samples when Mario walked in, holding the mail. 'What the hell are you doing?'

He ground his teeth. 'Giving you options, Dad. You said you couldn't choose paint from the sample chart so I've brought the samples to you so you can get a feel for what each colour will look like.'

'Your mother always chose the paint.'

'I know, and if she was still alive she'd have repainted twice since this paint went on.'

Mario grunted. 'I saw Meredith at the letter box. She asked how you were.'

Raf ignored the disapproval in Mario's voice and dipped the sponge into the pot labelled 'Ecru'. He'd been avoiding Meredith and Zoe as much as possible, because building the cot had almost undone three years of hard work. Almost undone him.

Over the last few weeks he'd waved to Meredith from a distance, left boxes of fresh produce from Mario's vegetable garden at her door when he'd been certain she hadn't been home and on the evenings Mario had invited her to dinner, he'd gone to the ambulance station for volunteer training.

'I need you to drive me to the wharf,' Mario said firmly. 'I want to get fresh flathead for dinner.'

'I've already made lasagne.'

'Meredith and I don't eat lasagne.'

Raf looked up from the wall, confused about the connections between Mario, Meredith and lasagne. 'What?'

Mario shrugged as if it was obvious and Raf was being obtuse. 'When your wife or husband dies, people cook you lasagne. Your mother's death killed lasagne for me.'

He thought about the times he'd made lasagne for dinner and realised they'd been some of the nights his father had insisted that he eat at the club. 'I didn't know that. Why didn't you tell me?'

Mario's face hardened. 'If you'd been here, you would have known.'

A red haze flared in front of his eyes. 'If I'd been here?' He heard his voice rise as he remembered how his father had retreated into his grief, locking everyone out. 'I was bloody well here. You were the one who left us.'

'*Dio mio*, are you crazy? You left the island. I stayed, running a business you didn't want.'

'That's rich, Da—' The sound of Raf's phone pierced the air with the noise of a siren slicing deep into the argument. He took the emergency call. 'Raf Camilleri.'

'Raf, it's Dr Jeglinski. Are you at home?'

This place is so not my home. 'Yes.'

'Good. Dispatch just called. There's an incident at Camilleri beach, near emergency beach beacon number six. The island's ambulance is returning from a hospital transport run to Wongarri but it's still thirty minutes away.'

'I'm on my way. How long until a doctor can get here?'

She sighed. 'I'm twenty minutes away and it's Gavin's afternoon off. God, we need another doctor on this island.'

As the GP cut the call, Raf knew his time of avoiding Meredith had just come to an abrupt end. 'Dad, call Bianca and mind Zoe until she gets here.'

From the top of the beach steps the small cluster of people below made it easy to identify exactly where the patient lay. Raf ran down the steps with the first-aid kit in one hand, and the portable monitor and defibrillator in the other. He heard running feet behind him and hoped like hell it was Meredith. As he reached the group, he saw a young man in his twenties lying on the sand with a massive gash through his wetsuit. Blood stained the sand.

'First aid, let me through,' he said, pushing his way forward. 'What's his name?'

'Mick,' a guy of similar age said, wringing his hands. 'Bloody shark took him off his board.'

Raf pressed his fingers to the patient's neck, desperately seeking a pulse.

He caught the scent of crushed mint and lemons, and then Meredith was kneeling opposite him, asking, 'How is he?'

Relief spun through him that he wasn't dealing with

this crisis alone. 'Unconscious. Weak pulse. Bleeding like a stuck pig.'

She flipped open the first-aid kit with a quick, confident movement and threw a tourniquet at him. 'Staunch the bleeding. I'll put in a line.'

He wrapped the tourniquet around what was left of Mick's left leg and then attached him to the monitor. His blood pressure and pulse ox were so low the machine immediately started beeping.

'Raf, call 000 and tell them we need the emergency helicopter. Now!' The grieving woman had vanished—the doctor was in control. Meredith thrust the IV bag into the trembling hands of Mick's mate and moved the control to fully open. 'Hold that high and don't move.'

While Raf made the call, he quickly pulled out the disposable bag and mask resuscitator and wished they had a portable oxygen tank, but air was all they had. He hoped it was going to be enough. He gave the dispatcher the GPS coordinates, stressed the extreme urgency of the situation and got off the phone.

'Mick,' he said, just in case the guy could hear him, 'I'm putting a mask over your face to help you breathe.' Securing the mask with his fingers and keeping Mick's jaw closed, he rhythmically pressed the bag as Meredith struggled to find another vein.

'He's shut down.'

'He's fit. Try his good leg.'

'Squeeze the bags of fluid continuously,' she commanded the two terrified men, who both held bags of Hartmann's solution. As she cut away the top section of Mick's wetsuit, she leaned towards Raf, her china-blue gaze seeking his. 'Are there only three bags of IV fluid in the kit?'

He nodded. 'It's usually enough.'

'Not today. Pray it's enough to keep him alive until the chopper arrives.'

'He's lucky you're here.'

Her mouth flattened into a resigned grimace. 'He's lucky we're both here.'

As if mocking them, the portable monitor beeped frantically and the ECG tracing morphed from rapid but neat PQRST waves into squiggles like a kid gone wild with a crayon. 'He's in VT.'

Meredith swore and grabbed the electrode pads, quickly applying them to Mick's chest. 'Everyone stand clear.'

Raf removed the mask, stood and stepped back. 'I'll take that.' He grabbed an IV bag off one of the terrified bystanders and squeezed it hard, forcing the fluid into Mick's veins, giving his heart something to pump.

Meredith scanned the area and then pressed the shock button. Mick's body twitched. The monitor screamed. Meredith fitted the mask over Mick's face and squeezed the bag, giving him air. 'Give him the last bag.'

Raf attached the last litre of IV fluid, running it in as fast as he and gravity could push it.

As the bag got down to the last hundred millilitres, Meredith yelled, 'Stand clear,' and sent another shock into the dying man.

They both stared at the monitor, willing it to show them what they needed to see. Show them that Mick had a chance.

'Sinus rhythm,' Raf said jubilantly, wanting to hug her.

Meredith's mouth stayed tight. 'He's still bleeding…'

Raf heard her voice in his head finishing the rest of the sentence, *and we're out of IV fluids.*

'Chopper!' someone yelled.

Everyone glanced up at the sky as a black dot in the distance quickly became a red and yellow lifeline.

'Thank God,' Meredith said quietly, as Raf checked the tourniquet. 'Now he's got a chance.'

Ten minutes later Mick was in the air and the stunned crowd was talking with the police officer who was taking statements about what type of shark had attacked. Raf packed up the sand-filled gear and sneaked a peek at Meredith.

Her hair was whipping around her face in the wind and her cheeks were pink. The shadows around her eyes, which seemed a permanent part of her, were still there, but she had a slightly different aura. He recognised it as the post-emergency buzz.

'Saving a life, it's a good feeling, yeah?'

She smiled widely. 'Oh, yeah. As a GP I don't see much trauma but Richard thrived on it.' She gave a soft laugh. 'He was an adrenaline junkie at work and at play and he expected everyone around him to share the addiction.'

She hadn't talked very much about her husband and his curiosity had been waiting for an opportunity just like this. 'Did you share the addiction?'

'At first I thought I did but over the years he got a lot more adventurous and did things out of my comfort zone. I was energised by skiing double black diamonds but he needed to go way off-piste to get the same buzz. I was happy to bush walk, he wanted to rock climb.'

'He sounds like he was an enthusiastic adventurer.'

She nodded, her expression reflective. 'I think that's what initially drew me to him. I was this quiet girl from the farm, raised to consider everything and make balanced and informed decisions. Richard just plunged in.

He had fearless energy that I admired but at the same time it also scared me. As a trauma surgeon he fought with death at work every day. It was like he had to give it the bird on his days off.'

She blew sand from the moveable trays in the first-aid kit then closed them with a jerky snap. 'People say at least he died doing what he loved, as if that's in some way helpful to me.' She stood up fast. 'It isn't bloody helpful at all. If he hadn't been skiing in an avalanche area he'd be alive and Zoe would have a father.'

Raf thought about the many things that had drawn him to Teresa—among them her convictions and steely determination—and how eventually those admired qualities had contributed to their undoing. 'If he'd been sitting glued to the TV, would he have been the man you fell in love with?'

She pressed her lips together as she tugged her fly-away hair behind her ears. 'I don't know. What made Richard Richard was both easy and hard to love in equal measure.'

She turned abruptly, as if she'd said more than she'd planned, and marched determinedly through the sand towards the stairs. Raf followed, wanting to tell her he understood, but if he did that he'd have to tell her about Teresa. He wasn't ready to do that so he silently followed her, carrying the gear.

As the sandy path to the car park broke through the ti-trees, he saw his father sitting on the salt-weathered red gum bench seat he'd built in memory of his wife. He was rocking Zoe's pram back and forth, gently bouncing it on its suspension in the age-old tradition of soothing a baby. His sister was talking to Laura Jeglinski.

Bianca rushed forward. 'Oh, my God, I can't believe

there was a shark attack on our beach. Thank God you were both here.'

'I second that,' Laura said with feeling. 'I don't even want to think about what would have happened if you both hadn't been so close.'

'Or if Raf didn't have his very own portable defibrillator,' Meredith said, huge question marks in her eyes.

'Mum died of a heart attack way too young,' Bianca said simply. 'When Raf made his money he—'

'Laura, can you call the Alfred later and get a progress report on Mick?' Raf said, cutting his sister off before their father heard her talking about their mother. 'They tell doctors a lot more than volunteer ambos.'

'Absolutely. I'll keep you both in the loop.' She turned to Meredith, her face full of queries. 'Are you living on the island now?'

She gave a faint smile as if the question was loaded. 'For the moment.'

Laura didn't seem to notice her reticence. 'I don't suppose you want to work one or two sessions a week at the clinic? Believe me, *any* time you could give us would be fantastic.'

Raf fully expected Meredith to say no. Hell, Zoe wasn't quite five weeks old and it was only nine weeks since Richard had died.

Richard? Really? You're on first-name terms with a dead guy you never met. A guy Meredith's still very much in love with.

Shut up.

'I'd love to do one or two sessions a week,' Meredith said, sounding more enthusiastic than he'd ever heard her. 'Can you recommend anyone who might be suitable to mind Zoe for three hours a couple of times a week?'

'I will mind *la bella piccolina*,' Mario said, his voice

booming around the group as if he was on his fishing boat, talking to his crew in a gale-force wind.

'Dad,' Bianca said gently, 'I know you love babies but one of your hands is weak and you still need the stable cane to walk. How can you walk and hold Zoe?'

His father's coal-black eyes flicked to Raf, filled with intention and instructing him to offer his help.

His stomach clenched. *No, Dad. I'm not ready.*

He willed his father to understand and gave a tiny shake of his head. 'Bianca's right.'

'Then again,' Bianca said thoughtfully, 'Raf's here for backup and it's better for Meredith and Zoe if she's minded by someone she knows.'

Raf, who'd always admired Italian hospitality, suddenly hated it with every fibre of his being. 'I have app specs—'

'Your time's flexible,' Bianca countered, and then dropped her voice. 'It's just backup and it will be good for Dad.'

It won't be good for me. Raf felt like he was in a room with the walls closing in on him.

'It's settled, then,' Mario said, his craggy face wreathed in a rusty smile.

'Really?' Meredith's eyes lit up like glorious sunshine breaking through dense, grey clouds.

Raf's heart gave a crazy lurch. It was like looking at a totally different woman.

'Are you sure you can spare the time, Raf?'

Tell her no.

What, and kill the first signs of her wanting to move forward with her life? I can't do that to her.

Then you're well and truly screwed.

'I'm just the emergency backup,' he said tersely.

'And I appreciate it very much.'

Her reasonableness chafed at the complicated mess of emotions that churned inside him without relief. He strode quickly away from the group, away from Meredith and her helpless baby who had the power to destroy him.

CHAPTER EIGHT

MEREDITH WAS EXPRESSING milk when her phone rang. She switched off the gentle *burr-click-burr-click* of the breast pump and accepted the call. 'Hi, Linda, how are things?'

'Hello, Meredith.' There was a moment's hesitation before her mother-in-law said, 'Do you find that a hard question to answer some days?'

She glanced out the window at the turquoise waves and unconsciously played with the hearts on her necklace, moving them back and forth against the fine sterling-silver chain. Mario had presented the gift to her the day she'd arrived back on the island, saying it was from both him and Raf to commemorate Zoe's birth. Their thoughtfulness had both touched and saddened her, merging together in a way that was now becoming a familiar part of her life.

It was the perfect gift—a beautiful representation of mother and child—and it had immediately sparked the question, if Richard had been alive would he have made her such a gift? Even in her grief she'd known that Richard and jewellery hadn't gone together in any shape or form. He'd have been more likely to present her with a sturdy baby backpack so she and Zoe could join him on hikes.

Over the last five weeks the necklace had become a kind of stress-reliever—her fingers reaching for it whenever she needed to think. 'I often lie,' she finally replied. 'People ask how you are but most of them are not really interested in the answer.'

For some reason she immediately thought of Raf who, from the very first time she'd met him on the wintery, windswept beach, had not only wanted an answer to that question, he'd wanted the truth.

'How's my lovely granddaughter?' Linda asked, obviously wanting to change the topic. 'It's been two weeks since we've seen her.'

Meredith heard the slight censure and disappointment in Linda's voice and guilt dug in. She knew she should take Zoe up to Melbourne to see Linda and Derek but the three-hour drive with a baby was daunting. Melbourne was daunting. 'Zoe's planning a football career. It doesn't matter how well I swaddle her, she's worked out how to kick her way out of her bunny rug and then kick off her quilt. It's been a bit tricky keeping her warm at night.'

'I saw these really cute drawstring nighties at the Prahran market,' Linda said enthusiastically. 'The bottom is like a little sleeping bag to keep her all warm and tucked in. I'll buy some and bring them down on Thursday.'

'Oh, I'm working at the Shearwater Clinic on Thursday afternoon. Would Wednesday or Friday suit you?'

'You're working?'

Linda's surprise buzzed down the line and Meredith's gaze travelled to the most recent letter from the bank and her solicitor. 'Just a couple of sessions a week.'

'When did this start?'

Meredith wanted to lie but couldn't. 'Two weeks ago.'

'Two weeks! Who's minding Zoe?'

'Raf and Mario Camilleri.'

'You're letting two *men* mind my granddaughter?' she asked, her tone incredulous.

Meredith's fingers reached for the hearts. 'Yes, because they're very—'

'Why didn't you ask me?'

The hurt in Linda's voice pierced her and she said gently, 'You're three hours away.'

'That is *not* my fault, Meredith. You have a house and a job here in Melbourne. If you want to work, come back here so Zoe can be minded by her family.'

Her fingers zipped the hearts back and forth across the chain fast. 'It's not that simple.'

Linda huffed. 'Of course it is.'

But how could she tell her mother-in-law that the house she'd shared with Richard chilled her with its stark reminder of everything she'd lost when she knew it gave Linda comfort?

Raf threw off the covers and got out of bed, despite the fact his bedside clock told him it was two forty-five a.m. He'd been tossing for hours, falling asleep only to dream about babies that vanished whenever he reached for them. He was completely over waking up in a hot sweat, heart hammering and with his jaw clenched. Not only was it exhausting, it was undoing three years of hard work. He was better off up and awake.

Bending down, he picked up a pair of old, soft track pants and the T-shirt he'd discarded on the floor before bed. As he pulled the shirt over his head he smelled baby shampoo with a hint of something else—Zoe.

He breathed in deeply.

Yeah, no. Just change the shirt.

He ignored his own advice and padded down the dark hall towards the kitchen, wondering if hot milk might help him get a dreamless sleep. A wide shaft of moonlight crossed the newly carpeted living room, showing off the pale green to perfection. For a moment he admired the carpet that represented a small win in his battle to modernise Mario in preparation for his own return to Melbourne, then he realised the light couldn't possibly be the moon because it was on the wane. He walked to the window and saw Meredith's house lit up like it was early evening and not the middle of the night.

Through the narrow, high window and the gap between the balcony rail he could make out Meredith's distinctive silhouette pacing back and forth with Zoe in her arms, and he steeled himself against the special sight of mother and child together. It was pointless—his heart lurched anyway.

His vow to have as little as possible to do with Zoe had worked well for two weeks but the previous afternoon it had taken a solid hit and he'd spent two hours pacing the floor with her in his arms. Mario had fed her, he'd used the tried and true 'jostle the pram' technique, swaddled her tightly and had cuddled her, but Zoe had kicked and screamed as if she was being tortured.

'Rafael, you try.' It had been the first time since Mario had been minding Zoe that he'd asked for help.

'Dad, I'm here to help you so that you can do the minding.'

Mario had glared at him. 'You think I like asking you to be my legs?'

'No,' he'd said, trying not to growl back at his father, 'but you know I don't have baby experience.'

Mario had placed his fist on his heart. 'No experience required. Hold her against your heart and let her feel the beat. Pat her back firmly and walk.'

Every part of him had yelled to walk away, but a screaming baby didn't care about his feelings so he'd followed instructions—held her high on his shoulder with her stomach pressed against him and patted her on the back.

'That's too soft,' Mario had said critically. 'Do it harder. She won't break.'

He'd increased the pressure until a dull thump sounded against Zoe's bunny rug and his father's shaking head started nodding. 'Are you sure this isn't too hard?'

'It's perfect. Just keep doing it and keep walking.' A minute later Zoe had stilled and a rare smile had creased Mario's face. 'And that, Rafael, is how you calm a baby.'

The praise in Mario's voice had been unexpected and it had settled over him, smoothing out one of the many dents in his hope that one day he and his father might get along better.

Every time Zoe's screams had settled, her little head would fall onto the crook of his shoulder and her sleeping breath blew warm kisses onto his skin. Each breath had arrowed straight to his heart, scaring the hell out of him, so he'd laid her in the pram more for his sake than hers. Each of the half dozen times he'd done that she'd woken up immediately, looked up at him from those enormous dark eyes of hers complete with a judgmental stare that had said, *I don't think so, buster*, and then she'd bellowed as if he'd stuck a pin into her.

Two very long hours later, when Meredith had arrived home from work, he'd carried Zoe home and passed her from his arms into Meredith's. That had been almost nine hours ago. Surely Zoe had slept for some of that time? But if she had, why was every light in the house on? He and Mario had struggled to care for Zoe and they'd shared the load and suggestions.

Leave it be. It's not your problem.

Meredith's alone. He searched for his phone.

Stop. Don't add to the nightmares.

Meredith's living a nightmare. He found the sleek device and his fingers tensed over the keyboard. The push of his conscience countered the pull of survival. He wished he could be a bastard and ignore this but anyone in distress tugged at him. That, and his mother's early death, had propelled him into volunteering and he could never walk away without offering help. He hoped like hell this time she'd refuse.

Are you OK?

He saw Meredith walk to the coffee table, pick up her phone and read it. She looked towards the house and his phone vibrated with a message: No.

His gut rolled. He had no choice now but to go next door and walk into the lion's den. Slowly he opened the front door, vaulted the low front side fence and immediately heard Zoe's ear-punishing screams. By the time he was standing at Meredith's door, so was she, with the door wide-open.

'I've tried everything, Raf,' she wailed, her usual composure deserting her. 'She just won't stop crying.'

Meredith looked utterly woebegone in her candy-striped flannel pyjama pants and a long-sleeved pink T-shirt, and the sheen of tears tracked down her pale cheeks.

It was the most natural thing in the world to reach out and brush the damp trail on Meredith's cheek with his thumb. Her silky, soft skin was warm and soft, and the curve of her cheek tilted his thumb inward and it skimmed the corner of her mouth. He desperately wanted to sweep it across the moist plumpness of her lips. Wanted to feel her mouth open under his touch, suck his thumb into that hot, dark place before closing around it. Wanted to feel the tip of her tongue tracing the sensitive pad and—

A whoosh of heat exploded inside him, popping and fizzing and rushing him with desire. God, he wanted her.

Meredith's lips parted slightly and then she suddenly stilled and swallowed hard. The blue of her eyes was obliterated by huge black discs and emotions spun in their depths—the predominant one shock.

Whoa, mate, what the hell are you doing? She's grieving. That's way too intimate a touch.

He pulled his thumb back fast from her cheek as if it had been burned and dropped his hand to his side. With another sob, Meredith pushed Zoe into his arms and the combination of his shame and pain killed his arousal. Lifting the squirming baby high up against his shoulder, he followed Meredith up the stairs.

His gaze went straight to her behind and not even baggy pyjamas could hide its pert shape that may as well have had a sign stuck to it that said, *Come and get me.* Raf closed his eyes to banish the seductive image of Meredith's bottom and sucked in a deep breath. His nostrils clogged with the sweet, fresh scent of baby, sending a totally different raft of sensations through him—sensations equally as dangerous as lusting after Meredith. Assaulted by the Dennison females from all sides, he was doomed.

He needed armour. *Be practical. Treat this like* any *St John's job.*

He marched up the stairs, wanting desperately to hand Zoe back, but Meredith needed a break. 'I'll pace. You make yourself a warm drink.'

Meredith tugged at her already wild hair. 'I've tried everything, Raf. I've fed her, I've changed her, I've walked miles back and forth across this room, been out on the balcony with the soothing sound of the waves, hell, I've even cried with her. She doesn't have a fever, she doesn't have a rash and I've given her something for colic but it hasn't worked. I have no clue what else to do.'

Zoe was now sucking furiously on his T-shirt. 'Could she be hungry again?'

Meredith's sigh sang with exhaustion. 'I don't know. She shouldn't be. Maybe.'

'How about you sit and try feeding her, and I'll make the warm drink.' He passed Zoe over to Meredith and walked behind the long, central bench into the kitchen.

While he waited for the microwave to heat two mugs of milk, he checked a reputable baby information website. When the microwave finally beeped, the only sound in the house was Zoe's vigorous sucking.

He carried the mugs over and sat down on the ottoman, facing Meredith. 'The nursing site says babies have a growth spurt around six to eight weeks. Apparently when they do, they're ravenously hungry and unsettled.'

Meredith stared back at him slack jawed, as if he'd just solved the world's most complicated mathematical equation. He smiled at her. 'Sound familiar?'

She rested her head on Zoe's for a second and then

looked back at him. 'Oh, God, I didn't even think of that. I thought she was sick but she's starving, the poor little thing.'

'You doctors,' he teased, 'always going straight to the bad stuff.'

'It's programmed into us.'

'You're also exhausted so don't beat yourself up.'

She gave a rough, throaty laugh. 'I don't have the energy for that. I'm not even sure I have enough milk for her.'

He rechecked the website, trying not to let the sound of her laugh pull the pin on his barely leashed desire. 'It says here you just have to focus on feeding her every three hours or so and Zoe's sucking will boost your milk supply. In a few days everything will settle down again.'

'A few days?' Her eyebrows hit her hairline and then her head fell back to rest on the couch, exhaustion radiating off every part of her. 'I may not last that long.'

He wanted to gather her into him—feel her head on his chest, feel her hair tickling his chin and her delicate citrus scent filling his nostrils. He wanted to run his hands along the soft, smooth length of her arms, tell her he was here now and everything was going to be okay. Not that he had any qualifications or even any right to do any such thing but knowing that didn't stop the longing to touch her or the need to reassure.

You saw her shock when you touched her. Her husband's barely dead and there's no way she'd want you.

Reality dumped over him like a rough wave, reminding him of his place in all of this—the friendly, helpful neighbour—and he handed her the mug of hot chocolate, making a big effort not to touch her. 'I guess you just take it one feed at a time.'

* * *

Meredith woke with a start, roused out of a deep sleep by a raucous sound. 'Coming, Zoe,' she mumbled as she sat up and swung her legs out of bed. The room tilted and then righted as her blood pressure caught up with the sudden movement. The shrill noise continued and through her slowly vanishing fog of sleep she realised it wasn't Zoe's cry at all but the cackling laughter of a kookaburra. She squinted into the sunlight and raised her fist, shaking it at the smug, blue-winged bird sitting on the deck rail on the other side of the sliding glass door of her bedroom.

'I was asleep, you beast. If you've woken Zoe, there'll be no more choice pieces of meat for you.'

She glanced at the clock and blinked in disbelief. Ten past eight. The last time she'd looked at it the green glowing numbers had read three forty-two—over four hours ago. With a tight expression, Raf had taken a fractious Zoe out of her arms and insisted she go to bed and he'd walk the floor. Exhausted, she'd lacked the energy to argue that Zoe was her responsibility and she should be the one to stay up and care for her. Instead, she'd taken the offer with both hands and run for her bed before he could change his mind. She'd been asleep the instant her head had hit the pillow.

She sat on the bed a bit longer, her ears straining for the sounds of her daughter, but all she could hear was the rhythmic rumble of the surf and the low whir of the fridge. Pulling a polar fleece over her pyjama top, she slipped her phone into her pocket and tiptoed along the glossy floorboards to Zoe's room. She peeked in but the cot was empty. She hurried into the open living area and stopped short.

Raf lay on his back on the leather couch, fast asleep with his long legs stretched out in front of him and his feet up on the armrest. His grey cotton sweatpants sat low on his hips but his chest was utterly naked except for her daughter, who was cuddled up against it, contentedly asleep. Zoe was anchored safely by the width of his broad hands and splayed fingers resting gently against her back. His breathing was full and slow and as his chest rose and fell it took Zoe up and down with it like the rocking of a boat on a gentle swell.

It was a picture of strength and protection imbued with gentleness and care. A funny sensation wound through her chest before moving down to her stomach and then washing outwards, warming her from head to toe. It was the same sensation she'd experienced a few hours earlier when Raf had wiped the tears from her cheek. A sensation that wasn't entirely platonic.

The delicious warmth immediately turned into a brick of guilt, which sat hard in her chest. She'd come so close to touching his thumb with the tip of her tongue and she didn't understand why. All she knew was that it was wrong on so many levels.

Wrapping her arms around herself, she rocked slowly back and forth on the balls of her feet and firmly put the fleeting zip of something that resembled desire down to exhaustion—physical and emotional. She was so wrung out by being a mother and father to Zoe, trying to stay on top of everything, dealing with probate and the daunting task of untangling their messy financial situation, desperately missing Richard—missing being touched and loved—and feeling so very alone that her body was obviously confusing helpful friendship with something else and reacting to it.

It had to be that.

Yes, that's the reason.

Doubt crept in on her as she thought about the

women at her mothers' group. Last week the conversation had veered towards sex and all of them had said they were so tired they had no sexual feelings at all. If happily married women couldn't rustle up any enthusiasm for sex, then she was the last person who'd be having stirrings of lust. Whatever the sensations were, they must be another form of grief. If she ever got any sleep and if she ever found any spare time, she was going to write a book about the strange, complicated and poorly understood physical manifestations of bereavement.

She fished her phone out of her pocket and took a photo of Zoe and Raf for the photo album she knew she should make but had so far lacked the enthusiasm to do so. By the time Zoe was old enough to ask, 'Who's that, Mummy?' they'd probably be living somewhere else and have lost contact with Raf. She'd have to say, 'He was a very kind man who helped us a lot when you were a baby.'

Raf's eyes opened and he turned his head towards her, his chocolate-brown gaze coming into focus. A smile curved into his salt-and-pepper stubble. 'Hey.'

His deep, sleep-filled voice rumbled around her like a cosy blanket. 'I can't believe she's asleep,' she said softly. 'You're an amazing baby whisperer.'

'I doubt that,' he said quickly, his face tensing.

For a quicksilver second his cheeks hollowed before smoothing out again. It all happened so fast she thought she must have imagined it but then she remembered. She'd seen that look more than once before—in his bedroom soon after Zoe was born, in this room when he was building the cot, and there'd been a flash of it when Bianca had suggested Raf help care for Zoe and again last night. It was as if his help came with regret. Did Zoe freak him out in some way?

She shook the crazy thought away and sat on the same ottoman he'd sat on the previous evening. 'I think you have magical powers because you got her to sleep and I couldn't.'

'There's nothing magical about it,' he said in a brisk whisper. 'It's just I don't smell of milk. Actually, I smell of her because she spat up all over me, which is why I ditched the shirt. Eventually, she just gave up and went to sleep.'

Zoe stirred, her legs kicking, and she gave a whimper. 'See,' he said with a grin, 'you're in the room and she has the olfactory senses of an African elephant.'

Meredith laughed and reached for Zoe. In the process of picking her baby up, her fingers brushed Raf's naked chest—all golden skin stretched taut over rock hard muscle.

A jolt of heat zapped her, sending heady sensations scudding into every part of her. Her head spun, her knees weakened and for a split second an ache throbbed deep down inside her in the best possible way. Then, with the speed of lightning, it passed through her and was gone, leaving her bewildered and confused.

Raf sat up fast, pulling the pillow with him and placing it across his lap before resting his elbows on it. He scrubbed his face with his palms. 'You go and…' He cleared his throat and when he spoke again the huskiness in his voice had vanished. 'And I'll go grab a shower and a clean shirt. By the time you've bathed and fed her, I'll have breakfast ready. Are you hungry?'

She was about to say no—it had become her default answer to offers of food ever since Richard's death had dented her appetite—when her stomach growled and grumbled so loudly the noise echoed around the room.

She laughed. 'It seems that I'm starving.'

CHAPTER NINE

As MEREDITH FASTENED Zoe's nappy, she could hear Raf humming and the occasional crash and bang of pots and pans. The combined aromas of freshly brewed coffee and bacon called her from the bedroom and she carried Zoe back to the living area.

'That smells amazing,' she said, settling Zoe on her baby play mat.

'You can never have too much bacon,' he said, removing a plate of hot, buttered toast from the plate warmer.

He served up scrambled eggs and placed the plates on the table, and then presented her with coffee.

'Cappuccino is the only part of an Italian breakfast I can stomach,' he said, sitting down at the table with her. 'My mornings used to be a run, a bowl of muesli and fruit, and into the office by seven fifteen.'

'What else do you do apart from being a volunteer ambo?' she asked, recalling the time at the beach when he'd interrupted Bianca just as she'd been explaining why he owned a defibrillator.

'IT.' His spoon clinked against the saucer as he laid it down. 'I designed a program that hospitals use to centralise appointments for patients with conditions that require they see a variety of practitioners in different departments. It arranges all the appointments for them on the same day with minimal wait times in between.'

'HospIT?' She gaped at him, not quite believing what she was hearing. 'You created HospIT?'

'You sound surprised,' he said mildly, his eyes twinkling at her. 'There's more to me, Dr Dennison, than just a pretty face.'

'Obviously,' she said, laughing. 'Wow, that's huge. I mean, HospIT's used in every public hospital in Australia.'

'Is it?' he deadpanned. 'I wasn't aware of that.'

'Hey, be nice,' she said, reaching out and gently socking him on the arm. 'I'm lacking sleep here and my brain is like sludge.'

She recalled Richard reading something from the business section of the newspaper to her about HospIT's sale—remembered it had involved a big number with a lot of zeros attached to it. 'How did you even come to design the program?'

He stared into his coffee, his friendly mouth flattening into a grimace. 'Pure frustration and a need to produce *something*.'

Angst bounced off the word, thudding into her hard, and she promptly wondered if there was a connection between it, an ex-wife and a handmade cot. 'What do you mean?'

He sighed, the sound weary and resigned, and when he finally lifted his gaze from the coffee she caught the vestiges of raw emotion there. 'Teresa and I spent a lot of time and money undergoing IVF.'

She immediately glanced over at Zoe and then back at him, meeting his gaze. 'That's tough on a relationship.'

'Yeah.' He drained his coffee and put the cup down with a clatter.

'We take it for granted we're in control of when we choose to have a child and that we'll be able to have one whenever we want one.'

He made a snorting sound. 'And the trauma of IVF makes you question if you ever wanted a child to begin with.'

'You decided you didn't want a child?' But even as she asked the question she knew she was wrong, because if he hadn't wanted a child, why had he made a cot?

'Teresa changed her mind about IVF.'

The clipped words carried his pain and she remembered those agonising few months when she'd wondered if Richard was ever going to say he was ready to be a father. 'That must have been hard for you both. I guess it precipitated your divorce?'

'No, we survived that.'

She wondered what could break a couple up if they'd got through IVF intact.

His fingers reached for the salt-and-pepper containers, fiddling with them and stacking them on top of each other. 'I don't blame Teresa for wanting to stop IVF,' he said, his voice dropping to a mutter. 'She was the one with a body that was perfectly capable of conceiving naturally.'

His hand suddenly jerked and she found herself flinching as he knocked over the tower of condiments, sending them tumbling. The action was so unexpected and so full of unrestrained emotion that she wanted to reach out and touch him and offer support. The twist of fury and pain on his face stopped her. He didn't want condolences, support or understanding, and she totally understood why. None of it would change a damn thing.

She watched his long fingers flicking the spilled salt

and pepper into a pile and slowly his mask of normality slid firmly back into place.

When he'd finally corralled the mixture of seasonings into a pile, he raised his dark burnished eyes and hooked his gaze with hers. 'Sorry.'

She shook her head. 'Nothing to be sorry about.'

'You flinched.'

'Automatic response to the unexpected.'

He huffed out a sound that could be interpreted as either agreement or disagreement. 'I hate feeling angry so I don't talk about it but I can feel the doctor in you wanting to know my diagnosis.'

He was half-right—she did want to know but it was a lot more than just professional curiosity. She'd wanted to know everything from the moment he'd mentioned he'd once built a cot. 'Only if you want to tell me.' *Please, please, tell me.*

Raf returned to fiddling with the salt and pepper, and the crunching, cracking sounds of the fridge's icemaker tumbled into the silence. He shifted in his seat. 'I've got...' he raised his fingers in the air, making quotation marks '...idiopathic infertility.'

'Idiopathic being Greek for no freaking idea. It's a term doctors use to make themselves feel better, right?' His lovely warm eyes hardened. 'It has to be, because it sure as hell doesn't make the patient feel any better.'

His words came at her like a spear barbed with grief, piercing and jagging through her and bringing his pain with it. A dull ache throbbed for him under her heart—pulsing for everything he'd lost. In her professional experience, no man coped particularly well with being told they were the infertile part of a couple. Guys seemed to take it as a hit on their masculinity.

The irony here was that Raf was a picture of good

looks and good health. He could be the aspirational poster boy for the modern man—fit, toned, square-shouldered, flat abdomen—and yet those salubrious looks hid something faulty that was so often impossible to fix.

'I've got an idea,' she said, thinking about how both of them were struggling with life's curve balls. 'Let's take the words *idiopathic* and *act of God* completely out of our vocabularies.'

The grim line of his mouth tweaked up slightly. 'Sounds like a plan.' He stood abruptly, picked up his cup and saucer and carried them to the dishwasher and loaded them inside. 'Do you want more coffee?'

No. I want to know more about you. But she could see the regret on his face that he'd already told her far more than he felt comfortable disclosing. 'I'd better not have any more coffee, but a pot of chai tea would be lovely. The wet mix is in the pantry.'

She watched him move around the kitchen, his actions sure and fast. It took every ounce of her willpower to restrain herself from rushing and saying something—anything—to fill the silence.

Concentrating on the food in front of her, she ate the deliciously fluffy eggs and the crispy bacon. The kettle boiled, the coffee machine hissed and then Raf was back at the table with a flat black for himself and a pot of chai tea, a cup and saucer, a wooden honey dipper and the honey pot for her.

She breathed in the spicy scent of cardamom, cloves and anise. 'It smells wonderful, thank you.'

His mouth curved into a half-smile. 'You're welcome.'

As she stirred honey into the tea he'd poured for her, she closed her mind to all the loud reasons why she shouldn't ask him exactly what had happened to him and Teresa. About him and the cot he'd made.

'If you survived IVF, what eventually undid you as a couple?'

Her blurted words hung in the air and she saw the moment his brain decoded them. His nostrils flared and his eyes narrowed, and for a moment she was convinced he was going to tell her to back off.

'I'm surprised Mario or Bianca haven't told you,' he said tightly, the tendons in his neck bulging.

'I might be nosy, Raf, but I'd never go behind your back and ask them. Not when it's your story to tell.'

His eyes studied her for a long moment as if he was looking for something deep inside her or perhaps he was searching for something inside himself. He released a long, shuddering sigh. 'Telling you I don't like talking about it sounds pretty lame when you have to revisit your grief every time you meet someone new who hasn't heard the news about Richard.'

Reaching into his pocket, he brought his wallet out onto the table, flipped it open and pulled out a photo. 'This is Teneka.'

She took it from his outstretched fingers and studied the chubby, dark-skinned baby who was sitting propped up on pillows, staring straight at the camera. 'She's gorgeous. Is she Maori?'

'Fijian.' He took the photo back and smoothed it gently with his thumb as if caressing the child before returning the photo to his wallet. 'When Teresa said she'd had enough of injections, hormone-induced emotional roller-coaster rides and invasive procedures, I understood but I wasn't ready to give up on our dream of having a child. I suggested we pursue adoption and she agreed. Looking back, I now recognise her agreement was reluctant, but at the time…'

This time Meredith reached out her free hand and gave his arm a brief squeeze. 'We only see what we want to see.'

'Oh, yeah,' he said with feeling, 'and all I could see was our baby. Pursuing adoption meant we replaced IVF with a different treadmill. Anyone can bring a child into the world no questions asked, but jumping through the adoption hoops is a different form of torture.'

He ran his hands through his curls, tugging at them at the roots as if he welcomed the physical pain. 'Don't get me wrong. I realise it's necessary to protect a child who has already suffered loss but to a childless couple, it's just another form of hellish torture for people who just want to open their hearts and home and welcome a child.

'After filling in a gazillion forms, having medical checks and blood tests, enduring social workers doing home assessments, couples counselling and individual interviews about our values, ethics and abilities to parent, we finally got the phone call we'd been waiting so long for. There was a little girl needing a home. Our home.'

'Teneka?'

'Teneka.' He swallowed, his Adam's apple rising and falling hypnotically before he cleared his throat. 'I went straight to the timber merchant and chose the wood for her cot. I spent every night for the next week in the garage, making it, so it was ready for her when we brought her home.'

Meredith could picture Raf infusing love, care and tenderness into the cot as he measured, cut and planed the wood.

His left hand suddenly fisted so tightly his knuckles gleamed white and then his fingers were outstretched and wriggling as if they were numb and tingling. When he spoke again, his voice was so soft Meredith had to strain to hear the words.

'Only I never got to bring her home.'

Her heart, which had been beating pain around her body for weeks, suddenly thrummed with a very different type of agony. Her arm instinctively tightened around Zoe. 'Oh, my God. She died?'

He shook his head hard, his curls shaking. 'No, no, M. Teneka's not dead. She's living with another family.'

'I don't understand.'

'Believe me, neither did I,' he muttered, as he stood up, the chair legs scraping raucously loud against the floorboards. He started pacing as if moving would make things easier. 'The cot was a surprise for Teresa and when it was finished, I installed it in Teneka's room.

'I told Teresa to close her eyes and then I walked her into the room and flicked on the light. I'd expected her to run her hands along the wood and picture Teneka in the cot, just as I had while I'd been making it. At the very least, I assumed she'd throw her arms around my neck and share the excitement that after all these years we were two days away from meeting our baby.'

He stopped walking and faced the ocean, his rigid back turned to her. 'She didn't do any of that. She just stared at the cot as if it was a ticking bomb and then she said, "I can't do it."' His voice cracked. 'I laughed. I thought she was talking about tucking the sheets in around the mattress and I put my arms around her and told her she'd be an expert in no time.'

A shiver ran across Meredith's skin. She knew exactly what it was like to be driving along the road of life with a glorious vista stretching out in front of her as far as the eye could see, only to veer off the road with no warning and career down a steep embankment that offered no way out. 'She wasn't talking about sheets.'

He turned slowly, his face haggard. 'No. Sheets were the very last things on her mind. She stepped out of my embrace and told me I'd always wanted a family more than she had and that the last three years had killed any desire she'd had to become a mother. She said if I really loved her, I'd let go of my need to have a child and go back to putting her first.'

Zoe squawked and Meredith picked her up. As she cuddled her tightly, she knew the impossibility of Teresa's request. She'd loved Zoe the moment she'd seen the pink plus sign on the pregnancy test and if anyone had asked her to give her up even as a bunch of cells, she'd have refused. She instinctively knew that Raf would have loved Teneka from the moment he'd seen her photo. 'Did you try and adopt Teneka yourself?'

He linked his hands behind his head as if he didn't know what to do with his body to try and stop the pain of his memories. 'I tried but there are strict rules and without Teresa I lost Teneka.'

And he still carried her photo with him. 'I'm so sorry, Raf.'

He shrugged as if the action would push all the pain of his memories away. 'It is what it is. I got divorced, threw myself into work and kept busy.'

'Sold a multimillion-dollar company?'

'Yep, did that. HospIT saved my sanity during IVF and the adoption process but once I lost Teneka it didn't have the same soothing effect. The offer to buy was unexpected, timely and generous. It's given me breathing space and freedom to try new things. I designed and built a house in Middle Park, I'm designing an app for a group of cardiologists that's generating a lot of interest and when Dad got sick, well, here I am.'

And here I am, she thought although, it made no sense why she'd think that.

He walked over and refilled her teacup. Zoe glanced up at Raf and burped. 'I think she's smiling at us.'

'It's probably just wind.'

'No,' he said emphatically. 'It was definitely a smile.'

Her daughter stared at her solemnly and then her little mouth curved upwards, filling out her cheeks until she was beaming at her with sparkling eyes.

Meredith's eyes filled with happy tears and her heart seemed to get just that bit bigger and fill more of her chest. 'Oh, my God, Raf, she's smiling. Look, she's really smiling.'

He pulled his phone from his pocket and held it up to his face. 'Hey, Zoe, smile for the camera.'

Zoe's smile faded and she frowned with the intensity worthy of a sentencing judge.

'Who's a gorgeous girl?' Meredith crooned. 'Smile at Mummy.'

Zoe squirmed in her arms, grunted and then noisily filled her nappy.

Meredith laughed and automatically glanced at Raf, whose face was split with a grin of delight. His rich baritone chuckle joined her higher soprano one, weaving together in a truly joyous sound. It felt so natural and so very normal that she embraced the feeling, holding on to it tightly—not wanting to ever let it go.

A moment later guilt bulldozed in over her happiness, flattening everything and reminding her that nothing about her life was normal. As if to reinforce it, Raf checked the photo he'd taken of Zoe and the laughter lines on his face smoothed out and sadness moved in.

He picked up his jacket. 'I need to go. Mario…'

'Sure. Of course.' He was running from her and Zoe. Her beautiful daughter reminded him of what he'd lost and her heart ached for him. Ached for him in a way it shouldn't. 'Thanks for your help.' *Help that costs you.*

'Yeah.'

She watched him walk away, head bowed. It was too much and she wanted to shake her fist at the universe that had stolen her husband, taken Raf's dream of a child and then with vicious irony had thrown them together in this impossible situation.

Sometimes life seriously sucked.

CHAPTER TEN

'WHERE THE HELL is my fishing rod?' Mario demanded, thumping his new cane on the floor. 'You know if you borrow things you have to put them back where they belong.'

Raf closed the lid of his laptop, having executed the sale of some shares, and gave his full attention to his father, who'd been ill-tempered since the rehabilitation team meeting that morning. Granted, the meeting had been delayed a couple of weeks due to staffing issues but now it had taken place Raf couldn't work out why Mario was so grumpy. He'd thought his father would be over the moon with the result as he'd been cleared to live independently again—pending the addition of some small house alterations and the installation of an extra rail and bar—but instead Mario had been surly and out of sorts. Not even the fact he'd graduated to a regular walking stick had cheered him up.

Raf decided to take the slow, calm approach, not wanting his last week on the island to be marred by arguing. He was no longer needed as a carer and as soon as he'd finished the occupational therapist's list of required fittings, arranged for a house cleaner and convinced Mario that a mobile scooter would be a good

interim idea until he passed his driver's test again, he
would head back to his life in Melbourne.

What about M.?

*What about me? I need the safety buffer of three
hundred kilometres.*

Since the night he'd fallen asleep with Zoe on Meredith's couch and the following morning when he'd stuck
his hand inside his chest and ripped out his heart by
telling her about Teresa and Teneka, something had
shifted inside him. Now he walked precariously along
a tightrope that was an emotional impasse as he swayed
between joy at spending time with Meredith and Zoe,
and the heartache it caused him.

It had become almost impossible to avoid Meredith.
Each morning he woke up with good intentions of keeping his distance and by nightfall he'd failed. Mario encouraged her to visit and she'd often call over in the
afternoons and quiz Mario on gardening tips while he
tended his vegetable garden. Raf had built numerous
large boxes, raising the beds so it was easier for Mario
to continue his special touch with everything from aru-
gula to zucchini.

The moment Raf knew she was on the property his
concentration for work would fade to zero. He'd always been proud of his intense focus on work, no matter what distractions surrounded him. Hell, it had been
his retreat during the darkest days of his life but now it
held no sway over his desire for Meredith and it was a
battle not to race from his temporary office like a kid
anticipating a present.

Occasionally, Meredith would reluctantly ask Raf for
his help when she'd tried and failed to fix something.
While he wielded a wrench or another task-appropriate
tool, she invariably mentioned Richard as if he needed

reminding that she was recently widowed. She told tales of Richard the trauma surgeon, Richard the adventurer, Richard the demigod.

How bad was it to be jealous of a dead dude?

Pretty bloody bad.

Of course, twice a week Mario minded Zoe in the afternoons while Meredith worked. The night Zoe had slept on his chest she'd unlocked his paternal instincts, which he'd thought he'd successfully forced down deep. They'd risen with the strength of a geyser. Despite his rational argument that it was unwise and potentially dangerous to his mental health to allow Zoe into his heart, he was fighting an increasingly losing battle.

There were times when he could hold back from Zoe for hours on end but the moment Mario needed some help and he had no choice but to hold her, he was rushed with such a force of feeling that it scared him.

Yes, it was definitely time to go back to Melbourne.

'Did you hear me, Rafael?' Mario said again, his tone curt and disapproving, the way it had been for years.

'I did. I was just thinking, did you lend the fishing rod to Leo?'

'What, are you crazy? You think I'd let a fifteen-year-old anywhere near my carbon-fibre rod?'

Don't react. 'Just running through the options, Dad. I didn't borrow it. Fishing really isn't my thing.'

'And you say this like it's news to me,' he said bitterly.

Anger sparked, igniting the resentment he tried to keep at bay. 'How long are you going to hold on to this, Dad? Yes, I disappointed you by not taking over the family business. Yes, I moved away. Yes, I disappointed you by not giving you grandchildren. Anything else you'd like to add to the list? I'd hate to think I'd forgotten something.'

Mario grunted, his face hardening. 'You left without a word.'

Raf shook his head. 'Oh, no, you don't get to play that card. Well before Mum died I told you I was going to uni. I told you every time you talked about me joining the business but you chose not to listen.'

Mario's dark eyes took on the stormy look of a winter sea. 'What sort of son leaves his father?'

And this was the crux of their problem. 'What sort of father leaves his son?' he ground out, suddenly determined to have this long-overdue conversation.

'Don't talk in riddles. You've lived in Melbourne for nineteen years.'

Raf shot out of his chair, hating that he felt like the needy, bewildered teenager he'd once been. 'Because you shut me out of your life.'

'Now you're just being ridiculous.' Mario's voice held the same disparaging tone it always did whenever Raf tried to talk to him about feelings.

'Am I?' He slammed a fist into his hand. 'Your disapproval greets me the moment my car crosses the bridge.'

Mario's cane hit the floor. 'You're wrong.'

'Not from where I'm standing. So tell me, Dad, if it isn't disapproval, what the hell is it?'

Mario breathed heavily as if he'd run a race. 'I'm…' The words came out slowly as if they were hard to form. 'I'm…proud of you.'

Raf didn't believe him. 'You've got a hell of a way of showing it.'

'You want me to be grateful to you for the few times you took time out of your important life to visit me?

That I know you're counting down the days until you can leave?'

The hurt in his father's voice hit him, fuelling his own pain. 'No.'

Anger and bewilderment played in the florid folds of his cheeks. 'What, then?'

Raf's chest tightened. 'You want to know the reason I didn't visit often? Every time I came, you pushed me away. Hell, Dad, you pushed everyone away. Bianca, Mum's friends, your brothers, everyone who tried to get close and help after Mum died. You're still doing it.'

Mario's hand gripped his cane and his lips thinned but he didn't say a word.

Raf turned away, staring out the window because he knew if he looked at Mario, he'd never be able to say the words that needed to be said. He fixed his gaze on the melaleuca with its weathered, salt-grey paper bark peeling back to reveal the fresh tan of the new layers underneath. Was his need to rip off years of distance between him and his father going to give them a fresh start or make things worse?

There is no worse.

The thought steadied him and he focused on trying to be impersonal and calm. 'When Mum died, I watched my father vanish into an impenetrable fortress of grief, leaving me floundering and bewildered. I've waited for him to come out of it and for about four years I worked hard at trying to reach him, but he blocked every attempt I made and he stayed away.' The memories hammered him and he lost control. 'Bloody hell, Dad, I was seventeen. I needed you.'

'Mio Dio.' His father's voice quavered. 'You have no idea what it's like to lose the woman you love.'

He spun around, struggling not to yell. 'Seriously,

Dad?' His fingers tapped his sternum so hard they hurt. 'You're talking to me, remember?'

'Divorce is not the same,' Mario said, his tone dismissive.

'This isn't a competition, Dad,' he ground out through clenched teeth. 'I lost a lot more than a wife.'

For a moment they just stared at each other—father and son both hurting, both trapped in the emotional mud that had deepened, widened and thickened with every passing year.

Mario's rubber-tipped cane tapped against the floor and then his hand gripped Raf's shoulder. 'Never think you disappointed me about grandchildren,' he said quietly. 'I'm sad for both of us.'

Raf's throat thickened. 'Yeah.'

'It's why I love having Zoe.' Mario dropped his hand and stared out the window. 'I still miss your mother.'

'I know.'

'She did the emotional stuff for both of us.' Mario cleared his throat. 'I got lost without her.'

He nodded, knowing all too well.

'I didn't realise how much I've missed you until you came back.'

Raf's head wrenched sideways as disbelief drenched him. 'You've enjoyed having me here?'

'Why sound so surprised?'

Raf couldn't stop his eye roll.

Mario's mouth twisted wryly. 'I know I'm not easy to live with. I hate it that my body has done this to me. I hate I had to give up the boat. I've hated needing help but I don't regret that it brought you back to the island. For that I can almost be grateful to the stroke.'

Raf had to work to keep his voice steady. 'I was happy to come, Dad.'

Mario snorted.

Raf laughed. 'Fair enough. Bianca guilted me into it but I don't regret coming. Sure, we've had our moments…'

'I've given orders all my life, Rafael. Boats sink without a captain.'

'True, but you don't always have to be the captain, Dad. Sometimes you can be crew.'

'It's not easy.'

'No.'

'Two men with strong opinions will always clash. Doesn't mean I don't love you.' Mario cleared his throat and walked to the table, lowering himself into a chair. 'I want to talk about the house.'

The message was clear—they were done with all talk of feelings and it was time to get practical, but the topic intrigued him. 'Sure. I'll grab some beers.'

When he returned with the bottles, Raf twisted the top off a lager and handed it to his father. 'What about the house?'

'You're right. It needs work but I don't have the heart to change it. I know if your mother was still alive she would have renovated it years ago but me doing it feels like a betrayal.' He sipped his beer. 'It's too big for one or even two so she'd have convinced me by now to move.'

Raf's thoughts pinged from total surprise at his father's disclosure to excitement that he might actually be looking forward rather than backward. 'So what are you thinking?'

'I want something new, something smaller and, like you suggested, a sea view. If I can't be out on the water, I want the next best thing.'

Raf thought about the townhouses in the small township of Princeton but none of them came with a view. 'That's a tricky combination.'

Mario shook his head. 'It's simple. I'm subdividing. I get a modern house, a view and a garden, and the sale of the second townhouse will fund all of it.'

Raf choked on his beer as disbelief poured through him. 'You're going to pull down this house?' *This shrine to Mum?*

Mario's mouth quirked up on one side. 'Thank Zoe for ruining the carpet.'

'I don't get it.'

'When you changed the carpet and paint I realised that the best memories are in the mind, not in outdated and fading furnishings.' He tapped his chest. 'Your mother's always with me.'

Wow. Raf hadn't expected any of this and he ran his fingers around the rim of the beer bottle, trying to take it all in. 'For what it's worth, Dad, I think it's a great idea.'

'Good, because I need your help.'

He stared at Mario. 'So who are you and what have you done with my father?'

'Ah. My son the comedian.' Mario levelled his dark eyes at Raf's, a slight twinkle in their depths. 'Don't give up your day job. Oh, that's right, you don't have one. You just play on your computer.'

Raf leaned back in his chair, recognising Mario was teasing rather than criticising 'Hey, I'm joint babysitter two days a week.'

Mario's silver hair glinted in the early evening light. 'We're a good team with Zoe.'

'Yeah, we do okay with project Zoe.' And that was the irony. He and Mario got along better when Zoe was in the house.

'So, will you help me with project townhouse?'

Raf leaned forward, half excited and half wary. 'Doing what exactly?'

Mario leaned back towards the sideboard, pulled open a drawer and lifted out a pale yellow manila folder. 'Everything from helping me navigate the application for council for the subdivision to advising me on the design for the townhouses, and when the building starts, being my project manager.'

'I did a lot of that for my house.'

'I know. It's why I'm asking you.'

It was an olive branch—the first one Mario had ever extended. It was a turning point in their fractious relationship and he wanted to take it.

It means staying on the island.

The thought struck him so hard that it sucked the air out of his lungs. Leaving the island to put a much-needed safety zone between himself and Meredith put paid to any hope of an adult relationship with his father. Staying meant living next door to Meredith and Zoe and no chance of respite from the emotional maelstrom that continuously churned inside him.

He was stuck between a rock and a hard place. Both options would inflict pain on him but only one would injure his father. He wasn't prepared to do that to the old man. 'I guess I'm staying on the island a bit longer. I'll order in some real office equipment for the spare bedroom.'

'Good.' Mario raised his bottle of beer and clinked it against Raf's. 'Meredith will be pleased you're not leaving.'

'Oh?' Somehow he managed to make the word sound vague and disinterested.

Mario nodded sagely. 'Finding someone you trust to mind your child is always hard.'

Raf hated the slug of disappointment that hit him hard in the gut.

* * *

'Hi.' Meredith walked through the back door and into Mario's kitchen, having come straight from work.

Mario was sitting at the Laminex table, snapping peas. *'Ciao, bella.'* He smiled as he rose slowly to his feet and kissed her in the Italian way before giving her his standard after-work greeting. 'How many lives did you save this afternoon?'

She laughed and gave her usual reply. 'Thousands, of course.'

She was getting used to the Camilleri way of greeting and farewelling people—a kiss on each cheek. At first it had felt odd but now she couldn't imagine Mario ever shaking her hand.

You're not used to Raf's kisses.

It was true. Whenever he saw her, his face would break into a gentle smile, and he'd lean down and kiss each cheek so quickly and with so light a touch she sometimes thought she was imagining it. But her body didn't imagine it—it heated up every single time and she could no longer hide behind thinking her reaction was some crazy manifestation of grief.

If she was truly honest with herself it wasn't just the brief kiss that made her heart race but the anticipation of both the greeting and the farewell. It made her feel giddy and a sense of lightness streaked through her, which was such a stark contrast to the heavy and dull way she felt most of the time that she welcomed it. Thankfully, Raf never seemed to notice her reaction, because that would be far too embarrassing. She wasn't supposed to be aroused by a perfunctory kiss that meant nothing more than hello or goodbye.

'How's Zoe?' she asked, forcing her mind away from the absent Raf. Often when she arrived to collect her daughter, she was sitting in her bouncer on the kitchen table, waving her plastic keys.

'Asleep.' Mario opened the door of the fridge and picked up a bottle of wine, tilting it in her direction.

She nodded and he poured her a glass. 'Wow. That's amazing. Did she—?'

'Dad…' Raf walked into the kitchen, head down, studying a piece of paper in his hand. He was wearing black-rimmed glasses that gave him a professorial look that was at delicious odds with his breadth and bulk. 'Have you got the S…' He glanced up and stopped short, surprise crossing his tanned face. He pulled off his glasses, and his wide and generous mouth curved upwards. 'Hello, M. When did you sneak in?'

'About a minute ago.'

He moved towards her to greet her with a kiss and expectation thrummed through her fast, quickly morphing into heat. She felt the glow burning deep down inside her and its rapid spread upwards and outwards. *Oh, God.* Her cheeks and ears would now be fire-engine red.

Feeling self-conscious and discombobulated, she leaned at the same time as he did. His mouth missed her cheek completely, colliding instead with her own. His lips were warm and firm as they slid across hers, leaving a sheen of moisture that carried his taste—sea spray, sunshine and a hint of sandalwood. Her body tingled and shivered, making her gasp and opening her lips a fraction of a millimetre under his. She felt him still. Did he think she'd just issued him an invitation to deepen the kiss? Did she want him to? The thought both thrilled and horrified her, although not in equal measure.

She tried to rescue the situation by turning her head to present her cheek to him but he moved at exactly the same moment and they bumped noses. Flustered, she tried again and this time his stubbled jaw scraped across her cheek, the raspy sting waking up every nerve ending in her body and setting them panting.

'M.' His voice was low and guttural with a hint of humour in it. His warm breath caressed her ear, threatening to buckle her knees and send her slumping onto his chest. 'For our own safety, stop moving and stay perfectly still.'

She tried to laugh, aiming for a light-hearted sound, except her throat strangled it. He rested his large hands gently on her shoulders and quickly—far too quickly—executed a very perfunctory kiss on each cheek and then stepped back.

The loss of his heat made her body want to sway forward to stay close and she had to work on keeping her feet glued to the floor. She grabbed at the glass of wine Mario had poured for her and took a big slug of the crisp and cold chardonnay, scrambling to find her composure.

It's wrong to crave him like this. The familiar voice of self-reproach boomed in her ears.

Why? A bolshie thought stomped across her mind, indignant and insulted. *Yes, my husband's dead and, yes, I am a mother but I'm still a woman.*

You know it's way more complicated than that.

'Just as well the two of you aren't choreographers,' Mario said dryly. 'You'd have the dancers crashing into each other.' He snapped open another pea pod. 'Zoe's sleeping and dinner's half an hour away so the two of you take the wine to Mama's seat and enjoy the view.'

'That doesn't seem fair to you, Mario,' Meredith said quickly, telling herself that the reason she'd spoken was to keep the peace between father and son. To try and avoid Raf grumbling at his father for organising them both without consulting them.

'Good idea, Dad,' Raf said, putting the bottle in a cold bag and grabbing a packet of chips from the pantry.

Meredith blinked in surprise. She'd expected Raf to object. He always objected. Damn it, she needed him to object because being alone with him on a small two-seater bench seat with a world-class view and a bottle of wine was far too dangerous for her struggling equilibrium. 'Weren't you in the middle of doing something?'

He smiled at her in that way of his that always made her question everything she'd ever believed about her life. 'Nothing that can't wait.'

She swallowed against a dry and scratchy throat. 'Zoe's bound to wake up the moment we leave. I should stay.'

'Nonsense,' Mario said briskly. 'I'll text you when she wakes.'

In the past when Mario had insisted she do things, like eat more or drink hot chocolate, Raf had always interjected on her behalf. Now he stood patiently by the screen door, waiting for her.

'Come on, M.' Raf opened the door. 'You spend a lot of time being Zoe's mum and being Dr Dennison. Take half an hour out to just sit and be yourself.'

And that was the problem. Being herself was the reason she didn't want to go.

She felt the dark and smiling eyes of both Camilleri men on her and read the delight on their faces that they were giving her something they thought she'd enjoy. Her fingers reached for the hearts on her necklace, sliding them back and forth. Refusing would be churlish and it would create in them a false concern for her. They'd already done so much for her and she didn't want them to worry unduly, especially when the reason was the opposite of what they'd automatically think. This wasn't about her feeling sad and missing Richard, and in a way that was exactly it.

How could she miss Richard and yet be attracted to Raf all at the same time? It was so damn confusing.

Raf ushered Meredith out into the early November evening with its daylight savings sun still high enough to keep them warm. They crossed the road and she walked next to him on the sandy, ti-tree-lined path, her flat shoes leaving practical-looking imprints. He had a ridiculous wish that she was wearing heels and then it would have been necessary for him to put his hand under her elbow to steady her on the uneven coastal surface.

Better yet, put his arm around her waist, pull her in tightly against him and revisit that accidental but amazing kiss that still had his blood simmering. God, he'd wanted to kiss her the moment his lips had slid across hers, collecting her taste of chardonnay and chocolate, and his nostrils had caught her fresh and invigorating scent along with a hint of antiseptic from her afternoon at work. Every part of him had told him to deepen the kiss, and had frantically urged him to flick his tongue against those soft, sweet lips. If Mario hadn't been in the room, he'd have done it.

She wouldn't have welcomed it. You heard her horrified gasp.

'Richard always enjoyed this view,' Meredith said, as if reading his thoughts and inserting her dead husband firmly between them.

A bright green flash lit up behind his eyes. 'I haven't met anyone who didn't.' He immediately regretted the trite remark and as the bitter taste of regret filled him, he fought against the unsettled feelings induced by jealousy. 'Mum loved it too, which is why Dad carved the seat.'

He tugged open the chip bag and placed it between them, then refilled her glass. 'Chin-chin.'

She clinked her glass against his and her very kissable mouth curved into a reflective smile. 'Mario's happy tonight.'

'Weird, right? But don't panic, he still has his moments. Has he told you about his plans for the house yet?'

She shook her head. 'What plans?'

'With council permission, he's going to subdivide, build two townhouses, live in one and sell the other. He's asked me to spearhead the project so I'm staying on the island for a bit longer.'

Her eyes widened in surprise. 'That's unexpected. How do you feel about it?'

A sliver of disappointment curled in his gut that she hadn't responded to the news with *I'm glad you're staying* and he fought against it. 'That sounds very much like the doctor is in.'

A frown carved two lines into her forehead. 'Not at all. I'm asking as a friend. Over the weeks, as we've walked miles with Zoe, we've shared a lot of stuff. You've hardly made it a secret that living with Mario isn't easy.'

He leaned back against the wooden slats of the seat and stared out to sea. 'We talked.' He felt his mouth twitch at the understatement. 'Well, when I say talked, there was quite a bit of yelling involved but it seems both of us were feeling hurt and abandoned in our own ways.' He sipped his wine and turned towards her. 'This project might be the sinking of footings that we can build a bridge on.'

'I hope it is.' She licked her lips, the tip of her tongue catching some grains of salt from the chips.

His gaze hooked on the movement. He imagined her tongue tracing the outline of his lips and then pulling down his bottom lip before gently sinking her teeth into the soft flesh. His vision blurred. Blood pounded in his ears, deafening him, before dropping in his lap and leaving his head spinning.

'...another babysitter.'

Her voice broke through his lust-induced deafness. 'What?'

She gave him a puzzled look. 'I said I'll have to find another babysitter.'

This is your out. As relief wound through him it immediately collided with guilt and protectiveness. He didn't really want someone else minding Zoe. 'Mario would never forgive me.'

'Are you sure you'll have time now you've added project townhouses to your workload with the app? You probably thought you were doing it for just a few weeks and it came with an end date.'

Her blue-on-blue gaze fixed on his intently, empathy glowing in their depths as if she could see the constant battle that waged deep inside him. 'I want you to tell me if it's too much or...' she hesitated a moment '...too hard.'

A lump formed in his throat. Society acknowledged the grief of infertile women but rarely did it give much thought to the men who wanted children but couldn't have them. 'It's not always easy but it's not easy for you either...'

'No.' She leaned in, her shoulder gently nudging him on the arm. 'We're both a bit of a mess, but thank you. You and Mario help more than you know.'

'You're welcome.' He stretched his arm across the back of the seat, stretching his fingers so their tips brushed the silk of her blouse. The wind blew strands of her hair across his cheek, their softness caressing his skin.

Her head tilted towards him. 'I'm glad you're staying.'

'Me too.' His hand curled around her shoulder, giving it a gentle squeeze as he savoured the feel of her snuggled in against him. Her soft curves fitted against him like she belonged there and weeks of his restraint broke free.

She looked up at him and he wanted her so badly that every part of him hurt. He tucked the stray strands of hair from her cheek behind her ear, and her hand came up to cover his.

Her warmth flowed through him, caressing him, and for a long moment their eyes locked.

Time stood still and her chin tilted up as he slowly lowered his head towards her red, rosy lips. Lips that called to him as strongly as the sirens on the rocks had called to the hapless sailors. Her hand tightened on his and then he felt the pressure of her other hand flat against his chest like a stop sign.

'You're an amazing friend, Raf.'

Friend.

If she'd stabbed him with a knife it would have hurt less and something deep down inside him ached and cringed. He withdrew his arm and she straightened, creating a space between them that she obviously wanted.

What the hell was wrong with him? How had he misread the signs? She'd talked of Richard and now she'd played the friend card, making it very clear exactly how things stood between them. Only he wasn't a friend. A friend wouldn't want to kiss her senseless. A friend wouldn't be jealous of a dead husband. A friend wouldn't dream about her naked and wrapped around him.

'I'm glad things don't have to change,' she said, her usually melodic voice sounding strained.

'Nothing has to change,' he replied dully, before raising his glass and downing the contents in one gulp.

There was just one problem—he wanted everything between them to change.

CHAPTER ELEVEN

'HERE'S MY TIMESHEET, Sue,' Meredith said to the Shearwater Island Clinic's practice manager, as she dropped the piece of paper into the clearly labelled basket. If she missed the deadline, she didn't get paid for another fortnight and right now she needed all the cash she could lay her hands on.

The woman, who was in her fifties, looked up at Meredith over the top of her bright blue glasses. 'Are you enjoying working with us, Dr Dennison?'

'I am. It's hard to believe this is my eighth week working here.'

'It's hard to believe it's the second week of December. It's now officially summer and that means accident-prone tourists, stressed locals and general silly season dramas. Is there any chance you could give us some more hours?'

Meredith felt torn. Financial reasons deemed she say yes and say it fast. The new mother in her wanted to say no. She loved work but Zoe was only thirteen weeks old and then there was the chestnut of childcare. To ask Mario and Raf for more help would be crossing a line. A line she'd drawn in an attempt to keep a handle on her growing feelings for Raf.

Ask Linda.

No. If she asked Linda, her mother-in-law would tell her to come back to Melbourne to live and work. 'I'll think about it, Sue.'

'Let me know by Wednesday, otherwise I'll place an ad for a locum.

'Will do.' She said goodbye and walked the short distance from the clinic to the pub on the corner of the main street and the esplanade, feeling the first evening heat of the summer. She bought her Friday night bottle of champagne to take to Mario's for the usual Friday night dinner with the Camilleris.

As she was walking back to her car, her phone rang. Warmth flowed through her as she saw the name on the screen. 'Hello, Emma.'

'Hey, Merry.'

She heard the clang of a tram in the background and immediately knew the gang from the practice would be walking to the Rooftop wine bar, as they did every Friday night. As she'd once done every Friday night.

'How are things down in the boonies?' Emma asked.

She glanced down the street and out to the harbour. A windsurfer tracked back and forth across the slight swell, leaving a white trail of spray in its wake. Closer to shore seagulls circled the end of the pier, having caught the scent of freshly caught fish and bait.

An odd sense of something that shared more with peace than distress rolled through her. 'There are worse places to live.'

'But you're not really living there, are you?' Emma's tone was slightly aghast. 'I mean, it's been three months. You're going to be home by Christmas, right?'

Christmas. A throb pounded at her temples at the

thought of Christmas spent with Linda and Derek and
the pall of Richard's permanent absence hanging over
them all. She shivered. An image of Raf sitting at the
big outdoor teak table and holding Zoe on his lap, Mario
with a glass of red wine in his hand and holding court
with the rest of the Camilleris laughing, talking and
constantly interrupting each other, filled her mind.

Pangs of guilt immediately vanquished the living
and breathing picture. 'I'm not sure what I'm doing for
Christmas but let's catch up over the summer. You and
Evan should come down here for a couple of days. The
beach is lovely.'

'You should be up here so I can look after you.'
Emma sounded hurt. 'Aren't you lonely?'

That was one question Meredith could answer truth-
fully. 'I'm only lonely for Richard and that doesn't
change no matter where I'm living.'

'Don't you need people around you who know you?'

She thought of Raf and the legacy of his grief for a
child he'd loved and lost—grief that lived in the lines
around his eyes. In a way, his pain mirrored hers. He
understood how life could suddenly end up so different from the naive plans one made. How it was ran-
dom misfortune and *that* was the worst thing about it.
It struck and departed, leaving people floundering and
flailing, unable to make any sense of it because there
was no sense to be made.

Despite the best intentions in the world, someone
whose life had not been touched by such catastrophic
change couldn't offer quite the same level of understanding, especially on the days when the melancholy
messes hit. Both Raf and Mario understood. Their presence in her life supported her in a way she needed.

'I've got lovely neighbours who look out for me. You can meet them when you visit.'

She finished the call and sat in the car, checking her messages, before she drove home.

Mario had sent a photo of a smiling Zoe in her bouncer and Raf with his handsome face covered in soot standing in front of the old wood-fired pizza oven. She was laughing when a text came in.

Meredith, I'm starting to think your Internet and phone are not working. When can we visit again? Linda.

Pangs of conscience stabbed her and the lightness vanished. It was like Linda had just witnessed her reaction to the photo of Raf. Meredith struggled to understand how she could be so attracted to him when she still missed Richard. Instinctively, she knew Linda would never comprehend her feelings because Richard had only been dead barely five months. This was partly why she'd been slow to call Linda and issue another invitation.

The Nichols had spent last weekend with her. She understood the need Linda had to see Zoe and she was fine with that. What she struggled with was that the visits always included questions about her plans for the future. Questions Meredith didn't have the answers for. Questions she didn't want to deal with yet.

She moved on to the emails.

Dr Dennison
    Please call me at your earliest convenience to make an appointment to discuss your mortgage options.
Samantha Lucas
Personal Banker

Her stomach lurched. She knew her mortgage options were very limited but why was everyone and every corporation rushing her to make decisions she wasn't ready to make?

The familiar tightness in her chest started and she rubbed her sternum. 'Richard, what was the bloody point of your detailed five-year plan when you're not here to make any of it happen?'

But the only answer was a heavy silence, which filled the car and pressed down on her with aching sadness.

Her phone beeped with a text from Raf.

Look left.

She glanced up and surprise tumbled over delight like the fizz of lemonade on her tongue. Raf stood by the car with Zoe's three-wheeled pram beside him and a backpack tucked into the sling underneath.

He opened the car door, his expression a cross between pleasure and worry. 'I've been watching you sitting here for a few minutes. Everything okay?'

His concern wrapped around her as it always did, like a snuggly blanket on a cool evening. 'A friend from Melbourne called and then I made the unwise decision to read my emails,' she said, thinking about the bank.

'Can I help?'

'Not unless you've got a spare half a million,' she said without thinking.

'Actually, I do,' His tone was as matter-of-fact, as if she'd asked him if he had a pen she could borrow. 'Do you need some help?'

An embarrassed bark of laughter broke out of her and she wished she'd never said anything. The last thing she wanted was Raf seeing her parlous financial situation. 'No, it's all fine. At least it will be when the insurance company pays up on Richard's policy.'

He frowned and gave her one of his searching looks. 'Insurance companies can be difficult, M.'

'Tell me about it.' Her laugh sounded false in her ears. 'My solicitor's confident so it's all good.' He didn't look convinced so she added, 'Really.'

Silence stretched between them for about ten seconds and then he sighed. 'If you change your mind just ask. Meanwhile…' He held out his hand.

She automatically took it and slipped out of the high seat until she was standing almost toe to toe with him and her eyes were level with a square of blue on his bright green-and-blue checked summer shirt. She tilted her chin to catch his gaze.

'Your evening awaits.' The timbre of his voice stroked her like velvet and then he was dropping his head next to hers, the tips of his curls sweeping across her cheeks and his lips skimming her skin as he greeted her the way he did every time they met.

Her heart hammered, her mouth dried and she locked her knees as she tried to make her voice sound like the rest of her was in control instead of declaring she was a jittery mess. She tried to marshal her thoughts. 'What are you doing here? I thought we were having our usual Friday night dinner?'

'It's our first hot night and Zoe insisted we get fish and chips.'

'Is that so?' She laughed as she stooped down to kiss her pink-cheeked daughter, whose chubby and dimpled hand was gripping a soft toy hammer. 'What else has she insisted on?'

Raf easily swung the stroller around. 'That we picnic on the beach and go paddling.'

'My daughter has a lot of opinions.'

'And I'm a sucker for a woman who knows her own mind.'

Something about the way he looked at her sent a bolt of electricity coursing through her before it exploded in a tingling sensation between her legs. Flustered, she reached into the car and grabbed the champagne, wanting to roll the cold bottle over her overheated body. 'Is everyone else at the beach?'

Raf shook his head. 'Bianca and co. have got a life-saving club dinner and Dad's having a boys' night at the club so it's just us.' He adjusted Zoe's hat, which she'd pulled over her face. 'That's if you like fish and chips?'

'Are you kidding me? There's nothing quite like crisp batter and creamy, crunchy chips. Just the aroma of hot oil and salt has me salivating.' She automatically licked her lips at the thought.

His Adam's apple moved up and down, and his dark eyes deepened to the jet black of ink as they flicked over her body from head to toe.

It was the first time he'd ever looked at her like that, and her skin heated and shivered at the same time. It was as if he was trailing a finger from her lips, sweeping it into the hollow at the base of her throat and feeling her rapid pulse before tracing it down between her breasts and across her belly until it reached the apex of her thighs. Her heart hammered, her breath hitched and the sun suddenly dazzled. God, her pupils must be dilated. She slammed her sunglasses into place to hide them.

He cleared his throat. 'Good to know.' A huskiness still clung to his words.

Zoe started to fuss.

'She's hungry,' Meredith said, snapping from arousal to mother mode and getting mental whiplash in the process.

'I'll go and buy dinner and meet you under the shade of the Norfolk pines,' Raf said briskly. 'There's a picnic rug and drinks under the stroller.'

'Sounds like a plan.' As they focused on the practicalities of life with a baby, relief and disappointment got all tangled up as the raw current of lust that had flowed between them faded.

'Back soon,' Raf said with a friendly wave.

She watched him—all straight spine, narrow hips and broad shoulders—but her gaze quickly dropped to the way his linen shorts moved across his tight behind. She instantly recalled the naked look of desire in the dark depths of his eyes. The thick and heady warmth of her own desire rolled back in.

'Oh, Zoe, I think I'm in serious trouble.'

Her daughter squealed as if she disagreed, and threw the toy hammer to the ground.

The following Monday afternoon Meredith was having a working lunch—munching on a tuna sandwich while scrolling through pathology reports—when Sue's usually unflappable voice screeched through the intercom. 'Someone's collapsed on the pier.'

Meredith grabbed her emergency kit and ran out onto the street. Quickly crossing the road, she cut through the Norfolk pines, her feet ploughing through the sand where she and Raf had eaten fish and chips on Friday night. Panting, she reached the crowd on the pier, calling out, 'Doctor. Let me through.'

The crowd parted and she heard a woman sobbing before she saw a small child lying on her side on the rough wooden planks. She wore an oxygen mask on her small face and Raf was kneeling beside her, a used EpiPen discarded by his side.

'It's okay, sweetheart,' he said, stroking the child's hair. 'You and your mummy are going to take a ride in an ambulance.'

Meredith crouched down next to him, noticing the angry, red blotches on the child's skin. 'What happened?'

'Anaphylactic shock.'

'Do you know what caused it?'

He shook his head. 'No known allergens and the child didn't complain of being bitten or stung but it was a classic reaction. She developed a rash, went pale and floppy, and had trouble talking. It was just lucky I was buying fish for dinner and had the first-aid kit in the car.'

Meredith checked the little girl's vital signs and breathing, which was still laboured. 'I'll establish a drug line.'

The child's mother hovered anxiously, watching Meredith's every move. 'Thank God you're here, Doctor. I was so scared when Stacey stopped breathing.'

'Actually, all the thanks go to Raf,' she said, giving his shoulder a quick squeeze as she stood up. 'His first-aid experience and quick thinking saved your child's life. Without his EpiPen, my arrival might have been too late.'

The screaming sound of an ambulance siren sounded and Raf scooped up the little girl into his arms, cradling her against his chest as if she weighed nothing at all.

The man emanated protection and compassion. If he cared this much for a stranger, what would it be like to be the recipient of his love?

The thought stabbed her through the heart and her

fast-diminishing kernel of resistance took another hit. It was getting harder and harder to think of Raf in terms of being just a friend and yet how could she allow him to be anything more?

Running from her thoughts, she concentrated on handing over their patient to the ambulance officer, made sure the mother was able to travel with her daughter and then she telephoned the accident and emergency department of Wongarri Hospital to notify them of their new patient.

Later that evening the surf rolled in gently on Camilleri beach, and Raf and Meredith sat staring out to sea.

Raf ran grains of sand through his fingers, his thoughts stuck at the pier. 'Sick kids scare the hell out of me.'

She glanced at him, understanding in her eyes. 'Me too, but you did great. God, I hope Zoe doesn't develop allergies. Richard didn't have any but my mother had asthma…'

Raf looked back out to sea. For the last fifteen minutes he'd been in both heaven and hell. On one side of the equation he was alone with Meredith and on the other side he was sharing her with a dead husband and a baby. It was totally screwing with his head. He'd been trying hard to be the friend she needed but he swore he was getting mixed signals from her. Usually, he read women well, but Meredith flummoxed him. Was the light that lit up her eyes whenever she saw him attraction or just sheer relief he was around to help?

There were moments like on Friday night, when her cheeks had gone pink and her eyes had got so huge in her face that he'd swear she'd radiated a level of arousal to match his own, but it always vanished so quickly that he put it down to him having embarrassed her some-how. And then there were moments like now, when she'd come and found him on the beach. Was it post-emergency professional concern for him or something more? He was losing his mind second-guessing her. Hell, he was losing his mind wanting her.

But his yearning was so much more than lust.

With each passing day the urge to tell her he was falling in love with her grew. At the same time he was also convinced that telling her was the worst thing he could do, given it was barely five months since her husband's death. All of it meant he was stuck in no-man's-land with no possibility of rescue.

How long did he need to wait before he could speak? After Christmas? After New Year? After the first anniversary of Richard's death? He stifled a groan. Why the hell wasn't there a step-by-step handbook on how to love a widow?

'How long have you lived in Melbourne?' he asked, wanting to add to the many but nowhere near enough things he knew about her.

'Since uni. I'd always thought I'd be a country GP but then I met Richard and his career was very city based. If we were going to have a relationship there had to be compromise.'

He remembered her once saying that Richard had been both easy and hard to love in equal measure. It was the only time she'd ever said anything negative about her husband and he had a crazy and unworthy need to know that the guy wasn't a saint. 'All relation-ships need compromise.'

'True.' She gave a wistful sigh. 'I would have pre-ferred it if our compromises had been a little more even in number but when you fall in love with a surgeon you have to share him with the world.'

Memories of Teresa lobbed into his head. Compromise hadn't been her strong point either and she'd hated sharing him with volunteering. 'That sounds like it might have been hard.'

'Sometimes it was. Well, not so much the surgery but Richard's need to seek out adventures ahead of me.' She gave a tight laugh. 'It feels wrong now to say it.'

He brushed his sandy hands on his shorts. 'Why? It doesn't mean you didn't love him.'

She gave him a sidelong glance. 'I do love him, flaws and all.'

'He had flaws?' he quipped, the words shooting out before he could stop them. *Idiot.* He'd have done anything to wind back time and not have spoken.

She looked back out to sea. 'Am I turning into a woman who glorifies her husband in death?'

He sighed at the thread of discomfort in her voice that he'd put there. 'I'm an idiot, M. Just ignore me.'

She looped her arms around her knees, which she'd pulled up to her chin. 'That's the problem, though, Raf,' she said softly. 'I can't.'

His heart leaped and skittered, and he scanned her face, seeking clues as to exactly what she meant. Her eyes burned for him but her expression was taut and warring emotions played across her face.

For the first time ever he saw a chance.

Do. Not. Screw. This. Up. 'Is that a good or a bad thing?'

Ever since the emergency on the pier earlier in the day, Meredith's head had been spinning with a crazy mixture of vignettes of Raf in his many caring roles, and all of them were interspersed with flashes of him shirtless and sexy.

All of it had her body craving him to distraction. When she'd got home, she'd acquiesced to Bianca's request to bathe Zoe, and when Mario had mentioned that Raf had been quiet all afternoon and could she please check on him, she'd practically run to the beach.

Now, sitting next to him, all the flimsy barriers she'd erected in the last weeks in an attempt to resist him had tumbled under the onslaught of her desire, leaving her shaking with longing. Her skin flashed hot and cold despite the warmth of the evening sun, her heart beat fast, making her all her movements jerky, and the unfurling of heat deep in her belly throbbed constantly, creating an ache that was different from the one that had lived with her since Richard's death. This ache promised it could be eased.

'Is that a good or bad thing?'

She heard the wariness in Raf's question and understood. Hell, she didn't have a clear-cut answer. 'It's both good and bad.'

'Does the good outweigh the bad?'

She gave an involuntary groan and fell back on the sand, rubbing her face with her hands. 'I don't know.'

He stayed sitting, his back straight and stiff as if he was steeling himself. 'What do you know?'

She opened her mouth to say, 'Not much,' but changed her mind and chose the truth. 'I know that when I'm around you I feel like I'm sixteen again.'

He turned, his gaze riveted to her face, a slight hint of a smile playing on his lips. 'Lurching between aroused and confused?'

And, oh, so guilty. And lonely. 'How did you know?'

He lay down beside her—propping himself up on one elbow—and reached his other arm over her and gently cupped her cheek with his hand. 'Because you've been making me feel like that for weeks.'

Relief and excitement flooded her. She turned her face, feeling his soft caress, and kissed his palm.

His hand slid to her shoulder and then he was rolling her into him. She went willingly—her craving to be held, to be touched and to feel like a woman again silencing the faint voices in her head that asked if this was wise.

Their legs tangled as their mouths meshed and he kissed her as if he'd been waiting for ever to do so. He explored her lips with the tip of his tongue, skimming their outline like they were priceless treasures and too much pressure would shatter them.

She sighed against his mouth, her own opening and welcoming him. He came in, his heat filling her along with his taste of salt, citrus and something that was eminently Raf, and he feasted on her own flavours. Ribbons of bliss streamed through her and the lightness that she'd always experienced around him lifted her up and took her away from her reality.

His hands ran through her hair as his tongue flicked and stroked. Each touch was like the spark of a flint on a taper—a line of fire snaking through her until her body went up in flames. As wondrous as it was to be encased in his arms and kissed into oblivion, she wanted more. She wanted him. She met his kiss with one of her own. Tongues duelling, they fought for ownership of the kiss, both desperate to know the touch, taste and feel of the other. Wanting to imprint it on themselves so it never vanished.

He gently nipped her bottom lip.

White lights lit up her head. Her hips lifted in response, moving against him, needing to feel all of him pressed along the length of her, and vice versa. He groaned into her mouth and rolled her under him.

She recognised the guttural sound—the visceral version of, *I want you, I need you, I'm taking you.* She kissed him harder and her fingers urgently wound their way under his shirt, seeking the heat and strength of his back.

As she trailed her fingers along each notch of his spine, his mouth planted kisses along her jaw and down to the hollow in her neck. She'd imagined him doing this but as his tongue dipped and stroked, no amount of imagining had prepared her for the bolt of pure need that tore through her. Her fingernails dug into his back as the wondrous pleasure and pain spun like a double helix, touching every part of her before settling insistently and seductively between her legs.

His mouth moved to the top of her bra.

Her breasts tingled and suddenly her bra was wet. *Oh, God.* Reality surged back and her hands gripped his shoulders.

Dazed and unfocused chestnut-brown eyes stared at her. 'What?'

She didn't go into specific details about a wet bra. 'We're not sixteen. We're on a public beach and it's a headline waiting to happen.'

His phone rang with Mario's ringtone and he made a guttural sound that was half laugh and half groan. 'You do realise we now have to sit down with Dad, Bianca and the twins and eat dinner.' He rolled away from her with a sigh. 'Being an adult sucks.'

Tell me about it.

CHAPTER TWELVE

RAF PACED BACK and forth, immune to the view of the glorious sunset from Meredith's living area. The last two hours had been the most drawn out he'd experienced in a very long time. He'd gone from almost tasting sex to an excruciating family dinner where Meredith had lurched between laughter and silence.

Usually happy to share Zoe, she'd held on to her all evening as if she was worried her baby would vanish, and the moment dinner had been over, she'd stood to leave. He'd insisted on walking her home. She'd unlocked the front door and disappeared into Zoe's room, and that had been fifteen minutes ago.

He swore for the tenth time, wishing that the conversation they'd had at the beach had taken place here. He was certain that if it had, they'd be in Meredith's bed right now. Instead, he was sterilising baby bottles and teats, and Meredith was putting Zoe to bed. A crazy laugh rumbled out of him. Wasn't this exactly the scenario guys with young children complained about—babies killing their sex life? Only in this instance he didn't think Zoe had anything to do with it. He'd stake his life that the break in proceedings had given Meredith time to think and to panic. Richard was firmly back between them again.

The sound of Meredith's footsteps made him turn. 'She's asleep.'

'Great.' He smiled and reached for her but his fingers skated across her waist as she spun away.

'Tea? Coffee?'

Disappointment smashed into him like a dumping wave. 'No, thanks.'

'Something stronger, then?' she said overbrightly. She ducked down and opened the cupboard at the end of the kitchen bench where she kept the spirits.

'Meredith,' he said softly, 'do you really think I want a drink?'

A flash of pain crossed her face. 'No, but I do.' With a pop, she pulled the cork out of a bottle of port and poured some into the small glass. She tossed the contents back in one gulp and then refilled the glass.

He sighed as sorrow pierced him like the touch of a thousand needles. 'If you need Dutch courage to forget who you're having sex with, then I think I should go.'

Her eyes widened in shock and surprise. 'It's the other way around.'

'What are you talking about?' He crossed to her and took the bottle out of her hand, putting it on the bench. 'I want to make love to you and remember every single detail.'

She took in a deep breath. 'I'm not sixteen.'

'Ah, no,' he said, treading very carefully because he had no clue where this was going, 'and, thank goodness, neither am I.'

'Yes, but you haven't just had a baby.'

'I don't follow.'

She gave him a withering look. 'Seriously?'

He ran his hand through his hair in exasperation. He knew he was on unstable ground and he had the feeling he was going to fall into a very deep hole at any moment. 'Just tell me.'

She closed her eyes and a long sigh shuddered out of her.

'M., please. You're scaring me.'

Words rushed out of her mouth. 'You have a gorgeous, buff body and I have stretch marks, leaky breasts, and you…' Pain crossed her face. 'You delivered Zoe. You…' A strangled sob clung to the words. 'You…saw me. I… It's… None of it's sexy.'

It's not Richard. Joy surged through him and he pulled her into his arms, burying his face in her hair, trying not to laugh with relief. He raised his head and cupped her cheeks with his hands. 'Believe me, M., when I look at you I see a beautiful woman with a lush, curvy body. You constantly taunt me with your sexiness.'

The worry lines on her forehead faded but her chin shot up. 'You're just saying that to get lucky.'

He laughed. 'And you're just saying that to get me to give you more compliments.'

She tossed her hair like an expert flirt and her eyes danced. 'I never said I was easy.'

His blood heated. God, she was amazing. 'Do I think you're sexy? Let me count the ways.' He ran the tip of his tongue around the shell of her ear and whispered, 'You kiss me like a woman who knows what she wants.'

Unadulterated lust rocked Meredith, making her writhe in Raf's arms, and his laugh was wicked and incredibly sexy. His mouth moved from her ear to her eyes, which fluttered closed under the kiss.

His deep voice rumbled around her. 'One look from these vivid blue eyes and I'm lost.' His mouth continued its gentle but intransigent assault on her. He kissed her throat and her pulse fluttered under her skin as his fingers expertly undid the buttons of her blouse, slid it off her shoulders and reached for the catch on her bra. As he lowered the bra straps, he pressed a kiss to the swell of each breast.

The bra fell to the floor and, despite trying not to, she tensed. He tilted her chin so she was looking straight at him. 'Your breasts are every man's fantasy.'

She was trying hard to believe him and not think about how she'd just fed Zoe, but she failed. 'But how can they—? Oh!'

Each of his hands now cupped a heavy breast and he was rubbing his thumbs back and forth over her nipples. Her knees buckled and her hands gripped his waist as a sharp jab of desire rocked her, followed by shimmers that whispered, *This is only the start.*

He unzipped her skirt and it fell in a pool at her feet and then he dropped to his knees, pressing kisses to her belly, slowly moving lower until his mouth kissed her through the cotton of her *so* not sexy underwear.

He looked up at her, his eyes dark and dancing. 'Okay, I concede one thing. The undies are not sexy but the contents totally are.'

She laughed but it changed to a gasp as his tongue flicked between her legs.

'Do you believe me now that you're a sexy and responsive woman?'

'Yes.'

'Good.'

The next minute she was upside down over his shoulder and he was striding down the corridor to her bedroom. 'Shh,' he said, as if reading her mind that making any noise and waking up Zoe was the worst thing they could do.

He lowered her onto the bed and then crawled up her body, his arms and legs encasing her. She raised her hand to his cheek. 'How come I'm almost naked and you're still dressed?'

He grinned and rolled away from her, stretching his arms wide. 'Take me,' he said with a laugh that promised her everything. 'I'm yours.'

A shiver of wonder ran through her that he was hers to explore. 'Do you have a condom?'

'I do.'

'Thank God for that.' She pulled his T-shirt over his head, dropped it to the floor and then ran her hands across his chest. 'You know, I've had fantasies about this chest.'

His eyes dazzled with his desire for her. 'Now, *that's* sexy. Tell me more about these fantasies.'

She dropped a kiss to his nipple and he stilled under her. 'What if I act them out?'

'Even better.'

Raf's body ached in the best possible way. Half of him was dazed and couldn't believe he'd just had sex with Meredith. The rest of him was high-fiving and indulging in the knowledge that the reality had far outstripped anything he'd imagined. Now he lay panting, trying to catch his breath, as if he'd just done a ten-kilometre run. He reached out his arm to her and hauled her back against him, wanting to keep her close.

Her head rested on his chest, her hair filling him with her scent of the sea and a musky post-sex smell that was part him, part her and as arousing as hell. He stroked her hair. 'You okay?'

'Yes.' She sounded slightly surprised. 'You?'

'More than good. That was amazing.'

They lay there for a few minutes, not talking, and he felt the delicious heaviness of sleep rolling through him. His limbs turned liquid, his body loosened and his eyelids fluttered closed.

'Raf?'

His eyes jerked open. 'Yes?'

She raised her head and looked at him, her beautiful blue eyes full of shadows. 'Thank you.'

He grinned. 'Any time.' He lifted his head and kissed her deeply, pulling her over him and loving the feel of her pressed against him. His body stirred and he wondered how she'd feel about going again.

'Any time sounds like a dream.' She pressed her lips against his chest, her tongue wetting the skin before she sucked it into her mouth.

He went hard instantly and he gripped her buttocks, loving the feel of their soft ripeness in his hands. She sighed against him.

Whoever's up there, thank you so very much.

'Raf, I want to keep this just between us.'

'You telling me you're not into threesomes?' he teased, as he stroked stray hair behind her ear.

She didn't laugh. 'I'm being serious.'

'So am I. Okay, we don't tell anyone,' he said, hating the idea so much that it cut into him like a jagged blade.

She kissed him on the mouth. 'Thank you.'

'No problem.' The lie sat on his tongue as rancid as milk left out in the sun.

The next morning, Meredith and Zoe went with Raf to the farmers' market, like they did most Saturdays, only today was the morning after the night before. The night when Raf had sent her flying into a state of weight-lessness where nothing had existed except blissful sensation. It had been like the ropes tethering her to her life had snapped and for a few blessed moments she'd floated above everything.

And then she'd thudded back to earth and opened her eyes to see Raf smiling at her. Despite knowing he wasn't Richard, a part of her had been shocked she'd been in bed with another man, and some of the pain and sadness of the last five months had rolled back. When they'd made love the second time, she'd been better prepared for the post-orgasm re-entry and she still got rafts of tingles whenever she thought about the few stolen hours they'd spent together.

When Zoe had woken up at three a.m., Raf had got up, changed her and then he'd brought her to Meredith. As she'd struggled up the pillows to receive her daughter, she'd felt cosseted and cared for in a way that had been totally unfamiliar to her. 'I'll see you two gorgeous girls later,' he'd said, before bending down and kissing Meredith goodbye with a kiss that had made her grateful she'd already been sitting down.

The local folk group played a rollicking jig as people strolled up and down between the rows of white tents. True to his word, Raf didn't show her any discernible public displays of affection, although as they made their way along the market stalls he found ways of touching her—a stroke of his hand across her back as he ushered her forward and his pinkie finger stroking her thumb as their hands rested on the pram handle.

Meredith leaned in close, her shoulder brushing his arm as she read the list Raf held in his hand. 'Avocado, goat's cheese, pancetta, basil, garlic, cherry tomatoes, salami and a big block of Parmesan cheese. Wow, that's some list.'

'The Camilleris take their pizza-making very seriously.'

She turned and caught his dancing eyes behind his midnight-blue glasses, which made him look like a thinking woman's sex symbol. 'I can see that.'

Raf's head dropped close, his mouth next to her ear and his breath intoxicatingly warm. 'We take everything to do with pleasure seriously.'

An image of him last night with his head nestled between her legs rocked her and her blood heated, taking hot, heavy and thick need into every part of her. Her body throbbed and ached for sex. For him. And the intensity stunned her.

'Frozen yoghurt,' she managed to splutter out, needing something cold to douse the unleashed desire.

They bought frozen yoghurt served with freshly picked raspberries and at Raf's suggestion they took it down to the boat ramp and sat enjoying the smooth and creamy treat. A delighted Zoe watched the pelicans being fed.

A group of tourists held up cameras and phones, busily taking photos of the impressive sight of whole fish sliding down the pelicans' pink gullets—glug, glug, glug. An older woman stood next to Raf, ignoring the pelicans completely and smiling at Zoe. When Raf adjusted Zoe's sunhat the woman said, 'Your little girl's such a cutie. It's lovely to see young families out together.'

Meredith checked for the tightness in Raf's face to appear, fully expecting him to say Zoe wasn't his daughter, but instead he smiled and said, 'It's a perfect day for an outing.'

An odd sensation filled her chest and she couldn't decide if it was good or bad so she scooped in a large mouthful of yoghurt to try and shift it. An ice-cream headache hit her fast.

'We should go and buy the prawns,' she said, needing to do something—anything—to try and shift the feeling.

Raf turned his head from the pelican spectacle and smiled at her. His eyes crinkled up, softening the deep lines that hovered permanently at the edges. 'Did you hear that, Zoe? Your mum's keeping us on schedule. Mario will be pleased.' He swung the pram around and they hiked up the sand, back to the path.

The co-op was busy, as it was every Saturday, with locals and holidaymakers vying for service, and the white-coated and white-booted fishmongers raced back and forth between the cold room and the counter. There was no such thing as a ticket system—it was survival of the fittest or, to be precise, the loudest. Raf's height and deep voice came in handy and a white paper package of green prawns was soon stowed under the pram.

They strolled back along the path towards the car and as they walked under the trees Raf manoeuvred her and the pram behind a Norfolk pine. With a quick glance around to check there was no one in sight, he pulled her close and kissed her fast and hard, before letting her go. 'I've wanted to do that all morning.'

Zoe squealed as if protesting that Meredith was getting all the attention. Raf laughed and bent down, dropping a kiss on her head. 'Yes, you're gorgeous too.'

It was just the sort of thing a father would do and Meredith's heart rolled with happiness. Her phone rang, the strident sound she'd assigned to Linda's number breaking into the moment. Guilt rode in, buffeting her heart until it rolled back the other way.

Raf gave her an odd look as the phone kept ringing. 'Do you need to get that?'

'No,' she said, clicking on the decline button. 'It can wait.'

He slid his hand into hers. 'Come on, then, we need to get going if we're going to fit in everything we need to do this afternoon.'

'What are we doing?'

He gave her an undeniably wicked smile. 'Making pizza dough and taking a nap when Zoe naps.'

She leaned into him and kissed him. 'I like the way you think.'

The next two weeks fell into a rhythm that on the surface wasn't very different from that of previous weeks, except she picked up extra sessions at the clinic and Raf spent a few hours each night in her bed. He'd return to his own bed in the early hours, usually when Zoe had woken them both. He teased that they didn't need an alarm.

He had suggested that if he stayed the whole night he could give her breakfast in bed the next morning. It had been deliciously tempting. A life with Raf was deliciously tempting, but guilt held her back.

'If you spend the whole night, that tells Mario we're sleeping together.'

He kissed her naked shoulder. 'My father's not a fool, M. After pizza night my entire family is very suspicious.'

'Why?' Her heart thumped fast in her chest. 'We've been really careful.'

He'd given her an indulgent smile. 'So much more

is said by inaction than action.' His words had sent a shiver up her spine.

The bank had followed up the email with two phone messages. She'd told them she was expecting the insurance payout any day, which wasn't exactly a lie—she was hoping desperately it would happen. At least the phone call to the bank had temporarily silenced the emails and calls, giving her some breathing space.

Linda was another matter. After hibernating in a delicious bubble with Raf and Zoe for a week, Meredith had finally called her and invited the Nichols for the following weekend. Linda had icily told her that Derek had to fly to Sydney for work and had Meredith returned her calls last week she would have known that this weekend would have suited them perfectly.

She'd opened her mouth to say she'd been busy and that time had got away from her when the image of her and Raf having sex had made her close it fast. Shame had battled with indignation, and duty had won out. She'd asked Raf to video her bathing Zoe and then she'd emailed it to Linda with a cheery message: I hope you enjoy this.

Her phone had rung at eight on Sunday morning, with Linda asking waspishly if it was Mario Camilleri's voice she could hear in the background. Meredith had made a spilt second decision and lied. 'Yes, it was Mario.'

'He seems to be spending a lot of time with Zoe.' The disapproval in her voice had crackled and snapped down the line.

'What are your plans for Christmas?' Meredith had asked, throwing herself on a pyre of her own making just to change the subject.

* * *

On Thursday night, Raf ran up the stairs of Meredith's house, a bottle of wine in one hand, flowers in the other and happiness streaming through him. Life was good. His days were bookended with Meredith and Zoe, and today had been a great workday. The cardiologist group was thrilled with stage one of the app and he'd lodged the first round of paperwork for the subdivision. He hadn't seen Meredith and Zoe since the early hours of the morning and he was looking forward to spending the evening with them.

Meredith had suggested he bring Mario over for dinner but when he'd extended the invitation, the old man had winked at him and said as long as Raf wasn't too disappointed he planned to eat at the club. Raf had laughed and told him he thought he could cope.

His feet hit the landing and he saw Zoe first. She was lying on her front and pushing herself up on her chubby arms, trying to reach a set of brightly coloured giant keys. 'Hey, poss.'

She squealed as he kissed her on the head and he laughed. It was a relief not to have to hold himself back from loving her, and with each passing day he loved her just that little bit more—just like her mother. As he straightened up he saw Meredith sitting on the couch, surrounded by papers and staring blankly out the window. Her expression was so tight her face looked like it might shatter.

He hadn't seen her look like that in weeks and a wave of concern washed through him, although he wasn't certain if it was for her or for himself.

He set down the flowers and wine. 'M.?'

She looked up as if it was the first time she'd realised he was in the room, 'Oh, God, is it six already?'

He leaned in and kissed her, breathing her in as if he still had to reassure himself that the last two weeks had been real and she was actually his to kiss. 'It's a quarter past, to be precise. I take it I'm not late.'

She groaned. 'I haven't even started dinner, sorry.' She hastily grabbed at the papers, shuffling them into an untidy pile, but not before one fell to the floor.

He bent down and picked it up. It was impossible not to see the prominent logo of a bank.

Not unless you have a spare half a million.

Her words came back to him and his concern eased. He couldn't solve her grief for Richard but perhaps he could help with money. 'Is everything okay?'

'Of course. Why do you ask? She almost grabbed the bank letter out of his hands.

The defensive tone in her voice slapped at him but he worked at keeping his voice light. 'Oh, you know, a couple of clues, like you sitting here staring into space, forgetting to start dinner and snatching that letter from the bank out of my hand.' He put his arms around her. 'What's the problem?'

For a moment she held herself stiffly but then she rested her head on his shoulder. 'Richard's death has left me with the responsibility of two mortgages.'

For two million-dollar homes. Surely the guy hadn't taken crazy risks with his finances as well as his life?

As if reading his mind, she added quickly, 'The debt should have been covered by his personal insurance policy.'

He sighed, knowing exactly how insurance worked.

'But they're arguing his death wasn't covered under the terms of the policy?'

Her eyes widened in surprise. 'Yes. How did you know?'

'Insurance companies will use any excuse to hold on to their money.'

'That's exactly what they're doing. They're citing a legal loophole. Richard was covered for snowboarding but because he died in an avalanche in the back country they're saying it wasn't snowboarding but an extreme sport and it's not covered. I'm fighting it but it's taking a lot longer than I thought it would.'

He'd had friends deal with insurance companies. 'The battle could be long and protracted.'

'That's what I'm learning, and meanwhile the bank's expecting mortgage repayments.'

No wonder she'd gone back to work and recently increased her hours, but even if she worked full-time he doubted she'd be able to afford the repayments on two houses. He could offer bridging finance, but even at a seriously reduced interest rate it was unlikely that was in her best financial interests.

'It could take two years to fight this and meanwhile do you really need two houses now? You've hardly spent any time in Melbourne since Zoe was born.' He pressed a kiss into her hair. 'And you seem happy living here.'

She spun out of his arms. 'I'm not ready to make a decision like that.'

A short, sharp pain zipped under his ribs. 'I could take a look at the sums and—'

She shook her head, her hair sweeping around her face like a veil and hiding her expression from him. 'I can't take money from you, Raf.'

Why not? I want you to. 'It wouldn't be a gift,' he qualified hastily to ease her concern. 'My lawyer would draw up a contract and we'd settle on a low-interest loan, which you can pay back either on resolution of the insurance policy or on the sale of one of the houses. Whichever comes first.'

'I said no.' It was Meredith's doctor voice—cool, calm and authoritative.

'Okay,' he said quickly, running through her fast-diminishing options. 'What about renting the Melbourne house? That way you can negatively gear it and the rent covers the mortgage.'

Her face blanched. 'I won't do that.'

Richard. Raf's balloon of euphoria, which he'd been floating on for almost two weeks, burst. Despite the fact she was living on the island and now virtually living with him, she was still clinging to the house she'd shared with Richard—holding on to it so hard that she was prepared to go into serious debt.

'Thank you for listening.'

Before he could say, 'But listening hasn't solved anything,' she stepped back into his arms and kissed him, her mouth warm and soft on his. 'Now, I'm going to cook you a rack of lamb and make those roasted potatoes with garlic and rosemary you love so much.'

His stomach rumbled at the thought. 'With sea salt?'

'Absolutely.'

'That sounds perfect.' He pressed his lips to her forehead. Despite the issue of her not dealing with her financial problems, he was taking the fact she knew some of his favourite foods as a positive sign. That and the fact she welcomed him into her bed each night.

She stroked his cheek. 'While I'm cooking, can you bath Zoe and put her into her pyjamas? She always squeals and laughs so loudly when you do it that it makes me feel like the boring parent.'

His heart leaped and all his concerns receded. Yes, she missed her husband but she shared her daughter with him as if she were theirs. Everything between them was good and he was worrying over nothing.

CHAPTER THIRTEEN

MEREDITH GLANCED AT the clock. She'd been running late since she'd started at nine that morning. Her first patient had been a distraught and bewildered young mother, and Meredith had hardly been going to bustle her out of her consultation room when her official allotted time had come to an end. As she'd chatted with Lucy, she'd realised how much she'd learned about life with a baby over the last fourteen weeks.

'Is there anyone who can help you?'

Lucy shook her head. 'Rick and I had already split up before I discovered I was pregnant, and my parents live in Queensland.'

'What about friends or neighbours?' she asked, thinking about Raf and Mario and how much they'd helped her, and not just with practicalities. Without them her life would be very different. *Without Raf you'd be desperately lonely.*

'My friends all work and when they're not, they're out having fun, like normal twenty-year-olds.' She sucked in her lips as if she was trying hard not to cry. 'There's no one.'

'I think you need some time with other young mums. One of the community health nurses runs a group that meets once a week. It would be a great support for you but right now you need a two-hour break from the baby so you can feel like yourself.'

'I just want to sleep.'

Meredith knew how she felt. 'I'll ring the occasional care and see if they can take Cruz for the afternoon and don't worry about the money, we have an emergency fund for stuff like this.'

Lucy burst into tears.

The rest of the session had been pretty standard—family planning discussions, an insurance medical check-up where she'd had to bite her tongue not to say something acerbic about the industry, vaccinating two excited twenty-year-olds who were flying out to South America for the summer and taking the time to listen to people who struggled with a variety of aches and pains, many of which she was convinced stemmed from loneliness. This time of year—with Christmas bearing down on them fast—seemed to exaccrbate a lot of issues for many people.

The clock read ten past three—more than two hours after her expected finishing time—and her stomach groaned in protest. She'd had to cancel lunch with Raf and Zoe, and their plans for spending the afternoon on the beach had been eroded. Still, if she left now, they'd have a couple of hours together before the Camilleri family Friday night dinner.

She texted Raf.

Leaving now.

'Dr Dennison?' Sue's voice buzzed through the intercom. 'Can you possibly see one more patient before you leave? It's just a prescription, promise.'

She sighed. It was never *just* a prescription but she

found it hard to say no. 'Sure, but this is absolutely my last patient for the day.'

Half an hour later, just as she was locking her car outside Mario's house, her phone rang. Raf's name appeared on the screen. 'Sorry! I've just pulled up,' she said, making her way around the car and into the driveway. 'Everything okay?'

Raf appeared at the bottom of the drive, phone pressed against his ear talking as he walked towards her. 'Zoe's fine,' he said immediately, to reassure her, 'but there's a bit of a situation.'

'Situation?' She noticed his curls seemed to be wilder than usual, as if he'd been running his hand through his hair. When she reached him, she brought her phone down from her ear and rose on her toes to kiss him. She caught the tension on his face. 'What do you mean?'

The sound of raised voices blasting out of an open window made her turn towards the sound.

'She's my granddaughter.' Linda's precise and clipped voice snapped like the glass neck of an ampoule.

'*Mio Dio.*' The frustration in Mario's voice was almost palpable, along with his steely determination. 'No one's disputing that. All I'm saying is that Meredith didn't say you were coming so Zoe stays in our care until she gets home.'

'Oh, God.' The pain in Meredith's chest intensified. 'Why didn't you call me?'

Raf frowned. 'I just did. Linda's only been here five minutes but she arrived with a head of steam. For some reason she's very angry that we're minding Zoe.'

'I've got no idea why Linda's even here. She told me she was going to Sydney with Derek. I'm so sorry.'

His frown deepened. 'It's not your fault.'

Snatches of conversations with Linda about Zoe and

the Camilleris came back to her and nausea made her gag. 'I think it is.'

'I doubt that.' He caught her by the hand. 'Come on, I know all about tricky families. We'll go in together and have it sorted out in no time.'

His optimism about Linda almost made Meredith smile. She stared down at his broad, tanned hand intertwined with her smaller and paler one. His hand was a very different shape and feel from Richard's thinner, smoother, long, dextrous-fingered one, but Raf's warmth and support licked through her like the flickering orange and blue flames of a fire dancing around a log.

She was about to return his gentle but reassuring squeeze when Linda's voice took on the sound of shattering glass.

'Let me make it very clear, Mr Camilleri. You are *not* Zoe's family. I am.'

Her heart sank to her shoes at the agony in Linda's voice and right then she knew that if she walked into the kitchen holding Raf's hand, she'd destroy Linda. No matter how prickly and difficult she found her mother-in-law, she couldn't do that to her.

She slid her hand out of his. 'I'd better go and talk to her.'

A zip of surprise rocked Raf as he felt Meredith's hand slip out of his. He immediately locked his fingers back through hers. 'There's no need for you to do this on your own, M. I want to be there.'

She shook her head. 'It will only make things worse.'

'Excuse me?'

Meredith gave him a small, apologetic smile. 'She's already upset that you and Mario are minding Zoe and if we walk in together it's only going to add to the problem.'

A chill ran through him. 'So now I'm a problem?'

'Don't be silly.' She squeezed his arm. 'It's just Linda's nowhere near ready to cope with the idea of me being with someone.'

'I see.' A prickle of unease crawled through him. 'When do you think she might be ready?'

Meredith tugged at her hair in exactly the same way she did whenever she was troubled.

His prickle turned into a collection of burrs. 'So, just to confirm, every time she and Derek come and visit, you're going to pretend we aren't virtually living together and send me home?'

Her forehead creased in confusion. 'I don't understand why you sound upset. We agreed to this and it's no different from what we've been doing with Mario this week.'

Except it was very different. 'You're kidding yourself if you think my family don't know. Dad knows, Bianca knows, and they're happy about it. Half of Princetown probably suspects and I want to tell the rest.' He wrapped his arms around her and softened his tone. 'M., I don't want to be a secret part of your life that you hide at inconvenient moments.'

Her fingertips played on the skin of his biceps. 'It's not like that.'

'It's starting to feel that way.'

'Okay…' She huffed out a breath as if he was an inconvenient problem she had to solve. 'We can tell your family we're seeing each other but not Linda.'

He felt caught between his desire for a peaceful life, which meant giving in to her again, and a rising frustration at feeling she'd just tossed him a bone to shut him up. 'Hiding me from Linda is wrong.'

Her mouth flattened. 'Believe me, it's necessary.'

He hated the idea of being excluded from parts of her life. 'And I'm saying that if Linda knew we were a couple she might not be having a meltdown right now and feeling as if her granddaughter was being left with strangers. She needs to know we love Zoe to bits.'

'Raf.' Meredith's eyes implored him to understand. 'I would never have got through these past few months without you and this last fortnight has been beyond wonderful.'

'It has.'

'So why does anything have to change?'

'Because I don't want to be on the edge of your life. I want to be smack bang in the middle of it.'

'You are.' Confusion and determination rode together in her voice. 'God, you've almost seen more of Zoe this week than I have.'

He brushed her cheek with his thumb. 'So tell Linda. Keeping me secret will only make things worse.'

'I can't.'

Her words came out on the hint of a wail and he automatically stroked her hair in a soothing gesture of love and protection. Her scent rose from the strands, filling his nostrils, and, like a key opening a lock, it released everything he'd been hiding for weeks. 'I want to share your life, M. Not just the fun parts and the sex. I want more than that. I want to share the tough and messy stuff. The family stuff. Linda.'

He cupped her cheeks with his hands, loving the softness of her cheeks against his palms. 'I love you, M., and I love Zoe.'

She stilled in his arms. 'Raf... I... Wow. That's... It's...unexpected.'

Relief burst through his anxiety that perhaps he'd spoken too soon. Sure, he'd stunned her but she didn't look or sound horrified. 'So?'

Her hands rose to rest on his as anguish twisted her pretty face. 'Please, can we just forget what you said and leave things the way they are?'

He could almost understand her point of view. He could almost agree with her that perhaps he should not have told her he loved her but the idea of being kept an indefinite secret—another problem in her life—hurt more than a horse kick to the chest.

Shock pinged Meredith's thoughts around her head as fast as shafts of air bounced balls in a lottery machine. No matter how she came at Raf's words, they were impossible to absorb. 'I care for you a lot, I really do. It's just...' She wrung her hands. 'It's too soon.'

'Sorry.' His acerbic tone stung as he stepped back from her. 'I should have read the memo about love coming with socially acceptable dates and times of when it could be activated.'

She thought about the many, many months she'd dated Richard before either of them had mentioned love, which only added to her confusion. 'But how can you truly love me? We've only been having sex for two weeks.'

'Hell, Meredith.' He threw her a withering look. 'You really think I'm that shallow? I've been falling in love with you from the moment I met you.'

An ominous sensation pushed in against her, making it hard to breathe. 'I'm sorry. I didn't know.'

He ran his hand through his hair. 'Yeah.'

His devastation rolled off him in waves that in turn battered her. She ached at the hurt in his eyes—at the pain she'd put there—and she scrambled to try and ease it. 'Please, Raf, just give me some time to catch up.'

Tension pulled his skin taut across his cheekbones. 'Time?'

She nodded quickly, taking his reply as an opportunity to explain. 'Yes. You're in a different emotional space from me right now.'

'You mean I love you and you don't feel the same way?'

His bland words hit her with the piercing sting of needles. 'Yes. No. Raf, I care for you. A lot. I really do. Can't that be enough for now?'

'So, to clarify,' he said softly, 'so we're both on the same page, you care for me and you want us to keep the status quo?'

Relief filled her that he understood and she reached out her hand. 'Yes. That's exactly it.'

He didn't move. 'For how long?'

'For how long, what?'

'How long do we keep the status quo? Six weeks, six months, a year?'

'I don't know. I guess it will become self-evident.'

'Self-evident?' He almost spat the word at her. 'Can you hear yourself? This isn't an experiment, Meredith, this is our life. Yours, mine, Zoe's.'

'Which is exactly why I can't rush into anything.' Why couldn't he get that? Raf had always been so compassionate about her and her situation, but right now she didn't recognise the man standing in front of her. 'You of all people should understand that.'

'If I should understand, then so should you,' he ground out. 'Here's how I see it. You want to keep me a secret from Richard's family and friends but at the same time you want me in your bed so you're not lonely and as a childcare provider for Zoe. And while I do this, I have to wait and see if you fall in love with me.'

He made the words sound ugly and she wanted to push them away. 'That's not fair.'

'Isn't it? It sounds like a pretty fair representation of the situation to me. I'm your hidden, secret life. I get crumbs and you get the whole loaf.'

Indignation spurted through her. 'When did this suddenly become all about you? My life's been turned upside down, first by Richard and now by you, and you don't have the right to stand here and demand decisions from me.'

'Yeah, well, we both know you avoid making big decisions,' he muttered, 'but you know what? Sometimes life demands that we step up and deal with them.'

His barb hit squarely on her procrastination to take charge of her financial situation and she fought back. 'This is my life and I will make the decisions about it when I'm good and ready.'

'I'm sure you will.' His voice was weary and the lines around his eyes deepened into ravines. 'The thing is, M., I still have some tattered pride left and I have the right to protect myself. I've already loved and lost one child and as much as I understand you feel rushed and cornered, I can't spend weeks or months getting more involved in your and Zoe's lives if at the end of it you're going to walk away from me.'

His heartache ran parallel to hers. 'But if we don't spend more together then you're denying us any chance. How can I know for sure if I don't have the opportunity to work it out?'

A long and agonising sound shuddered out of him.

'I don't think you have a hope in hell of working that out while you're cutting yourself off from your old life and hiding out here on the island, deferring every hard decision.'

She shook her head, her convictions rock solid. 'I am not hiding. I'm doing the best to live my life.'

His eyes sought hers, their gaze a combination of softness and steel. 'Tell me, can you even come close to picturing us as a family?'

She tried framing the three of them in her mind. First she saw herself holding Zoe. The moment she tried to stand Raf behind her with his hand on her shoulder, Richard appeared, with Linda marching behind him. Mario stomped in from the right and everyone glared at everyone else. Zoe started crying.

'I'm taking that painful silence as a no,' Raf said, the words ringing with resignation.

'What did you expect?' she pleaded. 'You know my life's complicated.'

'I do and I want to be part of it but you don't want me involved in any of the complicated stuff. I can't pretend any more that everything is fine when each day I care more and more deeply for Zoe. It's just too hard. I can't be here for you any more.' His expression turned to stone. 'You need time and I'm giving it to you. Goodbye, M.' He turned and strode down the driveway.

She couldn't believe he was walking away from her because, for as long as she'd known him, he'd always walked towards her. 'Raf!'

But he didn't stop or turn back—he just kept walking, crossing the road before disappearing into the ti-trees.

Numb, she stared straight ahead unable to move as the whooshing sound of her own blood filled her ears.

Fury and disbelief hammered her. How could he do this to her when he of all people knew what she'd lost? Why did he have to rush her?

Because he's lost someone too.

But the faint reminder was drowned out by the duelling and angry voices of Linda and Mario, which finally pierced her shock. She heard Zoe's penetrating cry.

She wanted to sink to her knees and join her.

Meredith snapped Zoe's jumpsuit closed and then she picked her up, breathing in her sweet baby scent, trying to use it to calm her chaotic thoughts and ricocheting emotions. 'Okay, Zoe. It's time to go talk to Nana.'

Linda was sitting on the couch, drinking a glass of wine, and she shot to her feet when she saw her. 'Do you want some cheese and biscuits? I brought some Roquefort.

Richards's favourite. The strong blue-vein cheese wasn't her favourite. 'No, thanks.' She settled Zoe on the floor in her favourite position in front of the huge window, and after placing her toys within reach she poured herself a glass of wine.

Ever since she'd escorted an almost hysterical Linda from next door, her mother-in-law had behaved as if everything was fine and that Meredith hadn't found her in the Camilleris' kitchen, screaming at Mario.

Exhausted, Meredith sat on the couch and wondered how to broach the situation. 'I thought you were in Sydney this weekend.'

Linda tucked her carefully coiffed blond bob behind an ear. 'I thought a weekend with my granddaughter would be far more enjoyable than being a trophy wife. I've done that for years and I've had enough.'

This was a version of Linda she'd never seen before. It was like her social veneer had been ripped away, leaving the real Linda raw, pink and fully exposed. 'I thought Derek was on a pathway to retirement? He told me back in July he'd cut his work back to half time.'

Linda's hand tensed on her glass. 'Everything changed in August.'

It had, and the three of them were trying to find their own ways of attempting to cope with Richard being stolen from their lives. Derek's was working. Linda's was being a grandmother. 'I'm sorry it's been three weeks since you were last down. I got distracted with…'

With Raf. She didn't even try to stop the guilt—she just let it roll in unimpeded. 'With work.'

Linda hacked some cheese off the block. 'I know I should say that's all right, but it's not how I feel.'

Meredith leaned back against the couch, feeling like she'd been pummelled by every possible emotion over the last two hours. What did it matter if she opened herself up to more pain? She owed her mother-in-law that. 'How do you feel?'

'Like I've lost my son and now I'm losing my granddaughter.'

But not me. Guilt and duty intertwined. She didn't have the right to expect that Linda might miss her when she'd been the one to leave Melbourne. It was hard but she reminded herself that she wasn't the only person to have lost Richard. 'I promise you, you're not losing Zoe.

Linda's jaw tensed. 'It doesn't feel that way.'

'I'm sorry.' She sighed and figured she had nothing to lose with telling the truth. 'None of the last five months has been anything like I pictured my life and I'm sure it's been the same for you. I've just been trying to get through each day the best I can. The house in Melbourne is a hard place for me to be and sometimes I struggle under the weight of your sadness. I understand it but I struggle.'

'I'm sorry.'

'No, please, you have a right to feel sad. We're both struggling to find a way and I didn't mean to make you feel left out of Zoe's life by coming down here. You're her grandmother and you will always have that role. I promise to get better at involving you with Zoe.'

'Thank you.' Linda sipped her wine and then she suddenly sat up straight. 'I'm so furious with Richard,' she said in a tone that was uncharacteristically critical of her only child. 'How could he take such risks and do this to you and Zoe?' She didn't pause for an answer and two hot spots burned on her cheeks.

'Of course I blame myself. He was brilliant, charismatic and charming, and I indulged him all his life. I should have done something to temper his very large selfish streak.' She patted Meredith's arm. 'I really don't think he had any idea what a gift he had in you.'

Stunned speechless, she stared at her mother-in-law, slack jawed. Today was a day of emotional bombshells blowing up in her face. 'I…' She emptied her glass of wine and poured herself another one.

'I know I'm not your mother, Meredith, and I'm not very demonstrative, but I do love you. In the last few years we saw more of you than Richard.' She made a snorting wet sound as if she was trying hard not to cry. 'Now Richard's dead, Derek's working longer hours than ever, you're living down here and I've lost my family completely.' Tears fell down her perfectly made-up face.

Meredith set down her wine and, as odd as it felt, she

hugged Linda. The normally stiff and self-contained woman sagged into her and something inside Meredith unlocked.

'I'm so sorry you feel this way, Linda. Me being down here is not a deliberate thing to keep you away from Zoe. I've just been trying to get through each day the best way I can.'

Linda straightened up and took a pressed white cotton handkerchief out of her sleeve and blew her nose. 'Has being down here helped you, dear?'

I can't be here for you any more, M. A sharp pain caught her under her ribs. 'I thought it had but now I'm not so sure.'

Linda picked up her hand. 'Christmas is coming.'

She heard the slam of car doors and the voices of the twins greeting Mario for Friday night dinner, and a wave of sadness hit her so hard and sharp that she almost cried out. Raf's ultimatum didn't just affect the two of them. He'd walked away and in effect he'd taken his family with him. How could she continue to live next door now?

She could go back to Melbourne. She had friends and family there and a house. Linda would be happier.

A thick wave of nausea churned through her. The idea of living in either house was unpalatable and unthinkable.

'At least come back for Christmas and New Year,' Linda pleaded.

She grabbed at the offer. 'That's a great idea. Can Zoe and I stay with you?'

The moment she'd said the words Raf's accusing voice boomed in her head. *You're hiding and deferring every hard decision.*

She gave him a metaphorical bird.

* * *

Raf spent a large part of Christmas Day kite surfing with the twins, teaching them to use the new rigs he'd given them. Anything to keep busy. He'd have done almost anything to avoid the manger scene in the main street and being cornered by Mario to join him in watching the replay of carols by candlelight. The camera always zeroed in on babies and toddlers asleep in their parents' arms, and it made his heart cramp and his arms ache.

He ached for Zoe. He ached for Meredith. He just bloody well ached and he'd been a fool to think walking away from Meredith and Zoe now would be easier than later. It was beyond hard every single moment.

'You wore them out,' Mario said, tilting his head towards the twins.

Looking five instead of fifteen, they were snuggled up watching the annual Christmas viewing of a British Claymation film about Santa's reindeer.

'That or they're just full of *panettone* and pistachio cakes.'

Mario smiled and picked up a bottle of citrus liqueur. 'Come, Rafael, drink a *digestivo* with me.'

He followed Mario outside. Tiny white lights glowed in the grapevine that made a natural canopy over the eating area. As he sat, his glance strayed to the dark house next door.

Mario poured the liqueur over ice in the chilled glasses Raf had carried outside. He raised one. *'Salut.'*

'Salut.' Raf clinked his glass and then spun it, watching the ice swirl. 'This time next year, if everything goes according to plan, we'll be sitting on the balcony of your new house and enjoying the view.'

'If Meredith was home we could be doing that now.'

Mario refilled the glasses. 'I thought it was strange she didn't call today to wish us merry Christmas.'

'I guess she's busy with the Nichols,' he said, backing up the story he'd told Mario after Linda's breakdown—Meredith was spending some time with her in-laws. 'I was thinking we should go and look at the display homes at Wongarri so you can get a feel for kitchen and bathroom layouts.'

'You love her.'

'Excuse me?'

Mario's dark eyes studied him. 'You love Meredith and Zoe.'

'Dad, I really don't want to talk about it.' He emptied the glass, slammed it down and stared at the grain of the wood on the table. 'It's over.'

'Help me understand,' Mario said calmly. 'I thought everything was going well. Why is it over?'

He ran the glass back and forth across his palms, feeling the chill on his skin. He could tell his father to back off but then he'd be doing to Mario what Mario had done to him for years.

He sighed. 'I told her I loved her and everything went to hell in a hand basket from there. Happy?'

Mio Dio. Of course I'm not happy. I love Meredith and Zoe and I love you. The three of you are good together. We're all happier with them in our lives.'

It was true. Meredith and Zoe had been integral in the healing that had taken place between him and his father, and her presence at the Friday night dinners had only changed the family dynamics for the better. Today there'd been an empty space without them.

His finger traced the spots of condensation on the table. 'The problem is, Dad, we've been a welcome diversion that's kept Meredith from dealing with some big

decisions. I want to step into the world with her and be
her future and she wants to stay in the diversion zone
where it's safe.'

'She needs time.'

'I know that, but you telling me isn't helpful because
you locked yourself down for years after Mum died.'

'And you can't wait too long because of Zoe.'

His head jerked up in surprise. 'Hell, Dad, I thought
you said Mum did all the emotional stuff.'

Mario squeezed his shoulder. 'Don't give up hope.'

'If I'm going to survive this, I have to.'

CHAPTER FOURTEEN

MEREDITH CAREFULLY CLOSED her bedroom door. Since coming back to Melbourne, Zoe was sleeping in the portable cot in her room at Linda and Derek's house.

Linda and Derek were sitting on the couch, watching the Melbourne to Launceston yacht race. Derek glanced up from the TV. 'She fell asleep quickly.'

'Must have been that walk in the park you took her on this afternoon.' Meredith sat on the club chair and popped a chocolate in her mouth from the tin Linda produced every evening.

For the last few days she'd been working full sessions at the Fitzroy Clinic, covering the generally quieter days between Christmas and New Year. It had been win-win-win, with Meredith earning much-needed money, Emma getting a break and Linda having Zoe time. It was hard to believe tomorrow was New Year's Eve.

'Zoe's a sweetie,' Derek said with affection. 'I'm looking forward to taking her to the beach when she's older and watching her feed the seagulls.'

'Will that be squeezed between briefs, darling?' Linda asked, raising her brows slightly.

'Actually...' he slipped his arm around his wife's shoulder '... I was thinking now that Meredith's living at Shearwater, we might look into buying a house close by.'

The chocolate caught in Meredith's throat and she swallowed hastily, feeling the lump make its way painfully down her oesophagus. Since arriving back in Melbourne she'd kept herself frantically busy so there was no time to think about the island and the Camilleris. *About Raf.*

She rubbed her sternum. 'I'm not sure I'm going back.'

Surprise crossed Derek's patrician face. 'Oh? I just assumed because you were staying with us and not in Fitzroy, this visit must be a holiday. In fact, I thought you were going to tell us you were selling the house.'

Linda had leaned forward, her eyes shining. 'You've decided to stay? This is exciting news. I've kept the house clean and dusted for you in case you wanted to come back so there won't be much work to do at all. We can move you and Zoe in tomorrow.'

'I'll get cracking painting Zoe's nursery,' Derek added, his face creasing in an indulgent smile.

Panic skittered through Meredith. Despite going to the house three times since she'd returned from the island, she hadn't got past the front gate. Instead, she'd sat in the car talking to Richard and not getting any answers. 'Really, there's no hurry, unless you want me gone,' she tried to joke.

Linda and Derek exchanged looks.

'You know you're always welcome here,' Linda said, 'but if you're going back to full-time work won't you want to be settled in the house first?'

She stared at them, finding it hard to breathe against the lead weight that was pushing down hard on her chest. *No.* 'I guess that is the sensible thing to do.'

'We know you've been in limbo for months.' Derek

squeezed Linda's hand. 'We all have but Richard's gone and we need to build a life around that fact. Zoe makes it a little easier because there's a part of Richard with us all the time.'

He cleared his throat. 'Of course we're thrilled you're staying in Melbourne but even if you weren't we'd work around it. After all, knowing Richard, there was no guarantee he wouldn't have decided to up sticks and move you both to America or the UK to take a job that excited him.'

Derek patted her knee. 'We've been worried about you and we're just pleased you're feeling ready to make some decisions.'

Their love and support made her feel uncomfortable. She hadn't actually made any decisions—she'd just reacted to a situation. Again.

Raf's unwelcome voice boomed in her head. *We both know you avoid making big decisions.*

She'd hated him for saying that. It had been unfair and unfeeling and over the last two weeks every time she'd thought about it anger had fizzed in her veins. She braced herself for it.

It didn't come.

All she could feel was a sinking feeling as if something catastrophic had happened and she had an overwhelming need to talk to Richard. She stood up. 'I need to go out for a bit. Can you mind Zoe?'

'Of course,' Linda said quickly. 'Do you need Derek to drive you or…?'

She kissed Linda's cheek. 'Thank you but I have to do this on my own.'

It wasn't completely dark when Meredith pulled up outside the Fitzroy house so she didn't need a torch to find the lock. Even so, sliding the key in wasn't easy. The heavy door swung open and cool air met her—the one benefit of thick stone walls in summer. She reached her hand inside and flicked on the bank of lights by the door, which instantly lit up the length of the long hall. Sucking in a deep breath, she stepped inside.

The scent of pine antiseptic hit her first and she wrinkled her nose. It wasn't a scent she associated with the house. She walked past her bedroom and Zoe's room until she was in the living room and standing in front of a large, framed canvas print of Richard snowboarding. 'Hey, honey.'

He didn't reply and she slowly made her way along the photos on the mantel, picking each one up and tracing her finger along the outlines. Richard and her trekking in Nepal, Richard on the day he'd been made a fellow of the Australian College of Surgeons, Richard scuba diving, the two of them laughing on their wedding day—so many pictures showing their life together. 'I love you.'

The last photo was one she'd taken of him just before she'd got pregnant when he'd been heading off to yet another adventure. The same residual sadness crept through her that he'd never got to meet Zoe. She wondered, if he'd still been alive, what photo she would have chosen to add to the collection. She'd never really seen Richard interacting with kids, and that had caused one of her biggest unspoken fears—that her desire for a child had outweighed his.

She shook away the unwelcome thought and went back to imagining the photos. Perhaps it would have been a picture of Richard holding Zoe high on his shoulder? Or with Zoe in the sling, nestled into his chest? But now as she tried to build each image it was always

Raf's dark smiling eyes and welcoming smile that she saw, not Richard's.

Her heart lurched. Was that wrong? Or was it okay?

It was like her life had been cleaved into two sections and Zoe was the demarcation line. There had been life with Richard and life with Zoe and Raf. Yes, Zoe was Richard's and her creation but Raf had shared her parenthood journey with her. Raf had been there from the start—he'd delivered her, helped her name Zoe and, as much as it hurt her to admit it, Raf had been far more involved with Zoe than Richard would have ever been. Raf had supported her and got involved despite Zoe not being his child.

When did this suddenly become all about you? My life's been turned upside down.

Bile made her gag as she remembered the bitter words she'd hurled at him. Oh, God. How could she have been so self-obsessed and said something so awful to him? He was right. She'd been hiding from her life, avoiding making any decisions and busy feeling sorry for herself. Yet, despite his own pain, having already loved and lost once before, Raf had risked everything in loving her and loving Zoe.

He'd risked his heart for her and she hadn't risked a thing. She'd taken everything he'd offered her, everything that had made her life bearable—no, she'd taken far more than that. Despite loving and missing Richard, she'd been happy with Raf. Very happy. It had seemed wrong and yet at the same time so very right.

She pressed her hand against the large, framed canvas photo, her palm resting against Richard's face. 'I wasn't even looking for love. Did you send him to me? If I'd died, you'd have grieved and then fallen in love again, wouldn't you? Would you judge me for it happening faster than society thinks is acceptable?'

Life is for the living, Merry.

It had been a favourite expression of Richard's, usually said when he'd been pitching an outlandish idea to her. Now she heard it in response to her unconventional suggestion.

'I will always love you, Richard, and I promise, you will always be a part of Zoe's life.'

She hoped against hope that Raf would be too.

Raf read the note on the kitchen table and instantly regretted not going to Melbourne for New Year's Eve.

It seemed that once the family knew he was staying in, they were all stepping out and using him to be their designated driver. Mario had booked him to drive him to and from the club, Bianca and Marco had booked him for a one a.m. pick-up from a party, and now it seemed Bianca was adding collecting the twins from the surf club at twelve-fifteen a.m. At least he was being useful.

Although a calendar date made no difference to his feelings, he thought he ought to at least attempt to embrace the psychological import of a new year and a fresh start. If that meant starting the New Year ferrying his likely tipsy brother-in-law and sister, so be it.

He still had the afternoon to himself before he turned into a taxi driver. It was too hot for a run but the conditions were perfect for a surf. He got changed into his boardies, found his wetsuit and hauled it on as far as his waist before yelling out to Mario that he was going to the beach.

He grabbed his waxed board from the garage, tucked it under his arm and as he closed the door he stopped short. His heart rolled in his chest. He could see the top of Meredith's car parked next door. For some reason—probably self-preservation—he'd assumed she wouldn't come back to the island.

Idiot. Moron. Fool.

The thought that the car would still be there tomorrow—the first of January—almost made him go inside, pick up his keys and drive to Melbourne. But he didn't. Instead, he sucked in a breath, repositioned the board in his hand, put his head down and started walking.

He saw her berry-painted toes first, nestled inside a pair of turquoise summer sandals. They were firmly planted on the concrete pavement of the driveway. The memory of sucking those toes and trailing his tongue along the length of her legs socked him so hard he saw spots.

'Hello, Raf.'

He hauled his gaze to her face and for a moment he didn't recognise her. She looked different, although the only change he could see was that she'd had an inch trimmed off her hair. 'Meredith.'

How's Zoe? Where's Zoe? He clamped his lips down, silencing the questions. That was the road to insanity.

Zoe's squeal drifted out on the afternoon breeze, followed by a man's laugh.

'Linda and Derek came with me,' Meredith said quickly.

'I'm surprised you're prepared to risk being seen talking to me, then.' The moment the words left his mouth he felt slightly reduced as a human being.

'That's what I want to talk to you about.' She gave him an unsteady smile. 'Could we go somewhere private and talk?'

'I doubt that's necessary. It seems you and I are

perfectly capable of having life-changing conversations right here in this driveway.'

She flinched and her smile dimmed. 'Raf, I'm sorry I hurt you.'

His skin prickled as the realisation that she'd come for absolution hit him. He didn't want to give it to her but he couldn't stand here and listen while she told him all over again why she couldn't love him so he did the one thing he hoped might stop her talking. 'Okay.'

Now get the hell out of here. He took a step forward, forgetting he was holding the surfboard.

Meredith jumped sideways, only just dodging the board. 'I haven't said everything I came to say.'

'Too bad. I've finished listening.' He kept moving, forcing one leg in front of the other, desperate to put distance between them. He couldn't risk touching her because he was scared if he did he'd allow himself to accept her terms and that would only destroy both of them and damage Zoe. If there was one thing he could do right, it was to protect Zoe.

With her heart in her mouth, Meredith watched Raf walking away from her. None of this was going the way she'd planned, and once before she'd watched him leave her. She wasn't letting it happen again. Ditching her speech, she scrambled to find words—any words—that might make him stop.

'I'm selling both of the houses.' She held her breath as he took another step.

He stopped and very slowly turned around, his naked chest gleaming in the sunshine and his face impassive. 'I'm glad you've made a decision.' He turned away again.

She jogged up to him and put her hand on his arm. 'Don't you want to know why?'

His gaze slid to her hand on his tanned arm and back to her face. 'I already know why. You reached a point of no return and you had to solve your financial crisis.'

'Yes, but there's more to it than that. Please, can we go sit on your mother's seat?'

He studied her closely and she saw the battle in his eyes—was talking on the seat going to mean more pain? 'I will regret this.'

She dropped her hand. 'I hope you won't.'

They crossed the road together and Raf propped the board up against the trunk of a ti-tree before sitting down and staring out at the ocean.

'Raf.'

He didn't turn to look at her and with a sinking heart she realised this was the wrong place to talk. How could she make him understand if he didn't have to look at her?

'I don't know where to start.'

He didn't offer a suggestion so she ploughed on. 'I spent two weeks hating you and missing you.'

His mouth twisted. 'Sounds familiar.'

'I thought you were being insensitive, asking me to make decisions. I thought that my grief gave me the right to let things run and that I was the only person who'd had their life turned upside down by losing someone. I was selfish and I was wrong and I hate that you think that I used you. I didn't intentionally do that.'

His head turned slightly. 'I'm listening.'

This is your shot. 'I lost Richard but you lost Teneka and yet you were brave enough to take a risk and put your heart on the line loving me and Zoe. I was selfish and thoughtless and I threw it all back at you.'

His mouth twitched. 'Only a fool falls for a woman whose husband died not quite six months ago.'

Her heart tore at the pain in his voice and she put her hand on his thigh, the neoprene cool on her palm. 'I love you.'

This time he looked at her, his face taut. 'Don't use words you don't mean.'

'I'm not. I love you.'

His eyes scanned hers intently. 'And you worked this out when, exactly?'

'Last night. I went back to the house Richard and I lived in and it felt like another life. I've spent weeks struggling with my feelings for you. I mean, one day I was happily married and then, bam, I was a widow. I couldn't see past the next hour, let alone envision a future that might involve me loving someone else. Suddenly there you were and I was falling in love with you and we were making memories together with Zoe. It felt like such a betrayal to Richard, to Zoe and to Linda and Derek.'

He picked up her hand. 'I don't want to obliterate your past, M. I love you and Zoe, and, of course, Richard and his family will always be a part of your life. By default, I hope they will be part of mine.'

Tears pushed at the backs of her eyes. 'Before I broke your heart, you told me that you wanted to share my life, the fun parts, the messy parts and Linda. Do you...' she forced out the words against rising fear '...still feel that way?'

He set her hand down in her lap and her heart tore a little more, despite the fact it was threadbare already.

'How do you feel about the fact that if we share our lives, Zoe will be your only child?'

She grabbed his hand again and with the other she

turned his cheek to face her. 'Rafael Camilleri, you listen to me. Zoe is *our* child. She belongs to you and me. We are her family.'

He blinked before burying his face in her hair for a long, long moment, and she felt his chest heave.

She stroked his hair, her love for him spreading through her like sunlight after rain. 'And who knows what the future holds? Medical technology is constantly doing amazing things but none of that matters. We have Zoe and we have each other. I don't need anything more.'

'I love you, Meredith Dennison,' Raf said, his voice thick with emotion. 'And it will be the biggest honour of my life to be Zoe's adoptive father.'

He heaved in a breath, his face creased with hope but with a hint of anxiety. 'Does this mean if I ask you to marry me, you'll consider it?'

Life is for the living, Merry.

This time she wasn't scared by the idea and her heart swelled so much it threatened to burst. 'Ask me and see.'

He cupped her face in his large, gentle hands. 'Meredith Dennison, will you make me the happiest man on earth and marry me?'

She nodded quickly. 'When Zoe can run down the aisle from my side to yours, then I'll marry you.'

He grinned at her. 'It's a date.'

'You bet it is.' She rested her forehead on his. 'Your love is a gift I'll never take for granted. It lights me up and makes me want to tell everyone how lucky I am to have you in my life. Let's go and tell Mario, Linda and Derek.'

'You do realise that will mean Linda and Dad trying to out-organise each other as they fight over who opens the champagne?'

She laughed. 'Get used to it. Derek's already talking about buying Mario's second townhouse.'

But Raf didn't complain—instead, his expression was contemplative. 'I love the idea of Zoe growing up surrounded by her extended family and the freedom of the island.'

'Me too. And despite your grumbles, I think you like being close to Mario. I know you have a brand-new house in Melbourne but how would you feel about living here?'

His eyes crinkled up at the edges. 'M., I can work anywhere I have an Internet connection. I hear there's a house going on the market next door that we could buy.'

She held her breath. 'So is that a yes?'

'That is a resounding yes.' He wrapped his arms around her, pulled her in tightly against him and kissed her. It was his pledge of love and support, an infusion of his care and protection and a promise that, no matter what came their way, they'd face their future together surrounded by family and love.

Her world steadied on its axis as their new journey began.

* * * * *

A LOVE
AGAINST ALL ODDS

BY
EMILY FORBES

Published in Great Britain 2016
By Mills & Boon, an imprint of HarperCollins*Publishers*
1 London Bridge Street, London, SE1 9GF

© 2016 Emily Forbes

ISBN: 978-0-263-25422-8

Our policy is to use papers that are natural, renewable and recyclable
products and made from wood grown in sustainable forests.
The logging and manufacturing processes conform to the legal
environmental regulations of the country of origin.

Printed and bound in Spain
by CPI, Barcelona

Dear Reader,

I have visited Christchurch on New Zealand's South Island several times. It is a beautiful city, but one which experiences a phenomenal number of earthquakes each year, and between September 2010 and June 2011 the city was left devastated by three powerful quakes. I was there in October 2010, not long after the first quake, and saw for myself the damage that Mother Nature can wreak. But along with the heartache and tragedy there were amazing stories of courage, survival and resilience, and Christchurch and her people are slowly recovering.

This is Maia's story, and it was inspired after talking to survivors of the quake: those who had chosen to stay and rebuild their city despite the dangers.

Maia thinks she's happy with her life—until it's turned upside down by two major upheavals. One is the return of her ex—a man who could once make her knees go weak with just a glance, and it seems as if nothing has changed in that respect. And the second is a devastating earthquake. These events force Maia to examine what she really wants out of life, but making a decision is difficult when she knows people are going to get hurt. Her head and her heart aren't always in agreement, and she's struggling to decide which one she should listen to. What if there's more than one right answer?

But Maia has to make a decision—because if she waits too long she could lose everything.

Enjoy!

Emily

For my gorgeous nieces: Sophie, Lucy, Kate, Sophie,
Grace, Zoe, Harriet, Portia, Lilly, Saskia, Henriette,
Alexandra, Charlotte, Georgia and Adelaide,
and in loving memory of Georgiana Rose.

Books by Emily Forbes

Mills & Boon Medical Romance

Tempted & Tamed!

A Doctor by Day…
Tamed by the Renegade

The Playboy Firefighter's Proposal
Wanted: A Father for her Twins
Dr Drop-Dead Gorgeous
Navy Officer to Family Man
Breaking Her No-Dates Rule
Georgie's Big Greek Wedding?
Sydney Harbour Hospital: Bella's Wishlist
Breaking the Playboy's Rules
Daring to Date Dr Celebrity
The Honourable Army Doc
A Kiss to Melt Her Heart
His Little Christmas Miracle

Visit the Author Profile page at
millsandboon.co.uk for more titles.

CHAPTER ONE

'CHRISTCHURCH HAS BEEN *rocked by the biggest earthquake we've had for some time. Just after five o'clock this morning a quake measuring seven-point-one on the Richter scale was recorded; its epicentre was forty kilometres west of the city and it occurred at a depth of eleven kilometres. Several old buildings have collapsed but, while there have been numerous injuries, there are no reported fatalities at this stage. Injuries have been caused by falling masonry and glass but—just repeating—there are no fatalities at present. We're crossing live now to our reporter...*'

Maia Tahana pulled the headphones out of her ears as she walked through the automatic doors of the emergency department of the Canterbury Children's Hospital, cutting the radio journalist off midsentence. The story of the quake wasn't news to her; she'd been woken by it, jolted out of a comfortable sleep by a deep bass rumble and the sound of breaking glass. Her heart had hammered in her chest as the house shook and the windows rattled in their frames. It had sounded as if a freight train was hurtling past the front door but Maia had known that was impossible. The closest thing to the house was the Pacific Ocean, fifty metres away on the other side of the sand dunes that ran at the bottom of the garden—but it hadn't been the pounding of the surf that had shaken the house and its foundations.

The noise had been frightening and the movement of the house disturbing but it wasn't an unfamiliar experience. Maia had lived in Christchurch, New Zealand, all her life; she'd been through this before. Christchurch experienced thousands of earthquakes each year. She remembered hearing it was somewhere in the vicinity of thirteen thousand, which seemed like an enormous number, but she knew that not all of them were felt by people. Some were only detected by seismic equipment, but it was still a huge number, and it wasn't unusual around here to feel the ground moving beneath your feet.

Minor quakes were something that barely caused the locals to blink, let alone miss a beat. If the power wasn't interrupted, if no one was hurt and if there was no major damage, then the tremors were mostly ignored. But this one had been big and much closer to the surface. There had been a couple of smaller aftershocks and Maia was pleased to hear there had been no fatalities. Perhaps she could expect a regular shift, if ever there was such a thing for an emergency-department nurse in a busy paediatric hospital.

The emergency department seemed quiet when Maia walked in but she was superstitious enough not to say anything. The moment someone mentioned the 'q' word always seemed to be the moment all hell broke loose. She decided to grab a coffee while she had a chance. She needed a double dose of caffeine after being woken by the quake. She and her sisters had been sweeping up broken crockery and glass since four this morning and she hadn't had a chance to go back to sleep. She checked her watch. She had time.

She walked into the empty kitchen and took a coffee cup from the cupboard. She had her back to the kitchen door but she heard it open as she lifted a new pod from the box on the bench beside the coffee machine. The room filled with the scent of cedar wood and citrus—grapefruit, not oranges. The scent was familiar to her. It was the scent of an ex-boyfriend. She closed her eyes and breathed deeply, letting the memories flood back. A slight smile played across her lips as she remembered Henry.

She opened her eyes and mentally shook herself. She didn't have time to waste on old memories. She dropped the coffee pod into the machine, waiting for the aroma of freshly brewed coffee to clear her mind. Henry was a long time ago. He was her past. Well and truly. Her life had moved on. She had changed. Life had changed her.

But as she pushed the button to start the coffee-making process she could have sworn she heard his voice.

'Maia?'

The rounded vowels of his English accent were instantly recognisable. No one else made her name sound like he did—sexy and desirable, full of promise and suggestion.

Her imagination was working overtime.

'Maia?' His voice repeated her name and this time she turned around.

Three years evaporated in the blink of an eye as her past collided with her present.

Henry was standing in front of her.

He looked exactly the same: tall, dark and still the most beautiful man she'd ever seen. His features were faultlessly symmetrical. His square jaw was chiselled and his full lips were perfectly shaped. His indigo-blue eyes were the exact same shade as the chest feathers of the pukeko bird. He stood over six feet and he was solid, but in a lean, muscular way. Not fat. He looked just like she remembered—his hair was cut shorter than usual, his dark curls tamed, but he was otherwise unchanged. He was incredibly gorgeous and he was standing five feet away when she'd thought he was on the other side of the world.

'Henry? What are you doing here?'

She wanted to reach out and touch him, to see if he really was real, to make sure it wasn't her imagination playing tricks on her but, if it was, it was extremely good. She resisted the temptation. She wasn't sure what would be considered appropriate behaviour.

'I'm back.' He smiled at her as he gave her his answer and Maia's heart skipped a beat. He had a little dimple in the centre of his chin that disappeared when he smiled—how had she forgotten about that?

She could see he was back. What she wanted to know was why and when and how long for but all she could do was stare at him.

'I didn't know you worked here,' he said to her.

Maia nodded. Her mouth was dry and her tongue appeared to have glued itself to the roof of her mouth. She forced it free and swallowed as she tried to moisten her throat so she could speak. 'I left the Queen Liz eighteen months ago,' she told him.

When Henry had left Christchurch three years ago Maia had been working in the emergency department at the Queen Elizabeth Hospital—they both had—but she had quit that job eighteen months ago after her father had passed away. She hadn't wanted to nurse adults anymore; she'd needed a break and the Children's Hospital had needed staff.

'I'm sorry about your dad,' Henry said, putting two and two together with the timing. 'He was a good man.'

Henry had always had an uncanny ability to read her thoughts and it seemed as if that hadn't changed.

'Thank you,' she said but she didn't want to think about her father. She didn't want to think about the last few months of his life. Her dad had suffered a stroke and Maia had helped to nurse him. It had been a difficult and emotional time, and his death had hit her hard. She had spent a vast amount of the past three years grieving. First for Henry and then for her father. She was only just coming to terms with it all now.

The coffee machine beeped at her and she turned away, grateful for the distraction, grateful for the reason to break eye contact and the chance to gather her thoughts. But her first thought was about Henry.

Why was he back?

The comms system crackled overhead. 'All ED staff to triage.' Maia heard the voice of Brenda, the ED director, summoning the staff.

Her hand shook as she added sugar to her coffee and picked up the cup. Henry held the door open and fell into step beside her. She wasn't going to escape the past that easily.

'What are you doing here?' she asked. When Henry had left Christchurch three years ago she had never expected to see him again. He had never mentioned coming back; he'd made her no promises. He'd gone off to save the world, leaving her behind, and Maia could only assume that she didn't feature in his future plans at all. That had been a bitter pill to swallow but she'd managed to do it eventually.

'I'm doing project work in disaster management and the New Zealand government offered me a grant to come back. I'll be looking at the systems in place in the hospitals and how they would cope with mass-casualty incidents. But I'll be attached to the Children's. I thought it was an offer too good to refuse.'

That surprised her. Not his project choice—he was an emergency-medicine specialist and she'd known about his interest in disaster management—but the fact that he was back at all was a surprise. When he'd left he'd had plans that were bigger than New Zealand.

'Well, your timing couldn't be better,' she told him. 'You got an earthquake to order.'

'Looks like I did but it hasn't caused too much havoc— and, although that's fortunate for Christchurch and her residents, it's not very useful for my purposes.'

'I guess you can't have everything.'

'I guess not.'

Henry's indigo eyes searched her face. He seemed able to look through her brown eyes into her soul and his gaze, intense, powerful and passionate, made her knees go weak. She remembered this look. It was the look he would give her when they'd made love. The look that had made her think she was the only girl in the world he would ever need.

She looked away.

That wasn't the case and she wasn't that girl any-more.

'When did you get back?' she asked.

'A couple of days ago. I spent yesterday in orien-tation and induction and now I hope I'm ready to go.'

Yesterday she'd been rostered off. Today her world was changing.

As she and Henry assembled in triage along with the other staff, Maia saw Carrie, her best friend, standing on the opposite side of the group. She raised her eyebrows in a silent question at Maia when she saw who was by her side. Maia gave a slight, almost imperceptible shake of her head. She didn't want Carrie asking questions.

'If I can have everyone's attention…' the ED Director said as she scanned the group, obviously deciding everyone was present and accounted for. Brenda waited for the conversational noise to cease before continuing. 'There's been an accident involving a school bus and we've got several ambulances headed our way.'

Maia shouldn't even have *thought* about it being quiet.

'Apparently the earthquake triggered a landslide which caused the bus to crash but I don't have any more detail than that. The bus driver has been airlifted to the Queen Elizabeth and the plan is to bring all the kids to us. There were sixteen primary school children on the bus. Varying injuries—fractures, cuts, bruises, some suspected head injuries and possible spinal injuries—and all of them will be in shock.' She glanced at the clock on the wall. 'ETA five minutes.'

'It seems you got your disaster after all,' Maia said quietly to Henry as Brenda went on.

'For those of you who haven't met him yet, I'd like to introduce Dr Henry Cavanaugh. Henry is a UK-trained emergency-medicine specialist with a special interest in disaster management. He did part of his fellowship in Christchurch at the Queen Liz but this time he is seconded to our hospital and he will be looking at our management systems, as well as taking on a clinical workload.'

Maia could see Carrie making a beeline for her and by her expression she could tell she was in for a grilling. She really needed to process Henry's return before she was ready for it to be dissected in a discussion with anyone, even her best friend. But she knew her chances of putting Carrie off were next to none so all she could do was ensure that the conversation didn't take place in public.

Henry was about to be swamped by other emergency staff who hadn't yet met him so Maia headed for the change rooms, deciding she would quickly change into surgical scrubs. Carrie followed her, as she'd known she would. She and Carrie had been best friends since their first year of high school. For thirteen years Carrie had been by Maia's side. She'd been through everything that had happened to Maia over the past three years and longer.

The moment the door closed behind them, Carrie asked, 'Did you know he was back?'

Maia stripped off her uniform and hung it on a spare coat-hanger, exchanging her clothes for hospital-issued scrubs. 'Who? Henry?'

'Yes, Henry,' Carrie replied as Maia stepped into a pair of surgical pants and tied the drawstring at her waist.

'No. You know we haven't kept in touch.' They had agreed on a clean break—that had been his suggestion, not hers—and she'd spoken to him exactly twice in three years. He had called her once when her father had suffered his first stroke and again when he had died. That had been their only contact. Henry wasn't part of her life anymore.

'How did your date go last night?' Maia asked as she tugged the pale-blue cotton shirt down over her head.

'Don't change the subject.'

'I'm not. Henry being back is not a subject. Not one that affects me anyway.'

Carrie raised an eyebrow. 'You sure?'

Even though Maia had known the fairy tale hadn't had the happy ending she'd wanted, and she'd pretended he hadn't broken her heart when he'd left, it had taken her a long time to recover. But eventually she'd been able to consign him to her past and to think of him without feeling like her heart was being ripped in two. They'd wanted different things in life. Things had worked out for the best.

'Positive,' she said as she lifted her hand to gather her long, dark hair into a ponytail, wrapping and tucking the end to make a messy bun. Her engagement ring caught the light, reminding her to remove it, and she slid it off her finger and onto the necklace where she wore it while she was working.

She was engaged to be married. Henry was an ex-boyfriend. Not the love of her life.

'He's an ex-boyfriend, that's all.'

Henry was her past. Not her future.

He wasn't her Henry any more.

CHAPTER TWO

TWO AMBULANCES PULLED into the loading bay as Maia and Carrie returned to the ED, creating a flurry of activity. Maia's fiancé, Todd, was a paramedic. He had a day shift and she peered through the windows of the closest ambulance and scanned the bustling medicos, looking for his familiar figure. Looking for his sturdy frame, his short, neat brown hair and his gentle hazel eyes.

A girl of about eight or nine was pulled from the back of the first ambulance. There was no sign of Todd. The girl's eyes were closed and she had a firm cervical collar around her neck.

'Carrie, this child needs a neuro consult, possible head injury. Jim Edwards is on his way down but can you monitor her until he arrives?' Brenda relayed the paramedics' summary of the girl's condition.

'Sure.' Carrie had worked at the Children's since graduating from nursing. She was one of the most experienced emergency nurses and there wasn't much she hadn't had to deal with before. She crossed straight to the first stretcher.

The doors of the second ambulance swung open and Maia saw Todd climb out. She headed for her fiancé, closely followed by Brenda. Despite the fact that he'd just come from what she imagined was a complicated

and messy motor-vehicle accident with multiple casualties, Todd looked as immaculate as ever. He was fas-
tidiously neat and somehow his uniform had remained
clean and still had perfect creases in the trouser legs.
In contrast Maia could sense that her thick dark hair
was already escaping from the bun she'd fixed it in.
She couldn't count how many times people had uttered
the phrase 'opposites attract' when they'd been talking
about her and Todd.

He pulled a stretcher from the back of the truck.
A young boy was sitting up on it. He was alert and
seemed quite fascinated by the whole experience. He
was dressed in his school uniform, shorts and a T-shirt,
and Maia could see that his left knee was swollen. The
paramedics had rolled up a towel and stuffed it under
his knee to support it.

'Adam has undiagnosed knee pain,' Todd told them.
'And he's unable to weight bear. Vitals all with normal limits.'

'Henry.' Brenda nodded as she called Henry over to
join them. 'Ortho injuries; can you take this one?' she
said as she pointed to Adam. 'Maia, you go with him.'

She wondered if that was a coincidence or if Henry
had requested to work with her. *Don't flatter yourself*,
she remonstrated as Todd handed her a little green
whistle-shaped inhaler.

'He's had the Penthrox inhaler on the way here,' he
said.

Maia nodded and tucked the pain-reliever alongside
Adam, then put her hands on the stretcher, ready to
wheel it away. Before she had moved Todd reached
over and gave her shoulder a gentle squeeze. 'I'll see
you later,' he said.

Maia saw Henry watching. His eyes moved from

Todd's hand to Todd and then to her face. Maia blushed under his scrutiny. She almost felt like she shouldn't have let Todd touch her. Not that she could have stopped him, nor was she sure why she would have wanted to, but his familiar gesture made her feel awkward and uncomfortable under Henry's gaze. His expression was unreadable but he gave the stretcher a push, starting it moving towards the entrance, and Todd's hand dropped from Maia's shoulder with the movement. Henry wasn't watching her now, he was focused on manoeuvring the stretcher, but Maia knew his movement had been deliberate. She said nothing as she and Henry wheeled the stretcher away and Todd turned back to his other patient, to the girl with the broken collarbone.

'Hey there, mate, what's your name?' Henry had always had a good bedside manner and everyone, young and old, loved him. He had an easy charm. People were starstruck by his arresting looks initially but he always won them over with his personality to match.

She needed to be careful. Before he'd left she'd had him on a pedestal; she couldn't let that happen again. But, listening to him chat to their young patient, she could tell he hadn't changed.

'Adam Evans.'

'Nice to meet you, Adam. I'm Henry and this is Maia,' he said. 'You've hurt your knee, have you?'

Adam nodded.

'We'll get you comfortable in here and have a look at it. Have you been in hospital before?'

'No,' he said. Maia grabbed a blank patient file from the triage desk as they wheeled the stretcher past.

'Seen it on telly?'

He nodded again as they pushed his bed into a

cubicle and Maia pulled the curtain around to give them some privacy.

Maia helped Henry transfer Adam to a hospital bed before she wheeled the stretcher into the corridor. She knew one of the ambulance crew would collect it before they left the hospital but she didn't want them to have to interrupt, especially if it was Todd. She wasn't ready to deal with two sets of inquisitive eyes.

'Maia will attach a few leads to you,' Henry told Adam as he washed his hands before pulling on a pair of disposable surgical gloves. 'She'll check your pulse and a few things like that but I reckon that'll all be pretty normal, seeing as you're talking to me.'

They had worked together at the Queen Liz when Henry had been doing his fellowship. They'd worked well together then and slotted back into an easy rhythm now. It didn't feel like three years since they'd worked side by side.

Maia took a hospital ID bracelet out of the file and wrote Adam's details on it before fastening it around his wrist. Next she snapped gloves onto her hands, connected Adam to the monitors and recorded his observations—blood pressure, oxygen sats and pulse rate.

'Do you know what day it is, Adam?' Henry asked as he shone a penlight torch into Adam's eyes and checked his pupils.

'Tuesday.'

'Do you remember what happened?'

'I was standing up in the bus when the driver swerved and I went flying, and my knee slammed into the side of one of the seats. It hit that metal bar that made up the seat frame. My brother was on the bus too. Do you know if he's okay? His name is Bailey.' Tears welled in Adam's eyes and Maia could tell he was trying to be brave. She could imagine how she would have felt if she'd been in his situation at the same age.

'Let's get you sorted and then we'll find out about Bailey,' she told him. She wouldn't tell him that she was sure Bailey was fine; she couldn't promise that when she had no idea of the situation. Promising to investigate was the best she could do.

'All right, Adam, I need to have a look at your knee, but first I want you to tell me about your pain. Can you give it a score out of ten? Where zero is no pain and ten is unbearable.'

'Maybe a six?'

'I need to have a feel of your knee but you can hold Maia's hand if you like and squeeze it tight if your knee gets too sore and you want me to stop. I reckon holding Maia's hand might help.' Adam blushed and looked away and Maia almost felt sorry for him until she realised that Henry had started palpating the knee joint and had successfully distracted Adam so that he'd been able to start palpating without Adam even noticing. Obviously he hadn't struck anything painful yet but as a technique Maia was impressed.

The pain-relieving inhaler was lying where Maia had left it, on the bed. She picked it up and offered it to him. 'You can use this if you like?'

But Adam shook his head. 'I'll be okay,' he said, still putting on a brave face.

'Good choice, Adam. I'd choose to hold a pretty nurse's hand instead too,' Henry added as he palpated the medial and lateral ligaments and winked at Adam, who grinned. Now it was Maia's turn to blush but she held out her hand and Adam latched onto it.

As the young boy squeezed her hand, Maia wondered

if anyone watching her and Henry would guess they had a history. Henry seemed relaxed; working with her didn't appear to be throwing him off-kilter. Perhaps it was only her on tenterhooks, only her who still felt the spark of awareness in the air. There was no denying she was still affected by his easy charm.

Henry moved his fingers centrally over the quadriceps tendon and muscle belly. There was marked oedema of this knee compared to the other and Maia watched as Adam grimaced, but he didn't cry out.

'Are you a cricketer, Adam?' Henry asked.

Adam nodded.

'So, you'd be getting ready to watch the World Cup?'

The World Cup was scheduled to start in India at the end of February. It was only a few days away and New Zealand's citizens could barely talk about anything else. Maia knew that Henry also loved his cricket. He would slot straight back into the Kiwi culture even if he did barrack for the wrong team.

'Do you reckon the Black Caps can beat my team—England?'

Henry was having difficulty finding the borders of the knee cap. Adam flinched and his fingers tightened their grip on Maia's as Henry's fingers probed his patella but his bravado remained strong as he replied, 'The Black Caps can beat everyone.'

'I like your confidence.' Henry laughed. 'I'm looking forward to watching some cricket. I've been living in America—they're not into cricket there. See if you can bend this knee for me. I'll help you.' Henry had again successfully distracted Adam but his assessment wasn't over yet. He slipped one hand under Adam's knee to support it. It was resting in about thirty degrees of flexion and he was able to bend it another thirty degrees before the pain got too much. But Maia knew that flexion of sixty degrees was well off the normal range of one hundred and forty degrees for thin adolescents.

But Henry praised his efforts. 'Well done, Adam. Now try to straighten it for me.'

Adam tried but he couldn't do it. His knee got stuck at thirty degrees.

'Can you lift it off the bed?'

Maia could see from Adam's expression that he was trying but his quadriceps wasn't following orders and his leg didn't budge.

'These kids are primary school age, yes?' Henry asked Maia. 'How old are you, Adam?' he asked when she nodded.

'Twelve.'

'All right. I reckon you might have busted your knee cap; we need to get that X-rayed.'

Maia frowned. Patella fractures weren't common in children and she wondered why Henry suspected that. He must have seen her doubting expression. 'I've seen a few in this age group, boys more than girls,' he explained. 'Once the patella has ossified it's susceptible to fracture. Can we organise an X-ray? AP and lateral views?' he asked.

'Sure. They can bring the mobile X-ray machine in to do that. But we'll need to get permission first, I suspect. Why don't you ask Brenda to organise that when you get your next case and I'll wait with Adam?' Maia didn't want to leave the young boy alone. He would be apprehensive, if not scared, and with the added worry of his brother's whereabouts and potential injuries. 'And see what you can find out about Bailey,' she added as Henry pulled the curtain back and stepped out.

She watched him leave the cubicle. His dark hair

was neat at the nape of his neck. His back was straight, his shoulders square. He seemed relaxed, unhurried, in control, and Maia knew his calm demeanour was good for the patients.

Henry turned to pull the curtain closed and saw her watching him. He grinned and winked as he tugged the curtain across, cutting off her view.

Maia busied herself checking Adam's obs again while she waited for the blush that stained her cheeks to fade. She needed something to occupy her mind; she couldn't afford to fill it with thoughts of Henry.

She heard the curtain move again. The sound of the plastic clips sliding in the rail made her look up. She was hoping to see Henry but it was a lady's face that appeared.

'Excuse me,' the woman said as she ducked around the curtain. 'Sorry to interrupt—I'm Amelia Cooper, the deputy principal at Canterbury Primary School.'

Maia spotted an identification badge hanging around Amelia's neck that had her photograph and the school crest printed on it. She hoped she wasn't a journalist with fake ID. That had happened before, on more than one occasion.

'Hello, Adam,' the woman said, and Maia decided she would give her the benefit of the doubt, although she wasn't sure what she was doing in her cubicle.

'Is there something I can help you with?' Maia asked.

'I need to make sure all the children are accounted for,' Amelia explained. 'The school is contacting the parents. Some are already on their way to the hospital, but I was told we might need permission for some treatments. The school has all that information on file.' She indicated the electronic tablet she held in one hand. 'It's all in here.'

She put the tablet down on the end of Adam's bed and took a thick marker pen from a clipboard which she had been holding in her other hand. 'I'm also supposed to correctly identify the children,' she said as she printed Adam's name onto a sticky label which she peeled off and stuck to his shirt. Some things obviously still had to be done the old-fashioned way, although Maia knew her method of identifying the children was more secure. Adam's arm would go wherever he went, unlike his shirt, which could easily be removed, taking his ID with it. But she kept quiet. The children could be identified at a glance and another form of ID wasn't going to create any problems, as long as it was accurate.

'And I'll keep a list of their injuries so the parents can check in with me as their initial point of contact. I'll be the liaison person, according to your ED director that will leave you all free to get on with treating the kids.'

That made sense. Maia filled her in on Adam's condition and Amelia flipped over the page of sticky labels and jotted a summary on another page of her clipboard.

'Do you have authority to give permission for Adam to have an X-ray?' Maia asked.

'I do,' she replied. 'I spoke to Dr Cavanaugh who was in here before and told him.'

'Okay. Do you have any news about Adam's brother, Bailey?'

Amelia ran her finger down the list on her clipboard. 'He's fine. He's got some cuts and bruises and he's waiting for some treatment to clean those up.'

Maia could see Adam relax. 'That's good news, isn't it?'

'I've got more good news, Adam,' Amelia said. 'The school has spoken to your mother and she is on her way.'

The radiographer arrived and Maia left him to do his job while she went looking for Bailey.

The waiting room had filled with parents and some of the less seriously injured kids who were still waiting to be treated. Maia scanned the room and spotted a boy who, despite the large dressing that was bandaged to the top of his head, looked similar enough to Adam that she walked closer to check the sticker on his shirt. It read, 'Bailey Evans'.

Maia sought out the ED Director next. She was standing at the whiteboard behind the triage desk, updating the list. 'Brenda, have you got anyone urgent for me or can I take Bailey Evans?' she asked. 'I've got his brother having X-rays taken and I think they'd like to be together while they wait for their mother.'

Brenda scanned the board quickly before she nodded. 'Sure,' she said as she added a note on the board beside Bailey's name. 'According to the ambos he's got a head laceration that might need stitching. Your call, once you've cleaned him up.'

Maia introduced herself to Bailey as she pushed his wheelchair into the cubicle beside Adam's. They could talk to each other through the curtain while she cleaned Bailey's cuts—she didn't think Adam needed to watch that—but once they were both taken care of she could pull back the curtain and they could wait together.

Maia gently lifted the dressing on Bailey's head. It was soaked in blood from a nasty cut that ran along his hairline. The paramedics had been right; the gash would probably need a few stitches. She re-covered the wound with fresh padding and called for a doctor. The wound would need to be cleaned but she knew the doctor would administer a local anaesthetic and she preferred to wait for that before she started cleaning. She would make a start on his other more straightforward injuries while she waited. She could see several cuts on his hands and knees as well as on his face and head.

'How did you get all of these cuts?' she asked him.

'Some of the windows in the bus exploded when the bus rolled over.'

'The bus rolled over?' Maia hadn't been aware of that part.

Bailey nodded his head.

'The bus driver swerved so hard to miss the land-slide that the bus crashed through the rail on the side of the road and rolled down the hill.' Adam's voice came through the curtain, explaining the sequence of events.

'You didn't tell me that part before, Adam.'

'That wasn't the bit where I hurt my knee,' he said matter-of-factly.

'The window next to me smashed,' Bailey added. 'And then some of us had to break the emergency window and crawl out that way. That's how I cut my hands and knees.'

Maia picked fragments of glass out of his wounds, disinfected them and bandaged them before she tackled his face and head. She cleaned the cuts and scratches on his face before she carefully unwrapped the dressing on his head.

The curtain rustled on its tracking, flicking open to admit Henry. 'This is Bailey, Adam's brother,' Maia told him. 'He's got a laceration on his head that needs cleaning and suturing.'

She removed the dressing again for Henry to take a look. He nodded, agreeing with her assessment.

Maia handed him the local anaesthetic, pre-empting his request, and then prepared a suture kit while they waited for the anaesthetic to kick in. They worked smoothly together, their moves practised as Henry chatted to Bailey about cricket and rugby. Maia loved rugby but didn't really understand the attraction of cricket and she wasn't interested in listening to them discuss their favourite teams and players. She was busy thinking about other things. She was standing beside Henry's right shoulder, snipping the thread each time he finished a stitch. She didn't need to focus; her mind was free to wander and she let it drift as she watched his fingers pinch and move as he deftly sewed up Bailey's head wound.

He looked like he was conducting a mini-orchestra. His hands moved to their own silent beat. His fingers were long and slender, his forearms were strong. He was wearing a short-sleeved surgical top, a dark blue one that made his eyes look even darker than usual, and his olive skin was lightly tanned, even though he'd just returned from a Northern Hemisphere winter. She wondered what colour the skin under his clothes was.

That was a dangerous direction for her thoughts to take. She quickly tried to think about something else. She breathed deeply as she tried to refocus her mind. But all that happened was she breathed in Henry. She was standing so close to him that all she could smell was the scent of clean laundry and that citrus-and-cedar aftershave, and every breath she took filled her senses.

'Henry?'

Brenda stuck her head around the curtain and Maia jumped. She felt a guilty flush steal across her cheeks even though she was guilty of nothing more than wayward thoughts. But Brenda's appearance was enough to break the spell. Maia took a small step back, putting a little bit of distance between Henry and her.

'Adam's X-rays are back.'

'Okay. Can you put the dressing on?' Henry asked as Maia cut the final thread. 'I'll follow up on Adam.'

Henry swapped cubicles and Maia breathed out. She hadn't realised that she'd been holding her breath but it must have been protective tendencies. If she couldn't smell Henry, she could think. It was good that he was gone. She needed a bit of distance. Despite telling herself that Henry's return didn't matter and that it wasn't going to affect her, she knew that was a lie. She hoped he'd spend a lot of time in Theatre and on the wards—anywhere away from Emergency. She didn't know how she could be expected to function normally if she had to work closely with him.

She put a new dressing on Bailey's head and pulled the curtain back so the boys could see each other. Henry had his back to her as he studied Adam's X-rays. He held them up to the light and Maia was about to leave him to it when she heard Carrie's voice on the other side of the curtain, and another stranger came into the cubicle. Another woman. But this time Maia knew immediately who she was. The boys' mother. It wasn't that she looked particularly like them but Maia could tell by the way she rushed in and ignored the adults in the room completely as she sought out her children. Maia might as well have been invisible. The woman hesitated for just a fraction as if trying to choose which of her sons to hug first but chose Bailey. He was closer.

Henry turned around at the sound of a new voice and Maia noted the woman's double-take when she saw Henry. As concerned as she was for her children, part of her, possibly just her female hormones, still couldn't help reacting to Henry. It seemed he wasn't quite as invisible as Maia was. Not that Maia could blame her. There weren't many people, men or women, who were

immune to Henry's looks. He was a strikingly handsome man. Maia's glance went instinctively to the
woman's left hand to see if she was single. Not that it
was any of her business. She tried not to care but she
didn't want other people noticing Henry. Although she
knew that was impossible.

'Mrs Evans?' Henry queried as the woman kissed
Bailey and then moved over to hug Adam. 'I'm Dr
Henry Cavanaugh,' he went on when she nodded. 'I'm
an emergency specialist at the hospital and Maia and
I have been treating your sons. They are both fine.
They've sustained relatively minor injuries but, all
things considered, they've been very lucky. Bailey has
a few small cuts that have been cleaned and dressed
but he also had one larger gash on his head which required ten stitches—just here.' Henry touched his own
head just at his hairline. 'He'll need to get those out in
a week. Your GP might be happy to do it or you can
bring him in here.

'Adam has a fractured knee cap,' Henry continued
as he slid one of the X-rays into the light box on the
wall. This X-ray showed a lateral view and Maia could
see the dark line indicating the break running across
the middle of Adam's patella. Henry traced his finger
over the line. His fingers were slender and capable, his
hands smooth and hairless. Maia forced her attention
back to the matter at hand and listened as Henry told
Mrs Evans what had happened. She needed to pay attention; she would need to write discharge summaries
for the boys.

'It's not serious. A transverse fracture of the patella is not particularly common but it matches with
Adam's age and the injury history. The physio will be
along shortly to fit him with a splint and we'll make an

appointment with an orthopod to review his progress in two weeks. He should expect to stay in the splint for four weeks and then he will need physiotherapy. You can take the boys home as soon as the physio has taught him how to use crutches.'

'Adam gets crutches?' Bailey sulked.

The boys' mother laughed. 'Now I know you're okay,' she said.

Henry high-fived both of the boys. 'Maia, can you ring Outpatients and set up a review for Adam in a fortnight?'

Maia nodded. They had worked well together. No awkwardness. There had been no time to worry about anything other than their patients. She was right— Henry being back wasn't going to affect her.

Henry scrubbed his hands as he prepared to go into Theatre, taking a few moments to collect his thoughts. He hadn't had a moment of solitude since he'd bumped into Maia earlier today. If he hadn't been working solidly with her all morning, he could almost have believed he was dreaming. They'd been treating their young patients nonstop for hours, and his day wasn't over yet, but he needed just a little time to think.

He hadn't been completely honest with Maia about his reasons for coming back to Christchurch. He'd been offered a grant, that much was true, but he'd been offered several and he'd accepted Christchurch partly because of her. He hadn't come back *for* her but because of her. He had actually been happy here and he had Maia to thank for that. It had been many years since he'd felt truly happy, before Christchurch or since.

Six years ago his world had collapsed and as he'd recovered he'd made a decision. He would save the world, one disaster at a time, and if he couldn't save the world then he would at least try to make a difference to one family at a time. That had put him on the path to emergency medicine and disaster management. He knew exactly how devastating losing loved ones unexpectedly in traumatic circumstances was and, if he could make a horrible, tragic situation better, then that was what he wanted to do. If it kept him busy day and night, that was a good thing. He had no desire to have a life of his own. His family didn't get that now—why should he?

He'd been rudderless, almost homeless, for six years now. He hadn't wanted to stay in one place; he knew that being settled without any family around would make him feel even more alone. Family couldn't be replaced. Not even by another family. The risk was too great—something might happen to them too.

He'd decided it was better to remain alone, even if it meant being lonely, rather than risk his heart on love.

And then he had met Maia and he'd been tempted to change his mind. But he hadn't been able to ask her to commit to a life of uncertainty with him when he hadn't even been sure if he wanted that commitment. Yet he hadn't been able to resist returning and so he was back in Christchurch. This city held some of his few cheerful memories, without any lurking ghosts, and he was sorely in need of some happiness.

CHAPTER THREE

MAIA LOOSENED HER hair from the bun she'd worn it in all day and let it fall down her back in thick, dark waves as she and Carrie strolled along the banks of the Avon River towards the Stratford-on-Avon. The pub's picturesque waterside setting, proximity to the hospital and well-timed happy hour all combined to make it a popular watering hole for the staff of the Children's Hospital.

'Can you stay for a feed tonight?' Carrie asked as they pushed open the door and entered the pub.

Maia shook her head. 'I'm singing tonight. The band has a gig at the Cathedral Square Hotel,' she said as they ordered two bottles of cider.

Maia loved to sing. If she'd been good enough to make a living out of it, she would have tried, but her father had convinced her to have a career as well and she'd discovered nursing, which she loved just as much. But she sang as often as she could with a jazz band.

The girls took their drinks out onto the deck that overlooked the Avon River. Willow trees lined the bank, their sweeping branches dipping into the calm waters. It was a pleasant spot on a summer's afternoon. They could watch the occasional punt taking tourists along the river or the university rowing crews on their afternoon trainings.

Today it was a rowing four that glided past as Maia asked, 'Are you still okay to come to the dressmaker with me next week?'

'Are you finally going to pick out the dresses?'

'No.' Maia laughed and sipped her cider. 'I'm hoping you'll do that.' Carrie was Maia's maid of honour and along with Maia's three younger sisters would form the bridal party. The wedding was only six weeks away. Maia needed to stop procrastinating and make some decisions. Todd had done most of the preparation work. Maia had given her opinion but she wasn't the one driving this.

'I'm surprised he hasn't given up on you,' Carrie said. 'You've made him wait for almost two years.'

'Maybe he thinks I'm worth it.' She grinned.

'I'm sure he does. But what do you think? Is he worth it?'

'He's a great guy, anybody would be lucky to have him. *I'm* lucky to have him,' she said but even she could hear the uncertain tone of her voice.

'You don't need to convince me,' Carrie replied.

Maia didn't answer; her mind was wandering, off on its own little tangent. They'd been engaged for eighteen months, since just before her dad had died. Was she lucky Todd was so patient or had she been secretly hoping that he'd get tired of waiting for her? Maia looked down the river as she pondered the question. The water was flat and green. A light breeze stirred the willow trees, making their leaves brush over the water. A rowing eight glided past, young, fit men wearing university colours disturbing the surface of the river as she stared off into the distance.

'My dad loved Todd. He became like the son he'd never had. He gave us his blessing before he died and you know how important that is to me,' she said, answering her own question. 'Family was everything to Dad.'

'I know that but are you sure you're marrying him because *you* want to, not just because your dad approved? Are you sure it's the right thing for you? Are you ready?'

She knew what Carrie was asking. She and Carrie had been friends for ever. They'd been friends before Maia's dad had got sick, before Maia had met Todd, before everything. They'd been friends before boyfriends, even, and Carrie had been there every step of the way. She knew which boys had been important, which one Maia had loved and which one had left her heartbroken.

Carrie knew her history with Henry. She knew that Henry had broken her heart—unintentionally, but it had been broken all the same. It had taken a long time for the cracks to heal and Maia knew they could easily be prised apart. But, despite heartache, life went on. Todd had filled a gap for her and somewhere along the way he'd helped her look to the future. A future that was different from what she had dreamed of and hoped for in some ways, but getting married was Maia's choice. She knew she'd been influenced by her father's thoughts and feelings, and by circumstances, but it didn't necessarily mean it was the wrong thing for her.

'It's a new year,' Maia said in reply. 'And my resolution was to look to the future and be happy with what I have.' Todd might not have been her first love but he would be a good husband. He was loyal, trustworthy, dependable and he adored her.

But, if she'd known the future was going to bring Henry back into her life, would she have made a different choice? It was too late to ask that question.

'Besides,' she continued, 'everything is booked—the cathedral, the reception venue, the cake, the photographer and the hairdresser.'

'It can always be un-booked.'

Maia wasn't so sure. 'We posted the invitations yesterday.'

The wedding was six weeks away. The sun kept rising and setting, the days kept turning over, and suddenly she was near the end of her engagement. This was it.

Maia closed her eyes as she started another song. It was one of her favourites, made famous by Ella Fitzgerald. She left the microphone fixed into the stand but steadied it with one hand as she swayed in time with the music. She'd chosen to wear a long, black dress tonight and it brushed her calves and ankles as she moved. It was cut low in the front and hugged her curves but a split up one leg to her thigh allowed for movement. Sequins scattered over the dress caught the light. There were more than a few men in the bar who were watching her with interest but, for the moment, she was oblivious to the attention as she let her mind drift.

Tonight the band was performing in the piano bar of the Cathedral Square Hotel in the city centre. This had become a semi-regular gig for her and the band. There were five of them tonight: the pianist, the bass player, the drummer, the trumpeter and her. The band had a different repertoire for the nights when she was unavailable due to nursing shifts and on those nights the pianist became the lead singer.

A spotlight was focused on her but she wasn't aware of it. When she sang she wasn't aware of anything except the music and the lyrics. It was one of the things she loved about singing. It transported her to another world where she wasn't thinking about work or weddings or loss.

The spotlight highlighted Maia's exotic features. Her English and Maori heritage had blended together, giving her the best of both worlds. Her shape and colouring was courtesy of her Maori background on both sides of her family. Her round face, round cheeks, generous bust and generous hips, along with her masses of thick dark hair and brown eyes, were definitely Maori, as was her skin, with its hint of coffee. Her facial features were the image of her half-English mother, with the same almond-shaped dark eyes, finely arched brows and narrow nose.

She'd done her make-up tonight to suit the atmosphere of the piano bar. She'd painted her lips red and gone with dark, smoky eyes. She wasn't normally much of a make-up wearer—she was far too lazy to bother most days and she never wore make-up to work—but she made an exception on the nights when she performed with the band. She enjoyed the chance to get dressed up and performing on stage was all about playing a role and she was determined to do her part justice.

Tonight's performance was going smoothly. The crowd was reasonable; their first set had been well received and the applause was reassuring. Some nights Maia felt invisible on stage despite the spotlight.

She was pleased to have this gig tonight; it meant less time to think about Henry's reappearance. Despite her reassurances to Carrie, Henry's return had unsettled her more than she was prepared to admit. She had been twenty-two when they'd met, he'd been her first love and it seemed that neither her head nor her heart had forgotten him. But in a day or two she was sure she'd be fine. In a day or two she would have recovered from the shock of seeing him again.

She was halfway through a song, her eyes still closed, when she felt an odd stirring in the air as if someone had opened a window and let a breeze in. The breeze floated past her, caressing her skin and whispering in her ear. She opened her eyes and looked out into the crowd.

He stood by the bar on the far side of the room, watching her.

She watched him back. There weren't many things that could distract Maia when she was singing, but there was always one exception to any rule, and she knew this man was it.

He had showered and changed after work and he wore a black business shirt with the sleeves rolled up. Maia's eyes swept across his chest and followed the line of his arms before drifting down to his narrow hips which were encased in a pair of dark jeans. He had one hand hooked into the pocket of his jeans and in the other he held a glass of beer. He raised the glass towards her in a silent salute. Maia felt the breeze brush over her again and this time it whispered his name.

Henry.

Her breath caught in her throat as their eyes locked and she lost her place in the song. Even at this distance she could see the intensity in his indigo eyes and feel the heat in his gaze. Warmth flooded through her, pooling in her belly, and she couldn't even begin to try to find the words to continue singing. She had been swaying to the music but now she was worried that her knees were going to give way beneath her. She gripped the microphone stand with both hands as she tried to keep herself upright. She turned her head to look at the pianist, breaking eye contact with Henry in the process. Sean, the pianist, mouthed the words to her and somehow she managed to pick up the pieces and finish the song with a breathless voice and her eyes tightly shut.

As the song wrapped she didn't give the band a chance to launch into the next one. The moment the music ended, she stepped away from the microphone and said, 'Can we take a short break, guys?'

'Is everything all right?' Sean asked.

Maia nodded. 'Everything's fine,' she lied.

Things were definitely not all right.

She didn't remember stepping off the stage or walking through the bar but she must have done so because now she was standing in front of Henry.

'Hello, Maia.' His British accent caressed her name and Maia's knees wobbled again. His voice was deep and gentle and his blue eyes were smiling.

Was it only today that he had come back into her life? It felt like he'd never left. It felt like everything that had happened since had been a dream, or perhaps she was dreaming now.

He took her hands and kissed her on the cheek. They were not in the hospital now; there were no concerns about protocol. She closed her eyes and held her breath as her limbs turned to liquid. This was definitely not a dream.

Her heart raced as his lips imprinted on her skin. What was it about him that could do this to her? How was it possible that a simple kiss on the cheek could leave her breathless and excited and make her feel as if she could melt away? As if she could dissolve in a pool of desire? One kiss from Henry and she could feel herself unfurling, coming back to life. She thought she had been doing okay but now she realised she'd been surviving, not living. She'd been getting through her days, but the days had had a dullness about them. One kiss from Henry and the colours began to return.

How could he affect her like this after all this time? How could she let him?

She stepped back as annoyance overrode pleasure and guilt replaced desire. She'd forgotten all about Todd. She found it irritating that Henry could return after three years and immediately influence her like this. But she wasn't sure who she was annoyed with—him or her.

She wouldn't give in. She wouldn't give him the satisfaction of knowing he still set her heart racing. It had taken her years to put her heart back together and she wasn't going to let one kiss reopen the scar where it had healed.

'What are you doing here?' she asked.

'I was on my way to my room and I thought I heard you singing. I thought I'd check.'

'You're staying here?'

He nodded. 'Just until I can find some decent short-term accommodation close to the hospital.' He pulled his room card out of his pocket. 'Have you got time for a drink? My shout.'

She shook her head. 'I'm working.'

'Just a quick one, for old times' sake. We've got some catching up to do.'

She looked into his indigo eyes and said, 'It's been three years, Henry. That's a lot of catching up.'

'Have dinner with me tomorrow, then.'

No. She couldn't do that, for so many reasons. She didn't trust herself. Or him. Her best defence was to stay as far away from him as possible, though that would be difficult, given they were working together. But she certainly didn't have to complicate things further by agreeing to have dinner with him. She glanced back over her shoulder. The stage had been abandoned. The band had taken advantage of her abrupt exit and were taking a break—surely one quick drink couldn't hurt? 'One drink.'

There was an empty table beside them. Henry pulled out a chair for her and she sat. It seemed she lacked the willpower to refuse his invitation. No, she admitted, if only to herself, she didn't lack the will power—she lacked the desire to walk away. She had never been able to resist him.

'What can I get you? A glass of Marlborough Sauvignon Blanc?'

'No. I don't drink wine if I'm singing.' There was always the risk that her sinuses would become congested. 'I'll have a vodka, lime and soda.'

Henry signalled to the waitress and ordered Maia's drink.

'How was San Francisco?' she asked, filling in the silence while she waited for her drink.

'Interesting. I really liked it.'

'You didn't want to stay?'

He shook his head. 'I left there a year ago. I've been in Tokyo for the last twelve months, studying the medical implications and response to tsunamis. It was time to come back and put what I've learnt about disaster management into practice.'

The waitress placed Maia's drink on the table. Condensation settled on the outside of the glass and Maia wiped it off with one finger as she thought about all the things that Henry would have seen and done over the past three years. The diamond in her engagement ring caught the light and Henry's eye as Maia ran her finger over the glass. He reached for her hand and just the barest touch of his fingers on her skin made her catch her breath. While she was connected to him she felt like she ceased to exist. As if nothing else mattered but the two of them. As if they were one.

She knew he shouldn't have this effect on her still. Three years was a long time. It should have given her time to forget. Time had moved on. *She* had moved on. But her body didn't seem to have received the same message.

His thumb rested in her palm as he turned her hand, and the solitaire diamond sparkled. 'You're engaged?'

She nodded. She'd taken it off her necklace and had slipped it back onto her finger as she was getting dressed tonight.

'Anyone I know?'

'Not really.' The rapid beating of her heart made her voice sound breathless.

'What does that mean?'

'You saw him today but there was no time to introduce you.' There'd been no reason to introduce them either but Maia knew she hadn't wanted to.

'The paramedic who brought Adam in?'

It seemed he had noticed Todd's hand on her shoulder. Noticed and remembered. Maia nodded.

'When is the wedding?'

'Six weeks.'

Henry sat back in his seat and let go of her hand. She noticed he hadn't congratulated her. What did that mean?

Probably nothing. She couldn't afford to read anything into the silence. It wasn't her place to speculate about his thoughts.

'Timing was never one of our strong points,' he said.

She studied his expression but it was difficult to read in the dim lights of the bar. Did he have regrets too?

Maia shook her head. 'No, it wasn't.' His regrets were no longer her concern. They couldn't be. Her life had changed when her father had died and it was naive to think things could ever go back to the way they were. Their lives hadn't fitted together three years ago; it was unlikely they would fit together any better now. Nothing he'd said made her think his priorities had changed.

'So things have worked out well for you?' he asked. 'You're happy?'

'Of course.' She was, wasn't she? She had nothing to be unhappy about. She was healthy, she loved her job, she had family, friends and a fiancé who loved her.

She didn't want to think about why Todd was last on her list. Was that where he fitted in her life?

She should be happy. There was no reason not to be yet she knew she was lying. If she was happy why was she sitting here imagining what her life would have been like now if Henry had never left? Or if she'd gone with him? But that had never been seriously discussed.

They'd known at the beginning that their relationship would have an end. Henry's plans had already been in place. He'd been in Christchurch for a limited time, she'd known the date he was leaving and she had known he wouldn't take her with him. He travelled alone. That was his choice and, while she didn't like it, she'd had to accept it. Then, just weeks after his departure, her dad had suffered his first stroke and Maia had known then she would have chosen to stay. But it had been tough, really tough, and in the end she had lost both her father and Henry.

'Things have worked out differently to what I expected but that's life, isn't it?' she said. 'Things change and you have to change with them.'

She could see the band members making their way back onto the stage. She pushed her chair back and stood. 'I have to go.'

Henry got up too and came to her side. 'I'll see you soon,' he said as he leant forward and kissed her cheek a second time, making her stomach flutter.

Oh, God, how was she going to handle this? How on earth had she thought she was over him? Just one kiss and she could feel herself falling again. She needed to get out of here.

Somehow Maia managed to get through two more songs. Henry had stayed for both before leaving the room. She doubted he'd return to the piano bar tonight but she didn't want to hang around to find out. She told the band she wasn't feeling well and made an early exit. An exit that felt very much like an escape.

The hotel doorman hailed her a taxi and she spent the ride home thinking about Henry. She thought she had managed to put him out of her mind. She would have thought three years was long enough to stop thinking about him and it should have been long enough for her body to forget him. But her reaction tonight proved that wasn't the case. Her body definitely hadn't got the message that three years had passed—her body had sprung to life as if it had been dormant these past few years.

Did her body have a memory all of its own? A memory that was independent of her brain?

She had no complaints about her sex life with Todd, it was pleasantly satisfying. But there was no denying that sex with Henry had been incredible. Those memories must have been repressed but not forgotten for them to return to the forefront of her mind so quickly.

Sex with Henry had been amazing. It had been passionate, all-consuming, powerful and never routine. Sex with Henry had been nothing like she'd ever experienced before or after. He could almost bring her to orgasm with just one look, one touch, one well-placed kiss. And now he was back.

Why now? Why not six months ago? Or never.

It was too late now.

Maia sighed. There was no point dwelling on missed opportunities. There were things she was never going to get to do and there was no point looking backward. Life had other plans for her.

'Experts are predicting that last week's quake was just a precursor to a more powerful and potentially devastating one. Obviously, they can't predict when but we need to be prepared and put plans in place. It's a case of *when*, not if, as far as the experts are concerned.'

Maia and most of the ED staff were listening to Henry as he spoke about disaster management in his smooth British accent.

'A mass casualty situation is something that would stretch our hospital, and others, in terms of managing the number of injured—for example, a major earthquake. Canterbury Children's already has good systems in place. The emergency department staff is exceptionally well-trained, but in the event of a major disaster we would need to call in additional staff from other areas of the hospital and we would benefit from improving some of our systems to assist those staff who are unfamiliar with the ED environment. The easier we can make it for them to slot into our workplace, the more efficient and effective we will be, which will mean lives saved.

'Our triage nurses will be stationed at the main entrances with security and they will be responsible for deciding which casualties come into the hospital and which ones are sent elsewhere.'

He had been back for ten days and Maia was coping. Just. She had found avoidance the easiest way of managing so far but this was an important presentation she hadn't wanted to miss.

He was wearing a set of dark blue surgical scrubs, the ones that made his indigo eyes look even darker than usual, and Maia was hard pressed to recall anyone who looked better in a pair of unflattering scrubs than Henry. The scrubs looked as if they'd been tailor-made for his broad chest and the pants hugged his hips and the rounded cheeks of his bottom.

'Internally we create teams of ED staff supported by staff from other wards or departments. Ideally we would have an ED doc, ED nurse, anaesthetist and a second nurse in each team. I would suggest using medical or nursing students to act as runners and they can also assist with making up packs—for example, assembling hyperkalaemia packs if we are expecting multiple crush injuries. Everyone will be given a job card which will explain who they report to. The ward doctor will report to the ED doctor in their team, the ED doctor reports to the ED doctor in charge and so on.

'We are also going to implement a mass casualty box,' he said as he lifted a large red box, the size of an archive box, onto the table in front of him. Maia watched his biceps bulge as he hefted the carton. He really was very sexy in a British way. He had a cool, calm exterior but she knew the passionate nature that hid beneath that collected facade. She knew he kept a tight rein on his emotions and he was extremely strong-willed but once she'd been allowed to scratch the surface his true character had been revealed—passionate, intense and heartbreakingly gorgeous. He really was divine.

'It contains all the patient identification paraphernalia you might need, including "unknown patient" labels, as it's very likely you will get patients who have not been formally identified.' Henry pulled various documents out of the box as he spoke. 'There are wrist bands, paper-based ED charts, lab forms, X-ray forms as well as patient-tracking forms and simple instruction cards. Brenda and I would like you all to familiarise yourselves with the contents of this box.

'We'll make use of social workers to act as patient liaisons. The hospital has HR personnel trained in media liaison—these professionals will keep the media and the families informed and this will free up all ED staff to do their jobs without interruptions.

'One major change to procedure that we are planning on implementing is that patients who leave ED, say for X-ray, don't come back but go directly to a ward or Theatre. The surgical team can decide that in radiology but this will help to keep the ED turning over and reduce congestion and hopefully waiting times.

'We're hopeful that these changes will make it easier for the ED staff to do their jobs and to assist staff from other departments to help us without complicating process and treatment. We want to streamline triage with the intention of saving as many lives as possible in the event of a mass casualty.'

Henry took questions at the end of his discussion but as the staff milled around him Maia chose to escape outside. His talk had been excellent, but she needed to put some distance between him and her wayward thoughts before she lost control. His focus was still very clearly on disaster management, on emergency medicine, on saving the world. His priorities hadn't changed and she would do well to remember that.

Maia lay on the grass that ran along the northern side of the emergency department. She was waiting for Carrie, who was finishing off some administrative work for Brenda, but the weather was too nice to waste by waiting inside. It was a glorious summer's afternoon and Maia figured she might as well work on her tan while she killed time. Her eyes were closed, her face turned up to the sun as she let it warm her skin. A shadow passed over her and she opened her eyes to find Henry standing in front of her.

'I brought you a coffee,' he said as he held it out to her.

Maia sat up, cross-legged, on the grass. 'How did you know I was here?'

'I saw you as I was going to buy some lunch. Sugar?' he asked.

'Thank you.'

He took a sachet and stirring stick out of the pocket on the front of his surgical shirt and held them out to her as he lowered himself onto the ground beside her. She removed the lid from her cup and emptied the sugar into her drink. He stretched out on the grass, resting back on his elbows, and groaned.

Maia smiled. 'You sound exhausted.'

'Public speaking *is* exhausting.'

She stirred the sugar into her coffee as she looked at Henry. His dark blue eyes seemed violet. They were stunning and she felt the now familiar increase in her heart rate and body temperature that occurred whenever he was nearby. But she decided she could enjoy his company for a few minutes; after all, he'd sought her out and there was no one around to wonder about the blush that stained her cheeks.

'Poor you.' She laughed. 'I suppose you've got to go back inside after lunch and save more lives on top of everything else.'

'Of course, don't you?'

'Nope, I've got the day off.'

'Did you come in just to listen to me?'

'I did.'

'I'm flattered.'

'Don't be,' she teased him. 'I have to get my continuing professional development points up but, if it makes you feel better, I thought it was worthwhile.'

'Thank you. Have you got something nice planned for your afternoon?'

'I'm waiting for Carrie; we're going shopping,' she said.

'Really? That's what you're doing on your day off? The Maia I remember always hated shopping.'

'I still do, but I'm afraid I'm on a deadline.' She was running out of time.

'Wedding shopping?'

Maia nodded. She was supposed to be going to look at dresses with Carrie. They needed to choose bridesmaids' dresses and she still hadn't done anything about her own dress. Or the flowers.

'How long to go now, four weeks?'

'Four and a half.'

'You're young to be getting married—bucking the trend.'

'I'm twenty-five, it's not that young,' she said. 'My

mum was married when she was nineteen and Todd is thirty-two.'

'My age.'

She wondered if Henry thought that was too young also. Probably. She knew how he felt about commitment and it didn't seem as if he'd changed his mind in the past three years.

'We've been engaged for eighteen months,' she added.

'Since your dad died?'

'Yes. Todd nursed my dad, that's how we met.'

Henry frowned. 'Isn't he a paramedic?'

'He is now. He was a nurse when we met but he was studying to become a paramedic and he was working in home care. He was one of the nurses who looked after Dad so that Dad could stay home like he wanted. My father lost the power of speech with his stroke but Todd was able to understand him. He and Dad got along exceptionally well, so after the first couple of months Todd was the nurse who came most often and between the two of us and Mum we nursed Dad.'

Which meant Maia had spent hours sitting by her dad's bed and hours talking to Todd. Todd hadn't needed to spend as much time as he had at their house, he didn't get paid for a lot of it, and Maia knew that he'd chosen to spend time at their house as a way of spending time with her. That had been flattering and she knew she'd encouraged it. The attention had helped divert her mind from a host of other things including her father's condition and Henry's absence.

She and Todd had talked about lots of things: their work, their hobbies, their families and their plans. All those shared stories had bonded them until it had seemed like a natural progression to spend their free time together too.

'Todd asked Dad for his permission to marry me just a few weeks before Dad suffered his second stroke. That was eighteen months ago.'

Todd had helped her gradually to let go of the idea of Henry, and even though Henry was back now she had to remember he wasn't part of her life. She had a new life. With Todd. A life she couldn't have with Henry.

Henry was the past. He'd left her once before and she knew he would leave again. She could feel it in the air around him. That restlessness, that distance. Just like she could feel the attraction. But she knew that his restlessness was still too strong a force to overcome with chemistry. He wouldn't choose to stay and she craved stability. She needed that commitment; she needed to know that she could depend on someone.

Maia had been there when Todd had spoken to her father. She'd seen her father's reaction, seen the delight in his eyes, and knowing that was the last thing that had made him truly happy before he'd died meant that she had accepted Todd's proposal. She knew he was pleased she was getting the security she wanted. Maia felt like it had been her father's dying wish that she and Todd marry. How could she do otherwise?

Maia had a guarded look in her eyes and Henry knew she wasn't telling him the full story. What had happened to her to put that look there? She was older, maybe wiser, but he knew she'd been hurt. Maybe her dad's premature death had made her wary or maybe she had reserved that look just for him.

His pager beeped, calling him back to the ED. He said goodbye to Maia and left her in the sunshine. He had to walk away. She was getting what she always wanted—security and commitment—and Henry imagined that after her father's death that was possibly even more important.

There was nothing for him here. Nothing for her either. It didn't matter how he felt—it didn't matter that he was still attracted to her or that there was still chemistry between them. It was clear that Maia had moved on. She was about to be married. Which was probably a good thing. His circumstances hadn't changed. He wouldn't commit and it was obvious that was still what Maia wanted.

He could ignore the stirrings of desire. He had walked away before. It had turned out to be one of the hardest things he'd ever done but that had been his choice and it would be his choice again. When he'd met Maia he'd been alone for years but leaving her behind had made him lonely. It had been a bizarre, unexpected feeling but his circumstances hadn't changed in the past three years. He still wasn't willing to commit to a place or a person. He still had nothing to offer her and he knew he would walk away again. Love was too big a risk. Family was everything to her, a concept he understood but no longer had time for.

He would be here for a while and he'd move on again. Alone. It was better that way. Safer.

He and Maia could both have what they wanted—but not together.

CHAPTER FOUR

'WHAT ABOUT THIS?' Carrie asked as she flicked through racks of rainbow-coloured dresses. They were surrounded by metres and metres of chiffon, silk and lace but Maia was not feeling particularly enthused. She really didn't mind what the girls wore and choosing something that would suit them all was proving to be a nightmare. Carrie was short, blonde and fair skinned. Maia's sisters were all dark, like her, in varying proportions. Pippi was tall and thin; she was almost sixteen and hadn't started to spread through the hips yet, like eighteen-year-old Ariana. At twenty, Lani, the second eldest, was big breasted but short. They had to find something that would suit three different body shapes and Maia didn't see why it had to be her decision.

'Maybe we should choose a colour and a fabric but have two different styles,' Carrie suggested. 'Pippi and I could wear the same dress and Lani and Ariana could wear something else but in the same colour and fabric?'

Maia rifled through the racks as she tried to drum up some enthusiasm. 'But what colour?' In her opinion that was almost the hardest decision. Black wouldn't be flattering on her sisters, and white wasn't a good colour on Carrie. Red would suit her sisters but wash Carrie out. Bright blue looked lovely on all of them but Maia couldn't imagine having her bridesmaids in a bright colour.

'How about green?' Carrie was holding out two different dresses in the same pale mint green. It was a pretty colour and probably would suit all the girls but Maia was over it.

She groaned and collapsed onto the sofa in the shop window. She could feel the beginnings of a headache. Maybe it would be best to get this sorted out quickly and then Carrie might let her out of the shop. 'You decide,' she said. She almost said, *I don't care anymore*, but stopped just in time. A comment like that would only invite more questions from Carrie and Maia was tired of thinking.

She felt like she was making decisions for someone else. Last night she and Todd had gone to dinner at the hotel where they had booked their reception. She'd wanted to cancel the reservation, to claim exhaustion, but guilt had made her keep to the plan. It wasn't Todd's fault that she was at sixes and sevens. It wasn't his fault that she felt like it was impossible to think straight, let alone make a decision. They had finalised the menu and the drinks, and the position of the dance floor and the table for the wedding cake, but this morning Maia couldn't remember what any of the decisions had been.

Her brain was completely addled and today was only making it worse. Today was a kaleidoscope of decisions about shoes, dresses, make-up and flowers. For someone who didn't love shopping *or* making decisions that weren't work related, it was proving to be a little overwhelming.

'Why are you so grumpy?' Carrie asked as she handed the dresses to the sales assistant and sent her off to find out what other styles and sizes were available in that colour. 'Is it Henry?'

'Henry? What does he have to do with anything?'

'I don't know. That's why I'm asking.'

'It's nothing to do with Henry. That was all over long before I met Todd.'

'Yes, I know, but now he's back. Are you telling me that hasn't changed things? Do you still have feelings for him?'

'I've moved on. We both have.' But even as she said the words a part of her wished things were different. 'I'm sure this is just a case of pre-wedding jitters.'

'Also known as cold feet.'

'Which is perfectly normal, everyone says so. Everything will be fine once we're married.'

Carrie was looking at her closely and Maia waited for her to say more but the return of the sales assistant interrupted their conversation. She had her arms full of dresses and she hung them on an empty clothes rack for Carrie to sort through. Maia waited as Carrie separated a couple of possibilities and the sales assistant stripped two store mannequins and redressed them with Carrie's choices.

Carrie stood back and studied the dresses while she spoke to Maia. 'Okay, I'll choose for the bridesmaids, but *you* have to choose your wedding dress.'

They had started off the afternoon looking at wedding gowns but Maia had tired of that quickly too. There had been a couple she'd liked—one was strapless with a heavily beaded bodice and full skirt, and the other was a far more simple, bias-cut satin that draped over her hips and had wide, simple straps that crossed her chest and showed off her shoulders. But they'd been so different she hadn't been able to choose between them so she'd given up.

'Stop worrying,' she told Carrie. 'Everything will be fine.'

'I'm your maid of honour—making sure you are doing the right thing is part of my job description.' She swapped one of the dresses on the mannequin for another as she continued. 'Wedding dresses are a bit like men. You don't need more than one. You can like different things about different wedding dresses, or men, but in the end you only need one wedding dress and you only need one man. I can't choose your wedding dress for you. Only you can do that. And only you can choose the right man. No one else can do that for you either. You just have to choose the man who's best for you. Not the one who can't live without you but the one who *you* can't live without.'

'It's all good,' Maia said. She was convinced that once she and Todd were husband and wife she would settle down. Once that day was over and the decision was final, she'd be happy. Her life, their life, would be smooth sailing; Todd would make sure of it. He would look after her. She loved Todd. He was kind and loyal; he loved her family. It didn't matter that she'd loved Henry first. Todd's priorities—work, her and family—were the same as hers. That was important. 'I know what you're thinking—that Henry's return has unsettled me—but that's not the case. Henry wasn't the right man for me.'

'Why? Because he left?'

'No.' Maia shook her head, trying to convince herself that she spoke the truth. 'I want a family. I want to be settled and I want someone I can depend on, someone I know will be there for me. Henry doesn't want a family; he doesn't want to settle down. He wants to save the world, one disaster at a time. That's his priority, that's his choice, and it was never going to include me. I've made my choice. I'm marrying Todd.'

But was Todd really the one she couldn't live without?

Maia was finding it difficult to concentrate. She had come to the Queen Elizabeth Hospital for a half-day seminar on advances in emergency medicine and this session was a discussion on latest practice in paediatric anaesthesia. The sessions had been good so far and she was looking forward to this one, the final one of the day. She was expecting it to be both informative and interesting but she was finding it hard to focus because in the darkened theatre, in the seat beside her, with his thigh brushing hers, sat Henry.

The lights had been dimmed and Maia was aware of the slides changing as the speaker went through her presentation. But she was more aware of the length of Henry's thigh in his stone-coloured chinos, the slight jiggle of his leg as he listened and the smell of his aftershave. The scent of grapefruit and cedar wafted over her and she could feel his body heat radiating from his arm where it rested next to hers on the arm of his seat.

Maia had to tuck her hands between her thighs so she didn't reach out and touch him. She could hear him breathing. She counted his breaths, trying to stop herself from thinking about touching him, but then she forgot to listen to the lecturer.

Occasionally Henry would lean towards her and whisper a comment to her about the lecture content. His breath was warm and soft on her cheek and his aftershave mesmerised her and pulled her in closer. She could feel herself leaning towards him until their upper arms touched, startling her and making her shift away. She wanted to touch him, she wanted to feel him. She wanted to rest her hand on his thigh. She wanted to sit in the dark and hold his hand. But she couldn't do any of those things.

Fifteen minutes into the presentation, Henry slouched in his seat, his knees relaxed and his left thigh bumped into hers. She was convinced she could feel his firm, muscular thigh even through the thin layers of their clothing. She could definitely feel the heat radiating from his skin. She pressed her knees together primly, trying to avoid temptation. But it was impossible to maintain that uptight posture, it was impossible to maintain that distance, and eventually, when it all got too much, she decided she would excuse herself to go to the bathroom and when she came back she would sit somewhere else. Somewhere that wasn't next to Henry.

She was about to stand up and sneak out when the lecturer finished her presentation and the lights came up ready for question time. She couldn't sneak out now. She would have to sit and wait.

She sat as still as possible and fought off the waves of guilt. She hadn't done anything, and didn't intend to, but knowing that didn't stop the desire. She could feel Henry calling for her, his body speaking to hers in their own silent language. Her skin longed to feel his touch, her lips longed to taste him, her heart wanted to beat in time with his. She wanted to breathe his scent and see his indigo eyes darken with longing for her and hear him call out her name.

But it couldn't be. She had promised her heart and her body to someone else.

Surely this desire would fade once she got used to having Henry back in Christchurch? Surely it was just the unexpectedness and the excitement of the situation that made her feel this way? Surely this spark of desire, this attraction, this sense of longing, would diminish with time?

Maybe once she was married she would be able to put him behind her once and for all. Surely that commitment to Todd would put an end to her inappropriate thoughts about Henry? That was how she would handle this. She could put this extra energy that Henry seemed to instil in her to good use—she could put this energy into planning the final details of her wedding. And she might as well start now. Once this seminar was over she would go to the boutique and make a final decision about her wedding dress. She only had four weeks to go. It was time to focus on what was important, on her future with Todd. Henry belonged in the past.

Finally question time was finished and the morning was over and she could escape. She stood up and collected her bag and her water bottle.

'Are you going back to the Children's?' Henry asked as he followed her out of the lecture theatre.

Maia shook her head. 'This is a professional development day for me. I'm not rostered on to work.'

'I have to be back at two, but if you've got time how about I shout you a burger at the Stratford?'

In her head she'd already planned her exit strategy. Having lunch together wasn't part of it. Spending more time with him wasn't going to help her resist temptation. 'I shouldn't,' she replied.

'It's just a burger, Maia, I'm not asking you to run away with me.'

How did he always know what she was thinking, even when her thoughts were completely inappropriate? She almost wished he *would* ask her to run away with him.

No, not that exactly; that would involve her making a conscious decision. She wished he would steal her away and solve her dilemma without her having to decide anything.

She hesitated as right and wrong argued with each other, as suitable and unsuitable behaviours clashed, and as desire, want and need fought with loyalty in her mind.

Desire, want and need won.

It was an absolutely glorious summer's day. There wasn't a cloud in the sky, the sun was shining and it warmed her skin. There was a light breeze but it wasn't enough to take the warmth out of the sun. To spend a little time outside after being cooped up in the darkness of the lecture theatre would be wonderful and Maia could think of nothing nicer than to sit on the deck overlooking the river and share a meal with Henry. The boutique would still be there after lunch. What could be the harm in sharing an innocent bite to eat?

'Of course.' She nodded. 'Just a burger. That sounds lovely,' she said, accepting his invitation.

They strolled together along the footpath, two friends going to grab some lunch. Only she couldn't pretend that was all it was. As far as she knew friends weren't so aware of each other. She could feel the air buzzing. They weren't touching but she could feel the pull of electricity that hummed between them and she was aware of every movement he made. They walked in time, falling into old patterns and rhythms, but she made sure to keep some distance between them. She couldn't afford to touch him.

They passed behind the Cathedral Square Hotel on their way to the square. 'Are you singing here on the weekend?' he asked.

Maia nodded. 'Saturday night.'

'Maybe I'll come and listen again.'

'Are you still staying in the hotel?' Henry had been back in town for almost two weeks and she'd assumed he would have found other accommodation by now even if it was just a serviced apartment.

'I haven't had time to view anything yet but the estate agent has lined up a few possibilities for me that I'll look at on Saturday. Hopefully by this time next week I'll be sorted,' he said. 'While I don't mind the on-site restaurant, bar and laundry service at the hotel, I'd like my own space—but finding something close to the hospital isn't easy, apparently.'

'Have you checked the hospital noticeboards?' she asked. 'Someone might be looking for a flatmate.'

'I haven't,' Henry admitted as they rounded the corner of the hotel and the Christchurch Cathedral came into view. 'I'm a bit past sharing digs. I was thinking more along the lines of a serviced apartment.'

As always the cathedral drew Maia's attention. It was a gorgeous building, a landmark in the centre of the city, and it dominated the square and never failed to catch her eye. She looked up to the very top of the silver spire. If she had been alone she would have detoured inside to light a candle for her dad but she didn't want to delay Henry. She didn't want to miss her opportunity to have lunch with him. She'd return later instead on her way back to the dress shop.

A flock of pigeons roosted on the cathedral roof. They were a permanent fixture, the bane of the church's existence, and while Maia watched them they all suddenly took to the sky. En masse they flew east away from the city and towards the coast. Maia frowned and wondered what had spooked them. She searched the sky for the telltale shadow of a falcon but the sky remained blue and clear and the air was still and eerily quiet. There was no longer even a whisper of a breeze. Something was wrong but she could see no signs and she shivered as a feeling of apprehension ran down her spine. She looked around but could see nothing.

Henry had walked ahead of her and was waiting in the square. She tried to shake off the foreboding of impending doom as she hurried to catch up but as she took two quick steps her right knee gave way underneath her. She righted her balance, assuming she must have trodden on an uneven bit of footpath, but then she heard the rumbling. It vibrated through the ground beneath her and she realised she hadn't missed her step or caught her foot but rather the earth was moving.

The footpath rose and fell in front of her, cracking along its length as she struggled to keep her feet. The ground shook violently and the road beside her undulated as if it was liquid, rolling away from her like a wave going out to sea, leaving behind volcanic peaks of bitumen, broken pipes and muddy craters. Maia watched in silent horror too terrified to make a sound, as the earth cracked open and enormous dust clouds rose into the air as buildings crumbled and collapsed around the square like decks of cards.

This was the one they'd been warned about. This was the earthquake the experts had predicted.

As Maia listened to the earth groan, and watched it heave as if it was alive and in pain, she wondered why they hadn't all left Christchurch long before. Although she knew the answer to that question—no one ever really expected this to happen. The human mind could not comprehend disasters on this scale.

But now it was here. The one they'd been dreading but couldn't possibly have imagined.

The writing and screaming of the earth was accompanied by other sounds: the crash of breaking glass and the thump of falling masonry as concrete collapsed and bricks and windows fell into the street; the loud blaring of car alarms and the strident blast of car horns. Maia heard metal being crushed as cars collided and above it all she could hear the high-pitched shriek of twisting steel as some of the buildings tried futilely to resist the power of the quake.

The ground bucked and heaved under her, making it impossible to stay on her feet. The rumbling increased in volume; it sounded as if a jumbo jet was going to land in the middle of the city. Maia knew that was impossible, she knew it was an earthquake, but she couldn't stop herself from looking up to the sky.

Above her the green, copper-plated roof of the cathedral bell tower was swaying violently and the silver spire which normally pointed up to the heavens was arcing like a pendulum. The earth continued to shudder and Maia watched in disbelief as stones began to plummet from the walls of the cathedral and the top half of the bell tower began to collapse.

It was falling.

It was falling and it was going to come crashing down right where she stood on wobbly legs but she couldn't make her legs move. She had no control over her muscles, her brain or her body. Her mind had shut down and all she could do was stand and watch as the bell tower and its silver spire fell towards her.

CHAPTER FIVE

'MAIA! MAIA!'

One moment she'd been frozen to the spot, staring death in the face, waiting for the inevitable. The next she was lying on the ground in a cloud of dust. But the ground was soft. She was in Henry's arms, lying on his chest, metres from where she'd been standing seconds before. As the dust settled, the extent of the damage revealed itself.

The silver spire had crashed to the ground and was resting on the cathedral steps. The pavers where she had been standing were buried under blocks of stone and the green copper plating from the top section of the tower glowed in their midst.

Her heart thudded behind her ribs as adrenalin flowed through her veins.

'Are you okay?' Henry's words were soft in her ear.

She coughed and sat up. She was shaking violently and the only thing keeping her in a semi-upright position was Henry. His arms were still wrapped around her, holding her close, keeping her safe.

'I think so.' Her voice wobbled but she wasn't hurt. Henry had saved her life.

'Can you stand?' he asked.

Maia had no idea. There was only one way to find out.

'I think so,' she repeated.

The earth was still shaking as Henry helped her to her feet. Standing was better; she'd felt vulnerable and exposed while lying on the ground even though she'd been with Henry. It would have been impossible to run if need be while they'd both been lying down.

Her legs took her weight but she didn't let go of Henry. She didn't think she could. She clung to him like a lone survivor to a life raft in a stormy sea and watched as Mother Nature continued to wreak havoc around them.

Across the square buildings continued to succumb to the force of nature as their facades separated from the rest of the structure and toppled into the street, burying sidewalks, parked cars and people.

The situation was horrifying and almost impossible to comprehend. They were in the middle of the city. It was lunchtime on a weekday. These buildings were shops and offices, cafés and churches. These buildings were filled with people.

One of the Christchurch trams had come to a stop alongside them. The tram tracks had become warped and twisted strips of metal, going nowhere. Tourists piled out of the tram, ejected into the centre of the chaos, where they stood, dazed and confused. People ran from the cathedral, running for their lives, only to come to a stop in the square. They had nowhere else to go.

The earthquake wasn't finished with the cathedral yet and Maia watched on in horror as the slate roof on the north-west corner of the building fell into the cathedral itself. Her knees buckled again. It felt like she was on a suspension bridge and someone was making the bridge wobble. She clung tighter to Henry to stop herself from falling. To her left a cloud of dust billowed up into the air and she buried her face in Henry's shoulder as the roof of the Press Building, on the edge of Cathedral Square, caved in.

Finally the world stopped moving. The ground stopped oscillating and the city stopped shaking. Maia found the sudden stillness and the quiet unnerving, almost as unnerving as the quake itself.

'Maia? Look at me.' Henry put two fingers under her chin and gently tipped her head up. 'Are you all right?' He brushed strands of her dark hair from her cheek and searched her face for an answer.

She nodded. She'd have some bruises tomorrow but otherwise she was unhurt.

The quake had probably lasted less than a minute but the damage was immense, incredible, unbelievable. There was no traffic noise. Everything had ground to a halt. There were only two sounds now, car alarms and people. She could hear people crying, people calling out, people dying. She could hear the awful sounds of things that should never happen.

Maia stayed in Henry's embrace and from there she was brave enough to look around.

The air was thick with dust. She could taste it. Her lips and throat were coated with it and it made her eyes itch but despite her watery eyes she could still see the carnage around them.

The dust obscured some of the drama and the damage but wasn't dense enough to hide the horror completely. Where city buildings had once stood was now nothing but rubble. Some of the buildings had collapsed in on themselves, others had fallen sideways onto neighbouring buildings or into the roads. Power lines and poles had come down and traffic lights were out. Cars had toppled into massive craters or had been crushed underneath ruined buildings.

The city of Christchurch was unrecognisable.

She hugged Henry tight, clinging to him, needing the reassurance that she could only get from touching another living soul. All around them people had lost their footing and had fallen to the ground. To her right she could see someone buried under a pile of debris but she instinctively knew there was nothing they could do to help save them—they were already too late. And that was the worst thing. In a disaster of this scale, knowing that there would be people for whom they could do nothing, that there were people who were beyond help, people who could not be saved, was almost more than she could bear.

And then people started to move. Some people wandered aimlessly, shocked and disorientated; some were on their phones, others were already dragging people from the wreckage. In the distance she could hear the sirens of the emergency vehicles as they began to respond to the crisis. The square and the surrounding streets looked like a war zone but people's responses were strangely orderly. There was no running, no mass panic. It was almost as if they had been through this before but Maia knew that wasn't the case. Christchurch hadn't experienced anything on this scale in her lifetime.

'Maia?' Henry's voice brought her back. 'Are you sure you're okay? We need to help.'

An elderly lady lay on the ground near Henry and Maia. A younger woman crouched at her side. The old lady was pale and trembling and the younger one looked up at Henry with tears in her eyes. 'Please, can you help us? I can't get my mother up.'

Henry went to her and Maia went with him, focusing her attention on the two women.

'Don't move her,' Henry said to the younger woman as he squatted down on the paving. The old lady's right leg lay at an unnatural angle and appeared shorter than the other. 'She's fractured her hip,' he told the daughter. The woman was wearing a summer dress and sensible shoes. Henry put his fingers on the inside of her ankle, feeling for a pulse. The woman's daughter frowned and looked at Maia, obviously wondering what Henry was doing.

'It's all right,' Maia told her. 'He's a doctor.'

'My name is Henry.' He was talking to the old lady. 'Do you know where you are?'

'No.'

Maia could see the confusion in the old woman's eyes.

'Is she normally alert?' Henry asked the daughter. 'She doesn't have memory loss or dementia?'

'No, she's perfectly normal. Why, what's the matter?' Maia could hear the tears in the daughter's voice.

'She could have hit her head when she fell,' Henry explained. 'Does she have any significant medical conditions?'

The daughter shook her head in reply.

'How old is she?'

'Eighty-one.'

Maia pulled out her phone and dialled 111 to call an ambulance as Henry continued to check the woman. Maia knew it was more than likely that all the ambulances would already be on the road but she needed to notify someone about the situation. Someone needed to be coordinating the trucks.

'Can you move your fingers?' Henry was asking.

Maia watched as the woman wriggled her fingers. That was a good sign.

The emergency operator patched Maia through to the ambulance call centre and she gave their location and as many details about the woman as she could. 'An eighty-one-year-old woman, probable fractured NOF, concussion, possible head and neck injuries.'

She pressed 'end' on her phone and spoke to the woman's daughter. 'An ambulance has been dispatched. They know you're here but I can't tell you how long they will be.'

Maia could hear people calling for help all around them. People called from the ruined buildings and they called from the streets, wanting assistance to rescue the survivors trapped inside the damaged structures.

Henry stood up, the desperate pleas for assistance galvanising him into action. 'I'm sorry,' he said. 'There isn't anything else we can do for her here. You'll have to wait for the ambulance. We need to go; other people need our help too.'

He was right. People had been killed—Maia could see more than one body. Those deaths were tragic but there wasn't anything they could do about them. It sounded harsh but it was the reality. She'd recovered from her initial dismay; there were others who they could help, others who needed their help.

They walked down the buckled road, dodging the detritus of the quake. The street was a mess of potholes and cracks. The surface of the road was strewn with lumps of masonry, twisted signs and fallen light posts. Several water mains had ruptured and the road and the footpaths were flooded with muddy water and filth. On the street corner a couple of old, pre–World War II buildings had collapsed. Bricks and chunks of concrete from the facades had fallen onto parked cars, partially crushing some. The driver's door of the car nearest to Maia was open. It jutted into the roadway and a woman lay in the middle of the street. A chunk of masonry and a child's dummy lay beside each other near her right hand. Maia couldn't tell if she was alive or dead but as she crossed the street the woman's eyes opened.

She sat up as Maia and Henry approached and Maia could see she was bleeding from a cut on her head. The left side of her face was covered in a gruesome, bloody stain, as if someone had tipped a tin of dark red paint over her. She was struggling to her feet. Henry took her hand and helped her up. Her blue eyes were wild as she scanned her surroundings, as if she couldn't quite understand what she was seeing.

And then she started screaming and staggered towards the partially crushed car. Her blue eyes were wilder still as she turned to Henry and clutched his arm. 'My husband and daughter are in that car.'

Henry looked at Maia. His eyes were dark. He looked worried. 'Wait here,' he said as he gently disengaged her hand from his arm. 'I'll see what I can do.'

But she wasn't listening. 'That's my family,' she said as she took another step towards the car and this time it was Henry's turn to hold on to her.

He held her by her elbow, forcing her to stop, forcing her to look at him. 'Your family will need a doctor.' He spoke slowly and deliberately, maintaining eye contact, and his voice was quiet and calm. 'I'm a doctor. Let me help you.'

Maia wondered how many more times he would say that today. She wondered what he would be able to do, but it seemed that people trusted doctors. They were prepared to believe anything he told them.

'Maia will look after you and I will look after your family,' he continued.

He nodded ever so slightly to Maia. She knew what he wanted. What he needed. He needed her to take care of this woman. She looked ready to collapse. Even without the head injury, the stress and anxiety were going to make her a liability. She was going to be more of a hindrance than a help. Henry needed her out of the way.

But Maia was worried about Henry. The situation was confronting. There wasn't much left of the car. Surely this tragedy would bring back heart-rending memories for him? He wasn't an impassive, unaffected bystander; the situation was likely to feel very personal. How would he cope? How could she help him?

'Are you sure you want to do this?' she asked.

'This is what I've trained for. It's my way of making a difference.'

'Okay.' Maia nodded. She put her arm gently around the woman's shoulders and guided her back a few steps, turning her slightly so that Maia's own body partially shielded her view of the car. She manoeuvred her out of the way. Not far enough that she felt too removed but far enough that she wouldn't compromise the rescue and, more importantly, far enough away so she couldn't see too much. Maia expected the consequences to be traumatic and possibly tragic. This situation might not have a happy outcome and she didn't want the woman falling to pieces prematurely.

There was not even a whisper of sound from the car. It was ominously quiet. Maia and Henry exchanged a glance as Maia stepped away. The circumstances were far from good. The passenger side of the car was so badly damaged that it was almost unrecognisable and there was certainly no chance that Henry could access the car from that side. It was buried under rubble and the roof had caved in.

'What's your husband's name?' he asked the woman. 'Mark.'

Henry nodded and turned back to the car. He crawled inside through the driver's door. Dust still billowed in the air but Maia could just make out his figure through the haze. She could only assume that he was checking for a pulse.

There was a baby capsule strapped in to the back seat. Maia saw him reach towards the capsule but she knew he wouldn't be able to do anything from that position. The roof of the car was only inches from the top of the capsule, inches from the baby's head; he wouldn't have room to lift the baby out.

Henry backed out of the car. He didn't say anything. Maia assumed he didn't want the woman to panic, but he didn't shake his head either, and Maia knew that meant there was still hope. He jiggled the handle on the back door but the car was bent out of shape from the impact of the rubble and the door wouldn't budge.

He quickly marshalled bystanders; he couldn't afford to waste time. There were several burly young construction workers who must have been on a worksite nearby and were more than willing to lend a hand. They waited for Henry to explain what had happened before they began to lift wreckage off the car. Street signs, masonry, window frames and twisted metal were tossed aside.

Maia could feel the woman shaking. She needed to sit her down; she didn't think she could support her weight if she fainted or fell. The woman bent over, and Maia thought she was about to collapse, but then she straightened, clutching her daughter's dummy in her left hand.

'I think you should sit down,' Maia said. The woman was trembling and Maia knew she was in shock. She guided her to a bench on the edge of the square, opposite her car. The woman didn't resist—in fact she was almost too compliant, something which worried Maia even more. She doubted she would be this calm faced with the same situation but Maia suspected it was the shock that was causing her composure. Shock could be fatal and Maia had no way of combating it if necessary. Not out here in these disastrous circumstances.

'My name is Maia,' she told her again. She knew Henry had already told her that but she doubted the woman remembered—she wouldn't expect her to—and Maia wanted to keep the woman focused on her. 'What's your name?'

'Susan,' the woman replied as she leant forward and put her elbows on her knees, resting her chin in her hands. She jiggled her knees up and down. Maia could tell she wanted to bury her face in her hands but was too afraid to take her eyes off the car. The car that trapped her family.

Susan stood up from the bench. She paced up and down liked a caged animal, worry and concern making her restless.

She stopped briefly and turned to Maia. 'Sienna is only thirteen months old. She has to be all right. This is all my fault.'

Maia stood up and put a hand on Susan's arm. 'This isn't your fault.'

'But it is,' Susan insisted. 'Sienna dropped her dummy. If I hadn't bothered to pick it up, we could have been on our way. We could have been gone from here, away from that building. Half a minute could have made all the difference.'

Maia didn't know what to say. She had no words of comfort. Despite the warmth of the summer's day, Susan was shivering, and Maia wished she had something to put around her, something that could trap some body heat, but she had nothing. Maia hadn't felt so useless since her father had passed away. She hated the sense of futility. She hated being unable to help. And then, in the midst of the car alarms, the yelling and the thump of bricks and concrete being tossed aside, they heard it.

A baby's cries.

Susan shot across the street, all traces of shakiness gone, as Maia followed in her wake.

Henry was back inside the car but there was no way he could lift Sienna out of the capsule from the front seat. There wasn't enough clearance. He'd have to remove the entire capsule but Maia didn't know how he would do that either. The capsule was firmly secured in the middle seat by the seatbelt and straps. Even if he could undo it he wouldn't be able to squeeze it between the two front seats.

Susan's arms were folded across her chest and she doubled over, as if in pain, as Sienna's cries continued.

Henry backed out of the car. 'Does anyone have a pocket knife of some description?' he asked the construction workers. 'I need to cut the straps on the baby seat.'

One of the guys, a solidly built Maori, stopped moving rubble and unclipped a pocket knife from his tool belt. He tossed it across the roof of the car to Henry, who caught it easily. He flicked it open before crawling back into the car and Maia could see him sawing at the straps that secured the capsule until finally it came free. Sienna had gone quiet. Maia knew Henry would be talking to her;

perhaps she found his voice soothing or perhaps the rocking motion as he severed the straps had calmed her down. Once again, he backed out of the car, and Sienna's cries started again as he disappeared from her view. He straightened up and pulled his shirt out of his trousers. He undid a couple of buttons and pulled it over his head. The construction guys continued to remove the debris but Maia had forgotten all about them. Henry was standing in the middle of the street, half-naked, his torso completely bare. What the hell was he doing?

He held his shirt in one hand as he climbed back into the car. He draped his shirt over Sienna's capsule, tucking it underneath so she was completely enclosed, completely hidden, before backing out of the car again. His movements were quick but deliberate. Measured. He picked up a brick that was lying by his feet and Maia watched the muscles in his back and arm tense as he smacked it against the car window. The glass shattered, scattering little squares of safety glass through the car, and Maia finally understood why he'd removed his shirt. He'd needed something to protect Sienna.

He knocked the last remaining pieces of glass from the frame and reached through the window. He pulled the capsule across the back seat towards him. He carefully removed his shirt from over the top of Sienna and shook the glass off. He undid the buckles holding Sienna into her car seat and lifted her gently out of the car. She was still crying but it was a good sound. It was the sound of life.

'Sienna!' Susan reached for her baby. Her arms were outstretched as she stepped forward to take her from Henry, when the earth shuddered again. The movement wasn't as violent, nor was the tremor as powerful as the initial quake, but it was enough to trigger more panic and have everyone ducking for cover. Rescue attempts were abandoned as people bolted away from the buildings and into the street.

Henry dropped to the ground and Maia's heart dropped with him.

CHAPTER SIX

HENRY CRADLED SIENNA to his chest as he knelt on the road, sheltering her as best as he could. Maia pulled Susan down to the ground too, glancing up to check Henry was all right. They were in open space but her survival instincts kicked in and made her want to make them as small a target as possible. Crouching on the ground probably wouldn't make any difference to their safety—surely the buildings around them couldn't collapse any further?—but it was her first response.

The tremor passed. This one had been of far shorter duration than the first, but the destruction wasn't over yet. Maia stood, aware that she was pulling Susan up with her, when she heard a second loud noise. She was on edge, which wasn't surprising, but it wasn't a very useful reaction. She recognised the sound now, it was becoming all too familiar: the sound of more buildings falling.

The destruction was overwhelming and Maia wasn't sure how much more she could take. She was desperate to get out of the city; self-preservation was a powerful motivator, but she wasn't prepared to leave Henry, and she knew Henry wouldn't be prepared to leave the city. He had unfinished business.

Once again everyone was stunned in the silence

immediately following the tremor and it took several seconds for people to snap out of the disbelief and to remember what they were doing before the aftershock had rocked the street. Maia looked to Henry for guidance.

He was standing in the middle of the street, still holding baby Sienna. He looked calm and solid, a cool head in the face of the disaster. She had no idea how he managed it but his strength made her feel safe and secure.

Susan left Maia's side and went to Henry. He passed her baby over and Susan took her anxiously before retreating back to the bench in the square where she sat, cradling her child against her chest. Maia wasn't convinced that the bench was a safe place—she didn't know where safe was anymore—but at least there were no tall buildings on this edge of the square. The worst that could happen here was damage to the paving underfoot. Maia shook her head; no, the worst that could happen was that Susan could be widowed, but she didn't want to think about that. She was close to tears already and thinking about that would surely push her over the edge.

She turned her back on Susan and the cathedral. She couldn't stand to look at the damaged church with its caved-in walls and its massive spire lying in a pile of rubble. She really hoped that no one had been in the bell tower. It was a popular spot for tourists to get a good view over the city and she couldn't stand to think of how many people could be buried in there.

People were starting to panic now. Before the aftershock they'd been trying to help, battling to reach those trapped, fighting on, but now the flight response was kicking in. People everywhere were scrambling to safety but not Henry.

Maia couldn't let him do this on his own. If he was going to risk his life, she wasn't going to let him do it alone. She wanted to be by his side. She dodged the cracks and holes, the broken pipes and the mud and masonry that made the road a minefield, and went to Henry. She needed the reassurance and comfort that being with him would bring her.

The earth was quiet again. The terrible rumbling had ceased once more, leaving further chaos and carnage behind. Henry looked around at the deserted streets. People had fled in all directions but despite the mass exodus he wasn't alone. Maia was with him. And that was all he needed to know to keep going. He had saved the baby but there was more he needed to do.

He went around to the passenger side of the car where Mark was still trapped. If he was going to have any chance of saving this man, he needed to get him out of the vehicle. He wasn't certain that they would be able to get him out alive but he needed to try.

But the situation was grim. The left-hand side of the car was unrecognisable, buried under the fallen façade of the building. The roof was flattened by debris and only the back right-hand corner still looked anything like a car should. Henry couldn't be certain but it looked as if the wreckage that the construction workers had cleared before had been replaced by more debris following the aftershock.

He would need to start again.

He picked up the nearest brick and tossed it aside. Time was of the essence and this task was too big for one man. What he really needed was some extra muscle.

One of the construction crew, the big Maori who had lent Henry his knife, was still in the vicinity. He nodded at Henry and started once again to move rubble. He didn't waste energy on conversation; he just pitched in to help.

The pieces of fallen stone and concrete were large and it was heavy, back-breaking work. Within a few minutes Henry was puffing. He could feel his muscles straining and his skin was damp with sweat but the construction worker tossed the enormous blocks of masonry aside as if they were made of polystyrene, not concrete, and Henry vowed to keep going for as long as it took. He wouldn't give in, not while he had help. Not while there was a chance of saving Mark. He knew he would need to rely on the adrenalin that had kicked in and was coursing through his system but he refused to give up.

His hands were filthy, his knuckles were scraped and bleeding, and the muscles in his arms screamed with the effort, but he kept working. As he rolled another stone out of the way he saw Maia crawling into the car through the driver's door. He wanted to tell her not to, he wanted to tell her it wasn't safe, but he didn't. He knew she wouldn't listen to him and he wanted to know if Mark was still alive.

'Pulse is present but very weak.' Maia's voice floated out to him. 'I'm not sure if he's breathing. Mark? Can you hear me?' Maia tried to communicate with the man. 'There's been an earthquake. You're trapped in your car but we're working to get you out.'

Henry couldn't hear a response from Mark.

'He's unconscious.' Maia continued to update him. 'His head has fallen forward. It might be restricting his airway. His head is bleeding and his legs are trapped. I'm going to try to call an ambulance.'

There was a pause in Maia's commentary and, while he laboured, Henry imagined Maia contorting herself inside the car to reach her mobile phone and punch in the numbers.

'The network is busy!' She sounded agitated. 'How can the network be busy? 111 calls are given priority.'

Henry knew that in an emergency the phone network could block calls, only allowing calls to emergency numbers to get through. 'There must be an enormous volume of calls if you're getting a busy signal,' he replied, struggling for air as he tossed another lump of concrete aside.

Despite the gravity of the situation, he realised that not one ambulance had been past. Not that he'd noticed anyway. How many injured were there? What were the emergency crews facing? He wondered if the old lady with the broken hip had been collected. It was quite possible that she wasn't at the top of the list of casualties and was still lying on the ground. How many had already been injured or killed? How many more might die because of a lack of resources? What level of disaster was this?

Henry knew it was bad, but just exactly how bad they probably wouldn't know for a while.

If they got Mark out alive and there were no ambulances, what then? Was this a futile exercise?

Finally he cleared the last piece of masonry which allowed him enough space to get access to Mark from the passenger side. The passenger door had been ripped off—it must have been open when the quake hit—but at least that meant there was room for Mark to be extricated. That was fortunate as they would have had no hope of prising him out otherwise without assistance. They would have needed to wait for the fire brigade and the 'jaws of life'.

Henry could see Mark and Maia. She was still in

the car. He wanted to get both of them out of there as quickly as possible. Mark needed urgent medical attention but Henry was also worried about more aftershocks. He didn't want to be on this street if there were more shocks coming and he definitely wanted Maia out of danger, out of harm's way. But Maia was still talking to Mark, who was still unresponsive.

Henry squatted down and reached into the car. His hands and nails were filthy—scratched, dirty and bleeding—but there was nothing he could do about that at present. He lifted Mark's eyelid with a dirty finger, first his left eyelid, then his right. It was difficult to see but he thought the right pupil contracted when exposed to light and wasn't so sure about the left. It was impossible to do a proper assessment, he didn't have the room or the equipment, but the situation was not looking good. Mark was barely breathing, he had a possible head injury, potential chest injuries and, from this side of the car, Henry could see that his left lower leg had been severely crushed by the compacted front of the car. He didn't like the look of that at all. In order for Mark to receive help they would need to negotiate getting him out of the car, but that looked almost impossible, given that the windscreen and dashboard had been compressed down hard onto his legs.

It was going to be a difficult and dangerous process to retrieve him and, depending on how badly damaged his left leg was, moving him could have dire consequences. Fatal, even. Henry could only guess at the amount of blood Mark had lost. Blood loss, an almost certain drop in blood pressure, shock, a possible head injury; Mark's odds of survival were decreasing by the second, and if he did survive Henry suspected it might cost him his leg.

'What do we do now?' Maia asked.

They were both looking at the mess, assessing the situation and trying to work out a solution.

'I don't know. It's going to be difficult to get him out of here and I really don't want to move him until we have an ambulance on standby. He's critically injured.' Henry was at a loss but he refused to admit defeat. There had to be a way.

He looked around him but there were no answers, only chaos. A policeman was crossing the square. Finally, someone who might be able to help. Henry whistled loudly and waved his arms, attracting attention, and the copper came over to them.

'Are you able to get through to the emergency services?' Henry asked. 'The network is blocked and this man needs to get to a hospital. He needs urgent medical attention and we need an ambulance.'

'There aren't any,' the policeman replied.

'What do you mean, there aren't any?'

'They're all busy. It's World War III around here. We've never needed so many ambulances all at once. There are more injured people than ambulances and the paramedics are working flat out.'

'This man is in a critical condition. Are you telling me there's nothing we can do?'

'I'm sorry, I know it's a tragedy, but I wouldn't count on getting an ambulance any time soon.'

'My ute is parked over there.' The construction worker interrupted Henry and the copper. 'It's no ambulance but do you reckon we could get him into the tray and I can take you to the hospital?'

It was a terrible option but it was also the only one on offer. Without urgent medical attention Mark would die, and Henry knew Mark wasn't going to get that attention lying on the street. He might not make it, but he *definitely* wouldn't make it if they didn't try something. But it didn't mean that this was Henry's decision to make. He would need Maia's help if he was going to have any chance of pulling this off but he knew she might decide the risk was too great.

'Maia, will you help me?'

'You want to take him to hospital in the back of a ute?'

She obviously thought he was crazy.

'With his wife's permission,' Henry said, as if that was all he needed for this to work. 'I have to do something. If I do nothing, he'll die on the street.'

Maia looked at Mark and then back at Henry. He could see the concern in her eyes but then she nodded. She would help.

Henry didn't waste any more time. He turned back to the construction worker. 'I'm sorry, mate, I don't even know your name.'

'Dean.'

'I'm Henry.' They shook hands—an automatic and ridiculously civilised gesture in incredibly uncivilised surroundings—while Henry continued. 'Can you back your ute up as close as you can get while I talk to Mark's wife?'

Susan was huddled on the bench. She looked fragile. It would be a good idea for her to be checked out at the hospital too. Henry sat beside her. 'Mark is alive but he's critically injured. He needs to get to a hospital but there are no available ambulances. We can try to get him out of the car and then transport him in the back of that ute.' Henry pointed at Dean's vehicle as he was backing it up to Susan's car. 'It's not ideal but I believe it's his only chance. But it needs to be your decision.' He wasn't positive that Susan was in any state to be making this call but her answer, when it came, surprised him. She sounded strong and decisive.

'I can't let him die here. We have to try.'

Henry nodded and returned to the car. Dean had manoeuvred his ute so that it sat at right angles to the rear of Susan's car. It was going to be an awkward retrieval. First they had to get Mark out of the car and then they would have to lift and carry him over the rubble. Henry hated to think of all the things that could go wrong. Were they going to do more harm than good?

But he didn't have a choice. If they did nothing, Mark had no chance.

'Okay. Let's do this.'

Dean had cleared some room in the back of his utility truck. Tool boxes, bags of cement and a ladder had been pushed to one side and amongst the tools Henry spied a length of rope and a tarpaulin.

'Dean, grab that tarp and that rope, we can use that,' he said as he started to plan the logistics of extricating Mark. 'Maia, I'll need you out here to help me.'

They really needed a cervical collar and a stretcher. A spinal board would be even better. A defibrillator and an airway might be handy. Pain relief. Fluids. The list went on and on, but they had none of those things, and they didn't have time to waste. They had neither the time nor the equipment to remove him with the utmost care. They would have to do the best they could.

'I need to fashion a tourniquet for his leg before we attempt to move him.' Henry was holding the length of rope in his hands. He was going to use that as his tourniquet. He slid the rope under Mark's thigh and ran it around twice, pulling it firm before knotting it as tightly as he could. The next problem was getting Mark out of the car. His legs were still trapped under the dashboard.

'Have you got a crowbar in your truck—anything that we might be able to use to remove this dashboard?' Henry asked Dean. This was when the jaws of life would have been really useful. 'We won't get him out like this.'

'I've got this,' Dean replied.

The car's windscreen was a spiderweb of lines. Smashed and damaged, it had shattered and was barely hanging on. Dean reached into the car and with one well-timed punch the entire windscreen fell out onto the bonnet. He moved around to the front of the car, reached over the bonnet and into the car through the hole where the windscreen had been moments before, grabbed the plastic dashboard and ripped it out with his bare hands.

'That worked.' Henry nodded in appreciation. 'Okay, next step. Maia, if you can support Mark's head and neck, I'll lift his body.' Henry worked through his plan aloud; it helped him to clarify the steps in his mind and meant that the others were on board with his plan as well. 'Dean, can you clear a bit of space behind us? We need a flat area to lay your tarp out; we'll use that as a makeshift stretcher to lift Mark into the ute.'

Henry left Dean to get on with that task while he had another look at the logistics of moving Mark. He saw his shirt wedged between the two front seats where he'd dropped it after lifting Sienna to safety. He pulled it free and wrapped it around Mark's legs, tying it tightly by the sleeves. Perhaps if he could support Mark's left leg by using his right, then all the pieces of Mark would come out of the car together.

'Ready?' He looked at Maia. Her face was streaked with dirt and her dark hair had come loose and curled around her face. The dark strands were coated with a layer of dust and she had flecks of paint stuck in her hair like confetti. Her brown eyes were huge in her face. She looked scared but she nodded. He was scared too. This was an awful situation.

Behind them Dean had prepared the tarpaulin. It was time.

Maia tucked herself in close to the car and reached carefully behind Mark, sliding her hands behind his head to cradle his head and neck. Henry stepped in beside her. His hips were touching hers as he slid one hand just above Mark's hips and his other hand above his knees. He was worried about spinal injuries but the real danger was with Mark's neck. As long as Maia held firm they would be doing their best to minimise the risk.

'On three?' he said.

Maia nodded.

Henry closed his eyes and said a brief, silent prayer, hoping they would get Mark out in one smooth, or smooth-ish, movement. He tightened his grip and counted. 'One, two, three...'

Somehow they managed to free Mark and lay him on the tarpaulin without mishap. It was probably a good thing he was unconscious. His pulse was weak, he was barely breathing and his chest was rising unevenly, but he was alive. Now they had to get him into their make-shift ambulance.

'Dean? Are you okay to give us a hand with this next move?' Henry asked. Dean looked big and tough; Henry just hoped he could stomach the rather confront-ing sight of Mark's traumatised leg.

'No worries.' He sounded confident.

'Great. We'll take one side each. Maia, you look after

Mark's head. Dean, roll up your side of the tarpaulin, get it as close to Mark as possible; that'll keep him stable.' Henry watched, making sure Dean followed his instructions to the letter. 'We'll put him into the ute feet first.'

Dean had dropped the sides of his utility down so they had easier access and with Mark cocooned in the tarp this part of the transfer was much easier. Henry and Dean slid Mark's unconscious form onto the tray while Maia kept his head as still as she was able. Once Mark was safely ensconced, Maia and Henry climbed in with him. They would have to act as the medical team en route to the hospital. Not that there was much they could do except try to stop him from being buffeted around too much.

Susan hovered by the vehicle. She kissed Mark's forehead before climbing into the cab, still clutching baby Sienna. Dean lifted the panels on the side of the tray, sliding the catches into place as Henry urged Maia to swap places with him. She looked wiped out. She'd done enough; he would take responsibility for Mark.

'We need to get him to the Queen Liz,' Henry told Dean. 'Do you know the way?'

Dean nodded.

'Take it carefully, not too slow, but avoid as many potholes and bumps as you can,' Henry instructed.

'No worries,' Dean said as he climbed into the front seat.

Henry sat with his legs either side of Mark's head and shoulders as he stabilised his neck. The metal tray of the ute was uncomfortable but he barely noticed. It was going to be a long, slow, bumpy ride to the hospital but what other choice did they have? They had none.

Maia sat on a bag of cement beside Mark's inert

form. She had her knees bent, her feet tucked against her bottom. She looked exhausted but she had coped brilliantly. He couldn't have managed without her. 'Are you okay?' he asked her.

She nodded. 'I think so.'

They were both filthy, covered in plaster dust and dirt, streaked white and brown. He licked his lips as he watched the world go by. His throat and lips were dry and his tongue felt swollen and was caked in dust. He could taste it. He would kill for a drink of water.

He was only vaguely aware that he was half-dressed, sitting bare-chested in the back of a ute as it crawled out of the CBD. His shirt was wrapped around Mark's legs, it was torn and bloodied and would never be worn again, and his cotton trousers were damp and splattered with mud. He could see some dark, dried blood on Maia's forearm and shirt. Neither of them had gloves or any sort of protection. His hands were filthy and he was worried about infection but again, with limited options, there was nothing more he could do until they reached the hospital—there was every chance that Mark wouldn't survive the journey anyway.

Traffic was moving slowly but the roads were dangerous. The bitumen was riddled with wide cracks and deep holes, and the traffic lights were all out, adding to the chaos. Dean had to negotiate the damaged roads as well as piles of fallen masonry, and dazed and confused pedestrians. Everyone was desperately trying to get out of the city. People were driving on the wrong side of the road, which increased the level of confusion, and pedestrians wandered like zombies onto the street without looking. It was like the apocalypse.

Red and blue lights flashed through the dusty haze. The fire department had joined the rescue effort. They had their ladders extended up building fronts and were rescuing people from windows and roofs of collapsed buildings, but their efforts were being hampered as several buildings had caught fire, adding to the danger. The burst water mains meant there was no water connected to the fire hydrants so the fires burnt uncontrollably.

Dean's ute bumped over the cracks in the mud-covered road and Henry could smell sewage and gas. Their vehicle joined a convoy of civilian cars heading out of the city as army trucks and the fire department's urban search-and-rescue vehicles took their place. Half a dozen water tankers followed the army trucks and Henry realised these were for the fire brigade. It was the only way they had to try to fight and contain the fires.

Helicopters, both army and media, buzzed overhead, and the sirens of the emergency vehicles could be heard near and far, but there was surprisingly little human noise. People were being assisted, and in some instances carried, from the rubble but along the side of the road Henry could see the shapes of those who had not been so lucky, their bodies covered with makeshift shrouds.

There were coordinated calls from search and rescuers—official and unofficial—but no distressed screams, no loud crying. Henry wondered whether people were afraid to add to the stress and tension, or perhaps they didn't have the energy to spare on superfluous noise or were too shocked. Even he and Maia were silent. But there was nothing for them to say. There was nothing more they could do.

He looked back at Maia. She hadn't moved. Her chin was resting on her knees as she stared into the distance and clutched the tarpaulin, trying to minimise the rolling motion. She looked sad and Henry longed to comfort her.

She was smeared with dirt and blood but she still looked beautiful. Heartbreakingly sad and beautiful. Her hair was a wild mess. Dark tendrils framed her face and fell over one eye and he wanted so badly to reach out and brush her hair back from her face. He knew exactly how traumatic these events would have been for her. He'd been through something similar before and he knew nothing could prepare you for the first time you experienced a disaster on this scale.

The breeze created by the movement of the vehicle carried a scent to him, the scent of frangipanis, sunshine and summer. Maia's scent. He'd missed her smell.

Was it really possible that he could smell her? It was ridiculous to think that he could smell something so sweet over and above the stench of the streets but he breathed deeply regardless, taking in his fill of Maia.

The idea was a pleasant distraction as they drove back to the Queen Liz. Back to where they had started their day. It was incredible to think it was only a few hours ago that they had been sitting in the darkened lecture theatre. Incredible to think about what had happened in those intervening hours. Thousands of lives had changed in that time, some lives had ended. It just demonstrated to him how important it was to make every minute count. Nothing could be wasted or taken for granted.

Maia had taken her mobile phone out of her pocket. She was typing a message with her thumb as she kept hold of the tarpaulin with her other hand. He wondered who she was texting. Her mother? Todd?

Maia paused and looked up at him, her dark eyes shining with unshed tears. 'How bad do you think this is?' she asked.

'I don't know.' He was supposed to be the expert but

he had no way of knowing the extent of the damage that the quake had caused. He suspected that the CBD had been hardest hit but that was only a guess. His gut was telling him it was bad but he wasn't going to share that feeling with Maia. He wasn't prepared to make a bad situation worse.

'I'm worried about Mum and my sisters. The phone network is busy but do you think a text will get through?'

That was something he did know. 'There's more chance that a text will go through—maybe not straight away, but it will send at some point.' He thought it would likely be some time before the phone network was free again but he knew how important it was for Maia to feel like she was doing something. He knew exactly how overwhelming and distressing the feeling of hopelessness and helplessness could be in these situations.

He could see her hand trembling as she pressed the keys on her phone. He was worried about her. She was shaking quite noticeably and he suspected she was in shock. That wasn't surprising, the events of the day had been extremely traumatic and the day wasn't over yet. He wanted desperately to take her in his arms and comfort her. To tell her everything would be okay. To tell her she'd been magnificent today. To tell her everything would be all right. But he couldn't do that. He didn't have the answers and, even if he had, Maia wasn't his to comfort. Not anymore.

The knowledge that Maia was marrying someone else was cutting him to the core. He hadn't been able to commit to her and she'd moved on without him. She was marrying someone else and there wasn't anything he could do about it. He wasn't the type to destroy someone else's relationship. If she was happy, then he'd be happy for her. He'd learn to be happy and, if he couldn't learn, he'd pretend.

He longed to comfort her but he had lost that privilege. Maia had moved on and he would have to accept that Todd had Maia's heart. For now, and perhaps for always.

CHAPTER SEVEN

DEAN PULLED HIS vehicle into the emergency entrance of the Queen Liz and came to a stop behind a row of ambulances. The ambulance bay was a hive of activity; medics were thick on the ground and Henry assumed they'd been going nonstop for some time.

'We need some help here,' he called out loudly, drawing attention to their arrival. He didn't want to be overlooked in the chaos, mayhem and madness. He couldn't afford any more delays. Not if they wanted to give Mark a chance.

Maia moved around to the rear of the tray and her hands replaced Henry's as she continued to stabilise Mark's neck. Their movements were coordinated and fluid as a silent understanding of what needed to be done passed between them. Henry leapt out of the ute and began to drop the sides as a trauma team joined them.

'Male in his thirties. Unconscious but breathing,' he said, giving them a summary of Mark's condition. 'Crush injuries, possible head injury, severe blood loss, major trauma to his left lower leg. We pulled him from a car but were only able to give very basic first aid at the scene.' He and Maia stepped back as the trauma team took over. Their involvement ended here but it was difficult to just walk away. They waited and watched while Mark was lifted onto a stretcher and rushed inside. Susan trailed in the wake of the medics, holding baby Sienna close. Blood continued to run from her head wound but Henry knew she wouldn't seek treatment until she knew that Mark was being taken care of.

Mark's stretcher disappeared through the emergency doors and two paramedics emerged in his place. One of them was Todd.

He didn't notice Henry, or if he did he didn't acknowledge him. His eyes went straight to Maia.

He was by her side in three strides. 'Maia!' He wrapped his arms around her and Maia burst into tears. 'Are you all right? What happened to you?'

Henry could see Maia shaking but it was impossible to tell if it was from shock or her tears. Despite the heat of the day he could see goose bumps on her arms and her tears made her incapable of speech.

Todd looked over her head at Henry as Maia cried against his shoulder. 'What happened?' he asked him. 'Is she hurt?'

'No.' Henry shook his head. 'She's fine. Just in shock. We were in the city on our way back to the Children's and got caught up in the middle of the quake. We're only here because we brought a casualty in to the hospital.'

Todd nodded, put his hands on Maia's shoulders and gently stood her back. 'Maia, sweetheart, are you really okay?' He brushed her hair from her eyes and wiped a tear from her face. Henry felt a pang of longing. He wanted to be allowed to do that. He wanted to be the one who had permission to comfort her.

Maia sniffed and nodded.

Todd pressed his lips into the side of Maia's head as

he cradled her face in his hands. 'I'm sorry,' he said, 'But I have to go. I have to get back into the city.'

Henry felt like a voyeur, witnessing this exchange, and he wondered if he should give them some privacy. But before he could drag himself away Todd turned to him again. 'Will you take care of her?' he asked.

'Of course,' Henry replied automatically.

Todd kissed Maia softly on her forehead. 'I'll see you later,' he said as he left her in Henry's care and returned to his ambulance.

'Do you need a ride somewhere or are you staying here?'

Henry glanced to his right. Dean was standing beside him. Maia still hadn't spoken and Henry was worried about her. She needed something to eat and a place to sit down and regroup. Todd had left Maia in his care, he'd given him permission to take care of her, but what Henry wanted was permission to comfort her, which was something entirely different.

Henry was conflicted. He thought he should probably take Maia inside to the hospital to get her checked out but he had a better idea. He knew she was only in mild shock. He'd keep an eye on her. She would be fine. He'd make sure of it.

'We're not staying here,' he told Dean. 'We need to get to the Children's Hospital.' He'd promised to take care of her and he'd be able to do that at the Children's. Maia should probably go home but Henry would be needed at the Children's and he wasn't about to send Maia off on her own. He didn't know how to get her home in any case and until he knew what the state of play was there for her he wasn't potentially going to put her into a traumatic situation. She'd heard nothing back from her mother as yet and he hoped that wasn't ominous. 'Could you give us a lift?'

'Course. No worries.'

Maia was wedged into the front seat of the ute, between Dean and Henry. She couldn't believe they'd managed to get Mark to hospital without killing him. When Henry had asked if she'd help she hadn't really considered the consequences. He'd needed her help and she'd offered it without a second thought. She trusted him, and if he'd thought it was a risk worth taking she wouldn't second guess him, but she couldn't believe it had turned out okay. So far. Who knew what would happen now for Mark? But at least they'd got him to the hospital alive. They'd done their best.

Dean had the windows up and the airconditioning on and Maia was feeling claustrophobic and cold. She was still shaking. She trembled against Henry's shoulder. She crossed her arms over her chest but she couldn't seem to stop the quivering.

Henry reached for the climate control and switched the airconditioning off. 'Do you mind if we have this off and put the windows down instead?' he asked Dean.

He wrapped his arm around her back and Maia tensed as his hand brushed the nape of her neck. If she'd been able to speak she would have asked him what he was doing but she was shaking so hard her teeth were chattering and talking was almost impossible. He rubbed her arms, attempting to warm her up, and her body responded to his touch, coming to life under his fingers. She could feel the blood begin to flow through her veins but his touch did more than warm her skin. His touch lit a fire inside her that spread from her belly to her limbs.

She was pressed against his chest. His naked, shirt-less chest. He was still half-dressed. His shirt had disappeared into the Queen Liz, wrapped around Mark's legs.

Henry had a nasty gash on his left pectoral muscle and several grazes on his abdominals. Maia tried to ignore them. She tried to pretend he wasn't half-naked and she wasn't pressed against him. No one at the Queen Liz had batted an eyelid at his semi-naked state—it wasn't the most unusual thing they had seen today or any day—and Maia had also forgotten that he was only semi-clothed. Until now.

She closed her eyes, trying to ignore his proximity. She couldn't move away. There was nowhere to go and she knew she didn't really want to. It was comforting to be held in Henry's arms. But, while closing her eyes meant she couldn't see his sculpted chest or the ridge of his abdominals or the light dusting of hair that covered his pectoral muscles, her other senses took over. Now she could smell him.

All three of them were coated with dirt and a trace of dust lingered in the air but Maia could smell something extra on Henry. He'd worked up a sweat trying to free Mark from the car and the sweat had dried, leaving something warm and a little bit salty overlaying his familiar citrus scent but there was something more: the metallic scent of iron. The distinctive smell of blood. His own or Mark's—she didn't know. It could be his. She would need to clean and dress those cuts and scrapes on his torso when they got to the Children's Hospital.

She finally stopped shaking. Henry's body heat and the touch of his hands had warmed her to the point where she could sit still. She thought she might even be able to talk again.

Her phone beeped with an incoming message. She fished it out of her pocket, trying not to move out of Henry's embrace as she swiped the screen. It was a text from her mother.

'Is everything okay?' Henry asked.

Maia nodded. 'It's Mum. She's fine and so are the girls, the house too. We have no power and no water but we do still have a house. She'll send updates on the extended family as she hears more.'

'Good news, then.'

It was very good news and Maia's heart lifted as Dean dropped them off in front of the Children's Hospital. She felt she could cope with anything else the day wanted to throw at her now that she knew her family and Todd were okay.

The contrast between here and the Queen Liz was remarkable. There was none of the chaos, no sense of drama and urgency, no evidence of trauma teams, no frantic arrival and departure of ambulances. One ambulance was just leaving and that was the extent of the activity.

They walked side by side into the emergency department. The waiting area was empty. Eerily quiet. Carrie was the only person there. She raced over to them as if expecting them to collapse at any moment. Maia wasn't surprised. She knew they looked like walking wounded. They were filthy, bloody and dishevelled.

'Oh, my God, are you two all right?'

'We're fine,' Henry said as he headed straight for the water cooler. He poured two cups of cold water and handed one to Maia before draining his own in a single gulp.

Water had never tasted as sweet nor as good, Maia thought as she washed away the layer of dust that coated her tongue and throat. They refilled their cups several times as Carrie paced impatiently, waiting for answers.

'You're not hurt?' Carrie looked them up and down, inspecting them for injuries. 'You've both got blood all over you, and Henry, you're covered in cuts.'

'They're not serious,' Henry said, shrugging off her concern. 'And most of the blood isn't ours. We were coming back through the city when the quake hit. We stopped to help.'

'According to the reports we've had the CBD has been hit hard,' Carrie said.

Henry nodded. 'It's a disaster. It looks like the images you see on the news of cities after a bomb blast. Was that where the worst damage was?'

Carrie nodded and confirmed Henry's earlier suspicions.

'It was the most horrific thing I've ever experienced,' Maia added. Despite the rather regular frequency of earthquakes in Christchurch this one really had been the most frightening one Maia had ever felt. The force of the quake and the scale of the disaster were like nothing they had ever experienced before. 'Buildings were collapsing like decks of cards; they fell on people and cars and buses. There were fires and floods and bodies everywhere. It was horrible. The bell tower of the cathedral is gone—we were almost under it when it fell—and the Press Building has been destroyed. It was terrifying.' Now that she was out of danger she could admit how frightened she'd been.

'Brenda's husband works in the Press Building,' Carrie said.

'Keith?' In the stress of the day Maia had forgotten that she knew someone in that building.

Carrie was nodding. 'Brenda hasn't heard from him.'

Her voice caught in her throat and Maia could see the question in her eyes. 'No news is good news, right?'

Maia wasn't so sure. She remembered the noise as the roof had caved in and the sight of tonnes of building material crashing into the office space below. She'd seen the devastation in the city and watched that building and others collapse. She'd seen the bodies of the victims lying on the street and she knew there would be more to come. But there was nothing she could do and what could she say?

She turned to Henry. She could feel herself starting to shake once more. 'What do we tell Brenda?'

'Nothing,' he replied. 'We don't have any details. Any facts. Hopefully she might not think to ask us. Anything we say would be supposition—that's not helpful. If she can't contact her husband, the police or Urban Search and Rescue are the ones who will give her any news, and only when they know for certain. She doesn't need to know we've been in the city.' He looked from Maia to Carrie. He knew what it was like to be given false hope and he didn't want to put someone else in that situation. He waited for their nod of agreement before he continued. 'We came back here to lend a hand but I didn't expect it to be so quiet.'

'We had a few patients brought in early,' Carrie said. 'But, touch wood, there doesn't appear to have been too many children hurt.'

Maia rapped her knuckles against her head in a superstitious gesture as Carrie continued. 'The epicentre of the quake was at Lyttelton, and the worst of the damage is on that side of the city through to the CBD, but we're expecting the overflow of adult patients from the other hospitals. There are already hundreds injured and of course that toll is expected to climb. I think we're about to be run off our feet. We're about to test your new system.'

'We need to get cleaned up, then,' Henry said, in control and in charge.

'We're running on generators and we've got no water for showers. The best you'll be able to do is the antibacterial hand sanitisers and then antiseptic wipes,' Carrie told him. 'Do you need me to get you anything?'

'I don't think so. Thanks,' Maia said as she and Henry headed for a treatment cubicle.

'Okay, I'll let Brenda know you're here and leave you to it,' Carrie said as she bounced off.

They were both filthy—dusty, blood-stained and sweaty. Hand sanitisers and wipes were not going to cut it. Maia took two empty bowls from a cupboard and told Henry to follow her. She filled the bowls from the water cooler and gave them to Henry to take back to the cubicle while she fetched two sets of surgical scrubs. She ducked into the change room and quickly stripped off her own filthy clothes before grabbing some hand towels from the linen supply.

She returned to the cubicle and dropped the clean scrubs beside the sink before soaking a towel in the bowl of cool water and handing it to Henry. 'The water might be a bit fresh but we'll have to wipe some of the dirt off before we can hope to get decently clean.' She soaked a second towel for herself and wiped her face and arms, removing as much of the dirt and dust as she could, while Henry did the same. She threw the towel in the dirty linen bag and took her engagement ring off to put it onto her necklace so she could clean her hands properly.

As she removed it she noticed that one of the claws holding the diamond into the setting had been bent. She must have caught it on something while they'd been evacuating Mark. She checked to make sure the stone wasn't loose and wasn't in danger of falling out before she slid the ring onto the chain and fastened it around her neck. She felt terrible that she'd damaged the ring; thank God she hadn't lost the stone.

She plunged her hands into the bowl of cool water and scrubbed her nails. Henry was still wiping over his chest and arms but she tried to keep her eyes averted. She didn't need that distraction. She was managing quite well until she heard him inhale quickly, as if he was in pain. She looked up and could see that the cut on his left pectoral muscle had started to bleed as he'd wiped the towel across his chest.

'Sit down and I'll do your back for you,' she told him. 'And then I'll attend to those cuts.' She had offered to help clean him up. She gave him a clean towel. 'Put some pressure on that cut,' she said as she took a second fresh towel, soaked it and wiped it over Henry's back. She ran the cloth over his shoulders slowly, enjoying the feel of his warm skin under her fingers. It was an intimate motion.

She finished his back and moved around to stand in front of him. He had always been muscular but lean—he'd played on the wing in the university rugby team—but he'd bulked up over the past three years and still looked good. Really good. His shoulders were square and broad, the muscles in his arms well-defined, his chest hair dark, his stomach flat and his abdominals ripped.

She wiped a few traces of dirt from his chest, avoiding the more serious cuts. She pulled on a pair of gloves and concentrated hard on cleaning his injuries, putting antiseptic and dressings on. There was a nasty gash on the inside of his right arm, another one on his left chest and several grazes over his abdominals from leaning into the car. Maia could feel his body heat radiating from him and her hands shook as she applied antiseptic ointment to the cut on his chest.

'Are you okay?' he asked.

'I'm fine.' It wasn't fatigue or even shock that was making her jittery now, it was her proximity to a semi-naked Henry that was making her wobble, but she wasn't going to admit defeat. She didn't want someone else to take over; she didn't want anyone else getting this close to him. She was perfectly capable of finishing what she'd started.

But, standing this close, she wasn't really sure where to look, what was appropriate. She focused on the dimple in his chin. She'd always loved that. Along with his full lips the dimple added a bit of softness to his very masculine features. His strong brow, chiselled cheekbones and square jaw were all softened by the dimple. She was tempted to run her thumb over it but instead she opened another dressing pack and carefully placed it over the cut on his chest.

All that was left now was the cut on the inside of his right biceps. She took his elbow in her hand and turned his arm out, exposing the paler flesh of his upper arm.

'Are you up to date with your tetanus shots?' she asked as she put the last dressing on and gathered up the rubbish.

'Yes.'

Maia turned to the bin to throw the rubbish away. 'You need to get…' She turned back as she spoke and was confronted by the sight of Henry bending over to pull his trousers off over his feet. He was wearing navy boxer shorts, she couldn't help but notice, and very little else. His bottom was round and firm and perfect.

He straightened up, holding his trousers in one hand.

He stood in front of her, now almost totally naked. His boxer shorts had a white band of elastic at the waist. It made his olive skin look darker than it would normally and drew her eye.

No, that wasn't what was drawing her eye. His shorts were a snug fit and left very little to the imagination. Not that she needed to rely on her imagination—she'd seen it all before. Many times. But she shouldn't be looking there now.

'I need to get what?' Henry said, reminding her that she had been halfway through a sentence, but Maia had completely lost her train of thought. She'd been completely and utterly distracted by the sight of a nearly naked Henry and her brain was having difficulty thinking about anything except Henry in boxer shorts.

She blushed and swallowed hard as she lifted her eyes to his face and tried to remember what she'd been going to say. 'Dressed,' she said.

He grinned; his perfect, full lips parted, showing off his even white teeth as he laughed. 'That wasn't what you were going to say.'

He was right, it wasn't. It wasn't even what she really wanted. But she shouldn't be so happy to stand here and ogle a semi-naked man, be it Henry or otherwise. 'No, I was going to suggest that you get some antibiotics,' she said when she remembered what the end of her sentence should have been.

'Sorry,' he apologised. 'I didn't mean to make you uncomfortable. I needed to change my clothes and I didn't stop to think.' He didn't look sorry. He was smiling, the dimple in the centre of his chin had disappeared and his eyes sparkled with amusement.

'It's okay.' She was a nurse after all. She'd seen plenty of naked bodies, although not many had been quite so spectacular.

Henry cleared his throat, and she realised her eyes had drifted south again, but there was nothing she could do. She was transfixed, mesmerised, hypnotised by the sight of him. His hips were lean, his thighs were strong and powerful, and Maia could feel her heart pounding.

She forced her eyes back to his face.

His eyes had turned dark with desire. She could see it in his expression. His indigo-blue eyes were devouring her, poring over her as if she too were naked.

He was standing mere inches from her. She had nowhere to go, nowhere to hide. She was trapped between the bench and a smiling and almost completely naked Henry.

CHAPTER EIGHT

HENRY REACHED PAST her and it took all her self-control and willpower not to step in towards him, not to close those last few centimetres and press herself up against his naked flesh. His arm brushed against hers as he reached for the clean set of scrubs that she'd left on the bench. This time he was touching her. It felt different from when she'd been touching him, from when she'd been running the cloth over his bare skin. Now he was in control. Before, she had held the upper hand.

She could feel his breath on her cheek as he leant towards the counter. She pressed herself backwards, and felt the hard edge of the bench top digging into her lower back, but the discomfort wasn't enough to distract from her reaction to Henry's proximity. Her nipples peaked in response to his breath on her cheek, to the touch of his arm. A ripple of desire shot through her, running from her breasts to the junction of her thighs, turning her legs to jelly. She pressed herself harder against the bench, knowing that was the only thing holding her up. Why was her body intent on betraying her? Betraying Todd? Because that was what it felt like. She'd made a promise to Todd but her body was making it difficult to keep.

What was she doing? She was engaged to be married. She needed to remember herself and her promises.

Her father would be shocked and horrified if he could see her now. He valued loyalty and family above anything else. He had considered Todd family and there was no greater sin than to be disloyal to your family. She picked up the scrubs and handed them to Henry, forcing him to move back as she stepped around him. 'You're all done.' Her voice wobbled as she tried to get herself under control. 'I'll see you outside,' she added before she fled from the cubicle.

By six in the evening Maia was physically and emotionally exhausted. She'd been working nonstop treating myriad patients, mostly adults who were being diverted from the Queen Liz and who were presenting with simple fractures, concussions, burns, chest pain and respiratory complaints. She wasn't having to deal with anything that was overly taxing medically but the emotional trauma for a lot of these patients was sometimes more harrowing than their physical injuries.

Hospitals around the city couldn't cope with the influx of injured, and people with minor injuries—cuts, abrasions and minor burns—were being turned away and sent instead to doctor's surgeries and first-aid facilities that had been set up in the suburbs. The injury toll was already into the thousands and continuing to climb.

Patients with more serious fractures or multiple fractures as well as internal injuries were being taken into surgery. The surgeons, including Henry, and theatre staff were being kept busy too.

Updates were coming through from the emergency services. The ambulance officers were the main source of information but there was also a battery-powered radio on the desk and, although the volume was kept low, it was enough to enable them to catch the occasional news broadcast.

The television screen in the emergency department which usually showed children's programmes was blank. No power in the city meant no television, which meant no live crosses to the disaster zones, which Maia thought was a good thing. No one needed to watch images of the disaster. They were living it.

Fifty-eight had been confirmed dead but still that toll was expected to rise. There would be no quick fix to the situation. The search and rescue and recovery would go on throughout the night.

Time was critical. Fortunately it was summer so the temperature and exposure to the elements weren't significant risk factors but the serious injuries people were anticipated to have sustained meant that the longer they went untreated or unrecovered increased the chance that they wouldn't make it. Death from trauma, asphyxia, burns and acute respiratory distress due to the dust in the air were all very real possibilities and infection would get more people.

But there wasn't time to think about what would happen in the next week or even tomorrow. Patients continued to arrive and as Maia finished with another case she got news that another ambulance was on its way. She headed for the loading bay.

'Maia, what are you still doing here?' Henry had been in Theatre for the past few hours but he appeared to be between cases now. 'You look exhausted. Why haven't you gone home?'

She felt dreadful but she didn't need to be told she looked it too. 'I can't get home. The buses aren't running and I don't have a car,' she told him.

'At least take a break, then. I'll figure something out but you need to sit down before you fall down.'

She wobbled on her feet as fatigue swamped her.

Henry caught her. He held her by her elbow and she leaned against him with relief. It felt good to have someone there to take care of her. It felt good that it was Henry.

'Have you had anything to eat?' he asked.

She frowned. They'd missed lunch. 'Breakfast?' That was hours ago, before the morning's seminar. Was it still the same day? It felt like she'd lived a whole week.

'The kitchen has just delivered some platters of sandwiches to the staff room. Will you please go and eat something? I promised Todd I'd look after you,' he said, reminding her that she wasn't really his responsibility and he wasn't hers to lean on.

'I'll just get this patient inside and then I'll have something to eat,' she said as the ambulance pulled in.

She saw Henry open his mouth, and knew he was about to argue his point with her, but before he could say anything the rear doors of the ambulance opened and Todd climbed out.

He looked like he'd been in the trenches. It was the only time Maia could remember that he didn't look immaculate. The knees of his uniform were caked in mud and his top was splattered with dirt and blood. But his first concern was for her. 'Maia, are you all right?'

Was he about to tell her how dreadful she looked too?

'She's exhausted. She needs to go home.' Henry answered for her before she'd had a chance to speak.

Great, now she would have two of them trying to tell her what was best for her. She opened her mouth to protest against being spoken about as though she was a child but she was too tired to argue. Add in some drama, fatigue and light-headedness from hunger, and she was really struggling. But she wasn't prepared to be sent on her way just yet. 'Don't worry about me,' she said. 'What have you got?'

Todd pulled a stretcher from the ambulance. A boy of about ten lay there, his face as white as the sheet that covered him. 'This is Patrick. Aged eleven. Crush injuries chest and torso, fractured arm, clavicle and probably scapula. BP one hundred over sixty. Pulse one-twenty. He was having a dentist appointment in the city and the building collapsed. He's had IV morphine, respiration monitored, rate fifteen.'

Poor kid, Maia thought; if he didn't like the dentist before he was going to hate it now.

Todd's paramedic partner, Jeremy, and Patrick's mum climbed out of the front of the ambulance.

'X-rays first,' Henry said as they wheeled Patrick into the hospital, where they were met by Brenda.

'I'll take over for you, Maia,' Brenda told her. 'You need to take a break, have something to eat. Have you boys eaten?' she asked Todd and Jeremy. 'There are sandwiches in the staff room,' she said. 'You can help yourselves once we've got this young man sorted.'

Maia didn't bother arguing. She went into the staff kitchen and looked longingly at a chair but she was reluctant to sit down. She was pretty sure that once she sat she wouldn't be able to make herself get up again.

Todd and Jeremy joined her but they didn't hesitate, sitting down and tucking straight into the food.

Maia gave in. She took an egg-and-salad sandwich and a beef-and-mustard one and sat while Todd got up and made coffee. She had just finished her second half sandwich and was debating about a third when Brenda came in.

'Thanks for your help today, Maia. I think we'll manage from here on. Why don't you go home?'

'Did Henry tell you to send me home?' Maia could tell Henry had been in her ear.

'Maia, you're not even supposed to be at work today,' Brenda went on. 'I appreciate your help, we all do, but I need you to get some rest. I need you back on deck tomorrow and I can't afford to have my nurses exhausted. Tired nurses make mistakes.'

'And what about you? When are you going to have a rest?'

'When Keith is found.'

'Has there been any news?' Maia knew that Brenda had been going flat out, trying to keep herself too busy to think about her missing husband.

Brenda shook her head. 'No and that's why I'm staying. I want to be here in case Keith is brought in. I'll feel better if I stay close to the action. I've asked the ambos and the Queen Liz to let me know if he's taken somewhere else.'

That was fair enough. Maia knew she would feel the same.

Todd drained his cup of coffee. 'We'll drop you home on our way back to the station, Maia. Have you heard from your mum? Is everything okay at home?'

She knew what he was asking. Was there a house and family to go home to?

'It's all good,' she said as fatigue finally got the better of her. Suddenly going home seemed like a very good idea. She didn't argue any further. She fetched her filthy clothes from the change rooms, and once Todd and Jeremy were ready to go she went with them. She didn't see Henry on her way out; he was probably back in Theatre, maybe operating on Patrick. She wondered if and when he'd get to leave.

Jeremy took a seat in the rear of the ambulance and offered Maia the front seat with Todd. Maia moved a bright yellow hard hat and high-visibility jacket to the floor and climbed up. Todd reached over and put his hand on her thigh before he started the engine. 'Are you really okay?'

'Yes, I'm fine.' Todd's hand was warm, she could feel it through the thin cotton of her scrubs, but his touch didn't make her heart race or her body feel as if it might self-combust. What was wrong with her? Was it just fatigue? Why didn't she respond to Todd in the same way her body responded to Henry? Was he too familiar? Was it the forbidden element with Henry?

She put her hand over the top of his as she tried to remember what she would do in these situations normally, even though nothing about today felt remotely normal. 'You're the one I'm worried about,' she said. 'You're the one who has to keep returning to the danger zone.' At least she could say the right things, even if she wasn't feeling them.

They turned left at the River Avon and skirted the city. The streets leading into the CBD had been blocked off with temporary barriers, set up in chicanes to allow only the emergency crews through. Todd could have driven the ambulance through the city but there was no need to. It would be quicker to circumnavigate it and he would be back to help soon enough.

'How are things looking in there?' Maia asked. She could see police cars, ambulances, fire engines and armoured troop carriers, as well as trucks transporting generators and floodlights. Being summer, the sun wouldn't set until late—it wouldn't get dark until around nine o'clock—but Maia knew the emergency crews would be working through the night.

'It's bad, Maia. Really bad. We've never seen anything like it. The quake was a magnitude of six-point-three, but it was only five kilometres below the surface and the damage is just incredible. You saw the buildings around the square. Multiply that tenfold. I don't think there's a building left standing in the CBD that isn't damaged, if it's been left standing at all.'

'Did you see the cathedral?' she asked. Even now, just thinking about the state of the glorious old building made her feel like crying. Their wedding was supposed to be held there in four weeks' time. That was one decision they'd made about the wedding that she hadn't minded. Although she would have been just as happy to get married in a park or on the beach, her dad had loved the cathedral and she'd felt that was a decision he would have approved of.

'I did.'

'I'm terrified to think how many people might have been in the bell tower when it collapsed.'

'The canine search-and-rescue team have been brought in. From what I've heard, the dogs haven't found any trace of people in there.'

Maia sighed with relief. Finally some good news. 'I don't think I could bear to get married in there if people have been killed.'

Todd looked at her very briefly. 'It's not a sign, Maia. It doesn't mean anything other than the building wasn't built to withstand a quake of this force. This was a natural disaster, nothing more. But I should tell you, I don't think we'll be getting married there regardless. There's no way that building will be declared safe.'

Of course it wouldn't. Maia had seen the devastation for herself but she hadn't stopped to think what it would mean for them. 'Oh.'

'Don't worry. I'll sort something out,' Todd was quick to reassure her. 'The only sign you need to worry about is the one that says we are all okay. You and me and your family.'

His comment made her think about all the other families that weren't so lucky. 'How are the people in Lyttelton?' she asked. The suburb at the centre of the quake was only ten kilometres from the city. She'd seen the extent of the destruction in town and wondered how much worse things were at the centre of it all.

'It's odd,' Todd replied. 'The worst of the damage is actually in the city. There haven't been any reported fatalities in Lyttelton itself, not so far anyway. I guess I'll find out more as the night unfolds.'

'You'll be working all night?' she asked. 'Won't someone relieve you?'

'I doubt it. There just aren't enough of us to go around. We can't stop until everyone is accounted for and it will take time for other crews to arrive from around the country to assist us. The airport is still closed. There are teams arriving by road from the rest of the country but they have to fly into the south island and then drive here. The Australians are coming too but until others arrive we'll have to manage. Even with help we'll be working through the night and possibly through many nights,' he said as he pulled into Maia's driveway.

Her house was at the end of a cul-de-sac and it was

usually a quiet street. The neighbourhood was on the northern beaches, a reasonable distance from the city, and didn't attract big crowds, but tonight the front lawn was packed with cars and there were people everywhere. The place was teeming with uncles and aunts and cousins. Not a crowd, per se, just relations.

'It looks like Grand Central Station,' Todd said as he switched off the engine.

Maia frowned. It wasn't unusual to have dozens of people at their place; she had a large extended family and family gatherings were commonplace. Once a month they held a *hangi*, a traditional Maori barbecue, that all family members were invited to, but that was always on the last Sunday of the month which wasn't until the coming weekend. The only reason there could be so many people here today was because of the earthquake. She wondered what had happened. She hoped it wasn't the worst that she could imagine.

Todd had hopped out of the ambulance and had come around to open Maia's door for her. He waited for her to climb out and then kissed her goodbye. 'I can't come in. I have to get back to work.'

'That's okay, thanks for bringing me home.' She actually didn't mind that he couldn't come in. She wasn't sure she wanted him to. As selfish as it sounded, she didn't have the energy to spend on anyone else, even someone as undemanding as Todd.

She needed some time to herself, she needed some space. Looking at all the people milling around the house, she realised she probably wasn't going to get it, but she had to try to sort through her feelings.

Why hadn't Todd's kiss made her heart race? Why hadn't it left her wanting more? Why didn't he make her feel like Henry did? There was none of the same excitement or anticipation or feelings of new beginnings. And she knew it wasn't just because they'd been together for over two years. Todd had *never* made her feel that way. She had thought that perhaps it was just circumstances but, now that she had experienced it again with Henry, she knew that wasn't the case. Henry left her feeling breathless, alive, wanting more. It was almost impossible to drag herself away from him and her body responded immediately whenever he was near. She was aware of Henry on so many levels.

This was bad.

She hoped her feelings were just a culmination of a stressful day. She was exhausted and emotionally fragile. She needed to sort herself out.

She gave Henry up three years ago. She couldn't have him back now. She needed to move on. She'd done it once. She could do it again.

By the following morning the power had been restored to Maia's house and to three quarters of the city but the restoration of power brought more bad news. Overnight the death toll had climbed to seventy-five, over two hundred people were still missing and the injury toll was in the thousands. Even more people had been made homeless either because their houses had been completely destroyed or because engineers had deemed the buildings unstable and therefore too dangerous to be in.

Her house had been total chaos. Not in the same vein as the devastation caused by the quake—her house hadn't been damaged in any way—but the chaos had ensued as a direct result of that because it was one of the few houses amongst her extended family that had escaped unscathed. Several relatives' houses hadn't been so lucky but fortunately no one had been badly injured. Accommodating an extra dozen or so was no problem and her cousins were happy to sleep on spare mattresses or camp in the garden.

But amongst the tales of woe were some remarkable tales of survival. After more than eighteen hours the Urban Search and Rescue teams were still finding survivors. People were being pulled from the wreckage alive. She knew that the first twenty-four to forty-eight hours were critical in that regard. After forty-eight hours, the chances of survival decreased rapidly until they were close to zero. Ninety-five per cent of people who survived entrapment were rescued within the first two days. The warm summer temperatures were a blessing, although that increased the effects of dehydration, but that could be counteracted as long as people were still alive.

Maia listened to the radio on her way into work. The bad news was interspersed with good but it was still difficult to listen to. There was so much pain and suffering, both physical and emotional, but she felt she needed to know what was going on. So much was happening so quickly. She almost thought she might prefer the bubble of denial that had been possible when there had been no power and limited communication.

The majority of the city still had no water and no sewerage, which meant infection control and gastroenteritis were going to be problems, along with the supply of fresh, safe drinking water. Even residents who had mains water were being advised to boil it twice before consuming it. Tourists were being evacuated, but at least the airport had reopened, which made that job a lot easier.

The community of Christchurch and the greater Canterbury area were rallying together as help came from further afield. Food and water were being brought in from other cities and the army had set up tents and temporary accommodation at several schools. Welfare centres had also been established at some of the local churches and sporting clubs, as well as the schools, and people were able to access food, water, shelter, and warm clothing and blankets. But just as importantly the welfare centres provided victims of the disaster with company and stopped the feeling of isolation that many displaced people experienced.

The aftershocks continued but they were lessening in frequency. There had been hundreds of small ones right through the night, but fortunately nothing like the main quake.

Maia waved to Brenda through her office window as she came into the ED. Brenda looked exhausted and Maia was surprised to find her still here. That could only mean that Keith hadn't been found yet, which wasn't good news.

The first order of the day would be a staff meeting to update the new shift about what was going on currently in the department. Maia headed for the kitchen. She'd make a coffee while she waited for the meeting to start. It would be her third of the morning. She was making up for the caffeine hits she'd missed yesterday due to the power outage. In lieu of a shower she'd made do with a swim in the pool at home and with a couple of coffees under her belt she suspected she might soon feel almost human.

She had just taken a mug from the cupboard when Henry walked into the kitchen. He had a surgical mask hanging from his neck and a theatre cap on his head. He snapped the ties as he walked into the room. He pulled the mask from his neck and threw it into the bin along with the cap.

Maia's heartbeat quickened at the sight of him. His dark hair was messy and he was unshaven. His beard grew quickly and the darkness of his stubble made his eyes look more blue and less indigo. She hadn't been able to forget the feel of his body under her fingers, the warmth of his skin, the firmness of his muscles or how it felt to be in his arms. She was having trouble sorting through her emotions. She knew it was partly because of the drama of the past twenty-four hours but the emotion was heightened by her reaction to him.

'You had an early start,' she said as she clicked a coffee pod into the machine and tried to ignore the traitorous stirrings of her body.

'I haven't left. I operated most of the night.' There was a plate of fresh sandwiches and another one of muffins on the table. Henry picked up a muffin. 'You got home all right?'

Maia nodded.

'And your family? Everyone is okay?'

'They're all fine. Some of them have lost their homes, so we've got a few extras camped out at our place, but everyone is physically okay.'

Maia handed him a coffee and his fingers brushed hers as he took it out of her hand. Maia had been expecting the contact, she'd prepared herself for it, but the shock of awareness still took her by surprise. She jumped and coffee slopped over the side of her mug.

Henry lifted a handful of paper serviettes from the dispenser in the middle of the table and passed them to her. She avoided his eyes as she cleaned up the mess, avoided looking at his lips as he bit into the muffin.

'Was Brenda here all night too?' she asked. 'She looked exhausted when I came in.'

Henry nodded.

'She must know that the Press Building collapsed?'

He nodded again.

'But there's been no news about Keith?'

'No.'

Maia sank into a chair as guilt swamped her. 'We should have said something yesterday. I should have told her about the Press Building. She might have been able to go into the city and find out more.' She'd said nothing to Brenda yesterday about the building. She'd been so busy but she also knew she'd chosen not to. She hadn't known anything definite and, as Henry had said, it wasn't her place to speculate. But she regretted it now. If she'd been in Brenda's shoes she would have wanted to know. 'I watched that building collapse,' she said. She was close to tears.

Henry stood up from the table and put his arms around her. She didn't resist his embrace. She rested her head against his chest and let him comfort her. It felt good. She didn't care if anyone walked in on them. Nothing was going to surprise people today.

'It's not your fault, Maia.'

'I know that but I should have said something. But if she knows now, why is she still at work? Why hasn't she been into the CBD?'

'She wasn't allowed in,' Henry replied. 'The CBD was closed off last night to everyone with the exception of emergency services.'

Maia had forgotten that, even though she'd seen it for herself when Todd had taken her home. But it didn't make it any easier. She wished now that she had said something. Guilt swamped her. Was it survivor guilt? Was she feeling guilty because she'd survived and so many hadn't? No, she refused to accept that Keith hadn't survived, not yet. But thinking of survivors made her think about Mark and Susan. She lifted her head to look up at Henry.

'What about Mark?' She was almost too scared to ask. Did she really want to know? What if it was bad news? 'Have you heard any news on him?'

Henry was nodding. 'I spoke to a mate at the Queen Liz this morning. He escaped without head or spinal injuries but they had to amputate his leg below the knee. But he made it through and by all accounts he's doing as well as can be expected.'

That was good news, in a way. She knew it was better than the alternative but it still wasn't great. Emotion and fatigue swamped her. She stepped out of Henry's embrace as the other ED staff members began to enter the kitchen ready for the morning update and wondered when the news would improve.

Brenda waited until the staff was assembled before telling them what they could expect this shift according to the S&R teams who were communicating from the exclusion zone in the CBD. Brenda looked wrecked but her voice was strong.

'Survivors are still being pulled from the rubble,' she said and Maia knew she was still hopeful that Keith would be amongst them. 'Like yesterday we expect to get the overflow from the general hospitals and the injuries will be at either end of the spectrum—minor injuries in those who might have been turned away yesterday and didn't present to the first-aid centres, or the more seriously injured if the other hospitals are at capacity and can't cope with the additional load. People are mainly presenting with fractures, respiratory conditions, concussion, dehydration and burns. I want you working in teams, as Henry outlined in his in-service, and there are job cards for everyone, including any ward staff we call in. As ED staff you will be the lead doctors and nurses for any cases.'

The meeting was short. Everyone knew their jobs. The routine was much the same as any other day with the exception being that many of their patients would be adults, not children. As Maia followed Henry and Brenda out of the meeting, she could hear them discussing the procedures for the day until Brenda paused midsentence and stopped in her tracks. Maia almost crashed into the back of her and, when she looked up to see what the problem was, she found two police officers waiting in their path. The officers—one male, one female—were holding their hats in their hands and they both had solemn expressions on their faces. They obviously were not here with good news.

'We're looking for Brenda Westin,' the female officer said.

Maia felt herself go pale as the blood rushed out of her head, leaving her feeling light-headed. There could be only one reason they wanted to see Brenda.

Maia saw Brenda's knees buckle but fortunately Henry caught her before she hit the floor.

'This way,' Henry said to the police officers, leading the way to Brenda's office as he half carried her. Henry closed the door behind them and he and Maia sat on either side of Brenda, ready to support her. Introductions were made before the female officer continued.

'A number of bodies have been recovered from the Press Building,' she said.

Maia felt sick. She'd watched that building collapse.

'Keith?' Brenda asked. 'Have you found Keith?'

Brenda had gone pale and Maia thought she might either vomit or faint.

'We have a list of people who have been reported missing along with their last known location, but we haven't been able to positively identify all of the victims. That's why we are here. We want people identified—we need relatives to come to the morgue.'

Brenda started to shake. Maia wrapped an arm around her shoulders as she fought back tears.

'Are there any survivors still trapped inside?' Brenda asked, holding on to hope.

'The USAR teams are still searching. There are still people unaccounted for, so there could possibly be survivors, but nothing has been confirmed at the moment.'

Maia could hear in the police officer's voice that she thought it was unlikely that survivors would be found but she wasn't going to say as much.

'Do you have someone who can go with you? A family member?'

'My daughter is on her way here from Auckland. I have no idea what time to expect her. Transport is chaotic. I don't want to wait for her. I need to know if it's Keith.' She turned to Maia. 'I can't ask Louise to potentially ID her own father! I couldn't do that.'

'Of course not,' Maia agreed. 'Would you like me to come with you?' she offered. 'I know Keith.' She refused to use past tense.

'Would you?'

'Yes, of course.'

Carrie knocked lightly on the office door and as she entered Henry pulled Maia aside. 'Maia, it's not going to be anything like what you expect.'

'I know but I've seen plenty of dead bodies. I work in emergency.'

'I realise that, but these bodies will most likely be severely damaged. Some will be unrecognisable. The information I've received is saying that we will have to resort to DNA testing to identify some. It's not like seeing someone who has died of natural causes. It'll be worse than car accidents. Let me go with Brenda. I can't identify Keith but I can support Brenda. I know what to expect.'

Maia could see the pain in his eyes. Henry had been in the same situation. He already had those memories.

Maia looked around the ED. It was still quiet. She knew Carrie would take Brenda's place as ED Director—she was the most qualified—so she asked, 'Carrie, if Henry and I take Brenda to the morgue, will you be able to manage without all three of us?'

'Sure. I can call in reinforcements from the wards as per Henry's disaster management plan.'

'Okay,' Maia said as she turned back to Henry. 'We'll all go.' She appreciated that he was trying to shield her but she doubted the process would be as easy for him as he was trying to make it out to be. He wanted to protect her but she also wanted to be there to support him.

'Where have you taken the victims?' she asked the police officers.

'We've had to move them to the morgue at the army base. Do you know where it is?'

Maia nodded.

'You'll need this pass.' The male police officer handed her a letter.

They took Brenda's car. Maia drove. She knew where she was going. The Children's Hospital was west of the city, the army base was to the south. The streets

weren't too badly damaged on this side of the city but
it was slow going due to the detours. Traffic was being
diverted to the streets that could take the cars as whole
other sections of the city had been blocked off. They
drove in silence.

The letter gave them admission to the base and the
army chaplain met them in the administrative offices
and accompanied them to the morgue. Brenda declined
his offer to accompany her inside.

They introduced themselves to the army surgeon
and the mortuary attendant, a routine that felt civilised,
yet slightly inappropriate. It seemed ridiculous to ob-
serve the niceties of society, given the circumstances,
but maybe, Maia thought, when your world was crum-
bling around you those traditions became the glue that
held you together.

The room was cold and brightly lit. It was like walking into a giant freezer. The walls were tiled and the
concrete floor had a large drain in the centre. Maia
didn't want to contemplate why the army had such a
large and modern morgue.

A wall of drawers faced them and a row of stainless-
steel tables lined the centre of the room. Two large sinks
were positioned up against a glass window that looked
into a smaller dissection room and surgical equipment—
knives, saws and pliers—hung on the wall. The bright
overhead lighting meant there were no dark corners,
there was nowhere to hide. There was nowhere to escape the fact that death surrounded them.

Bodies had been grouped together depending on
where they had been found. White sheets were draped
over the corpses but most had their feet exposed. Tags
had been attached to the toes of the victims noting
where the body had been recovered from. There were

five in a row with 'Press Building' written on the tag. The only further information was either male or female notation.

Maia took Brenda's hand in hers as the army surgeon led them to the first body in the group.

Brenda walked slowly along the line, looking at the feet. Maia walked with her, holding her hand. She could feel Henry behind them and she held her free hand out. She needed to have Henry with her too. He took her hand, reassuring her.

The fourth body in the line didn't have a toe tag. The feet were covered but the left hand was exposed and a tag was attached to a finger instead of a toe. It was a male hand. Maia could see neat fingernails, some age spots and a wedding ring.

Brenda stopped in her tracks. Her hand flew up to cover her mouth as she let go of Maia's hand. A choked sob escaped from Brenda's lips and Maia knew they'd found Keith.

Brenda stepped forward and picked up Keith's hand. The mortuary attendant was standing at the head of the table. He waited for Brenda to make eye contact with him before he folded back the sheet. Brenda closed her eyes as the attendant lifted the sheet and Maia heard her hold her breath.

From where she stood Maia could see the man's face. It was Keith. She felt Henry's silent query and nodded as tears welled in her eyes. The death toll had risen overnight to seventy-five, and with the bodies recovered today that toll was now even higher, but Keith was the first person that Maia knew personally to have lost his life. While she had friends and family members who were now homeless she hadn't, as yet, known anyone who had died.

Brenda's shoulders shook as she sobbed. She held Keith's hand and kissed his forehead. The mortuary attendant handed her a box of tissues as Maia hugged her.

'I'm so sorry, Brenda.'

The surgeon gave Brenda some time before he said, very quietly, 'Once you are ready, I'll need you to sign some paperwork.'

Brenda nodded but didn't look up, but eventually she was ready. Maia held her hand while she signed a form to formally identify Keith. 'Henry,' Brenda asked as she signed the papers, 'would you mind very much having a look at Keith? I need to know what his injuries are but I don't think I can bear to look myself.'

There was no report as yet so Henry had no choice but to look. He nodded and the mortuary attendant lifted the sheet once more. Maia saw Henry's expression change. He managed to keep his face neutral and it was only because Maia knew him well that she could see the tightening of his lips, the setting of his jaw, and she knew Keith's injuries were extensive. She wanted to go to Henry, to comfort him, but she couldn't leave Brenda.

Brenda had signed the papers and she gave Keith another longing look. 'I don't want to leave him here alone,' she said.

'We'll wait outside and give you some more time with him,' Maia suggested. 'Take as much time as you need.'

There was a row of chairs lined up against the wall outside the morgue. Five chairs with plastic seats and metal legs had been welded together so that anyone sitting on one was within a few inches of anyone else. There was no personal space but fortunately Maia and Henry were the only ones there. Henry was very quiet.

'Was it very bad?' Maia asked.

Henry nodded. 'His legs and chest were completely crushed. He probably died from internal injuries. He would have lost a lot of blood and he would have been in a lot of pain. Hopefully he lost consciousness first.'

Henry leant forward propped his elbows on his knees and rested his head in his hands. He sighed, expelling the air from his lungs in a loud whoosh. He'd been up all night with barely a break and this situation had to be taking its toll on him also. Maia knew what would be on his mind. This wasn't the first time he'd been in a room filled with the bodies of victims of a natural disaster.

She put her hand on his thigh. 'Are you okay?'

'I'm fine.'

Somehow she doubted that. 'Do you want to talk about it?'

'What?'

'Your family. I know you must be thinking about them.'

He was thinking of them. Of course he was, how could he not be? The 2004 Boxing Day tsunami was never far from his thoughts and the events of today had ensured that those memories resurfaced. But he wasn't sure if he wanted to talk about it. Maia knew his history, she knew he'd lost his family in that tragic event, but he had never spoken about it in detail. Not to her or anyone else.

'Was it like that in Thailand?'

'God, no, it was much worse.'

But how did he begin to describe what he'd seen? It had been an enormous thing to get his head around when he'd arrived in Thailand a few days after the disaster. He had struggled even when seeing it first-hand.

He still struggled with it. How would he explain it to someone who hadn't witnessed it? Why would he want Maia or anyone to have that picture in their head?

CHAPTER NINE

HENRY HAD NEVER spoken to anyone about the horrors of the tsunami that had claimed the lives of his family.

It had happened six years ago but if he closed his eyes he could still picture it all so clearly: the devastation, the destruction and the dead. There had been hundreds of bodies laid out in rows in the corridors of the hospitals, in the street and in makeshift shelters. He could see it still and he could smell it. The stench had been the worst thing. The bodies of strangers he'd been able to cope with but the smell had been horrific and it was still so potent in his memory. He could smell it now and the foul stench made him want to retch.

He coughed and opened his eyes, bringing him back to the present to confront a new disaster.

'Are you okay?' Maia asked, concern etched in her deep, brown eyes. 'Do you want to go outside and get some fresh air?'

He took a couple of deep breaths. 'No. I'm all right.' He shook his head, trying to clear the images from his mind. He'd never spoken in detail of the devastation or of the horrors of having to identify his loved ones. He'd locked it away inside himself and used the power of that loss to spur him on to make a difference in disaster management. But he'd never dealt with the emotional trauma, he'd never been able to let it go, and it festered inside him and contaminated all his relationships. Being stoic and independent had cost him his relationship with Maia.

Had it been worth it?

He knew he'd made a mistake.

'What I saw in Thailand was far more traumatic than what we've seen here, but I'm not speaking on behalf of Brenda when I say that. The next days or weeks or months aren't going to be easy for her or anyone else here—far from it—but the scale of the disaster will be more manageable, and the capacity of Christchurch and New Zealand to manage the catastrophe will be far better than in South-East Asia. Although, for the victims' families everything is relative, and for the people of Christchurch this is probably as bad as it gets. It'll certainly be the worst thing most of them have ever experienced and they'll need support to get through it.'

'And who was there to support you in Thailand?'

'Nobody,' he admitted. 'I thought I'd manage. I arrived in Thailand still pretending to be positive but it was already five days after the tsunami and I'd heard nothing. I hadn't completely given up. I hadn't wanted to believe the worst, but when I saw the devastation I knew it was hopeless. Roads were gone, trees were flattened, buildings destroyed, whole villages wiped out.

'Before I'd even had a chance to find my family, before I'd even got off the plane, I could see the damage and the chaos and I knew a miracle would be almost impossible. I'd refused to think of the worst-case scenario and that was a mistake. I'd seen photos in the news of the scenes but flying in and seeing the devastation was nothing like I'd imagined and I was completely unprepared. Pictures don't convey the smell, the chaos, the heartbreak, the despair.

'Huge boards had been erected displaying photos of the deceased and that was where we all started. There were hundreds of people searching for missing loved ones but so many of the deceased had drowned and were bloated beyond recognition, making identification difficult. My brother's picture wasn't on the boards, nor was my father's. I found my mother first and initially I'd been given false hope with reported sightings of my brother in one of the hospitals but it turned out to be another English boy. I had to go from hospital to hospital, morgue to morgue, school hall to school hall, searching and looking, and it took me two more days to find out anything at all. I kept hoping that entire time that my father and brother had survived but I eventually stumbled across my brother's body lying in a hospital corridor. That was the worst moment of my life. It was so unexpected and so confronting.'

'What about your dad?'

'His body has never been recovered. As awful as today was for Brenda, at least it was controlled. She had people she knew with her and she was semi-prepared to see Keith's body. She will have closure.'

'You shouldn't have come today,' Maia said as she tucked her arm through the crook of his elbow and reached for his hand. 'You should have let me look after Brenda.'

He squeezed her hand, grateful for the contact, grateful for the touch of a warm body. 'No, it's fine. Today hasn't upset me—it's brought back memories, certainly, but Thailand is never far from my mind and this was something I'd vowed to do after the tsunami. If I can help to ease other people's pain, either through treating victims and hopefully reducing the death toll, or at least supporting them when they need to identify loved ones, that is what I want to do. In Thailand, locals rallied and supported mourning Thais and tourists alike, and I know first-hand what a difference it can make just having another person there, even if they're a stranger, to lessen the loneliness and heartache, sadness and despair.'

Brenda emerged from the morgue as Henry finished speaking. She looked as though her heart was breaking. Maia's heart was breaking too, for Brenda and for Henry. She wanted to be able to fix them both but she knew there was nothing she could do. Brenda needed time and her daughter, and Henry wouldn't let her help him; he wouldn't let anyone close.

Despite the fact that years had passed for Henry he'd admitted the horrors of the tsunami were never far from his thoughts and Maia would bet every last dollar that he still hadn't dealt with the trauma. She knew it was that event that drove him in life. It was the tsunami and the loss of his family that had brought on his decision regarding his life plan and he was still on that path— the path to redemption. He was driven by guilt just as she was. Guilt that he hadn't been with his family, guilt that he hadn't perished with them, guilt that he'd survived. He didn't think he deserved to be happy and he didn't want to get close to anyone in case he lost them. He didn't think he could take that chance.

Maia and Henry took Brenda home and waited for her daughter to arrive before returning to work. Henry looked and sounded exhausted and spent most of the journey trying to stifle his yawns. Maia almost expected him to fall asleep in the car. It probably would have done him good. He'd worked all night and, while she thought he'd deny that the visit to the morgue had been harrowing, she suspected differently.

'I think you should go back to the hotel and get some sleep,' she said as she turned into the hospital car park.

'I'm fine.'

She'd known he'd deny any problem but she wasn't prepared to give in. He really needed to take a break before he collapsed. Physically and emotionally. 'Henry, you're exhausted, you can't work like this.'

'If it's not busy when we get inside I'll have a kip in an on-call room.'

'Surely the hotel would be better?'

'I can't go back to the hotel. It's in the exclusion zone. It's still standing, but until the damage is assessed and its condition determined no one is allowed in. I can't even collect my things.'

Maia frowned. 'So where will you stay?'

'At the hospital. I'll camp out in an on-call room. I had a message from my rental agent this morning. I was supposed to be looking at accommodation on Saturday but that's been shelved. She says it will be difficult, if not impossible, to find somewhere to rent now. So many houses have been destroyed and thousands more so badly damaged that they will have to be demolished, which will make accommodation scarce.

'So many people are homeless and, although thousands have left Christchurch, there are thousands more who are staying but need somewhere to live. People can't live in the school gyms and in tents indefinitely. Other residents are all taking in extra people if they can. I'm not a priority. I'm one person who isn't injured and hasn't lost anything, really, except a suitcase and a few clothes.' He shrugged. 'I'll sleep here. Buy some clean underwear and a toothbrush from the hospital gift shop and wear scrubs.'

Maia felt terrible. She'd spent last night thinking about Henry but not in a practical sense. Her thoughts had all been ridiculous romantic fantasies. She hadn't spent one moment thinking about anything useful, like where he was sleeping.

She wanted to help. She knew he was lonely, even if he wouldn't admit it. He professed to want to be alone but no one really wanted that, did they? She would help.

'Don't be silly,' she said. 'You can come and stay at our place. Half my extended family is camped out there. It's chaotic but if you can put up with that I'm sure I can find you a bed. We have no water, but there's a pool and the beach, and we do have power again. You can come home with me at the end of my shift.'

She didn't stop to think if she was making a big mistake. It wasn't until later that she wondered what had made her extend the invitation and what had made Henry accept. It had been a rash decision but they were the only sort she seemed to be able to make in her personal life. If she thought for too long about something, she ended up going around in circles, never coming to a decision. There were always too many things to consider and this situation was no different.

But she hadn't stopped to think. She'd just acted. And now she had to deal with the consequences.

Maia tied the straps of her black bikini top behind her back and adjusted the cups to make sure she was decent. She threw a red cotton caftan over her costume and headed for the beach. They still had no water and she needed a swim to wash off the sweat and the stress of the day. She could have taken a dip in the pool but the house was wall-to-wall people; it looked and sounded like a school camp site and the only way to get some peace and quiet after a distressing day was to head for the ocean. She opened the back gate and walked through the sand dunes onto the beach. The sand was warm under her bare feet and the air smelled of salt and seaweed. The ocean was dark blue against a paler sky and a gentle swell brought small waves onto the shore.

The beach was empty but for one other person.

She might not have complete peace and quiet but she didn't want it. Peace and quiet was only one attraction of the beach. The other one was standing in waist-deep water looking out to the horizon.

Henry.

He was all alone and once again she was struck by the thought that it wasn't right. No one should be completely alone. She'd seen the haunted look in his eyes after they'd been to the morgue. He'd said he was okay but there was no way on earth he could be. Not after today.

She stripped off her caftan and dropped it on the sand along with her towel.

The water washed over her toes. Despite the heat of the day the water was cool, and she stood in the shallows for a moment, acclimatising to the temperature as she watched Henry. He dived under a wave, not hesitating to get wet.

His head broke the surface of the water as he came back up. He turned around and pushed his wet hair back from his face. The beach faced east and at this time of the day the sun was low in the sky at Maia's back. The late-afternoon westerly sun hit Henry and the water glistened on his chest. He had removed the dressings that she had applied to his cuts yesterday and as he walked towards her she could see that the gashes on his chest and arm were already looking better. Her eyes travelled down the length of his body, following the trail of dark hair that disappeared under his board shorts. She had lent him a pair of her cousin's shorts as all his clothes were still quarantined in the hotel and the borrowed board shorts fitted him well. Extremely well. They sat snug on his hips and moulded to his thighs.

She shouldn't be looking.

She lifted her eyes back up to his face. His perfect face.

He was watching her too. She could see his eyes running over her curves and then his gaze came to rest on her breasts. She could feel her nipples harden. It was incredible. He didn't even need to touch her; just a look, just his indigo eyes caressing her, was enough to make her nipples peak and she could feel the warmth starting low in her belly and spreading outwards. She could feel every heart beat, every pulse, in her chest and throat and between her thighs. She was moist and shaky. Her reaction was enough to get her into the water. The cold ocean might calm her down before she did something stupid. Something she might regret.

Inviting him to stay had probably been a mistake but it was too late now. She'd have to deal with it. It was probably lucky that there were plenty of people around the house; there wasn't much chance that they'd be alone together.

Except for now.

Henry took another step towards her. She could see the desire in his eyes and knew it was reflected in her own. She needed protection from his gaze.

She dived under the water and started swimming,

buying herself some time to think, hoping the cool water would settle her down. She stretched out parallel to the shore in a strong over-arm movement but she had no chance of leaving Henry behind. He was swimming beside her, matching her stroke for stroke.

After several minutes Maia stopped. She was breathing hard and needed to rest. She flipped onto her back and floated in the salty water. Henry was treading water next to her. She wanted to reach out and hold on to him. No one could see them, they were several hundred metres from the house, but she resisted the temptation. She wasn't in a position to do anything with Henry. She closed her eyes and tried to ignore the stirring of lust and desire in her belly.

She could feel him watching her. He hadn't said a word but he didn't need to. She had seen the desire mirrored in his eyes—she knew he was feeling it too.

She desperately wanted to reach out a hand to touch him but she knew that would open a door that she might not then be able to close. She knew that if she moved towards him he would meet her halfway, but she would be making him compromise his values as surely as she would be compromising her own. Once she stepped through that door, she would be turning her back on the promise she'd made to Todd, and to be disloyal to Todd was not something she wanted. She had to be strong.

Somehow she managed to resist him. She wasn't free to give herself to Henry no matter how much she wanted to. And that was the problem. She wasn't his but she still wished she was.

She had been pretending to herself that she was over him. It had been easy to fool herself when he was on the other side of the world, but having him back in Christchurch was proving to be torturous, and inviting him to stay was only going to make things worse. It might have been the most stupid thing she'd ever done. Possibly only trumped by letting him go the first time.

Maia was unsettled by the events of the past few days and weeks—the quake, Henry's return and her feelings for him, as well as her impending nuptials. Everything had changed and, while she knew none of this was really Henry's fault, he was certainly, as far as she was concerned, at the centre of it all.

She hadn't been able to rescind her invitation to him to stay with her family so she coped by trying to limit the time she spent with him, or at least making sure they had other company, whether at home or at work, but the awareness never left her. She tried hard not to be attracted to him but it was a difficult thing to deny.

She needed to be busy. And she was. She needed routine and order to make sense of the chaos in her head but there was no sense of order and routine at home. The quake had thrown everything into disarray. Part of her wished she could just float in the ocean for days, until everything was back to normal. But what was normal going to be?

It had been five days since the quake and there was still no running water or sewerage. Half of the buildings in the CBD were going to have to be demolished, if they hadn't already been destroyed, and the death toll stood at one hundred and twenty-three but more were still unaccounted for. There had been no survivors found for the past three days but people were still talking about miracles. One hundred and ten alone had been killed in collapsed office buildings, six had perished in buses that had been crushed and the rest had been killed by falling rocks and masonry. There were too many bodies and some still hadn't been identified. Because of the extent of the injuries, the experts were sometimes having to resort to using DNA from toothbrushes and hairbrushes, tattoos, dental records or fingerprints, as well as personal effects found on the bodies—wallets, keys and the like—in order to positively identify the victims.

It was going to take a long time for the city and her residents to recover. It was going to be a long time before things were back to normal and, for Maia, her sense of normal was about to change forever. She was getting married in three weeks.

Maia picked up another sweet potato as she tried to imagine walking down the aisle. At the moment it seemed almost impossible. Some things were continuing on as they always had but it was difficult to picture holding a wedding amongst the devastation, although they were managing to host the family's regular monthly Sunday night *hangi*.

Her mother had decided that since the majority of the family was already staying with them they might as well go ahead with the regular barbecue as there was food that had to be eaten. *'Hangi'* was the Maori word for 'earth oven' and the barbecue feast was traditionally cooked in a pit which Maia's dad had dug at the bottom of the garden where the grass met the sand dunes. It was the men's job to get the fire started. It would take several hours for the wood fire to heat the volcanic rocks to a temperature high enough to create the steam that cooked the food, and while the oven was heating up the women prepared the food. Fish needed to be seasoned and wrapped in banana leaves, pork and lamb got wrapped in cabbage leaves, and potatoes and kumara were chopped up, placed in wire baskets, covered with wet cloth and then buried on top of the hot rocks and left to steam in the *hangi* for about four hours.

Maia was chopping sweet potato but she wasn't sure it was safe for her to be handling a sharp knife. She hadn't been eating or sleeping well since the quake; her concentration was shot and her hands were shaky. She was a bit of a mess. She was stressed over the wedding, her feelings for Henry and the changes to her world, both her immediate and larger worlds, brought by the earthquake and by Henry's return. Any one of those things was stressful enough to deal with and she was finding it difficult to cope with all of them en masse.

She had lost weight and was having recurring nightmares about the quake. The dream varied—sometimes she was trapped in the cathedral, sometimes she was on the street and would hear Henry calling her name, telling her to watch out as the cathedral tumbled around her, and sometimes she would be watching the walls fall around Henry. The dream varied but there were two things that were constant. She was always wearing her wedding dress—the irony hadn't escaped her that she hadn't actually chosen a wedding dress yet and she had no idea what to do about that, given that the dress shop had been flattened in the quake. The second constant was that it was Henry, not Todd, who was always in her dream.

She went to sleep each night worried that she would call out Henry's name and wake Todd. She lay awake for hours, feeling guilty that Todd was sleeping in her bed while she dreamt of Henry. A guilty brain was apparently a restless one and she was finding sleep hard to come by.

The knife slipped off the edge of a kumara, narrowly missing her thumb. She handed the knife to Pippi before she caused herself an injury and started to layer slices of lemon on to the whole fish that had been stuffed and seasoned, before wrapping them in banana leaves. This was an easy job, one she didn't have to focus too hard on, which left her mind free to wander—and, of course, it went to Henry.

Not only was he in her dreams every night, she was spending far too many of her waking hours thinking about him too. He just had to look at her and her legs would turn to jelly, her heart would tremble, her pulse would begin to race, leaving her short of breath, and her temperature would rise. She could think of nothing else when he looked at her with his indigo eyes.

How on earth was she going to marry Todd when her heart desired Henry?

She needed to get out of the kitchen. She finished wrapping the fish and stepped out into the back garden. It was crowded with family and friends. It appeared that her sisters had invited everyone they knew, although Maia had also invited a number of extras. She looked around the garden. Todd was helping with the fire—it looked like they were almost ready to start cooking—and she could see Henry talking to some of her cousins, along with some of the hospital staff. Carrie was there along with Pippi's school friends and Lani's boyfriend, as well as a couple of ED staff. The air sang with the constant murmur of conversation and the frequent explosion of laughter.

For the first time since the earthquake people seemed relaxed. Except for Maia. Having Todd and Henry in the same place was keeping her on edge.

She longed to go and stand with Henry but she had vowed to keep a respectable distance. Her mother was sitting on the patio under the kiwi fruit vine. That looked like a safe spot to be. She bypassed the ice boxes filled with beer—she wasn't drinking; she was worried that alcohol might loosen her tongue and she might say or do something she would regret—and sat beside her mum. 'What are you doing over here all by yourself?'

'Enjoying some solitude.' Neina laughed. 'In case you haven't noticed, it's been a mad house around here.'

Maia smiled. 'I had noticed.'

'I'm glad you're here,' her mum continued. 'I wanted to ask you about your wedding.'

'My wedding?'

'Yes. I assume since the damage caused by the earth-quake you and Todd will have to adjust your plans and I just wondered what you've decided.'

'Nothing definite,' Maia replied. 'I'm thinking it might be easier to postpone it. It seems wrong to be planning a wedding when people are in mourning, but Todd is keen to make alternate plans. He thinks it will give us, and everyone else, something to look forward to, but there is so much that has to be reorganised. The cathedral has been condemned, so we can't get married there. The hotel where we booked our reception has structural damage and won't be repaired in time, although they've said they can move us into a marquee in their garden, and the dress shop where our dresses were coming from has been destroyed.'

Maia was still coming to terms with the fact that if Henry hadn't invited her to lunch then she might well have been in the dress shop that day. The shop had collapsed during one of the aftershocks so it was unlikely she would have been hurt but it was still a close call. 'And I haven't had a chance to find out about the florist yet. Basically, we have to start from scratch, and it's more than I can handle at the moment.'

Reorganising seemed like such a huge task. Maia wondered if all of these obstacles were signs indicating that they should delay the wedding or call it off, even. She had a reason to postpone it, but really it would give her a chance to work out what she ultimately wanted. 'I'm doing the right thing, aren't I? Getting married, I mean?'

'Only you can answer that.'

'You've always told us that you knew the moment you met Dad that he was the one. How did you know?'

'He made my heart sing,' Neina said simply. 'He brought me to life. I was only nineteen but I couldn't imagine my life without him and that never changed. He was the one I couldn't live without. I never looked at another man again and I can't imagine that I ever will. He was my life—him and you girls. He gave me everything I ever needed.'

'Do you think there's only one right person in the world for each of us?'

'No, I don't. But I do think that there's one person, above all others, who fits you best. It doesn't mean that you won't be happy with someone else. I think there is more than one right person, but perhaps only one *perfect* one for each of us. I was just lucky to find my perfect love first and I can't ask for anything more. No matter what we say, all of us are searching for love and happiness. If you can find that at least once in your life, you've done well.'

Maia was worried that her marriage might be the end of her chance at finding true happiness rather than the beginning. Her parents hadn't needed to look elsewhere, neither of them had needed anyone else, but Maia was afraid that one man wasn't enough for her. Unless that man was Henry. She was talking to her mother about Todd but she was thinking of Henry.

'You have to follow your heart,' her mother said just as Henry approached.

Maia had been acutely aware of his movements all day but had deliberately kept herself out of his vicinity. It was the only way she could cope with the chemistry that still burned between them. But he was heading straight towards them now and she knew there was no escaping.

He was dressed in a blue polo shirt that lightened his indigo eyes and a pair of casual shorts that showed off his long, powerful legs.

'Just the women I wanted to see,' he said as he took an envelope out of his shorts pocket. 'I have something for you.' He handed the envelope to Neina.

Maia's mother slid her finger under the flap and prised it open, pulling out a clutch of tickets. 'What are these for?'

'They are a thank-you for giving me a bed for the past few nights. The Canterbury Racing Association have organised a charity event to raise funds for the quake victims. It's a day at the races—lunch, champagne, fashion parades—so I booked a couple of tables in support and I'd like you to take one. I thought it might be a fun day out for you all.'

'That's a lovely idea, thank you, Henry.' Neina stood and went to put the tickets somewhere safe, leaving Maia alone with Henry.

'Where did you get the tickets?' Maia asked him.

'Through Joanne Parker,' Henry replied. 'You remember her? She's an anaesthetist at the Queen Liz. She might have a room for me to rent. I was talking to her about that and she mentioned this fundraiser. Her brother is the CEO of Canterbury Racing.'

Maia did remember her. Joanne was petite, blonde, pretty and ran marathons. She was the polar opposite of Maia. She remembered Joanne very well and she wasn't happy to hear that Henry was considering moving in with her. 'I thought you didn't want to share accommodation.'

'I didn't, but accommodation is scarce at the moment, as you know. While I appreciate your hospitality, sleeping on your couch is hardly a long-term solution.'

'It's no problem,' she fibbed. The only problem was that Maia was having a hard time controlling her emotions. 'You're welcome to stay as long as you like.' But could the offer of a couch amongst a dozen other relatives compete with the offer of a bedroom at Joanne's place? Maia doubted it.

Henry smiled. 'That's very generous of you but I feel like I'm walking on eggshells.'

'What do you mean?

'I'm making you uncomfortable and Todd doesn't want me here.'

'It's not up to Todd.'

'If I'm going to be completely honest, I'm on edge too. I can't stand to see you with Todd but I know I can't compete. I have nothing to offer you.'

He could offer her his heart, Maia thought. And she would take it. But he had sworn years ago that he wouldn't give his heart to anyone.

Maia didn't want him to move out but she knew she was being selfish. Henry was being honest and she knew she couldn't say the same about herself. But if she was going to take a leaf out of Henry's book and be honest about how she was feeling what could she say?

Could she tell him that, even though he wouldn't let himself love her, she'd never really been able to let him go? Not completely. Could she tell him she'd been holding back a piece of her heart for him? That he had stayed in the back of her mind and in a corner of her heart for three years? That she had learnt to accept that he might always remain there, but that she was still hoping that one day she would meet the man who would fill her whole heart? That one day she might meet the man who would be able to wipe all traces of Henry from her heart and mind, but that Todd wasn't that man? That she'd been so afraid of being alone that she'd accepted Todd's proposal, but she knew now that logic and reason couldn't replace passion and love?

But she said none of those things. She wasn't in a position to tell him how she felt.

The racecourse looked gorgeous. It was a glorious early-autumn day. The sun shone in a cloudless blue sky, the freshly cut grass was a bright emerald green and the roses bloomed along the racetrack railing. The Canterbury racecourse was only eight kilometres from the city but there was no sign of the devastation wreaked by the quake out here. It was almost possible to forget what had happened just a little under two weeks ago.

Carrie had insisted that they use Henry's gift and she had planned a girls' day out which included Maia's mum and sisters and a few other girlfriends. In the end Maia had embraced the idea. She needed something to look forward to. She needed to let her hair down and have some fun and that was what she intended to do. She would forget about the wedding and the quake and all the things she'd been refusing to deal with. Everything could wait for another day.

She'd taken care with her outfit. She had chosen a stiff cotton sateen dress with a fitted sleeveless bodice and a flared skirt. It was white with large roses in varying shades of pink printed on it. Ariana had fixed her hair into a French bun and tucked frangipani flowers into her dark tresses. She'd completed the look with white strappy sandals, a pink clutch, bright pink lipstick, and a dash of mascara and blush. It was nice to make an effort, especially when she felt like she hadn't worn anything except her uniform, scrubs or bathers for two weeks, but who was she making an effort for?

Henry was seated at the table beside hers. He had filled the second table with his friends and Maia was trying to ignore him. She was trying to pretend he was just a handsome stranger at the adjacent table but that was almost impossible. His table was so close to hers that if he leant back in his chair his shoulder could brush against hers. Maia was totally aware of every movement he made, every conversation he had, every time someone laughed at one of his remarks. She tried to pretend his proximity wasn't affecting her but she'd been unable to focus on anything but his scent—citrus and cedar—the sound of his voice—quiet, deep and tuned just for her ear—and the way the air stirred around her every time he moved. How could she concentrate on anything else when he was near? There was no way of ignoring him or her reaction to him.

And, along with trying to pretend she was immune to Henry, she was also trying to pretend that Joanne wasn't sitting next to him—young, pretty, intelligent and recently divorced Joanne, whom Henry had moved in with just a few days ago. Maia refused to admit she was jealous. She knew she had no right to be. Nor would she admit that she missed having him around. But that hadn't stopped her from carefully considering her outfit.

She'd been surprisingly nervous about spending the day with Henry, while trying to maintain a respectable distance, but her nerves had diminished with her first glass of champagne. Or maybe it had been her second. She couldn't remember how many she'd had.

As the waiter cleared her plate Maia studied the form guide, pretending to be immersed in the finer details of horse racing when she actually had no idea what any of it meant.

'Are you going to place a bet?' Henry was standing behind her, leaning over the back of her chair, and the sound of his soft, deep voice in her ear sent a tingle along her spine.

She squeezed her knees together as the deep timbre of his voice lit a fire between her thighs. 'I was thinking about it,' she said as she looked up at him. 'But I might as well just give my money to the bookie. I have no idea what I'm doing.'

'Would you like to go and take a look at the horses? One might catch your eye that way.'

'You can see the horses?'

'Of course.' He smiled, making the dimple in his chin disappear. 'You can walk past the stables, and before a race the horses are paraded around the mounting yard.' He checked his watch. 'There should be some coming out about now for race four.'

Maia knew it wouldn't help her with her betting but if it meant a chance to have Henry to herself, away from the watchful eyes of her family and away from Joanne, she wasn't about to refuse that invitation. She was sure Joanne was perfectly nice but not for Henry.

She pushed her chair back, picked up her handbag

and prayed that her shaky legs would support her, but as Henry led her across the third-floor function room towards the lift she hesitated. 'Can we take the stairs instead?' she asked. She knew the emergency exit stairs were on the opposite side of the room. She'd come up that way. Since the earthquake she'd avoided elevators. She had a fear of getting trapped in a lift during an earthquake, and as the city was still experiencing aftershocks another quake was highly likely. Her sandals had high heels, but it was only three flights of stairs, and walking in high heels was preferable to being cooped up in a lift. Just in case.

He held the door for her and as she brushed past him she could feel the warmth of his breath on her neck. She gripped the railing as she willed her legs to keep moving. She focused on the stairs. One foot in front of the other. One step at a time. She knew how to get down a flight of steps.

They were halfway down when she stumbled.

Henry put his arm around her waist to steady her. 'No more champagne for you,' he teased.

His touch sent the now familiar surge of longing through her. She knew he was holding on to her to support her but his touch only made her more unsteady on her narrow heels as her hormones surged and her heart raced. She gripped the stair railing more tightly in an attempt to counteract the wobbliness that Henry's touch had triggered and felt the railing vibrate as she took another step. The vibration travelled through her, compounding her instability, then she heard the familiar, accompanying sound. She paused, frozen on the step, one foot in midair as the earth grumbled and groaned.

'Did you hear that?' she asked.

She let go of the railing and turned towards Henry,

thinking she'd rather be hanging on to him, when the staircase moved underneath her and the lights flickered and went out. Her arms shot out, reaching for something to hold on to. It was an instinctive reaction, elicited by the darkness and the odd sensation of a moving staircase. But she was grabbing at nothing.

The staircase disappeared from beneath her feet and she pitched forward into the shadows.

She was falling.

She was tumbling.

She was plummeting headfirst into the darkness.

Somewhere over and above the noise of falling concrete and rumbling earth she heard the sound of her own voice. She was calling for Henry.

Her arms were flailing but her hands and arms were making contact with nothing.

There was no railing and no Henry.

There was nothing there.

Nothing at all.

CHAPTER TEN

MAIA CRASHED WITH a thump onto the concrete landing between the two flights of stairs, expelling the air in her lungs in a loud 'whoosh' as she hit the ground. Somehow she managed not to hit her head but her left leg twisted underneath her; she came down hard on top of it and heard something crack. Searing pain shot up her leg and she thought she might pass out.

'Maia?'

Hearing Henry's voice calling her name was enough to keep her in the present but she was unable to speak. She was completely winded and gasping for air.

She couldn't breathe. She couldn't talk and she couldn't see either. The stairwell had no windows and now no lights. They were in complete darkness.

'Maia?' She heard Henry's voice again and felt his hand on her arm.

'Maia?'

She could hear a note of panic in his voice now. He was probably wondering if she was dead or alive. She still hadn't been able to catch her breath, she still couldn't speak, but she thought she might be able to move her arm. She bent her elbow, sliding her arm up until her hand was under his palm and then curled her fingers around his.

'Oh, thank God.'

The emergency lights above the exit doors came on as she heard Henry's sigh of relief. An eerie half light lit the dusty stairwell, barely illuminating their surroundings. The lights had a green tinge which made them look a little weird, like motion-sick aliens.

Henry's hand was on her chin; his fingers cupped her face and stroked her cheek. 'Maia, sweetheart, are you okay?'

She shook her head as the dust settled and she finally managed to gasp a lungful of air. Something hurt but it was hard to focus while Henry's fingers held her face.

Something was throbbing. She closed her eyes and concentrated on the pain. Her ankle. She opened her eyes and glanced down her leg, pointing towards her foot. She could see that her ankle was already starting to swell, and she thought she could see some purplish bruising, although it was difficult to be certain due to the ghostly green lighting. She sat up, trying to get into a more comfortable and less awkward position, but gasped in pain as she moved her left leg.

'Careful.' Henry dropped his hand from her face and took her by the shoulders, supporting her as she tried to sit up. He pulled his phone from his pocket and swiped the screen. A bright light beamed from the end of his phone as he activated the flashlight app. He scanned her with the light. 'God, Maia, you're bleeding.'

Maia looked down at her dress, the front of which was covered in blood. She had no idea how that had got there. She took a deep breath and her lungs filled with air. She could breathe easily now. There was no pain in her chest. At least there was nothing wrong there.

She lifted her hands and turned them over as Henry shone the light on her palms. Her palms were wet with blood, sticky but not sore. The blood was running down from her elbows. She'd taken the skin off the back of both her forearms when she'd crashed to the ground, but that pain was minimal in comparison to her ankle.

Henry took a handkerchief from the pocket in his jacket and wiped the blood away.

'That's not too bad.'

'Not as bad as my ankle,' she told him. It was funny how blood always caught the attention, yet she knew those injuries were minor.

The light from Henry's phone illuminated her left ankle which, in the past minute, had ballooned to twice its normal size.

Henry passed her his mobile. 'Can you hold this for me while I have a look?'

She took the phone and kept the light trained on her leg as Henry slid his hands gently down from her knee to the lower third of her shin. He ran his fingers along her tibia to the inside of her ankle. His fingers were soft, his hands gentle and his touch made the pain bearable. It receded into the background as she imagined how it would feel to have Henry's hand roam over the rest of her body.

'How's that?'

Fantastic, she almost said. 'That's all fine,' she said. 'But I felt something crack when I landed.'

Henry sat on the bottom step—it was about all that remained of the staircase—and lifted her foot into his lap. The heel of her shoe hung limply from the sole. It must have snapped when she rolled her ankle. He carefully slid her sandal from her foot and palpated gently below her lateral malleolus and over the bones of her foot. None of that bothered her but when his fingers moved up over the bump of her ankle she thought she might pass out with the pain.

'There,' she gasped.

'I think you might have a fractured fibula. Not compound, thankfully. You'll need an X-ray but hopefully it's nothing worse than that. Nothing else is hurting?'

'No,' she said as she shook her head. 'But I don't think I can stand on it.' The thought of putting any weight on that leg made her feel nauseous.

'That's okay, I'll carry you, but I have to see which is the best way out of here first.'

Henry took care putting Maia's foot on the ground before he stood up. Using his flashlight app, he could see down the stairwell. A pile of concrete, the remains of the stairs, lay on the next landing, completely blocking the remainder of the staircase and the door. The door opened into the stairwell; there would be no easy exit that way.

He shone the flashlight up but there was nothing above them. The stairs they had been standing on had totally disappeared but for the very last one. There must have been a weakness in the concrete— he could see the smooth edge where two sections had been joined and one section was now lying a whole flight below where it should be. The lower exit was blocked, so there was no point going down, but he couldn't go up either.

Looking at the mess, he knew it was lucky they hadn't been crushed. He hated to think what could have happened to them if they'd been standing on the other half of the staircase. They were lucky to have escaped serious injury. A broken ankle seemed manageable when confronted with the reality of being trapped in a concrete tomb.

He checked the screen of his phone. There was no reception. They were stuck here until someone found them.

'Can we get out?' Maia asked.

He shook his head. 'No. The door is blocked on the floor below us and there's nothing above us.' For all intents and purposes they were imprisoned in a concrete bunker. Not a tomb—he knew they would be rescued eventually; it was only a matter of time—but, for now, they were stuck.

'Can you call someone?'

He shook his head again. 'No reception,' he said as he held his phone up.

'How are we going to get out? If you've got no reception, how will they know where to look?'

'They'll know we're missing, the others will tell them. They'll keep searching until everyone is found.'

'That's assuming everyone else is okay.'

'Come on, Pollyanna, we'll be fine.' He tried to make light of the situation but the reality was he had no way of knowing what the situation was outside the stairwell. 'Someone will find us.'

'What's on these floors?' she asked.

'I have no idea. Offices, I think. Maybe storerooms.'

'So no one will hear us if we yell?'

'Maybe not yet, but someone will come eventually, and in the meantime I will take care of you.' He could hear the trace of panic in Maia's voice. He didn't want her to panic. It was his job to protect her. She had to know he wouldn't let anything happen to her.

But, his conscience argued, he already had, hadn't he? She was lying in front of him with a broken ankle.

He was still standing on the step. He shrugged out

of his jacket and hung it over the section of bent and twisted stair railing that hadn't fallen into the abyss. He stripped off his shirt.

'What are you doing?'

'I'm going to bind your foot for you. It might make it more comfortable. And then you should keep it elevated.'

He bit the button off one of his cuffs. He didn't want to press the button into her swollen leg. He squatted down and picked up her foot. In the light of his phone he could see that her toenails were pale pink; they looked like tiny shells glued to the end of her brown toes. Her skin was soft and warm. He cupped her foot in his hand and wound the sleeve of his shirt around her foot and up her leg, followed by the body of the shirt, compressing her lower leg, and finally he wrapped the other sleeve over the top and tucked the end in.

'Better?' he asked as he rolled his jacket up.

'Yes, much better, thank you.'

He put his jacket on the bottom stair and propped Maia's foot on top of the temporary cushion, elevating it.

He switched off the flashlight app to conserve his battery and sat with his spine against the wall, pulling Maia back so she could lean on him. It was stuffy and airless in the stairwell but at least he didn't have to worry about them being cold.

The air smelled of frangipanis. Maia had tucked the flowers into her hair. He breathed deeply; the scent was familiar and pleasant. He was more than happy to sit there for as long as it took with Maia lying against his chest.

'Do you think we should try making some noise? Someone might hear us.'

'I'm in no hurry to get rescued,' he said as he tightened his arms around her ever so slightly. 'I've got everything I want right here.'

Maia didn't reply, she just looked up at him with her enormous brown eyes. In the dim half light of the emergency lighting, he saw her throat move as she swallowed. When she kept her eyes focused on him and licked her lips, he almost groaned aloud with desire. He wanted her more than he had wanted anything else in his life.

He had panicked when Maia had plummeted down the stairs and he'd felt his heart stop momentarily with fright before the adrenalin had made it beat so hard in his chest, he'd thought it was about to burst through his skin.

It had stopped again when he'd found her lying on the stairs. He'd lost everyone he'd ever loved and he couldn't lose her too. He realised then that he couldn't let her go. Not now. He'd been given a second chance and only a fool would let her go twice. He was no fool—a bit misguided, perhaps, but not a fool—and he had a chance now to put things right. He couldn't bear to lose her, either to Todd or through his own doing. He had to claim her. If he didn't claim her he would lose her altogether.

He shifted a little to move around to her side. Her hair had come loose from the bun at the nape of her neck. As he brushed it back from her face, a flower came loose and fell into his hand. He lifted it to his face and inhaled its scent, knowing frangipanis would forever make him think of Maia.

He put it on the ground beside him and ran his fingers along the side of her face. He heard her sharp intake of breath as his thumb traced over her lips.

Her lips moved under his thumb. 'What are you doing?'

He bent his head towards her. 'What I've wanted to do since the night I got home.'

'We shouldn't,' she breathed but her voice was just a puff of air. It lacked any conviction.

'I don't think we can stop it.' His voice was a whisper in the silence of the stairwell. His heart had only just resumed its normal rhythm and now, under Maia's gaze, he could feel it starting to increase in tempo again. He could feel the blood pounding in his veins, flooding all his extremities, throbbing in his groin.

She was intoxicating and he was filled with longing, light-headed with need, burning with desire. 'I want you, Maia, more than I've wanted anyone or anything in my life, and I think you want me too. There is still chemistry between us. Plenty of it. I know you feel it. I can hear it in your voice and I see it in your eyes. I've felt it in the air and in your touch. This is our opportunity for a second chance.'

Another frangipani flower fluttered to the floor as Maia shook her head. 'It's too late. *You're* too late.'

'No, I'm not. Don't marry Todd,' he begged. 'Not if you still love me.'

'You were everything to me, Henry, but you chose a different life. You chose to save the world. You didn't choose me.'

'That was my mistake,' he said as he picked up the fallen flower and tucked it behind her ear. 'And I won't make the same mistake twice. Don't write me off. You know what the tsunami did to me—you know why I made the choices I did, why I needed to feel like I was making a difference. But these quakes have shown me that my life means nothing, my plans and goals and promises mean nothing, if I don't have you. Before I met you I was prepared to be alone. I thought I could manage—I thought I could deal with the loneliness, I thought that was what I wanted. I didn't want to love another person. In my mind loving people left me open to heartache and loss, and I didn't want to risk losing anyone else I cared about but I can't live without you. I don't want to. I would rather tempt fate than give you up voluntarily.'

'Oh, Henry, you have no idea how I missed you. How I longed for you. How I wished it was your arms around me. How I wished it was you in my bed at night, but it wasn't, and eventually I had to stop wishing. I had to move on with my life and Todd was there for me when I needed him.'

And you weren't. Henry heard her unspoken words but he wasn't done yet. 'Maia, don't do this. Give me another chance. Give us another chance. I couldn't give myself to you back then, I had nothing to give. I needed to save the world, to fight my demons, but I should never have left you. It was foolish of me to think that you might still be here, that you might still want me.'

'I did want you, Henry, more than I ever wanted anything.'

'And now? Do you still want me?' His heart felt as if it had lodged in his throat while he waited for her answer. He couldn't believe how nervous he was.

'I'm committed to Todd,' she said as his heart sank into his stomach and nausea replaced nervousness. 'I made my father a promise and I have given Todd my word. I know it was my father's wish for me to marry Todd. When he asked Dad's permission to marry me that was one of the last moments that Dad was truly happy before he died. How could I refuse Todd's proposal after that? How could I do anything else?'

'You're settling for a life that you think your dad wanted for you, but surely he would want you to be happy? Is this marriage going to give you the life you wanted? Is it going to make you happy? I'm begging you, Maia, please, don't do it. Don't marry Todd.'

'And what about when this disaster is over?' she asked. 'You'll want to move on to the next disaster and then the next. What will happen to me then? To us?'

'You can come too. Or I'll stay here. I'll do whatever you want if you'll agree to spend the rest of your life with me. I came back for you and I don't want to lose you. Not to an earthquake and not to another man. You've taught me to love again and now I'm more afraid of losing you than of risking my heart. If I were to lose you I would have lost everything.'

'I've made a promise to Todd.'

Could he hear her resolve weakening or was that just wishful thinking?

'There's no law that says you can't change your mind. It's all up to you. You can't tell me that you and Todd share the same chemistry that we have. You can't tell me there's nothing between us. We both feel it. Do you think Todd wants to be your second choice? You can choose your happiness or choose to spare Todd's feelings. You can choose our happiness or choose to keep a promise you think you made to your father,' he said as he ran his hand over the edge of her jaw and let his fingers trail down her neck until his hand was on the bare flesh of her arm.

He heard her sigh and knew he wasn't playing fair but he was a desperate man. He had one last chance. 'It's your choice, but I don't want to live my life without you. I need you. I love you.' His thumb traced the outline of her mouth. 'Marry me instead, Maia.'

Her face was still tilted up towards him. She was shadows and light. She had a bruise on her cheek and there was a question in her dark eyes, but a smile on her pink lips. He bent his head. There would be time for talking later.

His lips covered hers. She closed her eyes and sighed and, as the sigh escaped, her lips parted and he took that as an invitation. He deepened the kiss. His tongue explored and delved and tasted. She tasted of champagne and strawberries, of bubbles and goodness. She smelled like frangipanis, of summer and sweetness. She was soft in his arms. She felt like home.

Maia slid a hand behind Henry's head as he deepened the kiss, holding him to her as her body responded and the memories flooded back, and she remembered how life had felt when she'd been with Henry. Nothing had ever come close, before or since. She thought she'd been coping but now she realised she'd only been surviving, only half-living. A piece of her heart had wilted when Henry had left but now that little piece of her blossomed again, like wildflowers after rain. She could feel herself unfurling as blood pumped through her heart, flooding that wilted piece, and her body came to life. She could feel the power of his kiss repairing her heart and making it beat properly for the first time in years.

She had one hand behind his head and the other on his arm. His muscles were warm and solid under her fingers.

He tasted of peppermint. He smelled like grapefruit and cedar. He felt like her future.

She loved him still. She'd never stopped. She would wait for her heart to heal and then she would give it back to him.

'Hello?'

He felt Maia jump in his arms as a voice called down from above them. She pulled away, leaving Henry wanting more, but their time was up. The door to the flight above them had opened, the door to the flight of stairs that was no longer there, and the voice called out again.

'Hello? Is there anyone in there?'

'Down here,' Henry replied.

He was reluctant to leave Maia but he had no choice. He took a long look at her face. Her dark eyes were huge and solemn, her lips pink and swollen from being thoroughly kissed. She looked utterly gorgeous but sad. As he stood up he sensed that this was the end. They both knew it. Once he got up he might never get another chance to hold her in his arms but he couldn't prolong their isolation. Maia needed medical attention.

Henry directed the rescue mission. Because of Maia's ankle, they couldn't winch her up the stairwell—the angles didn't allow access with a stretcher—so the only way out was through the blocked lower-level door. Two firemen were lowered into the stairwell and together the three of them cleared the rubble. If anyone wondered why Henry hadn't started until now, no one voiced the question, but finally they had cleared enough space to allow them to open the door.

Todd was on the other side. Waiting. A reminder to Henry that Maia wasn't his.

Henry climbed the steps and returned to Maia. He picked up the fallen frangipani flower and put it in his pocket before scooping her up and carrying her down the stairs. He buried his face in her hair and took a last, deep breath, inhaling her scent as he paused, before getting ready to step over the last blocks of concrete. 'Choose me, Maia. Be mine,' he whispered to her as he carried her out of the stairwell.

It was time to hand her over but he couldn't bring himself to hand her to Todd. He laid her gently on the stretcher instead but even that felt like he was giving her up.

He followed the stretcher outside and watched as she was loaded into the ambulance. He waited for her to call to him, to ask him to go with her, but she said nothing. Her dark eyes kept him in sight until the doors were closed but there were no last words, no last-minute declarations. He took the frangipani flower from his pocket and held it to his nose as the ambulance drove away. He didn't want to believe this was the end but there was nothing more he could do. If Maia chose to marry Todd, Henry knew he would have to leave Christ-church. He couldn't stand the thought of seeing her but not being able to have her. He wasn't prepared to live his life watching Maia with another man.

The ambulance doors slammed into place, forming a solid, impenetrable barrier, separating Maia physically from Henry and taking her by surprise. Was he letting her go? Again? Were all his words just empty promises, platitudes? Was he going to let her leave?

Her fragile heart sat heavily in her chest. She wasn't sure if she was strong enough to cope with this. But what had she expected? Had she expected Henry to make a scene? To sweep her off her feet? To chase after her and swear his devotion while Todd sat in the ambulance beside her? Did she expect him to ignore Todd's part in this tableau? She knew he wouldn't do that.

Henry had been watching her closely as she'd been loaded into the ambulance. His blue eyes had been dark, unsmiling, haunted. He'd been watching her and waiting. She'd assumed he had more to say but now she realised he had said everything he needed to. He'd told her how he felt. He'd been honest. She could scarcely believe he'd come back for her. After all those years of waiting, of wondering how he really felt, he'd actually come back for her.

He loved her.

With every metre of distance the ambulance put between her and Henry, Maia could feel her heart tearing and breaking piece by piece. The freshly healed fragments of her heart weren't yet strong enough to cope with the pull of separation. As the ambulance carried her further away she realised he'd been waiting for her to speak. It was her turn now. The next move was up to her.

She wanted to tell the ambulance to stop, to turn around, to take her back to Henry. She could feel her future slipping out of her grasp with every yard, every corner, every street. Henry *was* her future. She couldn't give him up again.

What happened next was definitely up to her. She had to take the chance. She had to know she had done everything she could. She had to know how this ended.

She put her hand on her chest as if she could physically hold her heart together and two fat tears spilled from her eyes and rolled down her cheeks.

'Do you want something for the pain?' Todd's voice was earnest, his eyes kind and concerned.

She shook her head. It wasn't her ankle that was troubling her.

She looked at Todd and knew Henry was right. She was settling for a life that other people had wanted for her. She loved Todd but she wasn't in love with him. She'd been trying to fill a void left by her father's death and by Henry. She hadn't wanted to be alone, and Todd had solved that problem, but it wasn't the answer she was looking for. Life with Todd would be fine, she'd be okay, but she wanted more than fine—she wanted more than okay. She wanted it all. She wanted passion, laughter, love and joy. She wanted Henry.

'Is there anything you need?' Todd asked.

She nodded.

She needed Henry.

She didn't want to hurt Todd but her heart belonged to Henry. It always had and Todd deserved better than to be her second choice. He deserved to have someone who loved him unconditionally and completely. Todd was a good friend, a good man, but Henry was the one she couldn't live without. She had to fix this before she ruined everything.

She slid her engagement ring off her finger and pressed it into Todd's palm. 'There's something I need to tell you…'

EPILOGUE

MAIA FLEXED HER ankle as she sat in front of the mirror at her mother's dressing table. It was six weeks since she'd fractured it and she'd finally been allowed to take the moon boot off yesterday. Her ankle was stiff, she'd be walking with a limp, but at least she was walking.

An envelope with her name on it lay on the dressing table. She recognised Todd's handwriting on the front. She opened the envelope and read the short note, finishing just as her mother came into the room. She slipped the letter back inside the envelope and stuck it in the mirror.

'Is everything all right?' Neina asked.

Maia lifted her head and met her mother's gaze in the mirror. 'Everything's perfect,' she said. 'Todd was just sending his best wishes to us both.'

Neina slid Maia's wedding dress off its hanger and said, 'He's really okay with your decision?'

'He said he wasn't going to stand in the way. He could see that what Henry and I have is special. He wants that too. He deserved better than to be my second choice, my consolation prize.'

Maia held her arms up in the air as her mother slipped the simple, white satin sheath over her head. The fabric slid easily down her body, skimming her hips and falling to her ankles.

'Ready?'

Maia nodded as she removed the silk scarf that protected her hair and make-up and picked up her wedding bouquet, a simple spray of white orchids from her father's greenhouse interwoven with clusters of frangipani flowers, and walked with her mother along the path that led from their house to the beach.

White chairs had been set up on the sand and a space had been left through the middle, marking out an aisle. The aisle was lined with hurricane lamps, and fairy lights had been strung between poles that formed a border around the rows of seats. At the end of the aisle a simple wooden platform covered with a white muslin draped roof had been erected.

Maia could see Carrie and her sisters. Everyone was waiting for her. Her mother kissed her on the cheek. 'Be happy, my darling,' she said.

Maia hugged her mother tightly. 'Thanks, Mum,' she said, before waiting as Neina went to join her other daughters.

Maia would be walking down the aisle alone. But that was how she'd wanted it. A simple wedding, at home, with her family and friends. She didn't need anyone to walk her down the aisle. Everything she needed was waiting for her at the end of the sandy path.

She lifted her eyes and smiled at her fiancé.

Henry beamed back at her. He wore linen trousers and a simple white shirt. His skin was tanned and his indigo eyes were dark. Like her he was barefoot. She was having the simple wedding she had dreamed of; today was a celebration of their love and the beginning of their life together.

In the end her decision had been easy. In the end she hadn't really had a choice. She couldn't imagine living her life without Henry. She knew to have decided anything else would only have ended up hurting the people she cared about, Todd and Henry, both in different ways.

She moved down the aisle, past Brenda and her hospital colleagues; past Carrie; past her uncles, aunts and cousins; her mum and her sisters. She wasn't having attendants; she didn't need anyone other than Henry.

He was waiting for her under the muslin-draped roof. The late-afternoon sun shone on him, lighting the way forward. The air around her shifted and stirred as she got closer to him. It carried the scent of cedar and citrus to her and brought a feeling of anticipation and excitement. It whispered to her. It brought her home.

Henry reached for her as she stepped up onto the platform. A tingle ran along her spine and her nipples tightened in a visceral reaction to his touch. Her body had its own way of telling her what she wanted. But her head and her heart and her body all agreed. She wanted Henry.

The priest cleared his throat and Maia tried to focus as Father Alex began the service. She barely remembered walking down the aisle—all she could think about was Henry—but she did remember her vows. She hadn't had to rehearse them; she spoke from her heart.

'My heart belongs to you, Henry Alexander Cavanaugh. You are the man I can't live without. I promise to love you, respect you and be honest with you all the days of my life.' She waited for Father Alex to hand her the ring. 'In the name of the Father, the Son and the Holy Spirit,' she said as she slid it onto Henry's finger.

Then it was Henry's turn. 'Maia Grace Tahana,

thank you for agreeing to be my wife. I promise to love you and to share the rest of my life with you, to always be there for you and to be the best person I can be. For you.' He took the ring from Father Alex and touched it to the ends of her fingers as he continued. 'I promise to love you, cherish you and take care of you for the rest of our lives.'

Then Father Alex said the words Maia had been waiting to hear. 'I now pronounce you husband and wife. You may kiss your bride.'

Henry cupped his fingers under her chin and lifted her face up to his. Maia wrapped one hand around Henry's head and pulled his lips down to hers as she gave him her heart and soul.

As Henry kissed her Maia knew he would never let her go again. She could taste all his promises for their future together in that one kiss.

He smiled at her as their lips parted. 'I love you, Mrs Cavanaugh,' he whispered.

'I love you too, my husband.'

* * * * *

MILLS & BOON®

MEDICAL ROMANCE™

THE ULTIMATE IN ROMANTIC MEDICAL DRAMA

'The perfect Christmas read!' - Julia Williams

Jewellery designer Skylar loves living London, but when a surprise proposal goes wrong, she finds herself fleeing home to remote Puffin Island.

Burned by a terrible divorce, TV historian Alec is dazzled by Sky's beauty and so cynical that he assumes that's a bad thing! Luckily she's on the verge of getting engaged to someone else, so she won't be a constant source of temptation... but this Christmas, can Alec and Sky realise that they are what each other was looking for all along?

Order yours today at
www.millsandboon.co.uk

MILLS & BOON®

Man of the Year

Our winning cover star will be revealed next month!

**Don't miss out on your copy
– order from millsandboon.co.uk**

Read more about Man of the Year 2016 at

www.millsandboon.co.uk/moty2016

**Have you been following our
Man of the Year 2016 campaign?**
🐦 **#MOTY2016**